THE TRUE LOVE CLUB
A RED CALENDAR MYSTERY

THE TRUE LOVE CLUB
A RED CALENDAR MYSTERY

Kate Merrill

SAPPHIRE BOOKS

SALINAS, CALIFORNIA

using the production/publication for purposes of training A.I., artificial intelligence, to generate text that may replicate the author's style or genre similar to this work. The author retains all rights to use this work for purposes of generative AI training and development of any language learning system.

To the extent that the image on the cover of this book depicts a person or persons, such a person is merely a model and is not intended to portray any character feature in this book.

This and other Sapphire Books titles can be found at
www.sapphirebooks.com

Acknowledgements

Special thanks to Christine Svendsen and the staff at Sapphire Books for your continuing support and for launching my new Red Calendar Mystery Series.

As always, thanks to Tara Young for your careful and sensitive editing and to the amazing cover designers who bring my visions to life.

Dedication

For all women
in the
True Love Club,
regardless of age,
marital status,
or
sexual preference

Chapter One

The bad vibes began when Red Calendar parked on an innocent-looking expanse of pavement across from Mooresville High School. It was the exact spot where she'd witnessed her first violent death, when two freshman boys had been tossing a football. The ball rolled out in the street; one kid ran out after it. He never saw the big green Ford station wagon. The driver, tapping on the steering wheel and singing to the radio, never saw the kid. But every student unlucky enough to be loitering on the playground that perfect spring morning saw the boy squashed flatter than a tomato on the railroad track. The principal closed the school, sent everyone home, and even provided a trauma counselor, but Red never took advantage of that help. Many deaths later, two of them caused by Red's own hand, she'd finally wised up and realized she needed all the help she could get.

The bad vibes followed Red down the hall to the gymnasium. Everything in her old school seemed miniaturized, but the same fluorescent light still ricocheted off the rows of steel lockers and polished tile floor, dazzling her eyes. Familiar odors of toxic cleaning fluid and adolescent sweat punched her square in the gut.

Red hated coming to a stupid high school reunion, but the girls from the True Love Club had promised to be there. Once upon a time, she'd loved those girlfriends but hadn't seen them in ages. She'd stayed in touch via email and the occasional phone call, especially when her relationship fell apart. She'd passed on a few photos, complained about her job, and they'd been supportive—but it wasn't the same as personal contact. So when they begged her to attend, she couldn't say no. Fact was, Red was lonely. She had congenial co-workers, neighbors, and acquaintances but no close friends. Slipping into middle age, she suspected she might just need more in her life.

As she pushed through the heavy swinging doors leading to the party, the electric noise from the public address system vibrated off the hardwood basketball court and assaulted her ears. The discordant chatter of alumni milling around the banquet tables sent nervous shivers up her bare arms in spite of the early July heat.

Taking a deep breath, Red scanned the roomful of strangers. Everyone was thirty years older. Would she even recognize her former classmates, others dumb enough to return to the site of their teenaged angst? What would she say to them? She had nothing to brag about, no big achievements to flaunt, and as far as true love was concerned, Red was a dismal failure. Stifling a childish impulse to remove her sandals to avoid scuffing the court, she squared her shoulders, stood to her full height—an impressive six feet of offensive drive that had led her girls basketball team to win the North Carolina state championships three decades ago—and strode into the room.

"My God, Red! Is that really you?"

The little cannonball hit Red from behind, scaring her so badly she almost spun into a reflexive crouch. Red's gun hand twitched above the holster that, of course, was not there.

"Jesus, don't arrest me!" The petite Hispanic woman's glossy black hair framed a wide, pretty face. Her full lips parted as she belted out one of her famous belly laughs.

Red pulled her into the club's traditional mama bear hug. Her friend had put on a few pounds, but she was still the same spicy Salsa. "Sneak up on me like that again, and you *will* spend the night behind bars," Red told her.

"Yeah, right." Salsa snorted as she attached a plump hand to Red's wrist and dragged her to a table near the far basketball net. "That tough cop crap doesn't scare me."

Red followed sheepishly. Tonight Salsa was *hot*—pink with sequins—but Red knew Salsa's one true passion was the environment. Even when they were kids, all Salsa talked about was solar energy, water purity, and preventing global warming. Back then, Salsa's steady boyfriend was a nature kid in a kayak who vowed to save polar bears left homeless due to shrinking ice caps. Red suspected that even now, Salsa would seek men who were like-minded tree huggers.

"Everyone's waiting for you, Red. We've already finished one pitcher of beer, so you'll have to catch up."

As Salsa navigated through a crowd of dancers, bumping hips and shoulders, Red's nerves switched to high alert. Was she actually afraid to meet her old friends? Over the years, Red had achieved a few professional goals, earned a detective's badge in her district, yet she feared this reunion might make her regress to the self-conscious, big-footed tomboy she once was. In the end, what did she have to show and tell? Only a gold shield that looked like a toy and the depressing story of her stormy relationship and latest breakup with her only long-term lover.

"When did so many of these guys go bald?" Red asked Salsa.

"About the same time I started wearing a size fourteen," Salsa answered as they reached the TLC table, where Salsa tapped a pretty blonde on the shoulder. "Hey, Summer, look who's out on parole."

When Summer turned to smile, Red saw eyes as Carolina blue as the morning sky on a down-home July day. Summer was the only member of their club born in Mooresville. She had married her high school sweetheart, the star quarterback, right after graduation. Like Red, Summer had recently suffered a nasty breakup. But unlike Red, Summer was a struggling single mom with an eight-year-old daughter. That child had been a big surprise, born on Summer's fortieth birthday.

"Hey, Summer!" Red grinned. When she bent to accept Summer's hug, Red felt tears of joy on Summer's porcelain cheeks. "Hey, why are you crying? Have I changed that much?"

"Nope, you're still the same ornery old burning bush." Summer reached up and yanked at Red's hair.

For this occasion, Red had released her flaming mane, now sparsely populated by a few strands of gray, from its no-nonsense ponytail. She had disguised her freckles under a layer of base makeup and a dusting of powder.

"Have a seat, Red." Summer patted the empty seat between herself and a long-legged beauty who had been watching their exchange with wry amusement, from eyes that had always reminded Red of her mama's favorite sapphire earrings. "Go on, Red, sit beside Lila," Summer urged.

"What if she tries something?" Red joked.

"Sorry, honey, you're not my type." Lila winked as Red slid into the chair.

Instead of giving her fellow lesbian the traditional hug, Red took Lila's face into both hands and planted a solid kiss on her lips. By the time she came up for air, Lila was laughing so hard she choked.

"God, maybe you *are* my type!" Lila gasped. "Where were you in high school, Red? I could have used some support back then."

In high school, Red had been hiding so deep in the closet you couldn't find her with a broomstick and flashlight. She wasn't proud of it, but that was the way it was. Red had stayed silent when the girls in her clique whispered and made fun of Lila. She'd been a gutless wonder. Had Red chosen police work to make up for the courage she'd always lacked?

Hands down, Lila was still the most drop-dead gorgeous member of their group. Men took one look at her floating brown hair and graceful, willowy body and fell in love—or at least in lust. Needless to say, all those males were doomed to disappointment.

"Lady Lila's the new boss over at the Mooresville Art Depot," Summer informed them.

"Will you cut that 'Lady' crap?" Lila was the only club member who refused to go along with her nickname. She claimed she was no lady, and often, her rough language proved the point.

"Give it a rest, girls." The rich alto voice bubbled up from the shadows at the end of the table. "We didn't come here tonight to rehash the past."

Until that moment, Red hadn't realized that Boots was here. Their African American friend lifted her dark face from behind the lid of a laptop. Pulsing light from a spinning party ball sparkled on Boots's close-cropped ebony curls. It illuminated her bright eyes and perfect, ultra-white teeth.

Summer frowned at Boots. "Please close that computer and join the party."

"Yeah, Boots, be sociable for once," Salsa added.

Boots rolled her large expressive eyes, then sprinted around the table to give Red a big, bosomy squeeze. Red felt the soft tickle of her Afro and smelled her signature spicy, tangerine perfume. Boots was a computer expert, their resident geek, but she sure didn't look or smell the part.

"Hello, ladies, who wants a refill?" A deep tenor voice startled them all.

Boots jumped backward in surprise and almost toppled a middle-aged man balancing a pitcher of beer. "Oops, so sorry!" Boots cried when some of the amber liquid sloshed onto Red's favorite party jeans.

"No problem." Red quickly grabbed a napkin, but when she glanced at the waiter, the odd premonition of doom returned with a vengeance. The man seemed to be a hot-tempered redhead like her, and he seemed mighty peeved.

"Oh, shit," Lila muttered as she located a napkin and dabbed at her expensive silk bodice, which had also received a splash or two.

"Look, I'm really sorry." The unfortunate waiter patted Lila's breast with his towel.

Bad mistake. Lila slapped his hand away with a resounding crack that turned a few heads, and Red decided it was time to defuse the situation. For one split second, she'd seen a look of pure hatred in the waiter's eyes but couldn't tell if his fury was directed at Boots, who had bumped him, or Lila, who had smacked him. Either way, Red placed a soothing hand on his arm.

"Do I know you?" Red asked.

Once the heightened color drained from his face and his breathing returned to normal, the man smiled. "You don't know me, but I know you guys. I was a lowly sophomore when you all graduated, and now I teach here."

"And you also wait tables?" Summer batted her blond lashes, flirting with her sky eyes.

"No, only when I want to prove I'm one of the good guys."

"Well, don't quit your day job," Lila grumbled.

Red breathed a major sigh of relief when the flustered guy poured each a full glass, left the pitcher, and then made a quick escape.

Chapter Two

Jeez, Lila, you were really rude," Salsa said once the waiter was out of earshot.

"Yeah, I thought he was kinda cute," Summer said.

"Not my type." Lila yawned.

"Well, who the hell is your type?" Boots had returned to her chair and was performing the "booting" maneuver that earned her the name. Once her laptop came to life, she scowled at Lila. "Clearly, no one with a penis floats your boat, so you might need to look beyond our provincial village to find your dream girl."

Red took a deep swallow of draft beer and tried to shake the sense of dread. Clearly, the five of them had drifted apart. Aside from email communications at holidays, weddings, funerals, and divorces, they'd rarely spoken to one another. And as the alcohol numbed Red's emotions and the faceted silver orb spun out a dizzying blur of missed opportunities, she wondered if her old friends, who were drinking and bantering about lost lovers, ever got tired of moving forward.

Why was Lila so angry and bitter? The others had told Red that Lila's breakup with her partner of five years had been worse than a straight divorce and that without the legal contracts married folks enjoyed, Lila's stake in the big house they'd bought together on Lake Norman was in jeopardy. The story made Red grateful that at least her ex and she had no significant material property to fight over when they split.

"Now here's what I'm talkin' about, girlfriends!" Boots's excited words penetrated Red's thoughts. "Internet dating. It's the best way to find true love nowadays."

Red did a double take, then laughed out loud. "You're delusional, Boots. That stuff's for kids."

"Red's right," Lila agreed. "We're a gang of old biddies. That shit is strictly for young straight kids."

"Hey, who you callin' a *biddy?*" Boots drawled. "Besides, you're dead wrong, Lila. LGBTQ people love this site. You'd simply select 'woman seeking woman,' then take your pick."

Salsa said, "Young chicks don't need the internet like we do. They get all the action they want cruising the bars. Truth is, many users are folks our age."

Red was truly alarmed. "What exactly are we discussing here?"

"DATESCAPE.com," they answered in unison.

"My sister found her husband online." Boots shifted her laptop, so they all could see the flashy DATESCAPE homepage. "And my bro-in-law is one awesome dude."

"All the nurses on my shift are doing it." Summer stood and walked around the table for a closer look.

"You can even surf the profiles in Spanish," Salsa said. "My uncle in Cancun is seventy-two years old, and he found my new aunt online."

"Are you serious?" Red interrupted. "Listen, internet dating is for losers and rejects who can't find a partner in real time." Hadn't they heard about the dangers, the loss of privacy? Not to mention the shame in giving up and resorting to cyberspace.

Four sets of angry eyes stared at Red, like she

was from outer space. As the silence deepened between them and the party noise muted to an annoying buzz, Red felt like she'd reached a crucial edge in her relationship with these women.

Finally, Summer spoke up. "Well, maybe we should consider the possibility that we *are* losers and rejects."

"Not me," Salsa insisted.

"Me neither." Boots's lovely square jaw jutted in defiance. "It's all about efficiency. For once in our pathetic lives, we can choose the date we want—age, looks, religion, political leanings—hell, we can even choose the type of facial hair."

"Why waste time? Let DATESCAPE sort out the good from the bad and the ugly," Salsa said. "You're an artist, Lila. You can design your own woman."

Lila shrugged and seemed disgusted, but she did not outright disagree.

Red sensed the crucial edge in her relationship with these women had become a dangerous precipice. "What's *wrong* with you people?"

"So why did you show up tonight, Red?" Summer demanded. "We all agreed our new club would be like the old one—all about finding true love. Am I right?"

Summer's statement threw Red off balance. Didn't they realize they were now *The Over-The-Hill True Love Club*? Her friendship with everyone was teetering on the brink. Red had never actually *agreed* to seek true love, but if she didn't play along, she'd lose them.

"Okay, I'll think about it," Red grudgingly conceded. "One of my duties at work is studying cybercrime. I could approach it as research."

"God help us all." Summer groaned.

Chapter Three

Was Red a loser?

The depressing thought sloshed around her alcohol-soaked brain like a lost marble in a broken pinball machine. At the same time, she took extra care driving as she headed south on Interstate 77. She had already spotted one unmarked patrol car and knew the county sheriff loved to prowl this stretch of highway on Saturday night. What if she, an upstanding member of the Charlotte Mecklenburg Police Department, got busted on a DUI?

Besides, her brand new Dodge Challenger, a spirited update of the 1970 classic, had not one ding on its two-week-old skin, and she planned to keep it that way. Her dad, a retired cop now living in Sarasota, Florida, had restored one of those classics, and Red had spent every moment of her formative years helping him in the garage. Much to her mom's distress, she had lived her young life covered with automotive grease and stinking of car wax.

And now she was a loser.

At least that had been Summer's theory after their second pitcher of beer. But hey, Red was a senior detective in the competitive CMPD. Summer was a nurse. Salsa managed a successful family restaurant. Lila directed an art gallery, and Boots was a tech genius. So how were any of them really losers?

The answer was a no-brainer. They were all headed home to an empty bed and a solitary lifestyle.

Bummer. Red's mattress hadn't sagged under two women's weight for longer than she cared to admit, and the only support she got was from her Playtex bra.

She merged onto the beltway looping the city, then got off at Exit 3, near Twelfth and Brevard, in Charlotte's First Ward. Moments later, she eased through the gate to her upscale apartment complex, which had been transformed from a historic cotton mill.

So far, so good. No fender benders, speeding tickets, or other incidents to further mar an otherwise only mildly upsetting evening. Soon she'd be home free in her little nest with hardwood floors, exposed wood beams, and brick—all those luxury accoutrements that were supposed to make her happy. She passed the complex's cyber café and glanced through a plate glass window at the handful of hopeful young singles hunched over their laptops. They were chatting online, hoping to hook up. But Red had been observing these kids for almost six months now, ever since she split with Gina, and so far, they always ended up returning to their sad little nests alone—just like her.

So why in God's name had Red agreed to rejoin the club? Did the girls really expect to find true love online? They had all promised to meet again in one week, and everyone had agreed to have one cyber date lined up. If not, she'd be kicked out of the club or at least severely censured. Big deal. Red had already decided to quit.

She mounted the two steps to her first-floor apartment and inserted her key, but the heavy oak door swung inward of its own volition. *What the fuck?* Hair prickled at the back of her neck as her drunken bloodstream flooded with adrenaline. No way, no how. She always locked the door. Always. And for the second time that evening, she reached for her Smith & Wesson, which still wasn't there.

Oh, sweet Jesus.

As her eyes adjusted to the dark foyer, she noticed an eerie green light flickering on the far wall and realized the television was on, its sound muted. But she distinctly remembered turning it off before leaving that night. She calculated the distance from her front door to the bedroom drawer, where she kept her weapon under lock and key, but quickly realized she could never span that distance before the intruder intervened and tackled her—if he was still there.

Well, shit. The only sensible move was to cut and run, to return to her car, lock all the doors, and call 911. Red figured one of her patrolman buddies from North Tryon Division would respond, but then she'd never get the egg off her face if her apartment proved to be intruder-free.

Red had never been famous for choosing the sensible move. So she took a deep breath and hoped the intruder couldn't hear her heart beating a frantic tattoo against her ribcage as she inched forward in the dark. Good news was, she knew the layout of her furniture as intimately as she knew the contours of her own body. Bad news was, she sensed she wasn't alone the moment her sandals moved onto the relative silence of the living room carpet.

She couldn't hear him breathing, nor could she make out any silhouette or out-of-place shadow that remotely resembled a human being. Instead, she experienced that horrific vibe that occurs when one hears the soft click of a hammer cocking nanoseconds before the bullet leaves the chamber. And before the scream could leave her throat, a hand snaked out from the depths of the couch and grasped her ankle.

He brought her down in a heartbeat, then rolled on top of her. Red's scream was stifled by the brutal crush of his chest on her ribcage and his crazy laughter. Powerful hands pinned her wrists to the floor above her head. She felt his weight and smelled his sweat but prayed she could plant one swift knee in his groin before she passed out.

By the time she recognized the tangy scent of his body wash and the all-too-familiar odor of Canadian whiskey on his breath, it was too late. Her knee was already cocked, so she let loose and nailed him in the gonads with her shin. When he rolled off, writhing in agony and screaming obscenities, she searched her heart for one drop of pity but found only sweet satisfaction.

"Fuck, Red, are you trying to kill me?" The mighty Ricardo curled into the fetal position, cradling his balls like a broken baby. "Jesus Christ Almighty!" He groaned.

As the fear and adrenaline retreated from Red's flooded system, she panted, pulled herself upright, and leaned against the couch. "What did you expect, asshole? You're lucky I wasn't armed."

"Fuck!" He scooted painfully to a sitting position and propped up beside her, still cupping the family jewels.

"It's called breaking and entering," she pointed out.

"Not when you have a key."

She watched his misery in amused detachment. Ricardo "Rick" Molerno was many things—traditional macho Italian, ego-driven, trigger-happy cop, her ex-partner in the CMPD Sexual Assault Unit—but one thing he was not now, not ever: a man able to apologize.

Most significantly, Rick was also the brother of Gina, Red's longtime lover. He had introduced them and then freaked out when Red and Gina fell in love. Some would call it an incestuous relationship—the partner you depend on to watch your back also being your lover's brother. Certainly, Red's divided loyalties had caused many a family fight. The relationship had also prompted her to give Rick the key to her apartment.

"The key was a mistake," she calmly told him. "Give it back, and the situation is rectified."

He pulled out one of the white cotton hankies he habitually carried and mopped the damp forehead beneath his short, curly black buzz cut.

"If it's not just B&E, it's stalking," Red snapped. "You were lying in wait in the dark."

"It's two a.m. Where the hell were you?"

"None of your goddamn business." She rested her aching head on the cushion, pushed off her shoes, and massaged the carpet with her toes, just to be sure they still worked.

"You've been drinking and driving." He snarled. "You smell like a brewery."

Red recalled the moment the unlucky waiter/ high school teacher had doused her jeans with beer. "So what? You're stinking drunk. Did you bring your own Windsor, or did you drink mine?"

"All in the family, right, doll?" He quit nursing himself and punched her shoulder.

"Wrong." She slapped his hand away. Rick had lacked the guts to stick with sexual assault, so after ten years as Red's partner, he'd transferred to homicide, claiming it was easier to deal with dead bodies than rape victims.

"C'mon, I was only testing. If I was a real burglar, you'd be dead meat." He inched closer, so their arms touched.

She knew all his moves. Now that Gina had left her, Rick knew they were no longer "family," as he liked to put it, but he still felt entitled to check up on her, especially when he was drunk. "Back off." She growled.

They sat in total silence while their heart rates slowed to normal and the all-night cable news spewed out the latest gloom and doom. Red watched the newscaster's lips move on mute and figured Rick had come because he wanted something. He always had an ulterior motive.

"Okay, so why are you here?" she demanded.

"That was really stupid, Red. Driving drunk, then entering unarmed. The alcohol impaired your judgment."

She sighed and watched the ambient light from the television wobbling on the ceiling, pretending it came from a cozy log fire, like the one Gina and she shared in their former apartment.

"Cut the crap, Rick. What do you want?"

Rick's sigh matched hers. If she hadn't known him so well, she might have fooled herself into believing he was channeling his sensitive side.

"Are you gonna tell me where you were tonight or not?" he asked.

"Not."

"You were with a new woman. Did you fuck her?"

Red slapped him so hard his face jerked sideways and his brown eyes popped open in surprise.

She would've taken another shot at his groin, but his hurt puppy expression stopped her.

"Sorry, I was way outta line," he said as the red imprint of her hand appeared under his afternoon shadow of whiskers. "Forgive me?"

Rick wasn't one to apologize, so his professed regret was either the result of too much whiskey, or else he wanted something really big.

She almost felt sorry for him. "Chill, will you? I was out with my girlfriends."

"Which *girlfriends*?"

She considered her options. She had nothing to hide, but Rick had always hated the women of the TLC. That was mostly Red's fault. Over the years, she had described him via email to the girls as crass, controlling, and partly responsible for her breakup with Gina. So each girl had something nasty to say about him, and Red had made the mistake of telling him all about it.

But she figured, *what the hell*? "I was with the True Love Club."

Rick rolled his eyes. "I don't get it. Why in God's name would you want to reconnect with those bitches?"

She hated it when he rolled his eyes. "Look, tell me what you want or get out. Now."

They glared at each other, but Rick broke first. "Hell, I'm getting too old for this. I came here to ask you about a case." Using the sofa like a crutch, he hauled himself upright, then lifted a manila file off the end table.

That was truly bizarre. They didn't work together anymore, so Red figured it was some lame-brained trick.

"No, it's true." He caught her drift and opened

the file. "Check it out. We discovered a body tonight. Woman was found dead in her own bed."

"Tonight?" *So how did he get his notes together so quickly?*

"Hope you don't mind, but I used your PC to type up my preliminary. I printed out a copy for you."

Red's blood boiled all over again. How dare he help himself to her private computer? Damn! She'd neglected to change the stupid password, and Rick knew it by heart. Like the duplicate key, it was a mistake she intended to rectify immediately.

"You're in homicide, I'm in sex crimes. So what does your case have to do with me?"

He hung his head. "We've got some overlap. The woman was raped, then strangled. The killer left a letter opener shaped like a gold crucifix buried in her vagina."

Rick looked green at the gills, like he was about to throw up on her carpet, and she couldn't exactly blame him. The killer sounded like one sick dude, yet Red was intrigued in spite of herself. "Semen?" she asked.

He moved toward the powder room. "Crime scene's still on location. Appears he never got inside. Ejaculated all over her belly."

Now Red felt truly ill. No matter how many times she waded into the swamp where the sexual predators lived, she always came out feeling violated and dirty. The muck never washed off.

"So are you gonna help me?" He hesitated outside the bathroom door.

He was wasted, so was she. "Leave the file," she told him.

Rick dropped it on her hall table, then

disappeared into the john. As she listened to the toilet flushing, then water rolling around in the sink, the file gave off a poisonous glow. She knew that against her better judgment, she would open it. Not tonight. Maybe tomorrow.

By the time he emerged, Rick's cocky grin was restored. He crossed the room, took her hands, and lifted her to her feet. Red allowed him to pull her into his arms and used the moment to reach into his right trouser pocket but didn't find what she was looking for.

"Where's my key?"

He laughed. "You'll have to do a strip search."

She pushed him away. "Give it to me."

"No."

Okay, it wasn't worth it. She'd fight that battle another day. Ricardo Molerno was many things—the man who convinced her to become a cop, the guy who always had her back, her self-appointed protector. Unfortunately, because he was also her ex-girlfriend's big brother, he couldn't accept the fact that he no longer had a bookmark in her life.

"I want you to leave now."

Red was also many things. Above all, she was stubborn as a bloodstain in white carpet, and Rick knew it. Two minutes later, she was alone. She double-locked her door and set the security chain.

Chapter Four

Lila used to love Sundays, when she and her partner would sleep late and then make fresh-ground coffee and a special breakfast to share over the art section. They'd struggle over the *New York Times* crossword until they gave up and then chased their golden retriever through the lazy afternoons.

She poured a second cup of coffee and carried it to the sunroom overlooking Lake Norman, where boaters were churning up waves with their water skis and WaveRunners, but their joyous antics only intensified Lila's loneliness.

Thinking back, maybe her partner was right. They had lived an insular existence, wrapped tight in their own little cocoon with limited contact with the outside world, and their only friends were lesbians from their former lives. Their old friends were scattered across the country, thriving in metropolitan areas far different from Lila's tiny Mooresville.

"We live in the buckle of the Bible Belt," her ex had complained. "Or maybe we reside higher up in the red state anatomy—like the armpit."

Lila turned to her golden. "She was crazy, wasn't she, Georgia?" She rubbed the retriever's fuzzy stomach, then fed her a tiny bite of bagel with cream cheese. "We don't miss her at all, do we?"

But Georgia, named after the artist O'Keeffe, not the Peach State as most locals presumed, did not necessarily agree. At times, Lila believed her pet missed her ex more than Lila did. After all, her athletic lover was the one who threw the tennis ball, taught Georgia how to dive off the dock, and took her everywhere in her pickup truck. Now that truck was cruising around in New Mexico.

"You know what, Georgia? If I'd known the bitch was going to leave us, I'd have named you after *my* favorite artist, not *hers*. But then Salvador is a dumb name for a pretty little girl dog. Sally, maybe?"

Suddenly, the coffee tasted bitter on Lila's tongue, so she walked to the kitchen and tossed it angrily into the sink. She scolded herself for carrying on an endless monologue with her pet and hated to admit her ex had been right. They had lived too much alone. It was one thing for an artist like Lila to be perfectly happy spending the insular hours with her welding equipment, but her partner had been gregarious and social. She needed more people.

When the doorbell rang, Lila's funk escalated to where she wanted to throw all the breakfast dishes against the nearest wall. She was eager to see Salsa, but as usual, Salsa had arrived too damn early. "What's wrong with that woman, Georgia?"

Lila had no intention of joining the True Love Club, but she hadn't wanted to tell Salsa. Lila thought the internet dating scheme was pure nonsense, but she really wanted to see Salsa. Salsa's visit would prove to be a waste of time because Lila would simply tell her friend that she'd changed her mind about the club and send her away. And then Lila would be alone once again.

She braced herself for the inevitable tornado named Salsa, and when she opened the door, sure enough, Salsa blew in with gale force, closely followed by her golden retriever, Taco. The dogs went ballistic, wagging and mouth wrestling until the women stood clear, allowing them to bolt into the fenced backyard and compete for squirrels.

"Good thing Georgia's spayed," Lila muttered. "Otherwise, we'd have puppies."

"Would that be so bad?" Salsa laughed. "Georgia and Taco are in love, which is more than you can say for you and me."

Lila gave Salsa a sly, seductive smile. "Well, you and me never gave love a try. Maybe I can convert you."

Her Hispanic friend blushed to the roots of her black blunt cut and backed up one pace, but Lila pulled her into the mama bear hug. She allowed Salsa to struggle a moment, then held her at arm's length. "You look hot today, girlfriend." She stared at Salsa's revealing red halter top, then allowed her gaze to slither down to Salsa's cut-off denim shorts.

"Go away!" Still blushing, Salsa extricated herself and stomped toward the kitchen table. "We have work to do."

The feigned sexual tension was an old joke between them, but sometimes Lila's gaydar suggested that Salsa might actually be attracted to her, and hey, Lila was more than open to that. Salsa's energy level was off the charts compared to Lila's, but they did share a common interest in preserving the environment.

"God, I'm hungover." Salsa plopped down on a kitchen chair and hefted her laptop onto the table.

Lila eyed the computer suspiciously. "Well, it doesn't show." If her friend were any bouncier, the dogs would mistake her for a superball. And if Salsa launched into her DATESCAPE pitch, Lila would toss her into the yard and let the animals fight over her.

"I'm hungry. Watcha got?"

Lila did a mental inventory of the contents of her fridge. For a woman who ran a Mexican restaurant, Salsa was always starving, and for a moocher, her standards were unreasonably high. "Bagels and cream cheese," Lila offered.

"Processed? Preservatives?" Salsa scowled.

"I'm afraid so. How 'bout a smoothie?"

"Organic fruit and soy milk?"

"You got it." Lila took out her blender and got busy fixing Salsa's favorite snack. If she were honest with herself, she'd admit she kept these ingredients on hand because she hoped Salsa would stop by. The girl was annoyingly hyper and upbeat, she made Lila feel grouchy and old, yet Lila looked forward to her visits. One hour with Salsa was like being goosed up the backside with a battery charger, so she finished making the drink, poured it into a wide crystal goblet, and set it at Salsa's right hand. Her reward was a hundred-kilowatt smile.

"Yum." Salsa licked her full, fresh-bitten strawberry lips. "Okay, now let's get down to business..."

Lila hated to burst Salsa's bubble, but no way would she participate in online dating. To buy time, she asked how Salsa had enjoyed their high school reunion. "What did you think of the girls last night?"

Salsa looked up from the screen while she waited for Chrome to activate. "Gee, I don't know. Boots is always up, but Red and Summer seemed sad."

No kidding. Red had been singing the breakup blues, and Lila felt guilty about that. Recently, Lila had introduced Gina, Red's former partner, to a young woman named Amanda Rittenhouse, who was a metal sculptor, like Lila. Gina had invited Amanda to visit Asheville with her, so that Amanda could look at studio space there. When Gia and Amanda went off together, Red, always prone to jealousy, had assumed the two were having an affair. Lila knew for a fact that Gina and Amanda had never been lovers, but Red was unconvinced.

Summer had recently suffered a bitter divorce from her philandering husband, so like Lila and Red, she was single and lonely. Possibly, Lila, Red, and Summer understood the facts of life in a way Salsa and Boots did not yet comprehend—that lasting love was a pretty myth concocted for losers, like the three of them.

"What's wrong?" Salsa seemed to have read Lila's bitter thoughts.

"Nothing. People change."

Salsa shrugged. "Not really. They're just busy. Red's in Charlotte doing her cop thing, and Summer's a nurse with a kid. They haven't changed, they're just exhausted. Underneath, they're still like us, always looking for true love."

Lila groaned.

"What?" Salsa pulled out the chair beside her and patted the seat. "Sit down and pay attention, Lila. DATESCAPE's up and running, so check out this awesome guy I plan to hook up with."

Lila groaned again but took a seat. She couldn't argue with a force of nature like Salsa, so she yawned and glanced at the dizzying array of old geezers' mug shots scrolling across the monitor. Salsa double-clicked on a grinning man with big blue eyes, straggly long hair, and a Grizzly Adams beard. He was rangy, fit, and had a youthful attitude.

Salsa crowed. "Isn't he cute?"

Lila was appalled. "He calls himself *Bikerboy*?" She envisioned tattoos and a Harley-Davidson Hog.

Salsa laughed. "He rides *bicycles*. You know, pedals and handlebars? He rode all through Appalachia last fall and took field notes on the strip-mining operations. He's way into limiting carbon emissions, and he even got up a petition to lobby against Duke Energy's new plants."

"Good for him." Lila didn't mean to be sarcastic because this aging hippie sounded much better for Salsa than her former boyfriend, a retired naval officer with obscenely pumped biceps and an obsession with explosives.

"You're just jealous," Salsa said. "I chatted online half the night with this guy, and now it's *your* turn." Much to Lila's alarm, Salsa twisted the laptop in her direction, then typed in "woman seeking woman" and their area code. "What screen name should we use for you?"

"No, I won't do this." She tried to get up, but Salsa grabbed her wrist.

"Look, you don't have to sign up right now. You get a sneak preview for free. We'll look for women aged forty to sixty in a radius extending fifty miles from here. Does that sound good?"

If Salsa thought she'd find any middle-aged lesbians looking for love in their sorry neck of the woods, she was sadly mistaken. "Good luck." Lila sneered.

But then the screen suddenly lit up with one hundred thirty matches, a veritable yearbook page of female faces—butch and femme, some pretty, some not—but all were smiling hopefully.

"Shit." Lila stared in stunned disbelief.

"Too many?" Salsa chirped playfully. "Let's narrow the field. Do you want previously married, divorced, single, or what?"

Lila remained speechless.

Salsa said, "All right, you've told me that straight women who've had a change of heart are bad news, so we'll enter 'never been married.'" The field narrowed to eighty matches.

"I still don't believe it."

"Told you so! Now we'll choose 'spiritual, not religious,' since I know you're not into the church." The group dropped to twenty choices.

Lila was intrigued in spite of herself because some of the women were pretty damned interesting. She took over the mouse and selected candidates with graduate degrees, and lo, six women remained. Of those, one face stood out from the rest. When Lila double-clicked to view three more photos of that woman, she felt an odd sensation in the pit of her stomach.

"Do you know her?" Salsa leaned closer for a better look.

Lila stared into the smiling blue eyes of the mystery woman she'd seen at the art center. The match named *Waterspirit* was perhaps ten years older than Lila, pushing sixty, with charming laugh lines at the corners of her eyes and expressive mouth. She had soft, short white hair, and as Lila already knew, a passion for modern art.

"God, I always assumed she was married."

"So you *do* know her?"

"Not really."

The sensation in Lila's stomach intensified as she realized that yes, she'd always wanted to know this woman. Even when she'd been with her ex, Lila had noticed the stranger at every one of her exhibit openings. She'd been enchanted by her grace, her laugh, and her generous support of the emerging artists. In fact, she'd been so enamored of *Waterspirit* that she'd avoided her while her shy heart contracted into knots.

"Well?" Salsa demanded. "Why don't you join up and 'wink' at this woman?"

Shaken, Lila stood and silently turned her back on the computer. "No, I don't want to know her. Not this way."

Chapter Five

Summer's neighbor was a creepy kid from a horror movie. He stared from behind thick glasses, fidgeted with his hands, and picked his nose when he thought no one was watching. But he was a great babysitter, her daughter, Gloria, adored him, and he even loved the cat.

"So did you and Connor have fun last night?" Summer brushed Gloria's long blond hair. She was rushing to get the child ready for an afternoon and evening with her daddy.

Gloria nodded vigorously. "I guess. Connor let me win at Mario Kart."

"Maybe you won fair and square." Her daughter was a computer whiz, a geek-in-the- making, and although Neighbor Kid was an expert at video games, Summer sensed he'd never possess Gloria's reasoning skills.

"C'mon, Mom. You know Connor's a Zelda master, so of course he let me win."

As she brushed Gloria's hair into a ponytail and secured it with a red, white, and blue ribbon, Summer gazed out the window to the parking lot, where sixteen-year-old Connor was lurking in the shadows between buildings, sneaking a cigarette—or maybe a joint. Like Gloria, he was the product of divorce and had been raised by a single mom. Summer worried because Connor still clung to his mommy's apron strings. Likely, that was why his mom had worked overtime to get him a learner's permit and a beat-up old Toyota.

But who was she to complain? Last night, Neighbor Kid had even changed the stinking cat box while Summer was away at her high school reunion. The kid, his mom, and the countless other singles at Oakmont Apartments banded together and helped one another, so everything considered, she was in a good place.

"Will Daddy's girlfriend come along?" Gloria jerked away when Summer accidentally pulled her hair too tight.

"I 'spect so."

"Then I'm not going," Gloria whined. "I hate that slut!"

Slut? Where had Gloria picked up that word? Summer made a mental note to tone down the language when she was chatting with her girlfriends, at least when Gloria was around.

"Don't be callin' Jolene names," Summer warned. "I'm sure Daddy's friend is a nice lady, and you'll have fun."

Gloria scooted off the stool and stomped one red tennis shoe. "She's not a nice lady, and she hates it when I come along. Do I have to go?"

"Yeah, you do."

"But I hate fireworks. They hurt my ears."

Seemed like Gloria *hated* most everything these days, especially the fluffy little patriotic dress her father had requested she wear for the occasion. Her little girl preferred jeans and T-shirts, but today, she was decked out like a miniature American flag. No wonder she was irritable.

"You look real pretty, honey. You'll have a great time."

"Will not."

"Will so." Summer saw her ex glide up in his aging Jeep Cherokee. Back in the day, when his insurance company was flourishing, Ed figured the vehicle made him seem rugged and outdoorsy, figured folks would think he was a fisherman, hunter—whatever—anything but a pitiful paper-pushing quarterback gone to seed. "Look, Gloria, your daddy's here."

"Yeah, I see him, and *she's* with him."

The child dragged her feet on the way to the door, and Summer followed. Sure enough, the whore Jolene was hunkered down on the passenger side. Even at a distance, Summer saw the diamond engagement ring sparkling on her left hand as she performed contortions to wave with that arm. All right, the bitch had made her point. After twenty-six years of marriage to Summer and four years of divorce, Ed had finally settled on a favorite bimbo. He had popped the question, and that damned ring was worth a couple of months of child support, money Summer would surely never see.

"Lookin' good, Summer!" Ed hollered.

"Hey, Summer!" Jolene added. "Love the matching bathrobe and slippers. Don't tell me you're staying cooped up inside on this glorious day."

Summer gave Gloria a little push in the right direction, and as her daughter shuffled to the car, Summer treated Jolene to an icy look cold enough to freeze fresh dog shit. It was bad enough that Summer had to work in the same building with Jolene at Lake Norman Regional Medical Center, but adding insult to injury, Jolene had recently been transferred to Summer's wing, where she'd be mopping floors in the office where Summer worked for the hospital's chief gastroenterologist. Come Tuesday morning, after the long Fourth of July weekend, every nurse in the unit would know about Jolene's engagement and Summer's disgrace.

"Aren't you goin' to the fireworks display?" Ed called out.

"Nope, I have other plans," Summer hissed through clenched teeth.

"What a pity," Jolene crooned. "We were hopin' to see you there, share a plate of barbecue or something."

With those parting words, Ed got his Cherokee moving and eased out of the lot. Gloria looked miserable, hunched and scowling from the backseat, and Summer imagined how good it would feel to dump an entire dish of vinegar barbecue down Jolene's exposed cleavage.

At the same time, Neighbor Kid came skulking from the shadows and stood by Summer's side, scuffing the toe of his unlaced sneaker on the curb. "I'm goin' to the fireworks," he said. "It's up at the high school, you know?"

Yes, she knew. The event had been widely advertised at their reunion last night, but whether anyone believed it or not, Summer really did have other plans.

"You can go with *me*, ma'am." Connor stared at her hopefully.

Summer smelled marijuana on his breath. "You know that stuff will rot your brain."

Connor's habitually pale face turned crimson beneath a bad case of adolescent acne. He backed off several paces. "Please don't tell my mom."

She glared at him but decided that telling on the kid would likely result in the loss of a perfectly good babysitter. Besides, at his age, Summer had smoked more than her fair share of pot, so who was she to judge?

"Don't let it happen again."

Connor promised he'd never use pot again and disappeared into his unit, then Summer hurried into her apartment with as much dignity as a forty-eight-year-old matron with a date could muster. She snagged a Diet Pepsi from the fridge, then bustled into Gloria's bedroom to use the computer they shared.

She lifted a teddy bear off the child-size desk chair and ignored the sticky peanut butter and jelly residue on the keyboard. After disabling the child controls and entering her top-secret password, Summer checked her email to verify the bizarre change of fortune in her otherwise dismal social life.

Sure enough, Paul's message was still there, saved "as new," confirming their date for six p.m. that night. They were meeting for drinks at La Hacienda, the Mexican restaurant owned by Salsa. Undoubtedly, Salsa would serve as a vested chaperone, so how scary could that be?

Besides, Summer and Paul had already met—sort of.

In the wee hours of morning, when Gloria was sound asleep, Summer had sneaked in and joined DATESCAPE. She had been only slightly impaired by drinking with the TLC girls, so she recognized Paul immediately when his face appeared on her first page of perfect matches.

She took a deep swallow of icy Pepsi, then experienced a brain freeze along with the excited thudding of her heart when she navigated away from email, back to DATESCAPE, and gazed into Paul's deep blue eyes under an unruly shock of bright red hair. His screen name was *Bioteach,* and Paul was none other than the clumsy waiter from the reunion.

Both of Summer's parents were retired teachers, so she just knew they'd approve of Paul's credentials. Was that karma or what? She'd thought he was cute right off the bat, even though Lila had been rude to him, and she couldn't wait to see Salsa's face when the two of them strolled into her restaurant together.

The two of them. She liked the sound of it. Boots had been right all along—online dating was the way to go. She liked it that Paul was also a night owl looking for true love, and she liked how he gave up his name as soon as they emailed. None of that bullshit caution, not when they were already friends—kind of.

It wasn't like they were competing in a race, but Summer would bet a week's pay that she'd be the first to land a viable date. The others in the TLC would be jealous, to hell with the skeptics. And she didn't give a rat's ass that *Bioteach* was a few years younger than she. Likely, Paul didn't need Viagra to help him along.

So as Summer started a hot scented bath and decided what to wear, she cared only that she felt thirty years younger—like eighteen again.

Chapter Six

Red woke up in a panic when bright bars of morning light framed the shade at her bedroom window. She had forgotten to set the alarm, she'd be late for work, but when she hoisted up onto one elbow, she realized *no.* Today was Sunday, tomorrow was the Fourth of July, and she was midway through an unwanted holiday.

She had two options—flop back down and sleep away the emptiness or get on with it—in spite of the fact that days off were a punishment, not a treat. When had that happened? When the hell had Red decided it was more fun to show up at 601 East Trade Street, Police Central, and wallow in the miseries of women who'd just been raped, rather than stay home and build a life of her own?

What life? When she sat upright and swung her legs off the side of the bed, a jackhammer at the base of her skull reminded her of last night's excesses—too much beer with her old girlfriends. *Oh, shit.*

When the phone on her nightstand suddenly started screaming, the jackhammer went into overdrive, and her caller ID announced it was Rick on the line. *Double shit!* She massaged her temples and knew she'd have to answer. Because if Ricardo Molerno was anything, he was persistent. He'd keep it up until her head exploded like a melon in a microwave.

"What?" she barked into the receiver.

"Good morning to you, too, doll. Did you get

up on the wrong side of the bed?"

"Go away."

"Hey, Red, did you read the file?"

She drew a blank, but then remembered the manila folder Rick left on the hall table—something about a rape/homicide. "No, damn it, I did not read it."

"Too bad." He chuckled. "Sounds like you have the day off. No wonder you're in such a pissy mood."

He knew her too well.

"So why don't you read my notes? There's nothing like a good juicy crime report to fill the empty hours."

"Go to hell."

He laughed. "Does that mean you won't accompany me to the fireworks tonight?"

Another blank. Had she actually agreed to go with Rick?

"C'mon, partner, you remember. I volunteer each year. It's a benefit for Gang of One at the stadium."

Gang of One was the CMPD program for at-risk kids likely to get involved with criminal gangs, and Rick had been active in all their events.

"I'm not going anywhere," she told him.

During her eleven years in a tempestuous relationship with Gina, Rick had gotten too damned comfortable hanging with the two of them. He was the stereotypical *lonely guy* and was currently between wives. She knew he missed Gina and Red being a couple, but it hadn't been Red's idea to break up this time. "I have other plans," she told him.

"You said you weren't going anywhere."

"My girlfriends are coming over," she lied.

"Those clueless girls from the TLC?"

"Are we done here?"

She heard him breathing through the silence as he decided how to respond—blast her with an angry retort or hang up like a gentleman.

"Okay, then," he said at last. "Have a good day."

Red sighed in relief when Rick signed off. Maybe his anger management classes were actually helping. She climbed out of bed, but when she walked across the hardwood floor toward the bathroom, the old wound above her left knee reduced her progress to a painful hobble. The bullet had severed a ligament, but expert surgery had prevented her from becoming disabled. Still—she swallowed the bitter taste at the back of her throat—she had never expected to be limping at age forty-eight. No wonder the assholes were pressuring her to retire.

She entered the john, stood at the sink, and frowned at the wild, redheaded witch in the mirror. She washed her face, untangled her unruly hair with a brush, and pulled on her favorite T-shirt—an ancient cotton rag from her police academy days. She added a comfy pair of plaid shorts and flip-flops, then she was good to go—if one's standards were extremely low.

Ignoring Rick's file as she passed the hall table, Red spooned extra coffee into the maker, poured in the water, and fired up the machine. As every coffee addict knew, caffeine was the best remedy to tame a headache, but just in case, she swallowed two Tylenol for good measure.

Next she shook some corn flakes into a bowl, added a whole red mini packet of raisins, skipped the sugar in deference to her migraine, and then moistened the mixture to mush with a dollop of two percent milk. Once her gourmet breakfast was ready, she had two new options: move out to the patio to breathe fresh air and soak up vitamin D or boot up her Dell and check out the man she'd seen on DATESCAPE last night.

She chose the latter.

In truth, Red had been curious about the whole internet dating scene. She had attended a two-day seminar on the subject of online predators, and her boss had encouraged all the detectives in their unit to explore cyberspace to better understand how so many women fell into dangerous situations leading to rape, kidnapping, and worse. The girls from the TLC had given Red the perfect excuse to get this done. But instead of seeking the woman of her dreams, as they suggested, she looked at men. After all, not one statistic cited any internet woman-on-woman crime.

So Red had put on her straight woman hat, which fit quite well after years of practice, and then logged into DATESCAPE. She opted for another noncommittal freebee, typed in the same criteria she'd used the night before, and sure enough, the handsome *Paintercat* came up again. She stared at the mug shot of a man with intense blue eyes and expensively styled dark brown hair, with a dusting of gray at the temples. The caption said he was sixty and lived in Mooresville. Those claims seemed honest and accurate, although his face looked much younger. But folks who lie about their age never add on years, so likely, he was telling the truth.

It was his screen name that first intrigued her. The first part implied he was a *painter*, as in "artist," and she liked that idea because Gina was a painter. But the second part, *cat*, really captured her imagination. She had studied the natural history of North Carolina and knew the word "painter" was loosely used by mountain folk to describe the mountain lions or cougars that roamed the hills. When she peeked at *Paintercat*'s two other photos, her suspicions were confirmed. The name had a double meaning.

Both pictures depicted Red's match standing in his studio beside an easel displaying two works of art he had supposedly created. Both paintings were violent studies of mountain cats attacking prey. The first canvas showed a stolen chicken in the cat's jaws, the second a dead fox. The style was abstract, almost cubistic. The predator's teeth were a slash of white, his eyes a round glint of amber, with plenty of red to indicate blood. The powerful message came through loud and clear: This artist understood the primal aspect of life and death.

Red liked that. She could relate. So she decided to go in for the kill, to pay her money, join DATESCAPE, and learn more about the edgy *Paintercat*. But there was a right way and a wrong way to go about the hunt. First, she created a new email account that bore no resemblance to her regular address. If and when she received mail from *Paintercat*, it would arrive in this new box.

Next, instead of her true ZIP Code, she entered the code for an adjacent postal district. Instead of revealing she lived in Charlotte, she claimed to reside in Mecklenburg County—much less specific. She chose a screen name, *Firebird,* and instead of using a personal credit card to pay for the service, she used a PayPal account in her father's name. Her dad had created the account so Red could choose her own holiday gifts, making Dad's life much easier. If a clever hacker followed the money to the PayPal account, it would lead him directly to a retired cop living in Florida.

Feeling good, almost smug, she poured a third

cup of liquid caffeine and realized her headache was finally retreating. Red had learned these privacy protection tricks at that seminar on internet crime and hoped with all her heart that her girlfriends, had they decided to proceed with the mission, had also used some diversionary tactics.

Obviously, a determined predator could break Red's anonymity in spite of these minimal barriers, but she figured for a little harmless internet flirting, the precautions were good enough. If some psycho actually tracked her as far as a phone number, the only one listed anywhere online would connect him to the front desk at the police department. *Whoops.*

Next, whistling off-key, Red navigated into her computer's picture album in search of some photos of herself that made her look acceptably human. Sexy and attractive was maybe too much to hope for. Whatever. It was time to bait the *Paintercat.*

Chapter Seven

Boots spotted her stalker immediately. He was impossible to miss because his wooly, salt and pepper Afro floated above the restless crowd of bargain hunters lined up to bust down the doors at Best Buy. The Reverend Jonah Ellis looked like a retro civil rights activist from the sixties, his full, unsmiling lips pursed above a neatly trimmed goatee as his equine head rotated and his dark eyes sought hers. When he caught her sneaking into the store through the heavily guarded employee entrance, he practically whinnied and pawed the ground.

Oh, shit. Likely, the man had been waiting for hours, and not because he wanted a hot deal on one of their featured sale computers. Boots couldn't decide if she was scared, annoyed, or both. Mostly, she was exhausted from her late night with the TLC girls. She'd known all along she had to work at the crack of dawn, but the last thing she needed was this loser lying in wait to make her job a misery. Why wasn't he in church preaching?

"C'mon, get in here, Boots!" Her assistant, Jimmy, cracked the door just wide enough for her to squeeze through, then he locked it behind her. "That crowd is mean. I swear, some of those crazies at the front of the line have been here all night with their sleeping bags. They'd just as soon trample you as wait one more minute."

"Idiots," she muttered as she stared at the heavy

young man. He was sweating profusely and already looked like he'd been through the Fourth of July sale wringer. "Glad I'm not in charge of security."

"Amen to that."

As Jimmy waddled toward the office where he and the rest of Boots's Geek Squad hung out, she ticked off a mental inventory of her store's readiness. Security would soon open only one door, permitting the customers to enter in a tight single file. They had hired extra discreetly armed guards for the event. These guards would exhibit zero tolerance for anyone who pushed, shoved, or cut into a checkout line. The managers claimed the merchandise was readily accessible in a traffic-controlled pattern. Unfortunately, the in-stock quantities of the lost leader sales items were insufficient to satisfy the large crowd, so many buyers would be forced to place orders and pick up their stuff next week. Invariably, those who didn't achieve instant gratification would be pissed, but that wasn't Boots's problem.

No, her job was to hide behind the scenes and schedule Geek appointments at the homes and offices of the technically challenged, who would hopefully buy tons of electronics today. The nine remaining Geeks would man an information desk or circulate with the customers, to answer their questions, and sell them the higher-priced items.

Boots sighed and glanced outside to where the reverend was still craning his neck and scowling in her direction. She and Jimmy had met Jonah Ellis at his Church of the Holy Redeemer. His large congregation had purchased a truckload of sound equipment and a computer system from Best Buy, so it had fallen on Boots, as team leader, to oversee the complicated installation.

They had spent nearly a week working at the church, and during that time, the fifty-something divorced pastor's interest in Boots had escalated from mild flirtation to obsession. He cornered her in the pews and sat too close for their so-called "technical consultations." He followed her room to room, and once he had sneaked up while she was flat on her back, her head tucked into a cabinet to conceal some wiring. When she pulled out, he was standing over her, his feet planted on the floor on either side of her waist, effectively pinning her.

Jonah had stood with his arms crossed, his eyes burning like red coals above his clerical collar as Boots struggled to wriggle out from between the sturdy tree trunks of his legs. The maneuver caused entirely too much physical contact with parts of the pastor's anatomy she would have preferred not to touch. Once she was successfully upright and Jonah was guffawing into his beard, Boots experienced something akin to terror, so she never returned to Holy Redeemer. Instead, she forced poor Jimmy to finish the job alone.

She sighed again. The dim, cavernous store was eerily quiet, the calm before the human storm that would churn the ordered aisles into swirling chaos. Like Jimmy, she hurried to the sanctuary of her private office and firmly closed the door. She retrieved a bottled water from her mini fridge, took two Tylenol, booted up her powerful computer, and opened her scheduling file. In the meantime, she heard the sudden rush of the human tide beyond her wall. It began with a low buzzing, like a swarm of locusts, then became a tsunami. She put on her headset, which connected her to the information desk, and within ten minutes, her monitor was alive with requests for appointments.

Boots got lost in the frenetic challenge of juggling personnel and dates. The hours flew by, until suddenly a tentative tap to her shoulder pulled her back to real time. "Jesus, Jimmy, I didn't hear you come in. What time is it?"

"Nearly noon. I hate to bother you, Boots, but he's out there asking for you."

One look into Jimmy's wide eyes left no doubt as to who "he" was. "Don't tell me he's still here."

"I'm afraid so. He's been lurking around all morning."

This wasn't the first time the reverend had hung out at the store, just hoping to have a word with her. "Tell him I'm not here." She groaned.

"But he saw you come in. He claims the sound system in the sanctuary's out of sync. When they try to play music, it skips…or some such shit."

"So tell him I'm out to lunch."

"No can do. The Rev went straight to the general manager. It was the boss who told me to come get you." Jimmy squirmed with guilt. After all, he had witnessed Jonah's pathetic advances and would do what he could to protect her, which was precious little. "I'm sorry, Boots. Want me to stay close, in case he tries something?"

She had to laugh. Her chief Geek, a college freshman here for a summer job, had too many Big Macs under his belt to defend her against the likes of Jonah. One shove and Jimmy would curl up and roll down the aisle like a pop bug.

"Thanks anyway, but I'm a big girl. I can take care of myself."

"Okay, but why don't you step outside your

office to meet him?"

Maybe it was smart to have this potential confrontation in public, but Boots's head still throbbed and her feet were asleep. If she let him in but didn't bother to get up from her chair, even a jerk like Jonah would see she was busy and take the hint. "Let's keep the door open," she told the kid.

"Copy that." Jimmy saluted. "I'll be right outside if you need me."

While she waited for her unwelcome visitor, Boots closed her eyes and rubbed the pain at the bridge of her nose. She had hoped to sneak out to her car during break and fire up her iPod. She had a tentative chat date with *Avatar*, her very hot new DATESCAPE match. In fact, she hadn't been entirely truthful with the girls last night. She wasn't a newbie like them; she'd been internet dating for over a year. She had initiated two strictly sexual affairs, but now *Avatar*, whom she had not yet met, promised to be much more than a casual roll in the hay.

As always, she'd done a background check, and so far, everything *Avatar* had claimed about himself was true. He was youngish, black, and beautiful. He owned a successful chain of video game stores in and around Charlotte, and better still, he was a would-be game designer looking for a business partner. He needed someone like Boots to enhance the technical behind his creative genius. *Avatar* had two retired Nintendo designers on the team—one composer, one artist—so maybe this guy wasn't just a pretend action character, like his screen name implied, but the real deal.

Boots desperately hoped so because she needed a break. Her own entrepreneurial start-up, designing software for small businesses, had gone south with the economy, forcing her to take this nowhere job at Best Buy. She was as sick of the corporate rat race as she was sick to death of men like the Reverend Ellis hitting on her.

"Hello, Sister Boots, may I come in?"

Speak of the devil. The reverend was hunched in the doorway like an old black crow, backlit into silhouette by the blinding warehouse lights. "I am not your sister, Jonas, and what the hell's wrong with your sound system?"

"Please call me Joe. Everybody else does."

Then that was everybody else's problem. Boots didn't intend to encourage this holier-than-thou poor excuse of a preacher man.

"Be nice, Sister Boots. Your manager promised 'satisfaction guaranteed.'" The man was smiling, but the smile never reached his cold eyes.

A chill shot up her spine. "Listen, Reverend Ellis, you said your sound system was skipping. Now that can't be right. I hooked it up myself, and it's rock solid. Only way it's skipping is if your disc is dirty." She kept her fingers on the keyboard and refused to meet his dry ice eyes.

But he stepped closer and placed his big hands on her shoulders. "Maybe we should discuss this over lunch. After all, I convinced our junior pastor to deliver the sermon this morning so I could meet with you."

"I don't eat lunch." She felt his heat and smelled sandalwood incense, an odor that permeated his church.

"Now you know, all God's chillun gotta eat. Your body is a temple, woman. Respect it, and it will respect you."

Right. Like Jonah respected her body? The chill in Boots's spine migrated to her breastbone. "Look, can't you see I'm busy?"

One of his hands strayed to the back of her neck and massaged the hollow at the base of her skull. "Let's talk about my dirty dick," he whispered.

His words were barely audible, but she'd heard him loud and clear. "Jimmy, can you come in here?" she called through vocal chords frozen by fear.

Boots's young helper appeared instantly. His pudgy cheeks were flushed, but the kid was game. "What's the problem?" he stuttered.

Jonah removed his hands and backed up one pace. "No problem, son. We were discussing my sound system. The lady says I have a dirty disc."

Jimmy seemed confused as he looked to her for guidance. "Yeah, that could cause trouble, so…?"

"So what should I do about that, son?"

Boots felt Jonah's eyes boring into her back as Jimmy fidgeted and gestured.

"Well, you should spray your disc with a mild glass cleaner, then rub it gently with a soft cloth."

Jonah's evil laugh echoed inside her small office. Boots was suffocating, she'd had enough. "Get the fuck outta here, Jonah!" She spun around on her chair and jabbed at the charged atmosphere between them with a sharpened pencil.

The reverend laughed even harder, his crooked teeth glazed green by the computer's light. "Lordy, you should watch your mouth, woman," he said as he backed toward the door.

"I think you should leave now," Jimmy croaked.

"I'm going, son." He winked at Boots. "We'll discuss my issue at a later date, Sister, at a time when you are less distracted."

And then he was gone.

Boots couldn't seem to catch her breath.

"Are you okay?" Jimmy seemed at a loss.

She nodded and waved him away.

"You sure? What just happened here?"

Boots inhaled deeply, holding the oxygen in her lungs. She exhaled slowly. "Nothing special," she told her assistant. "Just some Fourth of July fireworks exploding way too early."

Chapter Eight

Red was bored out of her gourd by the time the fireworks started, so she took a pot of coffee and Rick's file out to her tiny patio and stared up at the night sky. Sure enough, all over the city, bursts of colorful light exploded, bloomed into patterns, and then dropped out of sight. The most extravagant display was above the stadium, and she pictured Rick in the thick of the action. He would be overseeing the event with sulfurous powder filling his flared nostrils as the kids from Gang of One cheered him on. More power to him.

Far as she was concerned, the cacophony, especially the firecracker strings, sounded too much like gunfire. The sound dragged her back into that dark alley when, in a moment of panic and confusion, she'd felt the bullet enter her leg and had fired off a round at her attacker. When the smoke cleared, a kid was dead, a boy much like the gang members Rick was trying to save. Her victim's lifeless eyes, filled with surprise, haunted her frequent nightmares.

Red placed the coffee and file on her round wrought iron table and lit a citronella candle. She hated the potent citrus stink but appreciated the lack of mosquitoes and the light it provided—just enough to read Rick's short preliminary. Next she poured a cup of strong Cuban blend, propped her hated reading glasses near the tip of her nose, and read the single page. She recalled only a few details about what Rick said last night, but as she scanned the information, the gruesome bit about a gold crucifix shoved up some poor woman's vagina rang an unpleasantly clear bell.

Jesus Christ. The coffee sent a wave of heartburn churning up her esophagus. No wonder Rick left the Sexual Assault Unit. Just recently, Red's boss had complimented her for retaining her capacity to empathize with rape victims. The very next day, the boss had singled her out from a group of seven detectives for reassignment to the Cold Case Unit. Red's co-workers considered this assignment a step up the ladder, but she felt it was a comedown. She'd be stuck behind a desk and buried under paperwork.

Plus, she'd done nothing to deserve a demotion. It wasn't fair. Her two kills had been ruled "clean shoots" by Internal Affairs. On the other hand, Red had needed excessive psychiatric counseling to pull herself up from the abyss. Had she become a liability in the field?

Certainly, Gina had begged her to retire at that point, even threatened to leave if Red continued to put her life in danger. Leaving was one of the few promises her sweet lover had actually kept.

At forty-eight, Red was eligible for a decent pension, and Rick was the only fellow officer who consistently reassured her that she was still at the top of her game. Impulsively, she picked up her cellphone and speed-dialed his number.

He answered on the tenth ring. "What's up, Red?"

She heard impatience in his voice, as well as the deafening concussions of fireworks in the background. "Sorry, I had a couple of questions about this file you left for me."

"And you want to discuss it *now*?" he snapped.

She wanted to shrink up and hide under the table. "Sorry, you're right. My timing is off."

"Way off, doll."

Red recognized a familiar female voice in the background. Her first thought was that Rick had taken Gina to the fireworks and that he'd invited Red to set them up. Ever since they'd split, Rick had tried in subtle and not-so-subtle ways to get them back together. As she began to hyperventilate, she suddenly realized the background voice belonged to Miranda, a very young, very hot new detective who worked with Rick in homicide.

"What's Miranda doing there?"

He laughed. "C'mon, I invited *you* first, but you blew me off. Besides, aren't you with those crazy TLC girls?"

Until that moment, she hadn't realized that Rick and Miranda were an item. "Yeah, sure, the girls are here," she lied. "I'll call you tomorrow." She hung up before he could respond.

Dumb, dumb, dumb. Not to mention pathetic. Red was so humiliated she tossed the remainder of her coffee into an innocent potted geranium. Rick was moving on with his life, and so should she. At the same time, she really wanted to talk to someone about the weird case Rick had dropped into her lap, and the only other person who came to mind was dear old Dad. Calling him had been on her to-do list all day, and since the Fourth of July was his favorite holiday, now was as good a time as any.

Dad lived in a retirement community in Sarasota, a facility populated mostly by other retired cops, so she figured that even if Dad and some of his buddies were engaged in some celebratory activity, like tossing empty milk bottles filled with lit firecrackers into the pool, he would still make time for his only daughter. She punched in area code 941, followed by his number, and Dad answered on the first ring. Not a good sign. She hoped he wasn't feeling as antisocial and isolated as she was.

"What's up, monkey?" He sounded cheerful enough.

"Happy Fourth. Whatcha doin', Daddy?"

"Nothing much. Just sitting at the shuffleboard court under a palm tree, waiting for a coconut to fall on my plate."

She giggled. More likely, her father was tucked into his den with his computer, backseat driving whatever baffling case the Florida SBI was currently working. He had started like her, as a beat cop in Charlotte, but then he moved on to Raleigh to become one of North Carolina's top profilers. When Mom died, Dad was transferred to the State Bureau of Investigation in St. Petersburg, and even now his associates who were still active in the bureau allowed him to keep his fingers on the pulse of their most interesting cases— strictly in an advisory capacity, of course.

After exchanging the usual pleasantries, especially fun stuff about her new Dodge Challenger, she told him what was in Rick's file.

"So this woman named Judy was found dead in her own bed," he reviewed. "She was a fifty-three-year-old, out-of-work librarian. Her branch had been closed due to the economy and a lack of funding. Is that right?"

"Yes. The forensic tech believes she died sometime late this past Friday night, but they won't know for sure until the medical examiner takes her liver temperature. Point is, our guys didn't get to her until late last night, almost twenty-four hours later, and they wouldn't have found her then if her elderly parents hadn't gotten worried and called. Seemed Judy always phoned them on Friday nights."

Dad silently digested all the facts. Red thought the oddest part of Rick's report was that at first glance, the crime scene seemed like a perfectly normal, well-ordered bedroom with nothing out of place. Even the corpse had been carefully dressed in a pretty nightgown, then tucked neatly into bed under the sheets and covers.

"But then they found the ligature marks on her wrists and ankles, the semen on her belly, and that damned cross up her vagina," her father angrily regurgitated more details, "and the cause of death was strangulation. That's interesting."

"They think so. Or else it was the trauma when he crushed her larynx." Red took a deep breath. "The preliminary says the killer didn't use the letter opener as a weapon. They found no damage to her vagina, more like the creep just left it inside her when he finished."

"Sick bastard." Dad snorted in disgust. "Maybe the pervert used that damned opener to tease, or terrify, while he was getting his rocks off."

Suddenly, the muggy atmosphere of the summer night made Red nauseated. "They think Judy knew her attacker, Daddy. They think she let him in willingly, and then he drugged her. The physical evidence implied she didn't struggle until he had her down on the bed. It sounds like a date gone way wrong."

"An understatement. Seems the killer was a religious nutcase. You'd be surprised how many of those we get these days. What about fingerprints?"

"Nothing obvious, but we don't know yet."

"Witnesses?"

"The detectives are still making phone calls, still canvassing the neighborhood around Judy's apartment."

"You haven't given me a hell of a lot to go on, monkey. I assume that worthless ex-partner of yours collected a big juicy paper bag of semen."

Finally, Red laughed out loud. The fake animosity between Dad and Rick was legendary, when in fact her father liked him. The two men were painfully alike, and while Rick and she were partners, Dad and Rick had been best pals. Unfortunately, Dad had major reservations about Gina and had never fully accepted Red's lesbian lifestyle. When Gina left, Red figured Dad was secretly pleased, so the net result was that they never discussed what really mattered.

"The DNA evidence is already at our lab," she told him.

"Glad to hear it. Once your guys have a result and you send it to CODIS, tell those feds to put a rush on it. Unless you light a fire under their asses, those lazy techs will put the entire criminal justice system on hold. These days, results are so delayed we have felons walking the streets whistling Dixie and planning their retirements because they know we'll never get through the backlog."

"Yeah, Dad, I know. I'm sure Rick's captain will get our sample compared ASAP." CODIS, the Combined DNA Index System, was the national database that stored DNA profiles of all convicted felons, as well as profiles of those who had never been apprehended. Red knew CODIS would play a huge role in her life once she got to the Cold Case Unit. "I only hope we get a match," she finished.

"Don't count on it. Your killer probably wore gloves, and that's why you didn't find any obvious, misplaced fingerprints on the scene. He came prepared with restraints and his religious calling card. Likely, he had a supply of chloral hydrate or some other depressant to put poor Judy to sleep. So the crime was organized and premeditated, but the jerk took no precautions when it came to his semen, so obviously, he knows he's not been identified in the database."

"Dear old Dad, always the pessimist."

"Always the realist," he countered. "And another thing, monkey, the act of strangulation is personal, as is this sicko's attempt to leave the woman looking like a sleeping princess when he left her. Your man has some serious love/hate issues with middle-aged women, possibly had a problem with his mother."

"Oh, please stop!" Dad's assessment sounded like yesterday's cliché. "At this point, we know next to nothing, so maybe it was just a date gone wrong, some sadomasochism got out of hand."

Dad chuckled. Hey, *you* asked *me*, remember?"

Once a profiler, always a profiler. "I'll keep you in the loop."

"Good, and I hope this one murder is the end of it."

"What do you mean?" Suddenly, an exceptionally loud round of fireworks, likely the grand finale at the stadium, brought Red's morning headache back full throttle.

"Never mind, honey," Dad said soothingly. "Just watch your back, and give Rick a swift kick in the butt for me, will you?"

As usual, he hung up before she could squeeze in the last word or even a civil goodbye. So what else was new? As she watched the last pyrotechnics sputtering out above Charlotte's skyline, where the skyscrapers looked alarmingly like giant phalluses, she decided it was time to call it a day.

Chapter Nine

By the time the long holiday weekend was over, Red felt like tearing her hair out strand by copper strand. She'd never been good at leisure, so she holstered her Smith & Wesson, clipped her badge to her belt, retrieved her handcuffs, and drove to the huge Charlotte Mecklenburg Police Department building on Trade Street, which was only a few blocks away from her apartment. Not surprisingly, she was one of the first to report to work that Tuesday morning.

The second floor was the hub of the city's law enforcement, with all major units quartered on both sides of a long hallway. She took the steps two at a time, ignoring the end of the building where Rick worked in homicide and continued on to the Sexual Assault Unit, where as of today, she would be officially reassigned to the Cold Case Unit.

Naturally, her supervisor was waiting to help with the transition. "Gladys will be here to show you the ropes, Red, and I know you've already memorized the CCU handbook," Sergeant Darling said. "You'll only be moving across the room, so it's no big deal."

The petite blond sergeant was perched on the edge of Red's old desk. The large, airy room was divided into cubicles, and for fifteen years, Red's cubicle had included a great view of the old City Hall and the Police Memorial. But suddenly, the sergeant hopped off the desk and led her to a brand new, larger desk, where she would be stationed with the other supervisors against an inside wall with no view at all.

"So this is it." Sergeant Darling hunched her shoulders and seemed uncharacteristically ill at ease. Darling had never been comfortable with emotional confrontations, and she knew Red never wanted this change.

Red smiled mournfully at her longtime boss, whose name—Darling—accurately described the woman's appearance but remained the antithesis of her tough, no-nonsense personality. Darling always played the role of "bad cop," convincing traumatized young girls who had just been raped to stand up in court and relive the painful details of their attacks to put the bastards who hurt them behind bars. By contrast, Red's "good cop" persona was motherly and nurturing, an approach that too often left both Red and the victim in tears. According to Sergeant Darling, that empathy had been a recipe for Red's so-called burnout.

"Don't worry, you'll do just fine," Darling reassured her. "But don't let Gladys make the coffee. I swear her stuff's even viler than the swill we drink in the SAU."

"Thanks for the tip." Red eyed the big new desk, which was depressingly free of clutter. For one frightening moment, it appeared Darling was going to reach out and give her a hug, but fortunately, the sergeant came to her senses and stuck out her small hand instead.

"Well, good luck then." She gave Red's large paw a firm shake.

"Yeah, thanks..." But before she could finish the sentence, Darling left. She didn't even glance back over her shoulder.

At least Red still had her gun and shield, and she

still worked in close proximity to the fellow detectives who were like family. But she'd be riding a desk from now on, and as she sank into her plush new swivel chair, she could already feel her butt getting fatter as it spread out on its comfy new seat.

Damn it to hell. She lifted her gaze and faced one of the most powerful computers in the state. Red had done her homework and knew this Mac would connect instantly to almost every cold case nationwide. She also knew that since Charlotte's CCU had been established in January 2006, they'd brought numerous perpetrators to justice.

So her job was to review old cases and uncover new leads that might point to the bad guys. She would examine the evidence coming from the crime lab, which was located upstairs. As soon as their excellent techs profiled a DNA specimen, the result would automatically upload to the local databases. If they got no hits, it would move instantly to CODIS, the national database, and regardless of Dad's pessimism, the CMPD usually had a result within five days to a week, and that was pretty damned fast.

If a match occurred, Red would review victim and witness statements and, when possible, reinterview people. Considering the fact that the CMPD had two hundred thirteen reported rapes last year alone, many of them unsolved, her task was an awesome responsibility. And even though last year's rapes were down twenty-five percent from the year before, the numbers were still staggering.

That was the job description, but Red had always been a hands-on kinda gal, so as she stared at the shiny keyboard and monitor, not to mention the unused stack of lined pads and a cup of freshly sharpened pencils, she was not impressed. Also, her new PC was outfitted with the best security money could buy. It was supposedly hack-proof, bug-proof, and fully loaded with spyware. This meant she couldn't fool around with DATESCAPE or any other personal stuff unless she wanted Gladys, the unit's senior watchdog, to turn her in to Internal Affairs.

And as she sat there feeling sorry for herself, she glanced back at the tall window beyond her old desk and saw a dark storm cloud creeping across the summer sky.

As Red watched the first flashes of lightning and continued to feel sorry for herself, her phone system began beeping and blinking. She hadn't yet been instructed in the complexities of how to answer, but she picked up the receiver and began wildly punching buttons. Eventually, she connected to a familiar male voice.

"Hey there, big shot. Are you enjoying your new job?" Before she could bitch, Rick continued. "I'm really sorry about the other night, but the fireworks made it impossible to talk, you know?"

Sure, Red knew. Rick had gone home with his lovely fellow officer Miranda, then spent all day Monday in bed with her. As a consequence, Red had spent those boring hours twiddling her thumbs.

"You're not pissed, are you? You want to discuss the case, right?"

"Right."

"Well, we know a little more. Not much…"

She listened quietly while Rick confirmed what her dad had already surmised. Yes, Judy had probably known the UNSUB. She'd likely been dating him. Unfortunately, they'd found no witnesses to confirm this because the neighbors in the victim's large complex were all deaf, dumb, and blind.

"It's like nobody ever saw Judy dating, let alone saw anyone suspicious. Even her parents swear Judy had no social life," Rick continued. "But the medical examiner did find traces of Rohypnol in her system, along with a partially digested seafood dinner in her stomach."

So, Red mused, first the fucker took Judy out to a nice restaurant and then treated her to his date rape drug of choice. The sedative effects of Rohypnol took effect in a half hour or so, and some victims never remembered events they experienced under its influence. She hoped that had been true for Judy, that she hadn't been fully aware when her victim tortured her, but somehow, Red feared the worst. Most violent perverts derive no pleasure unless they witness the terror in their victim's eyes.

"The UNSUB was wearing powdered latex surgical gloves, so we suspect the prints we've lifted will belong to Judy and her family members," Rick said. "You can bet your buttered biscuit they won't be the killer's."

"Buttered biscuit?" Red giggled.

"C'mon, you know what I mean."

"So what's next?" Suddenly, she felt uncommonly sad as the storm cloud outside her old window let loose and wept all over the city. "Will you stop strangers on the street and check their pants pockets for powder residue?"

"What's your problem, Red? Didn't your old pals in SAU leave candy and flowers on your new desk?"

She would not dignify his remark with a

response, so eventually, Rick continued.

"We're doing everything we can. The lab's already profiled the DNA sample and uploaded it to CODIS, so hopefully, we'll have a match in less than a week. We also impounded Judy's hard drive. You never know what our quiet little librarian was up to online. For all we know, she was having a hot cyber affair with the killer. Now that would be stupid, wouldn't it?"

Very stupid indeed. Red would mention the stupidity of internet dating to her girlfriends when they got together Saturday night for their first TLC meeting. In the meantime, she'd figure out how to live with her stupid new job as thunder clapped and lightning electrified the Charlotte sky.

Chapter Ten

The TLC girls had unanimously chosen Lila to host their first meeting because they wanted to see her new lake home and had heard she was a good cook. So Lila stood at her kitchen counter, stirring the onions, peppers, ground beef, and Italian sausage into the wok. Soon she'd add her famous homemade tomato and mushroom sauce and allow the mixture to meld until her guests arrived.

She couldn't understand why they all wanted spaghetti on a hot summer Saturday, yet she was glad the women had chosen her to host and cook something requiring a little effort. She figured her hospitality would put them in her debt, making it harder for them to kick her out of the club once they learned she hadn't joined DATESCAPE.

At the reunion, they'd all promised to join and to have at least "winked" at someone by this first meeting, and Lila knew for a fact that Summer was already dating a guy she'd met online, so Lila would have to do some fast sweet-talking to keep the others from shunning her.

"You've been a patient girl, Georgia." She patted the golden retriever head Velcroed to her shorts. Since she began cooking, Lila had been acutely aware of the warm puffs of doggie breath tickling her thigh. She tasted the small rounds of browned sausage she'd set aside on a napkin, decided they were cool enough, and then tucked one into Georgia's drooling mouth. "Was that good, sweetie?" She smiled in adoration as her pet thanked her by fanning her with her tail. Naturally, Lila rewarded her baby with a second, then a third.

Next she and her golden shadow moved to the sink, where Lila gazed out the window and Georgia dropped to the cool tiled floor. At six p.m., the sun was still glowing in the blue July sky. It cast long, dramatic shadows across the newly mown lawn and sparkled on the lake. Only last night, they'd been inundated by floods of rain. Lila told Georgia it was lucky they had a pontoon boat so that they, like Noah, could board their ark and survive. But then, around midnight, the rain had stopped, as though a heavenly hand had decided to spare them all one more time, and so Lila could have a beautiful day for her party.

"Oh, look, Georgia, your boyfriend is here!"

Sure enough, Salsa drove her green Honda hybrid into Lila's driveway and quickly liberated Taco. As Lila braced herself for the canine love fest, she watched Salsa trot up to her door. Her friend looked especially sexy in a peach sundress and matching flip-flops. The low-cut string top accentuated Salsa's voluptuous bosom, while its short skirt showcased her tan, athletic legs.

As they hugged in the foyer, Lila wished again that Salsa wasn't so determinedly heterosexual. Different as they were—Salsa being the scintillating sunshine to Lila's moody moonlight—they'd always been best friends. But pathetically, Lila wanted more.

"Hmm, you feel good," Lila said as she released her.

"Likewise." Salsa grinned. "But don't let it go to your head."

Off and on since high school, they'd played

this game, with Lila pretending to pursue, Salsa gently rejecting. And although for twenty years Lila had lived out of state, as far as possible from her Carolina roots, each time she came home to visit, she and Salsa had reconnected.

"Where's Georgia?" Salsa asked as Taco jumped up and slobbered on Lila. "Usually, she's right here at the door."

"I hope she's not counter surfing." Lila laughed. "She's been mesmerized by the spaghetti cooking." When Lila whistled, Georgia eventually approached, wagging her tail and licking her lips.

"Uh-oh, looks like she got something," Salsa said.

They watched the dogs meet and greet, with Taco sniffing Georgia's mouth, rather than her opposite end, as was his usual practice. Soon they booted them both out into the fenced backyard.

"So c'mon in," Lila said.

They automatically beelined for the kitchen, where the only evidence of Georgia's indiscretion was a shredded paper napkin on the floor. As Salsa slipped into her favorite chair, Lila poured a glass of white zinfandel—organic, of course. Then, as Lila had feared, Salsa got right down to talking about the internet dating deal.

"Okay, girlfriend, let's dish. I have a date tomorrow with *Bikerboy*. Long as the sun's still shining, we're going to meet at Lake Norman State Park and then bicycle until the sun goes down."

Lila snorted. This would be Grizzly Adams, the blue-eyed longhair Salsa spotted on DATESCAPE. "Sounds   like fun," she said, trying to drum up some enthusiasm.

"Well, yeah, it will be. But if you're not interested, I won't tell you one damned detail." Salsa sounded tough, yet her eyes sparkled with mischief.

"I'm interested." Lila dumped the sauce into the wok, gave it a good stir with her wooden spoon, and dialed the thermostat down to simmer.

"We'll see how it goes. *Bikerboy* looks good on the internet, but you never know. He may turn out to be a dud, like maybe he stutters," Salsa said.

"I bet he has pimples on his butt." Lila poured herself some wine and sat across the table, grinning at Salsa.

Salsa was not amused. "How about you? Did you contact your art-loving mystery woman, *Waterspirit*?"

Lila took a long swallow. Of all people, Salsa should know Lila would never hook up with someone through an internet date. "Nope, I haven't done anything yet."

"Why not? The girls will kill you!"

Lila shrugged. "Then I'm dead, and no one gets supper."

"But I thought you had a thing for this woman. You said she was hot when you saw her at your gallery, right?"

Lila shrugged again. "DATESCAPE is not my thing." She felt no need to confess that since she'd discovered that *Waterspirit* was online *and* a lesbian, Lila had been obsessed. She had combed through the gallery's art sales slips until she found the mystery woman's name, address, and phone number. Next Lila had shamefully Googled directions to her house and even done a drive-by.

Salsa helped herself to another drink. "Well, I want supper, so I'll try to run interference for you with the others. Where the hell are they, by the way?"

Before Lila could answer, the dogs barked, and an engine growled up the driveway. When Lila gazed out the window, she saw an old tan station wagon stop and park.

"Summer's here."

"Cool. Now *she* has a real story to tell," Salsa said. "And I witnessed the whole thing—at least part of it. Summer had her first date with her internet guy at *my restaurant*, so I got to meet him, even sat with them at their table for a while."

"Did you like him?" Everyone in the club knew Summer had been on a date, but no one knew the details.

Salsa wriggled her shoulders. "He seems okay, not my type, but apparently, he's really into Summer. He's a quiet, clean-cut guy, you know?"

"What's wrong with that? His hair isn't long enough for you? Did he not believe in global warming or hate polar bears?"

"Oh, give it a rest."

They raced to open the door for Summer, who looked as fresh and radiant as her name in a pale blue tank top, which brought out the color of her eyes. She wore an ankle-length patterned India skirt and sandals. When they pulled her into the club's mama bear hug, Summer's long, floating blond hair smelled like shampoo.

"You look great, Summer," Lila said as both dogs crowded at the hem of Summer's skirt to sniff for cat trace. Everyone had heard stories about Summer's ornery cat. They were almost as commonplace as her tales about her precocious eight-year-old daughter, Gloria, her philandering ex-husband, Ed, and the creepy neighbor boy who babysat for her.

Unlike Salsa, Summer and the other women in the club had never visited Lila's home, so as they guided her toward the kitchen, Summer hesitated to inspect the bold primitive art on the walls and to touch Lila's favorite African sculpture—a carved wooden fertility goddess with jutting breasts and a prominent, bare buttocks.

"Whoa, you better cover this girl with a sheet or something if I bring Gloria to visit."

"Really, Summer, kids should learn at an early age that the human body is beautiful, nothing to be ashamed of," Lila said.

"Even so." Summer frowned. "We didn't raise our girl that way."

Lila sighed. Okay, so she and her old high school friends had little in common, but they were still good company. And as her ex had often pointed out, Lila was too much alone.

The sun had dropped lower in the sky when they entered the kitchen. Six thirty. Lila checked out the window, hoping Red and Boots would come soon. Summer refused the wine and opted for a beer. While Lila prepared a plate of crackers, a selection of soft cheeses, and black olives, she listened to Summer's enthusiastic recounting of her date with Paul, who proved to be the clumsy waiter who had splashed beer on Lila's blouse at the reunion.

"God, he's so smart, a biology teacher. He's sweet and funny and such a gentleman. He even opens doors and pulls out chairs for me."

"Has he ever been married?" Salsa was into it.

"Nope, but says he's been close a few times." Summer blushed. "And something tells me he's ready now. He loves kids, so tomorrow he's dropping by to meet Gloria."

"Aren't you moving a bit too fast?" Lila grumbled as she lifted a frozen loaf of garlic bread out to thaw.

"Hey, girls, in case you haven't noticed, none of us is getting any younger," Summer retorted. "How many guys out there are looking for women pushing fifty?"

"I don't care how many *guys* are out there." Lila took lettuce, tomatoes, and other salad materials from the fridge.

"No, I'm sure you don't, and I think you're jealous."

Salsa interrupted to defuse the tension. "Listen, I spoke to Red, and I think she's planning to wink at a man called *Paintercat*, who claims to be an artist."

"An artist? Good luck." Lila groaned. "But why the hell is Red winking at a *man*? We all know she's playing on my team, so what's she up to?"

Salsa shrugged. "Red claims it's a work project. She told me she made up a profile pretending to be a divorced woman on the make. She implied that she was looking for sex and wasn't too picky about the men she met."

"Or maybe Red's come to her senses and wants to find out what she's missing," Summer said. "She wasn't gay in high school. I think that Gina woman got her off track."

"Grow up, Summer." Lila rolled her eyes.

Salsa said, "Hey, guys, Boots is hooking up with this awesome dude called *Avatar*, who owns a chain of video game stores in Charlotte. I spoke to her Wednesday night, and for all I know, she's met the guy by now."

Lila refreshed her guests' drinks and poured another large zinfandel for herself. As she assembled tomato juice, vinegar, and crumbled blue cheese for her dressing, she knew she was in trouble. Everyone would hate her once they discovered she hadn't "gotten with the program," and what was she doing with these straight women, anyway? She wished Red would arrive to support her because Red would understand her reluctance to bare her soul in the very public, maybe dangerous world of the internet.

As the minutes ticked by, Lila felt anxious. She accepted that Boots might be delayed because her managerial position at Best Buy often prevented her from leaving on time, but Red supposedly had this Saturday off, so where the hell was she?

Chapter Eleven

By the time the sun slipped below the horizon, leaving a golden stain in the sky and on the water, Lila realized they were all drinking too much and, in spite of the snacks, getting a wee bit tipsy. She knew this because the conversation had disintegrated from excitement over their new boyfriends to complaints about their current lives.

Salsa was upset because her new all-organic menu at the Mexican restaurant was failing to capture the public's imagination, and sales were down. Summer was bitching about her ex-husband's new fiancée, an apparent slut named Jolene, who mopped the floors in Summer's office at the hospital and made Summer's life a misery.

Lila was mainly concerned about feeding everyone before they all got drunk. "Maybe I should put the pasta water on the stove."

"Shouldn't we wait?" Salsa said. "I'll give them a call and see what's keeping them." She took out her cellphone and dialed Red and Boots, but both calls went to voicemail.

"I think we should eat." Summer's pretty forehead creased with worry. "I only have Connor until ten."

Lila filled the pot with hot water, added a drop of olive oil, and switched on the burner. "Let's get started without them. That's the good thing about spaghetti. We'll keep the sauce warm, and they can eat when they get here."

By eight o'clock, the three had finished dinner, but no one ate with gusto. The absence of Red and Boots weighed on their spirits like a tropical depression, and as they carried the dirty dishes to the sink, everyone was unusually quiet. Salsa had called their absent friends again, but again her messages went to voicemail.

"I don't get it," Salsa said. "Why don't they call back?"

"Yeah, it's really rude. Everyone carries a cellphone nowadays," Summer added.

Lila pushed the sad, uneaten scraps into the garbage disposal and began rinsing plates. "It's not like either one of them. Something must have happened."

By nine, the dishwasher was humming on auto dry, and the girls were sipping distractedly at their coffee.

"I'm sure they didn't just forget about our meeting," Salsa said.

"Of course not." Lila figured she'd better bring Georgia and Taco in, as it was now fully dark and the dogs would be hungry and thirsty. Hopefully, they would distract her guests with doggie antics because otherwise, her party was dead in the water.

She excused herself and stepped outside, hoping against hope to see Red's new Dodge Challenger drive up the road. When she whistled, both dogs began charging toward her but then put on the skids and reversed course when they heard a car turn onto Lila's dead-end street.

Lila ran to the gate, accompanied by wild barking, but then stopped cold when she realized the automobile that swung into her drive, then parked was not Red's Dodge, but rather a white Ford Crown

Victoria. She was instantly apprehensive because Lila never had unexpected company. She squinted at the two profiles in the front seat just as a tall female figure unfolded from the passenger side and strode toward her. In the pause of several heartbeats, Lila recognized the woman as Red.

"Where the hell have you been?" she shouted. "Don't you know what time it is?"

But Red simply held up both hands in a gesture of peace and kept coming.

"Is that Boots with you?" Lila shrieked, unable to control her inhospitable expression of relief. "It better be!" But when she peered again into the car's interior, now dimly lit, she saw the driver was male.

When Red came through the gate, gently pushing the dogs away with her feet to keep them from escaping, Lila knew right away that something was terribly amiss because Red wore her badge, handcuffs, and a mean-looking gun holstered under her jacket. She was definitely not dressed for a party.

"What's wrong?" Lila gasped.

"Let's go inside."

Salsa and Summer were hovering inside the front door with expectant smiles on their lips, but when Red and Lila stepped into the hall, Red's slouching, defeated body language wiped the joy from their faces. When they moved into the bright kitchen, they saw that Red, who never cried, was holding back tears.

Lila placed her hand on Red's trembling arm. "What?" she gently asked.

Red almost choked on her words. "Boots is dead. She's been murdered."

Chapter Twelve

Red stayed only ten minutes because she couldn't abide all the questions and tears, especially when she had no answers. They exchanged hugs, then she escaped through the backyard, wriggled past the dogs milling at the gate, and slid into the passenger seat.

"Take me back to the scene," she said.

Rick's dark eyes glistened in the dim interior. "Bad idea. The team has it under control, and you're too emotionally involved."

"But I never said goodbye. I owe Boots that much."

"Trust me, you don't want to see her."

They fastened their seat belts. Rick started the engine, and as they backed out of Lila's driveway, Red saw the girls' faces, framed like three desolate ghosts in the window. When they drove down the lane, the lake was black and still, glazed by moonlight.

"I was a coward, Rick. I should've gone in."

"You did the right thing."

Rick had gotten the call from Northeast Service Area about the time Red got home. She was just about to shuck off her uniform and dress for Lila's party when Rick called. He explained that although the reporting officer had given few details about the homicide, Rick had recognized the victim's name. When he told her it was Boots, Red had dropped everything, begged him to pick her up, and let her ride along. But when they finally arrived at Boots's condo, Red had been too distraught to view the scene. Instead, she'd cowered in the unmarked car like a blubbering baby.

"Please take me back, Rick. I want to talk to that kid who called it in. I'm sure he's still there."

He groaned and ran his fingers through his buzz cut. She knew he was weakening because while Rick was a wuss when it came to dealing with rape victims, he loved all the forensic details at a murder scene.

"Okay, but all you do is interrogate the kid. You don't enter the condo, agreed?"

"Agreed."

Boots lived in a village of one-floored condominiums built in three-storied tiers. The housing groups were nestled in an attractive, park-like setting, including woods, tennis courts, and several ornamental ponds. Mostly young, upwardly mobile singles resided there, attracted by the proximity to Interstate 77, which gave them easy access to Charlotte and the rapidly growing Lake Norman area. Had Boots's condo been located a stone's throw farther north, it would have been outside the CMPD's jurisdiction.

"Sure you want to do this?" Rick asked as he parked near a perimeter strung with yellow crime scene tape. The lot was brightly illuminated by strobe lights from a half dozen police units, and the usual clots of curious onlookers had assembled for some Saturday night entertainment.

"Stop worrying. I'm okay."

An ambulance was discreetly parked off to one side, and Red realized that soon they'd be bringing her old friend out in a body bag. She had no time to lose, so before Rick could react, she unclipped her seat belt and charged toward the scene. Ignoring his angry calls, she ducked under the tape and flashed her badge at Boots's front door before Rick could stop her.

"C'mon in, Detective."

Red was instantly recognized by a pair of cops from Eastway Division and by Harold Fishbein, the medical examiner. Harry the Fish was a tall, stork-like man, all wrist bones and Adam's apple, with the serious, unsmiling demeanor of an undertaker. But his forensics skills were legendary, and he had served the department well during his long tenure.

"Hello, Red. Rick told me you knew the vic. I'm so sorry."

She took a deep breath and warned herself, *Do not think of Boots. Pretend this corpse is just another casualty of the fucked-up society we live in.* But as she walked through the small, neat rooms with minimal furniture and maximum high-tech equipment, she couldn't help but visualize sweet-natured, geeky Boots sipping wine in front of the oversized OLED television or hunched over the streamlined keyboard of her PC.

"Obviously, this wasn't a robbery," Harry said. "These electronics are worth a small fortune."

"Boots worked at Best Buy," Red mumbled as she followed. By then, Rick was on her heels, trailing like an overprotective guard dog. With each step, the closed space smelled more deeply of death, so Red braced herself and hesitated outside the bedroom door.

Rick pulled out the micro-recorder he carried in his breast pocket and began speaking into it. "Apartment is in good order, no signs of a struggle. We believe the victim knew her assailant, no evidence of forced entry."

"But she was subdued with a stun gun," Harry interrupted. "We found a raw, red patch of skin on her stomach. The killer zapped her in the hall, then dragged her inside and tied her down on the bed." The ME pointed at the almost-imperceptible drag marks on the recently vacuumed carpet. "Of course, that's only a theory."

"Sounds about right to me," Rick grumbled.

It took every ounce of willpower Red could muster to enter Boots's bedroom, where two crime scene techs were bagging trace evidence and dusting for prints. The photographer was the only official looking at the body, and the faint clicking of his camera's shutter, followed by the popping explosions of light from the flash made Red dizzy. Noticeably absent was the usual nervous banter from the cops, which so often accompanied a rape homicide. Were her fellow officers subdued because they knew Red was Boots's friend? Or were they respectful because a horrific crime scene had stunned them to silence?

Harry the Fish gently appropriated Rick's micro-recorder and held it to his lips. "Livor mortis is fixed, and she's in full rigor. Given the fact that the apartment is heavily air-conditioned, and until we do the vitreous potassium tests to confirm, I put the time of death at approximately twenty-four hours ago."

"She was killed last night this time?" Rick asked.

"I believe so," Harry confirmed.

Rick turned to Red, a pained expression on his face. "The kid named Jimmy reported Boots missing. He works with her at Best Buy and was worried when she never showed up this morning, but he waited until the end of his workday to drive here. When he saw her yellow Volkswagen in the lot, but she didn't answer her doorbell, only then did he call 911."

Harry shrugged. "Doesn't matter. The lady was

long gone by the time Best Buy opened this morning. Cause of death—manual strangulation."

"Just like Judy the librarian's murder last weekend," Rick commented. "Gotta wonder if the two are related. Both deaths occurred on a Friday night. Both vics were middle-aged women who apparently knew the killer, let him come inside, and were then strangled."

"One big difference," Red said.

"Yeah, what's that?"

"Boots was African American."

"Maybe the UNSUB has no racial preference. He's an equal opportunity killer."

Harry cleared his throat, then continued speaking into Rick's recorder. "Bruising on her wrists and ankles indicates she was bound to the bed frame before death, likely when her muscles had been immobilized by the stun gun. Vaginal area shows signs of penetration with an unidentified sharp object, but the sick fuck apparently ejaculated on her clothing."

"Sounds like the same killer to me," Rick broke in. "Only this time, the asshole didn't bother to undress her, just pulled her panties off."

Red sank into a chair at Boots's dressing table and hoped against hope that the unidentified sharp object was not another bloody crucifix. She felt faint as she stared into her lap and couldn't look up to the mirror for fear of seeing the bed reflected there. She hadn't yet looked at the body, but she knew by the anger in Rick's voice that the scene was not pretty.

"At some point, the lady regained consciousness and put up a fight," Harry said. "We found traces of skin under her fingernails. She got a bite of him, too, judging by the blood residue—not hers—on her teeth."

Leave it to Boots to retaliate, Red thought proudly. Likely, that was when he killed her. If it was the same pervert, he liked his women drugged and helpless, not fighting back.

"Did you find anything *religious* around?" she weakly inquired.

Harry blinked in surprise. "Only a gold cross around the victim's neck."

"That wasn't Boots's cross," she firmly informed him. "Boots rejected religion back in high school, as a protest against her folks' insanely strict Baptist upbringing."

"High school was a long time ago," Rick pointed out. "Maybe your girlfriend got herself *saved* over the years."

He was right. What did Red really know about Boots or any of the TLC girls after all this time? "But I still say it's not her cross. The killer put it around her neck after he strangled her."

Harry nodded. "You could be right. Had the chain been around her neck during the attack, the pressure from his hands would've left an impression of that chain on her skin."

"This jerk didn't dress her up pretty, like he did Judy. Maybe it's not the same guy," Rick said.

"The DNA will tell us real quick, boss," one of the techs said. "Either they match, or they don't."

"You are right, my man." Rick then turned to Red, his eyes filled with concern. "There's nothing more we can do. Let's split and let the experts take it from here."

"First I need to say goodbye." This was the moment Red had been dreading. As her hands trembled in her lap, she saw movement in the mirror when Harry covered the body with a large white sheet. When she stood and began walking, she was grateful her legs still worked.

A hush fell on the room as Red reached the bedside. She bowed her head a moment and closed her eyes. When she opened them, she saw Boots asleep on a pillow. The sheet was pulled up to her chin, and Boots's dark, intelligent eyes, which Red would forever remember as sparkling with mischief, were blessedly closed.

Had it not been for the odd angle of Boots's naked arms, bent at the elbows and lying flat on the bed, framing her head in a triangle, her wrists cocked outward in the caricature of a Japanese Kabuki dancer and for the stiff jutting of Boots's always stubborn jaw and the ashen gray pallor of her beautiful ebony skin, Red might have been fooled.

But as it was, she reached out and touched Boots's soft, close-cropped Afro, then bent over and kissed her cold, purple lips. *Farewell, my friend.*

Red left the bedroom and sensed Rick's anger as he stalked her through Boots's small condo. When they reached the door, he stepped wordlessly into the night to give Red an opportunity to compose herself. Rick had always been propelled by anger, especially in situations where he felt relatively helpless. The anger motivated him to succeed as a cop, but it had been disastrous for their work relationship. Especially when Red's response to his fury had always been an icy, nonverbal calm.

She felt that calm now—a gut-deep determination to avenge Boots's death. Like a dog with a fresh, bloody bone, she would clamp down and growl like hell if Rick tried to pull it away. By rights, this was his case. As homicide's lead detective, the murder was his baby, but as the former senior member of the Sexual Assault Unit, Red figured she should get joint custody.

As she waited for her pulse rate to slow and pondered her next move, she noticed something out of place from the corner of her eye—a small, card-like object that had apparently fluttered from Boots's hall table down to the tiled floor. Red knew she shouldn't touch it, yet she took a tissue from her purse and carefully retrieved the photograph mounted in a decorative cardboard mat. Holding it under a lamp, she was stunned to see five familiar, animated faces— the TLC girls enjoying their high school reunion. The candid shot captured what now felt like a bittersweet moment, with Summer, Salsa, Lila, and Red seated at their table. They were laughing and drinking beer, while Boots stood above them, her laptop open on the table between them.

It captured the instant when Boots introduced them all to DATESCAPE. The intense memory squeezed Red's heart like a strong, icy hand and brought tears to her eyes as she took a closer look. They were so happy and carefree, with no premonition of the horror waiting just around the corner.

Who had taken this picture? Had a wandering entrepreneur capitalized on the event, figuring alumni would purchase their likenesses? Was the photographer one of Boots's friends, a former classmate kind enough to gift Boots with this special memento?

Suddenly, Red wished she'd stayed in touch and been more sociable, wished she had a photo of her own. Envy escalated to greed. After looking over her shoulder to be sure no one was watching and against all rules of protocol, she almost slipped the souvenir into her pocket. Fortunately, her good angel intervened and told her to behave and consider the consequences, so she returned the treasure to the tiled floor.

Chapter Thirteen

Rick was waiting impatiently outside the condo. "Lucky for you, the kid's still here." He pointed at a heavy young man standing alone, off to one side of the circus still performing in the parking lot. "You should've stayed out here, like I told you."

"Shut up, you're not my boss." Maybe it was her guilt talking, but Red wasn't in the mood for his bullshit. "I'll talk to him now." Without waiting for permission, she ducked under the crime scene tape and ignored Rick panting on her tail.

"Slow down, Red. We're on the same team here, believe me. You take the lead, and I'll play second fiddle while you interview the kid."

Did that mean Rick would allow her to work the case? Instead of playing the aggrieved bitch, she adjusted her attitude. "Promise not to interfere?"

"Absolutely." His dark eyes gleamed beneath his black buzz cut. "I want to work with you on this."

Red was intimately familiar with all Rick's signals, and by the way he nervously massaged the heavy afternoon shadow on his square jaw, she knew he was sincere. And she was mightily relieved. "Partners?" She held out her hand.

"Partners." He shook on it.

When they reached the kid who called 911, Red noticed he was sweating like a pig at a barbecue. "I'm with the Charlotte Mecklenburg police." She smiled and handed him her card. "Are you Jimmy?"

"Yes, ma'am...uh, Detective Calendar. I'm James Allen, a freshman at Mitchell College, but right now, I work with Boots at Best Buy. She's my boss."

"*Was* your boss." Rick snorted.

She shot Rick a warning look. "So, Jimmy, you were worried when your boss never showed up at work today, right?"

"Yes, ma'am." He mopped his flushed face with the back of his hand. "I can't believe she's dead." He glanced nervously at Rick.

"So you came here right after work, saw Boots's Volkswagen in the lot, rang her doorbell, and when she didn't answer, you called 911?" Red continued.

"Yes, ma'am, that's right."

She watched the boy anxiously. Obviously, he was scared out of his mind and trembling uncontrollably in spite of the repressive heat. "Are you sick?"

"Yes. I mean no—I'm not sick. I just can't believe she's dead." Jimmy blinked back tears as the coroner's ambulance backed up to Boots's door. Two EMS workers opened the van and lifted out a portable gurney. "Oh, shit." The kid groaned.

"You seem nervous." Rick rocked ominously back and forth on his heels.

"Yes, sir. I've never seen anything like this before."

Jimmy was hyperventilating. Red feared he would faint, so she took his arm and made him sit on a brick retaining wall. "Relax and tell us what you know."

"Yeah, Jimmy, how'd you feel when you saw your boss's body?" Rick moved in close, his face sinister in the pulsing light from the spinning cherries on the patrol cars.

"Jesus Christ! I never went inside," Jimmy

croaked.

"Sure you did. Boots wouldn't open her door for a stranger, but you were her friend, weren't you, Jimmy?" Rick was relentless.

"God, yes, I was her friend." The kid gasped. "I loved Boots!"

Red delivered a vicious elbow jab to Rick's ribs, but he kept up the brutal interrogation.

"But Boots didn't love you back, did she, Jimmy?" Rick paused while the EMS guys slowly brought the gurney, now weighted with a black body bag, bumping down the steps to the ambulance. "You couldn't take rejection, so you killed her," Rick finished.

The kid's eyes stretched wide with shock as he watched his boss being loaded. Suddenly, he hunched over and began coughing into his hand. Red was sure he would vomit. She took hold of Rick's arm, her fingernails biting into his flesh, and dragged him aside. "What the hell do you think you're doing?" she hissed. "I thought this was *my* interview."

Rick shrugged. "Kid said it himself. He loved Boots, but she was way above Jimmy's pay grade. That age, boys are hornier than hell, so his puppy love got outta hand."

"Bullshit." Red dug in harder as Jimmy continued coughing and the ambulance pulled slowly away. "You'll give that boy a heart attack."

Rick shrugged again, so she shoved him away in disgust. "Back off and keep out of my way." She returned to the stricken boy, who had finally stopped coughing. "Are you all right?" she asked gently.

Jimmy nodded. "I loved Boots."

"So you said." Red gazed at the night sky. "And you didn't kill her?"

Surprisingly, Jimmy climbed to his feet and squared his wide shoulders. "No, Detective Calendar, I didn't kill her, but I sure as hell know who did."

Chapter Fourteen

Red had never been able to cry. After years of holding back, she feared once she started, the tears would overwhelm her with hurricane force, and she'd never be able to stop. As Rick drove her home to her condo, she came close to letting loose, like the torrential rain that began the moment they took the off-ramp at Exit 3. The downpour continued while he dropped her off outside her apartment.

"Sure you'll be okay here alone?" Rick asked, a mischievous glint in his eye.

"Hell, yes. Why wouldn't I be?"

"Yeah, right. Good night then." He saluted, then drove off into the soggy night.

Naturally, Red had no umbrella, so she ducked her head and sprinted up the two steps to her door. On emotional overload, paying no attention, she suddenly bumped into a dark figure sheltering under her overhang.

"Jesus Christ!" The impact more surprised than frightened her, but when she got a better look at the intruder, she was truly terrified.

"Sorry, Red, I didn't mean to scare you." The rich alto voice was intimately familiar. Lamplight from the walkway glowed in her smoky, gray-green eyes, and raindrops glistened on her pale face. "Rick called and told me what happened. He thought you could use some company tonight."

Red's beloved Gina was shivering in the heat,

her arms folded across her chest in a defensive gesture, like she didn't know if Red would hit her or embrace her. Red didn't know, either. She was in full-blown shock.

"Don't be angry. I'm so sorry about Boots. I know how close you two once were. Will you let me in, please?"

Red hesitated, her heart pounding double-time. *Let Gina in?* How many times had the woman deserted her? How many tears to fill a bucket?

"I'll only stay a minute, promise, but I need to know you're all right," Gina pleaded.

Red hadn't seen Gina for almost a year, but the pain of her leaving had never stopped. Knowing full well she was making a terrible mistake, hands trembling, Red took out her key and opened the door, taking care not to touch Gina as she ushered her into the condo, which Gina had never seen.

As Red turned on the lights, heat radiated from Gina's wet clothes, and her short, spiked black hair glistened with raindrops. For once, Gina seemed terribly vulnerable.

"Really nice place," Gina said. "I've driven past several times, but I was scared to ring the bell."

No way! Red thought that she'd been the only stalker. During the first few months of their separation, Red had checked out their former apartment on a regular basis. She had hoped to catch a glimpse of Gina and had fervently hoped she wouldn't see signs that a new woman had taken up residence. When neither sighting occurred, Red had stopped, given up hope.

"Where's your bathroom?" Gina carefully removed her wet sandals and left them on the welcome mat.

Red couldn't speak, so she pointed and watched Gina's bare feet, which she had always adored, tiptoe down the hall with cat-like grace. Red took off her own shoes, and because she was a glutton for punishment, followed Gina and found her standing at the sink, facing the mirror. Gina pulled off her soaked purple tank top, and as always, she wore no bra. Red stared at the tiny four-leaf clover tattoo on Gina's left shoulder. As Gina toweled her hair, her small perfect breasts bobbed above her flat belly, and their gazes locked. Gina had always liked Red to watch.

Over the years, the slow strip in their bathroom had become a ritual, tops first. Red hesitated only a moment. She removed her jacket and holstered her gun, then unbuttoned her shirt. Shockingly, she sensed the pent-up tears pushing behind her eyes. The violent loss of Boots and the sudden appearance of Gina sent her emotions spiraling in dizzy circles.

Red's fingers trembled as she finished her last button and dropped the shirt on the laundry hamper. As her eyes burned with those unshed tears, she saw Gina's expression of surprise as Red faced her directly.

"Are those tears? You don't cry." Gina took two steps, closing the distance between them, and Gina's fingers sought Red's face. "Want to talk about it?"

Red's skin hurt where Gina touched her. Did she want to talk about Boots or ask what the hell Gina was doing back in her life? Red would rather chew on aluminum foil than discuss either topic. Red shook her head, then removed the cuffs and badge from her belt. She unsnapped her bra, let it fall, and then pulled Gina into her arms.

Choking back those pathetic tears, Red held Gina tight, her larger breasts cushioned above Gina's.

She felt the rapid beating of Gina's heart. In the beginning, Red had worried about how they would fit together. Red was taller, clumsier, and yes, eight years older than Gina. But from the first time they'd made love, they had combined like an easy jigsaw puzzle, and each time, it got better, deeper, and more explosive than before.

Red moaned when Gina's small, strong hands caressed Red's back, pulling her closer. Gina buried her face under Red's chin and kissed her neck. In turn, Red traced the delicate contours of Gina's shoulders, hesitating on the clover tattoo. Gina's hair still smelled like honeysuckle after a rain, and she tasted like salt.

What the hell was Red doing? Knowing it was all wrong, she unzipped Gina's shorts and slipped them down over slim hips. Gina stepped free of them with the skill of a ballerina. Returning the favor, Gina unbuckled Red's belt and tugged at the waist of Red's trousers. Gina managed not to giggle as Red struggled to get her long legs and big feet free of the pants, with much less grace than Gina.

Seconds later, when Gina's fingers slipped inside Red's panties and found her warm wet core, Red knew she was lost.

"Where's the damn bed?" Gina huskily demanded.

Once in the bedroom, Gina released Red momentarily, so that Red could retrieve her pistol. Gina still remembered the drill. She waited while Red locked the gun in her bedside table before they shakily made their way to the queen-sized mattress.

Red didn't have time to feel guilty about not making the bed that morning. Besides, Gina already knew Red was the world's worst housekeeper. They peeled back the rumpled top sheet and fell right in.

They had always taken turns, but that night, Gina started on top. Illuminated by a bar of light from the bathroom and the glow from the parking lot, Gina made love to Red like a woman possessed. Gina worked her way down from Red's lips, lightly teasing their inner linings with her tongue, and Red's belly clenched with need. Gina licked the hollows at the base of Red's throat. Holding Red's wrists down on both sides, Gina found Red's breasts, then nipped and sucked until Red arched with desire. When Gina released Red's wrists, Red gripped the sheets while Gina purposefully traveled down between Red's thighs. And when Gina's tongue played the game she knew so well, Red moved with her until the unbearable rhythm finally unlocked the dam, and all the months of need—of love and loss—broke loose in Red's shuddering climax.

Sometime in the wee hours of morning, Red realized that they were both sobbing. When Gina stroked Red's arms, kissed her eyelids, and whispered her name again and again, Red rolled on top of Gina and blanketed her with a raw, new self, whom Red had never met before.

Chapter Fifteen

The next morning, Rick and Red sat in the last pew as cheerful sunshine made the stained glass glow electric around the iconic image of Christ on the cross. Birds chirped outside in the courtyard of the Holy Redeemer Church, while the Reverend Jonah Ellis preached a fiery sermon condemning sex outside marriage. The contrast between the joyous light and hopeful sounds of a perfect summer day and the agonized dying savior made Red's teeth ache. The heavy odor of sandalwood incense snorkeled up her nasal passages, and her body throbbed with the satisfying ache of last night's lovemaking. She stifled a huge yawn.

"Is the sermon boring you?" Rick whispered. "I know you're a lapsed Catholic and hate organized religion, but try to behave yourself, will you?"

Red smiled. A few hours ago, when she woke up in Gina's arms, Red realized she'd overslept and rushed to make breakfast. When Gina asked why she was in such a tearing hurry, she'd explained she'd be "late for church."

Gina had reared up from her pillow, her sleepy eyes wide with shock. "God, what happened to you? I'm gone a few months, and you've become a fucking Christian?"

Rick seemed curious and continued to stare at her. "Hey, did you hook up with Gina last night? I hope you don't mind, but I asked her to check up on you. I was really worried."

Red smiled again. Gina wasn't one to kiss and tell, so unless Red spilled the beans, Rick might never find out about Red's relapse with his sister. Sadly, Red feared their sweet reunion might be a one-night stand, a "mercy fuck." Gina had carefully avoided talking about Red's retirement from the police force, which had been Gina's final ultimatum, so that impasse remained unresolved. Red had carefully kept her unreasonable jealousy under wraps. Red knew Gina was a natural flirt. Likely, Gina had been with other women since they split, but Red asked no questions about Gina's love life. Their sweet night together had been intense but fragile. Red didn't want to break it.

"Yeah, Gina called, and we had a nice chat," Red lied.

"So you're not mad?"

"No, but don't do it again," Red told him with a stern look. If Gina were to re-enter her life, it would be on their schedule, not Rick's. And since she was in a church, though having little faith in God's intervention, Red prayed for a miracle that would keep Gina in her life.

Rick squirmed, sighed, and loosened his tie. Red knew he was pissed because this visit to the church had been her idea—not his. He had conceded that the best time to confront a preacher was directly after his sermon, when he was surrounded by parishioners and not likely to pitch a hissy fit. Yet Rick still hated to make a scene in a holy place. Unlike Gina and Red, he remained a devout Catholic. After the testimony by Jimmy Allen, they both considered the Reverend Ellis a prime suspect, yet Rick still fought the idea. He had insisted the venue was inappropriate, unprofessional, and that it would be far better to bring Ellis to the police station rather than meet him on his own turf. Only in deference to Red's obvious grief had he finally given in.

"Bullshit," Red muttered under her breath.

"What's bullshit?" Rick whispered gruffly.

Red touched her ear. "Listen to that music." As the elders passed the collection plate, the many state-of-the-art speakers discreetly mounted near the ceiling delivered a bell-clear guitar instrumental of *Amazing Grace*. "The sound is perfect."

"So?"

"So Jimmy claimed the Reverend Ellis came to Best Buy complaining how the sound system they installed was skipping. The complaint was just an excuse to harass Boots."

He shrugged. "As hard evidence, that stinks."

Rick fished a five-dollar bill from his wallet, then jabbed Red with his elbow until she took a fiver from her purse. They slid their money into the plate, which was carried down the center aisle to a table near the pulpit, where Red saw little dollar signs register in the greedy preacher's dark eyes.

"He took in lots of cash today," Rick commented. "It seems the congregation supports the good reverend."

"Or else they figure they can buy their way to heaven."

Rick chuckled. "Yeah, that was one scary sermon about the evils of fornication outside matrimony."

"Well, in my opinion, Ellis is the worst kind of hypocrite. Jimmy said the preacher was divorced, but that didn't give him a green light to hit on Boots against her will."

Red closed her eyes as the gospel choir sang an upbeat recessional urging everyone to *Go with God,* and she tried to banish the awful images of the dead Boots by reviewing the evidence they had collected so far.

The crime scene techs had confirmed the similarities between Boots's killer and the UNSUB who murdered Judy the librarian the previous Friday night. Again it was likely the killer had worn gloves since no misplaced fingerprints had yet been found. Like Judy, Boots had apparently known her attacker and invited him into her house. He had come prepared with restraints, strangled his victim, ejaculated on her belly, and left a religious calling card—if Red's theory about the gold cross hung around Boots's neck was correct.

But there were also distinct differences between the two crimes. Instead of drugs, the jerk had subdued Boots with a stun gun, and unlike poor Judy, Boots had fought back hard, even bitten her attacker. Had Boots's resistance prompted the killer to a more vicious assault? Maybe the killer's violence surprised him so much he forgot to lay Boots out like a perfect princess. Red knew sexual predators' viciousness often escalated with each success. They were creatures of habit who sometimes freaked when their carefully planned routines were interrupted—as Boots had done. Hopefully, that was when they made mistakes.

Red opened her eyes. "Was anything stolen?"

"From Boots's condo? Nothing obvious. Seems like this killer's not into souvenirs."

She was twisting the church bulletin to shreds as the congregation filed from the church. "What about

Boots's computer?"

"Yeah, sure. It's been impounded. If Boots was half the geek she seemed to be, it might yield a clue or two."

Red watched Ellis make his way toward the rear. He was strutting like a tall parade stallion, high-fiving the parishioners and grinning through crooked yellow horse teeth. "What about Boots's new smartphone?"

Rick blinked in confusion. "What phone? Like an Android?"

"I think it was a Verizon Desire or some such thing." Red recalled how Boots had shown the new phone around the night of the reunion, bragging how it could do everything: email, photos and video, web surfing, and global positioning. "Boots carried it in her purse."

"Nope. It wasn't in her purse."

Suddenly, Red was certain that the damned phone was the key. "Shit. Maybe the asshole takes souvenirs, after all."

"Relax, it'll turn up. They'll find it in Boots's desk at Best Buy or maybe in her Volkswagen."

Nope. The phone was gone. It had been Boots's new baby, and like a cherished infant, Red was positive Boots would keep it close.

"Ready to rock n' roll?" Rick asked when the last worshipers trailed outside and the good reverend pranced toward their pew.

"Ready as I'll ever be."

Chapter Sixteen

R ed tried to analyze the laser-sharp focus in Ellis's eyes. Clearly, a Caucasian couple like Red and Rick wasn't the norm here, but was Ellis's focus curiosity or animosity?

"Welcome to Holy Redeemer," Jonah Ellis said in his deep bass voice. He extended a huge brown hand.

Rick and Red climbed to their feet. Rick shook Ellis's paw, but Red flinched when the preacher's gaze traveled from her face and lingered on her breasts. Jimmy was right. The man was a womanizer.

"Do you have a moment to talk, Reverend Ellis?" Rick asked.

"Please call me Joe, everyone does."

Red figured the best way to move Joe's eyes off her chest was to flash her badge. She pulled it from its wallet and held it up to his face. "We're with the Charlotte Mecklenburg police, sir, and we're here on official business."

The maneuver achieved the desired result, and when the preacher's eyes lifted, the lascivious heat had been replaced by two frozen lumps of coal.

"How can I help?"

"Can we speak in private?" Rick suggested.

"Follow me."

Skipping further pleasantries, Ellis took long, rapid strides toward a door behind the altar. With his black robe swaying around him, he reminded Red of an angry crow stalking to its nest. As they trailed him through the door, the nest proved to be the church kitchen, with the leftovers from a Sunday school breakfast tempting flies. She noticed a waste can overflowing with paper cups stained by juice and coffee, a plate bearing several uneaten Danish pastries, and a bowl of fresh fruit.

"Please help yourselves." Ellis gestured without enthusiasm.

"No thanks," they answered in unison.

"So to what do I owe this honor?" The pastor sighed, then perched one hip on a windowsill overlooking the churchyard.

Rick cleared his throat and formally introduced them. As Rick dispassionately explained the bare bones of an unnamed woman's murder, Ellis stared out at the rustling leaves of a poplar tree, apparently more interested in the garden than the story.

"That's very sad, but what does this abhorrent crime have to do with me?"

"The dead woman's name was Boots," Red snapped. "And I understand you knew her, maybe not as well as you would have liked."

Jonah Ellis's reaction was immediate and violent. Red watched closely as his indifferent eyes betrayed surprise, then shock, then deep sadness. Either he was truly stunned, or he was one hell of an actor. She strongly suspected the latter.

"Oh, my, this is very bad news." Ellis slowly shook his large head and ran fingers through his graying Afro. "I'm so sorry. I was quite fond of Sister Boots."

"So I've heard," Red said. "We understand from Boots's assistant, James Allen, that you were harassing Boots, trying to press her into a relationship she didn't want."

Again Ellis shook his head, as though he personally carried the weight of the world on his holy shoulders. "I was praying for Sister Boots so that she would forsake her promiscuous ways. She was meeting with strange men from the internet. I fear she lay down with the devil."

Red's cheeks flooded with heat as Ellis's pious tone fueled her fury. At the same time, Ellis had a point. Along with all the women in the True Love Club, Boots was guilty of cruising the internet, yet somehow Red felt Boots's devil came disguised as a Lamb of God. As Ellis gauged Red's reaction, he also eyed her breasts. The intrusion sent a shiver of fear up Red's spine.

"Where were you Friday night, Reverend?" Red ventured.

Ellis's body stiffened, and his protruding Adam's apple bobbed several times above his white clerical collar. She felt the man's animosity as he abruptly stood erect and crossed to the counter, where he picked up a small, excessively sharp fruit knife.

Rick and Red glanced at each other.

"Surely, you don't believe that *I* was in any way involved in Boots's death." He pointed the knife at them.

"Please, just answer the question, sir," Rick said.

Red ignored a swift chug of adrenaline as Ellis redirected the weapon and began cleaning under his fingernails. Her knee-jerk reaction to the implied threat was entirely irrational, but her heart began knocking back and forth in her chest. Something about him made her want to hide under the table.

"I'm a minister," Ellis intoned. "Where would I be Friday night but preparing my sermon? I was alone in my study, of course."

"Did anyone see you?" Rick asked.

Red heard the hesitation in Rick's voice, and she wondered if that knife had caused Mr. Macho Ricardo Molerno to experience a little adrenaline chug of his own.

Jonah Ellis placed an innocent apple on the chopping block and sliced into its white flesh. "Our Father in heaven saw me." Jonah smiled. "What better witness do I need?"

He has no alibi, Red thought. She couldn't look away from the slice of apple as Ellis lifted the wedge to his full lips, licked it, changed his mind, and then returned it to the block. There was something both obscene and dismissive about the gesture, and sure enough, shortly thereafter, Red sensed the interview was over.

"I'm afraid you must excuse me." Ellis glanced at his watch. "I'm due at the nursing home—lunch with the shut-ins, don't you know?"

Again Rick and Red locked gazes in understanding. At this point, they had nothing on the man, no reason to detain him.

"We understand, sir," Rick mumbled to Ellis's retreating back. "We'll be in touch if we have further questions."

As Rick trailed away in Ellis's wake, Red quietly folded the saliva-laden apple wedge into a napkin and tucked it into her purse. At the same time, she offered up a heartfelt prayer that the DNA on the apple would provide a dead-on link to the killer.

Chapter Seventeen

Salsa woke up to severe pain centered behind her eyes. Dragging her lids open, she saw pencil-thin lasers of light stabbing between the slats of the Venetian blinds, tasted the sour remnants of white zinfandel at the base of her throat, and heard the ear-splitting shrill of the landline on her bedside table. Phone, not alarm clock—she'd forgotten to set it. Sunday morning. Day off. She fought past the hangover to answer, and about that time, the full horror of last night's tragedy caused Lila's spaghetti to roil in her stomach. Dear God, their beloved Boots was dead!

Swallowing the nausea in her esophagus, Salsa glanced at the caller ID and saw that her restaurant, La Hacienda, was calling. Jesus Christ. Groaning, she remembered that sweet little Lucy, the biology undergrad she'd hired for the summer, was managing all day Sunday, and the lunch shift was about to begin.

Salsa answered through her tears. "What's up?"

"Do you know what time it is?" Lucy demanded.

Not really. Salsa squinted at her digital clock and realized it was indeed noon. "Is there a problem?"

"You sound like shit," Lucy said.

Salsa sat upright and slowly swung her legs off the bed, but the new position did nothing to ease her symptoms. All she could think of was Boots, but no way could she tell Lucy what had happened. Not yet.

"Are you listening, Salsa? Your dad forgot to take the chicken from the freezer, and you know all the customers will want *pollo* this or that..."

Salsa tried to concentrate. Until last year, she'd lived with her parents and cared for her aging mother. But when Mom died and they sold the family home, Dad had moved in above the restaurant. Since then, the poor man couldn't seem to do anything right.

"So thaw it in the microwave," Salsa said.

"Yeah, sure, but frozen chicken's the least of my worries," Lucy whined. "Some guy was here looking for you, and he was way pissed."

"What guy?" Even as she said it, Salsa realized she'd screwed up—big-time.

"He didn't give his name, but he had a mountain bike strapped on his Subaru and claimed you two had a date."

"What did he look like?"

"Kinda cute, for an old guy. Long gray hair tied back in a tail, retro beard..." Lucy paused to smirk. "You know, your average aging hippie."

Oh, shit, Bikerboy. Salsa struggled to her feet on rubber legs and massaged the bridge of her nose. "What did he say?"

Silence. Salsa pictured Lucy, all ninety pounds of her, tugging at her earlobe and deciding how best to torment her boss. "Did you really meet this dude online?"

"What did he say, Lucy?" As Salsa began to pace, she woke up Taco, who'd been sleeping beside her.

"He claimed he was a vegan, like me, so that's cool."

The golden retriever slid to the floor and licked Salsa's bare leg. "What did he say, Lucy?"

"Will you give me a raise?"

"No, but I'll fire you if you don't start talking."

Lucy giggled. "Internet dating is so pathetic, but hey, this guy seemed harmless enough. And I didn't give out your phone number, even though he asked."

Okay, that was their company policy, but Salsa panicked and hoped that she'd entered *Bikerboy's* cell number into her phone. She also made a mental note to murder her employee. "Lucy?" she demanded.

The girl sighed. "Okay, here's the deal. Said he'd packed a lunch for you guys and that he was going up to Lake Norman State Park to wait. Said he'd meet you at the boat launch, as planned, and he'd wait until one o'clock, but not one minute later." Lucy paused to greet a customer entering the restaurant. "So are you gonna meet him, or what?"

"Goodbye, Lucy, and don't forget to put the damned chicken in the microwave."

Once disconnected, Salsa hurriedly let Taco out the back door to pee, then rushed into the bathroom to do the same. As she sat there, she booted up her Blackberry and found, much to her relief, *Bikerboy's* number in her contacts. Salsa tapped his name, heard the ring, but her call went directly to voicemail. Damn! After leaving an urgent message for him to call, she realized she was out of time. Either she could rudely not show up, or she could put in an appearance and cancel their date in person. No way could she spend time with *Bikerboy* after just losing Boots.

Oh, lord, she had to get dressed. Pronto. Salsa quickly washed her face, ran a brush through her tangled black hair, ignored the ugly red rims lining her bloodshot eyes, then almost tripped as she hopped foot to foot trying to squeeze into a pair of new shorts that suddenly seemed too small. She pulled on her favorite T-shirt, the one she'd worn to weed the garden yesterday, then slipped into her flip-flops. Hey, this wasn't a date. She wouldn't even get out of her car.

"Taco!" she screamed, as her dog sauntered inside in slo-mo. She quickly filled his bowl with dry food and tapped *Bikerboy's* phone number as her dog ate slowly, wagging his tail. Still no answer. "Taco, will you get a move on?" But the retriever seemed determined to take his time as he leisurely lapped his water.

It was already twelve thirty. Salsa had intended to leave Taco outside in the fenced yard. After all, it was a beautiful day. But as the seconds ticked by, a desperate idea occurred. "Hey, boy, wanna go for a ride in the car?"

Bingo. Taco streaked through the house like a golden wildfire and was panting at the front door before Salsa could locate the keys to her Honda hybrid. This was never the original plan. The park didn't allow loose dogs, and Salsa deliberately left the leash behind. That way, *Bikerboy* would take one look at her pet and realize, in no uncertain terms, that their date was off. As she and Taco sprinted toward her car, Salsa glanced unhappily at her bike chained to the picket fence. No way, not today.

As she backed out of the driveway, Salsa stared at her bungalow and again thought of Boots. This house would belong to Salsa in thirty years or so, once the mortgage was paid off. The fruit trees she'd planted would be mature, her organic garden would have yielded many healthful meals, but today the concept only made her sad. Homeownership had been Boots's dream, too, but Boots had enjoyed her new condo for less than a year.

The mist in her eyes made Salsa feel like she needed the windshield wipers as she sped north on Perth Road, crossed the bridge, and soon turned left into the big wooded park with moments to spare. What the hell was she doing, today of all days, meeting some meaningless stranger instead of licking her wounds at home? She should be at Lila's, helping Lila cope with her grief.

Last night, long after Summer had left the party to rescue her daughter from the weird babysitter, Lila and Salsa had shared wine, tears, and memories of their friend Boots. Somehow, Salsa had wound up in Lila's arms as they finished the last bottle. They were lying together in the big hammock on the screened lakeside porch, watching the moonlight through blurred vision when Lila kissed her. It was not the platonic kiss it should have been, far from it. And to be honest, Salsa found the sensation of Lila's warm, wine-sweet lips on hers not altogether unpleasant. Nice, sexy even. But way wrong.

Salsa had left in a hurry after the kiss, not wanting to give Lila a false impression, not wanting to lead her on in any way. But now, in the clear light of day, Salsa thought she maybe owed Lila an apology. She had left the woman stricken not only with grief, but also guilt, and that was the last thing Salsa intended.

Just then, Taco nudged Salsa's arm, jolting her back to reality as she slowed the car and entered the picnic area near the boat ramp. "Well, here goes nothing," she murmured as she began scanning the lot for the Subaru Lucy had described.

When Salsa spotted the station wagon, hideously dirty from off-road travel, she noticed the bike was absent from its rack and figured *Bikerboy* had gone on without her. But then she saw a lone figure down on the dock. He was hurling bits of what appeared to be French bread into the water to a grateful group of Canada geese. By his body language, the stranger was angry, frustrated, or both.

Salsa slowed the Honda to a crawl and crept within shouting distance, then powered down the window. Taking a deep breath, she steadied her voice and called out, "*Bikerboy*, is that you?"

When the man lifted his elbows from the railing and stood to his full height, he was considerably taller than Salsa had imagined and more powerfully built. Maybe the guy had been to the gym, bulked up some since he took his DATESCAPE photo. As he turned and strode toward her, Salsa couldn't see his face because the brilliant July sun was behind him, backlighting his expression into shadow.

"Hey," he called. "I figured you stood me up." *Bikerboy* approached quickly and rapped the hood of her car with both hands. "Where's your bike?"

His voice was deeper, older somehow than Salsa had anticipated, and something about his aggressive stance made her cringe. "I'm sorry, but plans have changed. I didn't bring my bicycle because I can't do this today."

"Oh, yeah? What's with the dog?"

When the man lowered his face to the open window, Salsa saw something in his expression that scared her speechless. She smelled his sweat and sensed his rage. So what if she was late? *Bikerboy* had no claim on her, and his attitude did not bode well for a future relationship.

"I tried to call, but you didn't answer your cell," she said.

"Well no, I didn't. It's locked in my car. I never carry it while I bike, and I've already been 'round the track twice."

Was this her fault? Salsa was shocked when Taco began growling deep in his throat, something he never did, not even with strangers. "I'm really sorry," she said again.

"Yeah, me too." He frowned at Taco, and before Salsa realized what was happening, he reached into the front seat, latched on to Taco's collar, and gave the dog a little tap on the rump. "Hop in back, buddy. I need to talk with your mommy."

Much to Salsa's surprise, Taco did precisely what the man asked and jumped into the backseat. "Listen, *Bikerboy*, or whatever your real name is, I'm leaving now!"

"What's your hurry?" With one swift motion, he lowered his hand and popped the automatic door locks. Suddenly, he was sitting beside her, so close she could feel his heat.

Salsa cast a desperate gaze around the parking lot, but the two elderly gentlemen she'd noticed when she drove in had apparently disappeared into the men's restroom. "Get the hell out of my car!" she screamed.

But *Bikerboy* reached across her lap, brushing her breasts with his elbow, and pulled the keys from the ignition.

"What do you want?" she cried.

His eyes were nothing like the innocent blue pools she'd seen in his internet profile. They were more like an angry sky before a storm, and by the way he looked at her, Salsa feared she knew exactly what he wanted.

Chapter Eighteen

Summer had already decided to skip church, though the decision went against her grain. The turmoil of the previous night—Boots's murder and all—had left her wondering, not for the first time, why God allowed awful stuff to happen to decent people. She was mad at Him and figured a timeout from religion was a fine idea.

Gloria agreed. Instead of being trapped in a prickly crinoline dress and don't-you-dare-scuff-me patent pumps that morning, she was dressed in her Hannah Montana PJs while she picked the blueberries out of her pancakes.

"This is awesome, Mom. I hate Sunday school. Can we go shopping?"

Unlike most eight-year-olds, Gloria never asked to buy toys at Walmart or Target. She preferred Best Buy, where she could test the latest video games, a habit that usually cost Summer half a week's groceries if she gave in to Gloria's desires. Unfortunately, Ed, Summer's stingy ex, never contributed to their daughter's video game fund. Instead, he'd take Gloria out for a cheap ice cream date and drop her off with a sugar high to drive Summer crazy.

The thought of Best Buy made Summer sad all over again as she remembered poor Boots. Bad dreams had kept her up half the night, and once, after a particularly gruesome image of her raped and murdered friend jolted Summer awake with a scream, she'd thrown up Lila's spaghetti and given up on sleep altogether.

"Are you sick, Mom? You look awful."

"Thanks a bunch, honey. No, I feel fine."

"Does this mean Paul's not coming today?"

Summer stared at her daughter's plate. The kid had lined the blueberries up in a perfect row and was systematically squashing them with her spoon. "I asked Paul not to come."

"Bummer." Gloria made an ugly face.

Summer wished to God she'd never told the kid about Paul. Summer's new boyfriend had talked to Gloria exactly once on the phone, but somehow, he'd managed to win Gloria over in record time. Maybe it was the teacher in him.

Summer shuffled to the sink in her slippers and bathrobe and fed her uneaten breakfast to the garbage disposal. Oddly, even as her stomach did flip-flops, the thought of Paul made her spirits soar. She hated to cancel their date, but no way did she want him to see her like this. She glanced at their cat slinking into the laundry room, where they kept his litter box, and figured she looked, as they said, like something the cat dragged in…maybe worse.

"But I thought you *really* liked Paul," Gloria whined. "He wants to meet me."

"He'll meet you, sweet pea, but not today."

As Summer finished rinsing her plate, the doorbell rang. She figured it was creepy Connor coming to get paid. Last night, she'd been so upset when she got home, she'd forgotten to give him the two twenties they'd agreed on. The cost of babysitters was going through the roof, and Summer wondered bitterly how much a baggie of pot cost these days because sure as shootin', that's how Connor would spend her hard-earned cash.

"I'll get it, Mom!" Gloria tore off toward the living room, but when Summer listened to the silence as the door creaked open, she knew something was wrong.

"Who are you?" Gloria squeaked.

Summer's temper flared. Likely, it was more of those obnoxious Jehovah's Witnesses come to save her soul. Last time they showed up, the damn cat got loose and didn't come home for three days. But when Summer stomped out to do battle, the sight of Paul framed in the entryway brought her heart to her throat, and she panicked. Christ Almighty!

Stifling an impulse to hide in the closet, Summer watched in shock as Paul introduced himself, then solemnly bent over to shake Gloria's hand. What was he doing here? The man's pretty red hair was wet combed with a perfect part. He wore neatly pressed navy trousers, a white short-sleeved dress shirt, and a maroon patterned tie. Good Lord.

"Are you going to invite me in, Miss Gloria?"

Fleetingly, the child looked to her mama, but then, without waiting for permission, Gloria practically curtsied as she ushered their visitor inside.

"Sorry, Summer. I should've called first." Paul's fair face blushed pink under his freckles, and he smiled that crooked smile. "But when I saw the morning news, what happened to your friend, I just jumped in the car."

For once in her life, Summer couldn't come up with a snappy retort. When she'd canceled their date that morning, she hadn't told Paul about Boots—didn't have the heart. But now he'd gone and found out anyway. As he moved tentatively into their space,

Summer couldn't decide whether to kiss him or kill him.

"Yeah, but you should've called," Summer grumbled.

"What happened to your friend, Mommy?" Gloria piped up, yet her eyes remained riveted to the handsome stranger.

"Never mind, honey, we'll talk about that later."

Paul gazed down sheepishly at his spit-polished oxfords. "Want me to leave?"

"No!" Gloria shouted.

Yes, Summer thought, but her mama never raised her to be rude. She turned to her daughter. "Why don't you show Paul your games while I get dressed?"

"Yes, ma'am."

Whoa! As Summer scuttled into the bedroom, firmly closing the door, she marveled at how fast a little brat like Gloria suddenly got manners when a male entered the room. Lordy, she'd have to watch that girl when she became a teenager. Yet Gloria was starved for a father figure, someone other than Ed, and Paul was nothing like her ex. Paul was smart, polite, a real gentleman, and he claimed to love children.

Summer realized she was hyperventilating, so she took a deep breath. She rushed into the bathroom, washed up, and put on makeup so fast she broke a lipstick. Ignoring her haggard expression, she dribbled Visine into her ravaged blue eyes, vigorously brushed her long blond hair, and then slipped into a flowered sundress and sandals—nothing too sexy because even after one date, she sensed Paul disliked loose behavior.

It was hard having a younger boyfriend, a guy too perfect to be true, but Summer figured she was overdue for some good luck. So she put on a smile, raced out the door, and was back on track faster than Dale Earnhardt could say NASCAR.

Paul stood from the couch as soon as she entered the room. He'd been playing on the Xbox Series S with Gloria, but he carefully set his remote on the coffee table and whistled in soft appreciation.

"You look mighty pretty, Summer."

"Thanks." She shyly accepted the compliment. "What's the plan?"

"Do you two lovely ladies want to go to church with me?"

Gloria groaned, while Summer felt her jaw drop open in surprise. She'd never expected Paul to be a religious type. "You go to church?"

"Yeah, sure. I attend Lakeside Baptist, just up the road."

Summer groaned. She and Ed had attended Lakeside Baptist for years, right up to the divorce, but now Summer went to Living Waters, a much smaller church the opposite direction on River Highway. Plus, she'd heard from her old friends in the congregation that stupid Ed now brought his slut, Jolene, to the services.

"No thanks." It seemed strange that Summer had never noticed Paul at Lakeside Baptist, but maybe he joined after she left.

"Good call, Mom." Gloria approved the decision. "Let's do something fun."

Paul shifted uneasily, a worried frown on his face. "You know, sometimes church can be a comfort at times like these."

He was referring to Boots's death, of course, but Summer couldn't go there. "I agree, Paul, but not today."

An uneasy silence descended as colored light flickered from the muted Xbox game. Finally, Gloria turned the thing off. "I'm hungry! Can we go to McDonald's?"

"You just ate breakfast," Summer said.

Paul laughed. "Why don't we go to the buffet at Golden Corral? I like the way Gloria thinks."

Summer had been overruled, and as she looked back and forth from Gloria to Paul, they looked like eager children. "Okay, we'll go. Go get dressed, sweet pea."

"Yes!" Gloria winked at Paul, then streaked to her room.

"Kids," he said. "You gotta love 'em."

Summer smiled, not knowing what to make of this new man in her life. "Let's wait outside."

Paul followed Summer through the kitchen and out to the tiny patio, where Summer was suddenly ashamed of the dead plants in the pots and last season's charcoal growing mold in the grill. Still, the sun was shining, and it was a beautiful day. She almost jumped out of her skin when Paul came up from behind and wrapped his arms around her waist.

"Hey, I'm really sorry about Boots," he whispered against her ear. "I didn't know her well, though. Because remember, I was two years behind you girls in school. In all these years since, I hadn't seen Boots until the reunion when she bumped into me and made me spill that beer."

Summer had almost forgotten the incident. "I can't believe she's dead. Fact is, I didn't know her real well, either." Of all the girls in the TLC, Summer knew Red, Salsa, and Lila much better. Summer didn't want to believe it was a race issue because she truly didn't believe she had one ounce of prejudice in her heart, but somehow, she and Boots had never gotten close.

Paul ran his index finger down Summer's bare arm. "When I spilled that beer, your friend Lila slapped me, remember? Is it true she's a lesbian?"

Summer shivered, and not just because of Paul's seductive touch. Why would he bring up the subject of Lila's sexual orientation? "Well, I guess she's a lesbian, but so what?"

He shrugged. "Nothing. I just don't get it."

Truth be told, Summer didn't get it, either, but she believed in "live and let live." Come to think of it, she'd never been that tight with Lila, either.

Paul's hand strayed to the back of Summer's neck, where he gently massaged the tense muscles at the base of her skull. "It's an awful shame about Boots," he said. "What a waste. You gotta wonder if she got in with the wrong crowd."

"What do you mean?"

Paul removed his hand and sighed. "Oh, you know, I saw her profile in DATESCAPE, and it was pretty suggestive. Unfortunately, the world is full of perverts just looking for an opportunity, and maybe Boots came on too strong."

Summer pulled away. "Are you saying Boots asked for this? She asked to be raped and murdered?"

"Oh, God, no! It's dangerous, that's all. Haven't you heard about the Craigslist Killer?"

Sure, Summer had seen the Lifetime movie—something about a psycho who killed girls who advertised their escort services online. The killer figured he was ridding the world of prostitutes. "Why were you looking at Boots's profile, anyway?" she demanded.

"Hey, that's how I found you, right?" Paul lifted both hands in self-defense. "And I'm sure glad I did."

Summer wasn't sure she liked where this was going, and suddenly, she felt dirty for being on DATESCAPE. "I canceled my subscription," she told him, and it was true.

"Good, me too." Paul moved closer. "I found what I want. I don't need it anymore."

Summer wanted to believe him, hoped it wasn't just a line, but somehow, she couldn't quite relax into his arms. As she looked across the lawn surrounding her apartment complex, she noticed their sixteen-year-old neighbor leaning against the basketball standard. Did kids like Connor cruise DATESCAPE? Was there a minimum age requirement to join? As usual, the boy's eyes were following Summer's every move, and as they stared at each other, she despised the idea that Connor might have read her profile.

"Who are these sick people?" she said aloud.

Paul followed her gaze, nodded at Connor. "You never know. Maybe that kid over there is a serial killer."

Summer laughed nervously and leaned back into Paul's arms. What was this world coming to? She didn't know, Paul didn't know, but for now, this minute, she'd let someone else worry about it.

Chapter Nineteen

By late Sunday afternoon, Lila was crawling up the walls. Georgia sensed her distress and clung to her heels, until Lila gave her a rawhide chew. Distracted, Georgia dragged the shin bone-sized treat onto Lila's bed and got busy gnawing, while her mistress locked herself in the bathroom.

Stepping into the shower, Lila turned up the water pressure, shampooed her long brown hair, and hoped the pulsing stream, mixed with salty tears, would wash away some of the sorrow and guilt. The sorrow of losing Boots, of course—the horror and the waste— would likely not ease for some time. But the guilt for the way Lila had behaved toward Salsa last night—that kiss in the hammock—was another matter entirely. Confusing. Shameful. Yet how much was Lila willing to blame herself for succumbing to an attraction that had been there all along, maybe as long ago as high school?

As she lathered with body wash fashioned of lavender, chamomile, and ylang-ylang—whatever the hell that was—Lila realized that even the damned soap was Salsa's idea. The original nature girl, Salsa, had insisted the combination would "calm and relax." Fat chance.

Thing was, maybe Lila had made a terrible mistake returning to Mooresville five years ago. Originally from Manhattan, she'd lived most of her life in big cities, enjoyed many lovers, and had never before worried about being judged, ostracized, or even condemned for her lifestyle.

She'd spent only her last two years of high school in Mooresville, when she met Salsa, Red, Summer, and Boots. That move to rural life would never have happened if Lila's mom hadn't divorced her dad and married a builder from Charlotte, who happened to be one of the movers and shakers who developed Lake Norman. Lila had fled North Carolina immediately after her senior year and begun her world travels.

So why had she returned to Mooresville? As the soapy water swirled down the drain, taking precious little of the sorrow and guilt with it, Lila had to admit the decision to return to North Carolina was a foolish attempt to recapture a brief moment when she'd actually felt secure. Stupid, but true. After all, Mom was dead now, so Lila had no family connection here. Lila's partner had never wanted to make the move. So God help her, had some delusional little brain cell guided Lila back because of Salsa?

She left the shower and punished her skin with a towel. Last night, she'd frightened her best friend with the sudden flood of emotion that turned physical. At one point, Lila had actually believed her passion was being returned, but seconds later, Salsa was standing upright in panic. Minutes later, Salsa had run from the house like a three-alarm fire was licking at her heels.

Lila had stumbled, stuttered, and apologized to no avail, and as she watched Salsa's Honda speed from her driveway, she was mortally embarrassed. Had an actual fire engulfed her home just then, Lila would have jumped into the flames.

She opened the bathroom door and stumbled from the steam into the chill of the air conditioning.

Georgia was still chewing her bone on the bed, so Lila flopped down naked beside her. "Do you still love me, girl?" She ran moist fingers through the tangle of golden fur, but the dog never looked up nor did she wag her tail.

The goose bumps prickling Lila's flesh seemed inadequate punishment for last night's misbehavior, but she welcomed them and closed her eyes. She listened to the lazy drone of a lawn mower in the distance. She wondered if she should try Salsa's cellphone—bad idea. She tried to concentrate on her grief for Boots, but it hurt too much. And she told herself that if she had one ounce of gumption, she'd get dressed and go to the shed to work on her sculpture. The current project was an abstract steel seagull in flight. But shaky as she was, Lila feared she'd burn her hand off the moment she lit the welding torch.

As she shivered and listened to the steady thrum of the air conditioner, Lila wondered why her ex, now living in Santa Fe, had left a needy, cryptic message on Lila's answering machine a few days ago. Lila would never return that call. And lately, at unexpected times and in several different places, Lila had felt like someone was watching her, stalking her. Putting her paranoia aside, her thoughts again returned to Salsa, and she was overwhelmed by an irrational fear for her friend's safety. What was that about? The fear went deeper and deeper, pulling Lila into its chilled vortex until finally she succumbed to a cold, numb sleep.

❧❧❧❧

Demons and devils.

Lila's subconscious mind drifted into a recurring

dream of loss. It was always the same. She was locked inside a large metal building resembling the warehouse in Manhattan where she'd learned the art of welding. It was dark when the cheerful classes had actually taken place. Instead of laughing students flowing freely through the garage doors onto the bustling city streets, Lila was alone, and the building had no doors.

She was trapped in the eerily silent, cold, and cavernous space, and she'd lost someone. Lila, too, was lost as she searched through steel tunnels with no exits. As her panic escalated, the drum-like thudding of her heart echoed against the walls, and a ghostly, faceless figure floated past the high widows stalking her, following her rat-maze progress with malicious intent.

Suddenly, she couldn't breathe as a hot, heavy body landed on her chest. The wet tongue covered her mouth with kisses, strangling her. And just when Lila thought she would die, she was startled awake by her own scream, and the thudding echo of her heartbeats became the thumping rhythm of a wagging tail.

"Jesus Christ, Georgia!" Lila shoved the golden retriever off her sweating torso. "You almost smothered me, what's your problem?"

In answer, Georgia barked excitedly and leaped off the bed. As Lila watched her dog streak from the bedroom into the hall, heading for the front door, she got a grip on reality and heard the same lawn mower still buzzing in the neighbor's yard. The sun beyond the curtains had dropped deeper in the sky, so Lila reasoned the nightmare had ridden her late into the afternoon, and to make life more miserable, someone was ringing her doorbell.

Oh, shit! Likely, it was a pair of religious zealots

come to convert her. On the other hand, it might be a friend with more news about Boots's death. Lila struggled into her bathrobe and belted it tight. She hurriedly brushed her hair and pulled on her slippers.

"Coming!" she hollered as she padded down the hallway. Georgia spun with glee as Lila pressed her eye to the peephole. From Georgia's response, the caller was more likely friend than foe.

Sure enough, the first thing Lila saw was a panting pink golden retriever mouth magnified by the peephole, and she recognized Salsa's dog, Taco. But when she unlocked and opened, as the animals greeted each other in ecstatic growling and mouth wrestling, Lila was shocked to be face-to-face with the pale, ghostly apparition from her nightmare. Salsa's dark bob was disheveled, and her cheeks were streaked by the tracks of tears.

"What the hell happened?" Lila gasped as Salsa dropped   into her arms.

Salsa buried her face in the soft folds of Lila's robe. "God, Lila, a man tried to rape me!"

Chapter Twenty

Monday morning, Red rode the elevator to the second floor of the CMPD on Trade Street, rather than racing up the stairs, as was her habit. Only last month, she'd begun a rigorous shape-up regimen that included a brisk run around her apartment complex before breakfast, followed by a monastic bowl of high-fiber cereal and grapefruit juice, finally enhanced by the full-tilt race up the stairs to the Sexual Assault Unit. Her goal was to push back against the almost-fifty blues, to tighten her abs and firm her calves, to generally replace the workout she once got from aerobic sex with Gina. But since the Fourth of July, when Judy the librarian had been strangled and left with the gold crucifix inside her, all Red's good intentions had slipped to hell on a banana peel.

As she exited the elevator, guiltily hugging a white paper bag containing two breakfast burritos and a caffeine super-charged latte, she picked up the pace to avoid the end of the building where Rick worked in homicide. She fast-walked down the long hallway leading to her unit only to be confronted by Gladys, the team's senior secretary, a woman whose main function was to pry into the detectives' lives, gossip, pass judgment, and cause trouble for anyone perceived not to be putting in a solid day's work. Gladys scowled at her watch as Red signed in.

"I made fresh coffee, Detective Calendar," she said with a frown.

"No thanks, I'm good." Red held up the white bag containing her shameful meal. Everyone knew the brown tinted water Gladys brewed was weaker than a widow's tears, so no detective in her right mind would be caught dead drinking the swill unless she wanted to fall asleep on the job and make Gladys's day.

"Detective Molerno clocked in early," Gladys pointedly announced.

"Good for him." Clearly, the secretary knew how to push Red's buttons. Any and all news about Rick's job performance, his dedication to excellence felt like personal criticism.

Gladys followed Red all the way to her new desk in the Cold Case Unit. The desk facing the windowless wall still felt empty and unused, in spite of the powerful Mac computer and shiny new phone. With all the confusion and tragedy of the past two weeks, Red hadn't made the space her own. She shucked off her jacket and draped it around the shoulders of her fancy new chair.

"I'm sorry about your friend," Gladys continued. "What an awful way to die."

Gladys was referring to Boots. Bad news traveled fast in their small community, and likely, Rick had filled everyone in on the gruesome details the moment he clocked in early.

"I don't want to talk about it."

"Understood, dear. Detective Molerno explained how close you were to the victim. In his opinion, your emotions will likely prevent you from working the case."

"Rick said that?" Red eased into her plush new swivel chair, and her temper flared to high alert. The night of Boots's death, Rick had promised. He'd said,

"We're on the same team here. I want to work with you on this." They'd shaken hands and vowed to be partners in the investigation.

Gladys gave Red's shoulder a motherly pat. "Don't worry, dear, Detective Molerno's on top of it. He even filed new DNA evidence with the lab."

"What the hell are you talking about?"

Gladys clucked her tongue in disapproval of Red's language. "The piece of apple, of course. Rick said the saliva would likely link to the killer."

Red gripped the armrests and bit her tongue. Son of a bitch! That was *her* evidence, *her* licked apple. She had lifted it from the Holy Redeemer Church only yesterday morning, and the good Reverend Jonah Ellis was *her* suspect. All along, Rick had pooh-poohed her suspicions, but that hadn't stopped him from storing the sample in *his* refrigerator. He had condescendingly bagged it and shelved it beside his beer and leftover pizza for "safekeeping, just in case." Red sure as hell never expected the jerk to take full credit for *her* work.

"Contrary to what Rick might have implied," Red fumed, "I will in fact be working both cases in conjunction with homicide, so please let me get to it, Gladys."

"That's not what Miranda said." Gladys winked. "She arrived with Detective Molerno."

Red's hand strayed to her shoulder holster. Had she not been a law-abiding citizen, she'd shoot Gladys between her arched gray eyebrows. Instead, Red unbuckled her weapon and locked it in her empty drawer. Everyone on staff knew about Red's volcanic split from Rick's sister. They knew Red was a lesbian but never talked about it. At least not to her face. They also knew Rick was sleeping with Miranda, the hot new recruit in his unit. People like Gladys, who didn't approve of Red's lifestyle, seemed to think positive news about Rick's career or love life would somehow upset her. They were wrong. Although Red was now buried in Cold Case, she still wished the best for Rick. And as far as her love life was concerned, well, it was confusing. After their passionate one-night reunion, Gina had left after breakfast—no commitment, no promises, no resolution. God only knew how it would shake out.

Red shrugged. "Thanks for the news bulletin, Gladys, but I have to get to work."

"Suit yourself, dear." Treating Red to one last sympathetic smile, Gladys squared her shoulders, tucked an exposed bra strap back under her blouse sleeve, and then soldiered off to make some other officer's life miserable.

Red exhaled slowly and placed both hands on her desk. Truth was, she really didn't know where she stood, personally or professionally. Red couldn't bear to think about Gina, so she glanced at Sergeant Darling, who had just walked briskly into the unit across the aisle. Darling smiled and waved encouragement in Red's direction. Would Darling approve of Red's continued involvement with the dual murder investigation? During the fifteen years Red had been part of the SAU, she'd routinely worked cases involving both rape and homicide. Cold case might not extend Red the same courtesy.

It could be argued that two incidents meant a serial killer was loose in the Charlotte area. If this were true, Red's continued involvement might be justified. She could comb the cold cases to see if the UNSUB had done this before. If he'd resurfaced after a period of inactivity, then Red's research could be key to an apprehension. She would pursue that angle as soon as her computer booted up, and she would convince Darling.

Fact was, Red wouldn't tolerate being left out of the loop. She had considered resigning when they reassigned her. If the brass refused to let her participate in Boots's case, then maybe it was time to turn in her shield. Certainly, Gina would applaud her quitting, and Gina's approval was uppermost in Red's mind. Was a future together still possible?

Red's fingers trembled as she took out a lined legal pad and eyed the sharpened pencils in her cup. While organizing a plan of action, she opened her food bag, lifted out the latte, and figured she'd done two things right in the past twenty-four hours. The first was opening herself to Gina, the second was not sharing their reunion with Rick.

The bastard. Had Rick now gone back on his promise? Red's fingers continued to wobble as she lifted out the cold burritos and arranged them on a soggy napkin. The latte was also cold, bitter on her tongue, and somehow, she'd lost her appetite.

She stared at the phone and considered calling Rick. She'd tell him where to stick it. She'd threaten to cut off his balls and fry them up for dinner if he didn't let her work Boots's case. Instead, Red took a bite of congealed sausage, flour, and cheese, then almost jumped out of her skin when the phone rang—not the police line but her personal cell. All day yesterday, Red had waited for Gina to call, but she never did. Lila and Summer had called, but she had ignored them. Red wasn't up to talking about Boots's death, and selfishly, she hadn't wanted to tie up her line in case Gina called.

Her throat went dry. "Hello?"

"Jesus, Red, we've been trying to call you!" Summer yelped.

"Who's *we*?"

"You know, the girls from the TLC. Well, just Lila and me."

Red blinked and tried to focus. Her friends never called her at work. "What's up?"

"You don't know about Salsa?"

Blood drained from Red's brain. She felt faint and feared the worst. *Dear God, not again.* "What the hell happened?"

"It was awful, Red. The guy would have raped her! You know, *date rape*? Lila called and told me all about it."

As Red processed Summer's words, she realized that Salsa hadn't been murdered, after all. "Is she all right?"

"Duh, no! She's not all right. Salsa's real shook up. That's why she didn't call you herself. She went to meet some guy from DATESCAPE. He trapped her in her own car, and…"

As the bizarre story unfolded, Red was so relieved Salsa was alive, she couldn't quite absorb the details. Something about a verbal fight, some roughhouse, and in the end, the dog intervened—or had two men who came out of the park restroom saved Salsa? According to Summer's breathless account, Salsa had spent the night with Lila, and she was safe.

"Can you please repeat all that, Summer?"

"Sorry, I gotta go. Gloria's late for day care. But the man's screen name was *Bikerboy*. Can you check him out?"

"Can you give me something more? Did Salsa

report this attempted rape to the police?"

"Nope. What could she say? Since nothing actually happened, it would've been a he said/she said situation. Look, I've really gotta split. Catch you later. And by the way, I can't believe you haven't already heard." With that, Summer hung up.

Red slumped in her chair and massaged the headache brewing behind her eyeballs.

Yeah, that's me. Always the last to know.

Chapter Twenty-one

By early afternoon, Red had studied numerous cold case files, brushing elbows with the dirtiest serial rapists and killers to terrorize the area in the past several decades. As she worried about Salsa and tried to decide what to do about it, she sifted through evidence boxes stored on location and perused microfiche of the older files. The really old records had been moved to Cold Stone Mountain, North Carolina, but she didn't expect to need those.

Three retired officers who volunteered their time to help with case overload had assisted Red—two men and one woman. The senior member, with a shock of unruly white hair, was Carl Manning, nicknamed "Manny." Bald Morris Stover was "Mo," and feisty little Sylvie Jackson was "Jackie." So they were named for a celebrated trio who sold auto parts in the Northeast back in the day. Manny, Mo, and Jackie had all agreed it was useless to go back more than fifty years in the cold case records.

"Listen, Red, let's say your guy started acting out when he was twenty, it's not likely he'd resurface at age seventy with much of a sexual urge." Manny shook his white mane.

Red grinned. "Are you speaking from personal experience, sir?"

"Just sayin'…"

Several years ago, on January 16, 2009, the serial rapist Gilbert McNair, the man called the Myers

Park Rapist, had been caught after eighteen frustrating years. Yet McNair, and countless others like him, had never escalated to murder.

In July 2009, Patrick Burris, who had killed at least five residents in North Carolina, was shot to death near Charlotte after being paroled in April.

"Happens all the time," Jackie said. "Why they let these animals back on the street is beyond me."

Back in March 1994, Henry Louis Wallace was arrested in Charlotte after raping and murdering eleven young women. Wallace was a crack cocaine addict whose victims had mostly worked with him at Taco Bell or Bojangles. He had put the women in a chokehold, raped them at gunpoint, and then killed them.

"But those guys were nothing like my killer." Red moaned. "Besides, they're all dead or cooling their heels at the taxpayers' expense. My man's still out there."

Red had plugged in all the appropriate search keywords: restraints, strangulation, and ejaculation without penetration, middle-aged victims, date drugs, and religious tokens. But none of her computer searches turned up any unsolved local cases involving more than two of those criteria.

"You realize this guy has to kill three times before we consider him a *serial* killer." Mo rubbed his bald head.

"How do you know he hasn't killed three times?" Red countered.

"How do you know he has?" Jackie asked. "Maybe your two murders aren't related."

But Red's gut said they were. Maybe Boots's and Judy's murderer wasn't Jeffrey Dahmer, the Zodiac

Killer, or the Son of Sam, but his MO did resemble Harvey Carignan, who was convicted of murdering three women. Carrigan claimed that God told him to kill "whores and harlots." He hated women because he thought they were dirty and declared he was God's savior put on this earth to do away with the evils of this world.

"Maybe my killer's not from the Charlotte area," Red ventured.

"So are we wasting time sorting through our archives?" Jackie wondered.

Red hoped not. If she couldn't contribute something to the conversation, they'd take her off the case. She knew some serial killers were geographically stable, while others moved around, cropping up in various parts of the country. Sometimes years passed between their atrocious acts.

"I need to talk to my father," Red muttered aloud.

"Hey, I knew your dad," Manny said. "Profiler outta Raleigh, right? Don't tell me he's still working."

"No, he's retired, but not so you'd notice." Red made a mental note to call Sarasota as soon as she got home. At the same time, she realized sadly that she hadn't had an opportunity to tell Dad about Boots's death. He had known Boots when they'd all been in high school, and Dad's sorrow and outrage at hearing the news were guaranteed to be explosive.

The afternoon dragged on. Red continued to obsess about the actions she'd take to identify Salsa's would-be rapist, and every time she tried to approach Sergeant Darling about staying on the case, her old boss was too busy to talk.

The team finally called it quits around two p.m.

They had come up empty-handed, so all Red had to show for her efforts were filthy clothing and a slimy sense that she'd been permanently dirtied by the proximity to so many depraved histories.

"Don't sweat it, Red. Maybe the killer's DNA will give us a direct hit," Manny said. "And by the way, are you hungry?"

The mention of food made Red's stomach churn as she recalled the breakfast that wound up in her trash can. Yet she did need sustenance, some fuel to power her brain cells and chase the headache that had taken up residence at the base of her skull. She knew Manny, Mo, and Jackie would eat at Suds N' Sandwich, the pub across the street.

"Go ahead without me. I'll catch you later."

"So you're coming?" they pressed.

"Yeah, I'll try to meet you there."

But Red had no intention of keeping that promise. Instead, she waited until the gang drifted laughing down the hall and entered the elevator. Once the coast was clear, she retrieved her weapon, strapped it on, and quietly took the rear stairs out the back of the building to pursue her own agenda.

Chapter Twenty-two

Red hadn't planned to drive all the way to Mooresville, but she wanted to nail the jerk who tried to rape Salsa yesterday and needed to hear the details directly from Salsa's lips. A quick phone call established that Salsa was working at her restaurant, and although Salsa's voice trembled when she mentioned the assault, she had urged Red to come and even offered free food.

Food was an offer Red couldn't refuse. The very thought of Salsa's fresh Mexican meals made her stomach clench with need. Anything Salsa dished up would be way better than the fast food burrito that wound up in her trash can that morning. As an added bonus, the jaunt also offered some fresh air, after spending the morning sorting through musty cold case files.

She felt guilty about skipping out on Manny, Mo, and Jackie, but she knew they'd go ahead and eat without her.

Mooresville was way out of her jurisdiction, and since Salsa never reported the attack to the authorities, Red couldn't pretend she was following up on a crime. Screw all that. She called in as soon as she cleared the Charlotte city limits and told Gladys she was taking a personal day. Enough with the guilt.

She eased off the expressway at Exit 36, then steered east into the old part of town. When she slowed to enter the old residential district, the houses seemed shabbier than when she was in high school, and the streets were sleepier. Since Duke Energy created Lake Norman on the west side of the highway, old Mooresville had been left behind. All the action, wealth, and trendy new shopping centers had followed the waterfront, so the original businesses on Main Street were fast becoming a ghost town.

The town council was trying hard to lure new restaurants, boutiques, and art galleries—bribing them with incentives generated by taxes paid by the rich lake dwellers, but given the economy, Red feared any new venture's chance of survival was pretty slim.

She drove her new bronze Dodge Challenger down a nearly deserted Front Street to La Hacienda restaurant, taking some comfort in the fact that a half dozen cars were parked in the lot. Hopefully, Salsa's restaurant would make it. The family business had been in this same location for years. Salsa's parents ran it until her mother died, and now their nutrition-conscious daughter was making some drastic changes, betting that the organic ingredients in her nuevo cuisine would attract the upscale new residents.

Red parked in the shade of an ancient magnolia tree alongside Salsa's Honda. As she collected her purse and laptop, she decided to leave her gun and badge in the car. Removing both, she carefully secured them in the console. In her experience, a locked and loaded cop entering any place of business made customers nervous, and Salsa didn't need any added aggravation.

So she eased her long legs out of the Challenger, stretched, tapped the keypad to lock her car, and put on her best, non-threatening persona. Then, as she strolled through the small courtyard toward the stucco entryway, she was startled by a deep, familiar voice.

"*Buenas dias*, Big Red. Is that really you?"

The elderly man was sitting at a table on the porch, drinking a Corona. When he climbed stiffly to his feet, she saw his kindly face was wrinkled with age, and his thick black hair had gone snowy white. But his smile was exactly the same.

"Hello, Papa, it's great to see you!"

When he pulled Red into a hug, she smelled beer and lime on his breath, while the spicy scent of his aftershave reminded her of the crush she'd had on Salsa's dad many years ago.

"How are you, Papa?"

He shrugged as a flicker of sorrow crossed his eyes.

"I am well, *gracias*, but I am old."

"Not so old," Red objected. But she knew the loss of Papa's wife had hit him hard and that he now lived alone above the restaurant.

"Salsa said you were coming, so I made mole poblano especially for you."

"Oh, my God!" The dish was Red's favorite—chicken breast cooked in a dark sauce made with dry peppers, chocolate, and spices, then topped with sour cream. Usually, it was served with rice, beans, and flour tortillas.

"You will eat, *si*?"

"*Si*, yes, I will eat! Won't you join us?"

He shook his head. "You and Salsa need time alone."

She kissed his leathery cheek. "Okay, I'll see you later."

Red left Papa and entered a dim, air-conditioned space where diners sat quietly eating, drinking, and whispering at intimate tables adorned with candles and white cloths. The sight prompted fond memories, even though the place had changed. Certainly, it wasn't the loud family cantina she remembered from her youth, but she approved of the upgrades. Salsa had done an amazing job, and so Red expressed that opinion to the college-aged waitress who greeted her.

"Yeah, the boss works hard. Are you Red? She's waiting for you back in the kitchen."

The girl's nametag said "Lucy," so Red thanked her by name, then carefully wound her way back to the double swinging doors, which she knew led to the heart of the beast, where all the food was prepared. When she eased through those doors, the temperature climbed about fifteen degrees, as did the noise level. She spotted Salsa leaning over an enormous stove barking orders at a young Hispanic man with his dark ponytail folded up in a hairnet and bird tattoos perched on his long bare arms.

"Hi, Red!" Salsa left the stove and opened her arms. "Thanks so much for coming."

Red bent down to receive Salsa's bosomy embrace. As they hugged, Red noticed Salsa's arms were hot, and like her dad, she smelled of lime and spices. She wore a sequined blue sleeveless blouse and a patterned peasant skirt. Her glossy black hair swung freely around large gold hoop earrings and were it not for the deep circles under her big brown eyes and the tension lines at the corners of her generous mouth, she would have perfectly looked the part of a jolly Mexican hostess.

"Are you all right?" Red searched her eyes.

Salsa's shoulders slumped as she released her. "Not really. It's been a helluva week, don't you agree?"

"You got that right." Red's spirits drooped as

she thought about Boots. "But it's been worse for you than anyone."

"Not really. I'm alive, aren't I?"

"Thank God." For long moments, they stared at each other. Red felt the young cook's sympathetic gaze and figured Salsa had told the man about Boots's death. But she was certain Salsa hadn't mentioned the attempted rape to anyone. "Hey, where's my mole poblano ?" Red demanded, hoping to lighten the atmosphere.

Salsa laughed. "So Papa told you. Are you hungry?"

Red trailed Salsa to a large warming oven built into the wall. Salsa slipped on a heat mitten, lowered the door, and lifted out the steaming plate containing her heavenly dinner. "Aren't you eating?"

"Not hungry." Salsa sighed. "I haven't wanted a bite since Boots died. Lila tried to make me eat, even fixed my favorite—scrambled eggs with Texas Pete. I turned that down, too."

Red remembered that Salsa had spent the night with Lila after the attack. "I'm glad Lila was there for you. How's she holding up?"

An odd expression settled in Salsa's eyes, something between wistful and confused. Her dark pupils expanded as she searched for an answer. "Lila? Well, she's really torn up about Boots, but she's a strong lady."

"Yeah, she is."

Salsa shouldered through the back door, which opened onto a private patio. Red followed her out to a wrought iron table set for one. She saw a chilled bottle of red wine and two glasses. Taco was curled up under the table.

"Does Taco always come to work with you?"

"Nope. But he helped save me yesterday, and he's still upset."

He's upset? Yes, the golden did seem subdued, but Salsa was clearly projecting. *She* was the one still upset. "You need some food, Salsa." Red slid into a chair, then set her laptop on the flagstones at her feet.

In the meantime, Salsa turned on a small electric fan. Its humming blades sent a stream of air wafting at the table. "Thing is, I'm really worried about Lila."

"Why?"

Salsa plopped into the chair across from Red, then poured them both generous glasses of sangria. Salsa took a big sip. "She seems so unhappy."

Red refrained from commenting because what could she say? Sure the woman was unhappy. Lila's longtime partner had recently left, her dear friend Boots was dead, and now Salsa had narrowly escaped a brutal attack.

"I think Lila wants something I can't give her," Salsa confided.

Well, duh. Again, what could Red say? Even back in high school, Red felt the vibes. Lila had always had "a thing" for Salsa, but apparently, Salsa was the last to know.

"You understand Lila better than me. What should I do?"

Red couldn't advise her. Just because Lila and she were both lesbians, it didn't give her any special insight into affairs of the heart. Personally, she felt Lila was asking for heartache if she pinned her hopes on a straight woman, but what did Red know?

"I'm sorry, Salsa, your relationship with Lila is none of my business. You'll have to figure that out for yourself. I came to talk about the guy who tried to rape you, so why don't you start at the beginning and tell me exactly what happened?"

Salsa drank more sangria as she worked up the courage to speak.

Red shoved a basket of nachos at her. "If you don't eat something to soak up the alcohol, you'll be snockered before you can tell the story."

"Yes, Detective." Salsa gave a mock salute, then ate a chip. One chip led to another.

Once Salsa was eating, Red felt free to indulge. She lifted a forkful of mole poblano and shoveled it into her mouth, where it exploded in a gastronomic orgasm of chocolate, spices, and tender chicken breast. She began to gobble, couldn't help herself, until the plate was half empty. "Yum, I've died and gone to heaven." She groaned. "Remember when your mom used to make this? We'd sneak little bites of the dark chocolate until we made ourselves sick."

"Yeah, then we were too full to eat dinner, and Mom was furious."

Red slid her plate across to Salsa and handed her the fork. Much to her surprise and pleasure, Salsa took a little bite. She kept eating until all but one morsel was gone. In the meantime, Red kept her mouth shut. Many years of interviewing assault victims had taught her not to push because a woman would talk only when she was ready.

Shadows stretched across the patio as the sun dropped lower in the sky. Salsa slipped the last bite under the table to Taco, and in turn, the dog slowly wagged his tail against Red's legs.

"I don't know, maybe it was partly my fault," Salsa began.

Red tensed in frustration. Another commonality among abused women   , upon second-guessing their attacks, was they too often found reasons to blame themselves. Yes, Salsa was a flirt and sometimes she came on strong, but no way had she provoked any normal man to such inexcusable behavior. "Please, just tell me what happened."

As Salsa relayed her story, a terrifying account unfolded of how the internet date called *Bikerboy* flew into a rage and forced his way into Salsa's car, apparently because she was late and he was angry.

Red fought to keep her temper under control. "So then what did he do?"

"Oh, God, Red, it was horrible!" Salsa's small, expressive hands fluttered like agitated butterflies. "He pushed me down and reached under my shirt, and the whole time Taco was barking his head off, snarling, and lunging to get up front with us."

"Did Taco bite him?"

Salsa giggled hysterically. "Taco never bites, but *I* do. When the asshole shoved his hand between my legs, I bit into his upper arm, and he squealed like a pig."

"Jesus!" Red was proud but shocked. Typically when a victim fought back, the violence escalated, often with fatal results. "Then what?"

Salsa wiped away a stray tear with her fingertip and seemed confused. "It all happened so fast, I'm not really sure. He was screaming, he hit me, but then someone was pounding on the car. It was the old guys. I saw them go into the park restroom before it all happened. They must've heard Taco barking and come over to check it out. One man had a big hiking stick, and he kept beating on the roof…

"All at once, *Bikerboy* pulled off me, opened the door, and climbed out like nothing had happened. He raked his fingers through his hair, waved at the two guys, and trotted off to his car. A few minutes later, he drove away."

Red exhaled, stunned by the outcome. "You were very lucky."

"Tell me about it. The old guys urged me to call the cops, and believe me, I wanted to, but what the hell would I say? That some stranger I met on the internet got a little rough, then went away?"

Red groaned in exasperation. The Sexual Assault Unit had no statistics on the number of assaults never reported, but if they were available, the numbers would be staggering. Thousands like Salsa never spoke up, and unfortunately, she was right, it was hopeless. Without hard evidence that the event lacked mutual consent, she had no case.

"He won't get away with this. We'll locate him on DATESCAPE, track him down, and then nail him to the wall." This was the moment Red had been waiting for. She hefted her laptop onto the table, booted up, and found Wi-Fi available at the restaurant. Sure enough, she was able to connect immediately.

Chapter Twenty-three

S alsa said, "Free Wi-Fi was one of my improvements. Papa thinks I'm crazy, but the younger crowd loves it."

"Impressive." Red quickly logged onto DATESCAPE and started a new search. Knowing Salsa as well as she did, the keywords were no-brainers: *cares for the environment, organic foods, animal ethics, energy efficiency.* As she furiously typed, she was so anxious to crucify the lowlife rapist she could almost feel the hammer and nails in her hand. But throughout the process, Salsa remained strangely detached.

"You're wasting your time." She moaned. "Once the police find out I met him online and agreed to a date, they'll have zero sympathy."

Unfortunately, Salsa was right. Many of Red's co-workers believed anyone seeking love in cyberspace was asking for trouble, herself included. This stupidity their club had bought into was pathetic behavior for intelligent adults—particularly for a female police officer. Of course, she had an official motive. Originally, Red had only wanted to understand the mechanics of how women connected with potentially dangerous strangers, but now that Boots had been murdered and Salsa attacked, her interest was much more personal. Last night, she had again exchanged emails with *Paintercat*, the artist who depicted wild cats mauling their prey. He looked good on the monitor, so she understood the allure. In fact, she was considering a meet-up to complete her research.

She strongly suspected Boots's killer, certainly Salsa's attacker, habitually met victims online. The internet selection process allowed the criminal to not only choose his physically ideal target, but to also learn pretty much everything about the woman's   likes, dislikes, even her politics and religion. Armed with this knowledge, the predator could design a personal profile to attract anyone he wanted, gain her trust, and then lure her into his trap.

"You think victims are targeted through DATESCAPE, don't you, Red?"

"It seems likely. We know the first casualty, Judy the librarian, was a member. The techs haven't finished with Boots's computer yet because her security was state of the art. But if she fulfilled the club's pledge, it's a good bet her killer was a DATESCAPE date."

"Yeah, he was at least *one* of her many dates. Boots was deep into it. She's been hooking up with guys that way for over a year, so once they crack her code, you'll have a long list of suspects."

"No doubt. But right now, all I care about is locating your *Bikerboy*." Red lovingly stroked her laptop. "Once I analyze his profile for clues, put those together with Subaru station wagons in the area, plug it into the criminal database—I'll get him, Salsa. Just wait."

"You're wasting your time."

"Have a little faith, girlfriend. When I interface this laptop with the PC in my office, you'll appreciate the awesome power of police technology. We'll have this scumbag's real name in no time."

Then, suddenly and inexplicably, Salsa began hiccoughing with laughter. She reached into the pocket of her peasant skirt and pulled out a small slip of paper. "That's what I've been trying to tell you, Sherlock. You're not the only detective in the club. I already know his name."

Feeling foolish, Red snatched the small piece of paper from Salsa's hand. Even Taco seemed energized. He crawled out from under the table and chased a small lizard across the patio. When the lizard hid behind a potted plant tucked against the wall, Red took a closer look at Salsa's clue.

"Whoa, check it out!" The paper proved to be a payment receipt from Duke Energy, a stamped stub including not only the guy's name, but also his home address in nearby Troutman. "Who the hell pays his electric bill in person these days?"

"Tell you what," Salsa said smugly, "maybe the kind of guy who has no checking account, no credit cards, and would prefer to pay cash rather than leave a paper trail."

Red stared at her friend. Salsa's dark eyes were focused in angry concentration, her full lips compressed in determination. She looked less like a victim, more like a woman bent on revenge. "I'm impressed. How'd you get hold of this?"

Salsa threw back her head, tossing the bangs off her face. "Found it this afternoon wedged between the seats of my car. My memory's kinda ragged, but at some point, he took one hand away to reach into his jeans for his wallet..."

"The asshole was looking for a condom!"

Salsa snorted. "Right, but he was totally clumsy. He dropped the damn thing, and the stuff from his wallet flew everywhere. He took a couple of seconds to scoop up the change and bills, but somehow, he missed that receipt."

"Lucky for us." Red was already typing his name, George R. Burgiss, into the North Carolina felon database. If that didn't work, she'd go national and pray to God he wasn't using an alias. The prayer worked. "Bingo!" His name, mug shot, and a long list of petty offenses popped up immediately. She rotated her laptop so Salsa could see. "Is this our guy?"

Salsa squinted and nodded. "Absolutely. That's *Bikerboy*. Only he's about ten years younger in the mug shot and a few pounds lighter without all his hair." Salsa explained that the man she dated had long blond hair streaked with gray, pulled into a ponytail. The photo depicted a crew cut, neo-Nazi type with steely blue eyes. "It doesn't seem like him, except maybe the eyes. How could he be so different?"

"Maybe he figured the aging hippie look was less threatening."

"Well, he was right. What crimes did he commit?"

Red rapidly scanned Burgiss's rap sheet. "Mostly drug-related. He was convicted of selling crack cocaine and sentenced to two years. Unfortunately, he was recently paroled."

"What about assault?"

"Nothing in his record, but that doesn't mean it never happened."

Salsa seemed crestfallen. "Maybe that's because cowards like me never got arround to reporting him."

She sensed Salsa was close to tears, and Red preferred Salsa the fighter. "Yeah, but maybe George's luck just ran out."

"How could a man with a criminal record get a job as an environmentalist? He said he was a paid lobbyist fighting against strip mining and coal-fired, carbon-emitting power plants."

"And that's what attracted you to him."

"Yeah, sure."

"That's what you wanted to hear, so that's how George the Jerk designed his profile. He became Mr. Green to impress you. He spotted you online and gave himself an environment-friendly makeover. For all we know, predators like him have multiple personalities ready to go, so when the right woman comes along, he can pose as Jekyll or Hyde or all his cousins."

"So it was all lies. I wonder what he *really* does for a living."

"We're about to find out." Red couldn't help Salsa feel less guilty about falling for George Burgiss's lies, but she could do what she did best. As her fingers flew across the keyboard, Red located the parole officer responsible for monitoring George, and as luck would have it, she knew the man. They had gone to high school together.

"The Iredell PD has your boyfriend on a short leash. That means George is required to check in with his parole officer once a week. We both know Officer Bill Hoffman from Mooresville High, so let's give him a call."

"I don't remember him." Salsa climbed to her feet and began pacing, while Taco mounted a fresh attack on the hiding lizard. "Maybe we should wait and call him tomorrow. He's probably left his office."

"That's why God invented cellphones." Red took out her phone, brought up her contacts, and touched the number on the screen. When Hoffman answered on the second ring, she switched to speaker so Salsa could hear.

"It's been a long time, Bill," Red began, and then she gave him a quick recap of everything that had transpired in the past few weeks, with special emphasis on how his parolee had terrorized Salsa.

"Are you talkin' about Salsa from high school?" he drawled. "Cute girl. I asked her to my junior prom, but she wouldn't give me the time of day."

"Sorry, but Salsa doesn't remember you," Red said in exasperation. "Can you tell me if George Burgiss had anything in his juvenile record regarding assault? There's nothing mentioned in his file."

Hoffman clucked his tongue. "You know those records are sealed. Maybe if Salsa remembered me, I'd be more inclined to bend the rules."

Suddenly, Red understood why Salsa had refused to date this bozo back in the day. "Okay, Bill, can you tell me where George works? We agree that's not top secret, right?"

"He works at Lowe's. Is Salsa gonna press charges, or what?"

Salsa stopped pacing, rolled her eyes, and leaned in over the phone. "Hi there, Billy, this is Salsa. And you can bet your sweet ass I'm gonna press charges. We already know where George lives, so if you don't go round him up pronto, Red and I will pay him a visit and shoot off his balls!"

Red blinked in surprise, and for several heartbeats, Officer Bill Hoffman was stunned silent.

"Whoa," he said at last. "Now that sounds like the Salsa I remember, but tell Red we don't work that way here in the sticks. They may believe in vigilante justice in Charlotte, but here in Mooresville, we do it the old-fashioned way—innocent until proven guilty."

"It's possible George is guilty of much more

than his assault on Salsa," Red continued.

"You mean those murders?" Bill said. "Hate to bust your balloon, but in my opinion, he's not a killer. Maybe I do recall something about him being a bad boy and harassing some schoolgirls way back when, but that was the extent of it."

"So now you're the expert?" Red snarled.

"Not hardly." Bill yawned. "But if Salsa's really pressing charges, I reckon I'd best locate George ASAP."

"You do that, Billy," Salsa hollered at the phone. "Or I'll tell your mama how you cheated off me on the math final. I see her every day at the BP, you know."

"Hey, so you *do* remember me? Cool. Soon as I hang up, I'll call Lowe's and talk to George. According to his schedule, he should be restocking the paint department about now."

Before Red could get in the last word, cautioning Bill not to warn the suspect and set him running, the parole officer hung up.

Salsa sighed. "*Bikerboy* stocks the bloody paint department? Guess he's not an environmental lobbyist, after all."

Red also sighed. "Did you actually tell that cop I'd shoot off George's balls? Guess you don't know I've gotten a little gun-shy in my old age."

"Bill will call us back and let us know what happens, won't he?"

"Oh, yeah, and next time, he'll ask you for a date."

Red poured their glasses full to brimming with the remaining sangria, and then they waited. As she considered all the bizarre twists and turns these cases had taken, she feared Bill was right about George

Burgiss—guilty of assault, not murder. She still liked the Reverend Jonah Ellis for Boots's homicide. And what if none of these crimes was related? Maybe the entire Charlotte Mecklenburg Police Department was fishing in the wrong pond.

As evening approached and a cooling breeze ruffled the leaves of the big magnolia out front, Red noticed more cars parking in the restaurant lot. The noise level picked up inside the kitchen, then suddenly, Lucy poked her head out the door.

"Sorry to interrupt   Salsa, but can you lend a hand at the bar? Some guy ordered a whiskey sour but complained I brought him a daiquiri. Truth is, I don't know shit about mixing those drinks."

"Sorry, Red, I better go." Salsa's voice was filled with regret. "Promise you'll come get me the minute Bill calls back."

"Will do."

Taco whined when Salsa left, but he wasn't about to leave his post at the potted plant. Red seriously doubted the smart little lizard was still hiding there, until suddenly, the reptile jumped out and slithered across the tiles with Taco on its tail. It slid under a mound of pine straw mulch stacked off the edge of the flagstones, narrowly escaping extinction.

"Be patient, Taco, you'll catch him someday."

The phone rang while Taco was lunging at the mulch. As Bill told her what had transpired, she could hardly contain her disappointment. "Are you *sure*?" she demanded when Bill finished apologizing.

"Yeah, I'm sure. But maybe we'll catch up with him. He's only been gone twenty-four hours."

But Red knew the suspect could be halfway around the world by now. "Thanks for trying, and good luck, Bill."

She hung up. "Shit," she told the retriever.

"What's wrong?" Salsa stood wide-eyed, framed by the kitchen doorway.

"He's gone. *Bikerboy* flew the coop. When Bill called Lowe's, the manager told him George never showed up for work last night. Next George cleaned out his apartment and split without paying the rent. What's worse, it seems George was working the Friday nights that Judy and Boots were killed. His fellow workers confirmed it, so he's not the murderer."

"But they'll catch him, right?"

In the meantime, Taco dove head first into the pine mulch. After a round of growling and barking, he crawled out backward with a limp lizard hanging out either side of his jaw.

Good job, Taco, Red said to herself. *At least someone gets it done.*

Chapter Twenty-four

Wednesday morning, Red rode along with Rick to Boots's funeral. She had wanted to attend alone, to deal with her grief and remember her friend, but that was not to be. Although Rick claimed he was going to pay his respects, she knew he was going as a cop, to watch the mourners and calculate their responses, to perhaps detect the killer among them gloating over his crime.

"How much farther?" Rick asked when they left the interstate and drove through the outskirts of Statesville.

"The church should be about a mile and a half up the road." She glanced at the GPS.

"Are you sure? This looks like farmland."

The thermostat on the dashboard registered ninety-eight degrees, and the glaring sun beat down on the Crown Victoria's white hood, nearly blinding them. "Hope this church is air-conditioned," she said.

"Amen, sister." Rick gave her a sly look from the corner of his dark eyes and loosened the tie at his throat. "I talked to Gina this morning. She's worried about you. Think you might want to give her a call?"

From out of the blue, his words chilled her in spite of the heat. For the past two days, Red had agonized about the night she'd spent in Gina's arms. Even working full tilt on the Boots murder, she couldn't suppress the sweet memory. But in the final analysis, she was still Detective Red Calendar, and until that changed, what could she say to Gina?

"Did you hear me, Red?"

"I heard you. Do you think Gina might want to give *me* a call?"

Rick growled and shook his head. "No wonder it didn't work. It's like you two are in this crazy stare-down contest, and neither one will blink."

So Red stared at him and kept it up for a full mile, until he finally broke the silence.

"Okay, you win," he conceded. "Not my business."

Eventually, they got around to discussing Boots and realized they'd never been to an authentic African American funeral. Yes, they'd attended traditional services for two black officers who died in the line of duty, but those had been very formal affairs. They suspected this would be much different.

She told Rick that Boots had forsaken her family's religion years ago. Indeed, that fact had been the rationale for Red's theory that the cross found around Boots's neck had been placed there by her killer.

"I'm not sure Boots would've wanted a big service like this," she mused as they approached a large warehouse-like building that proved to be Family of Christ Church. "I'm sure all this was her mother's idea."

Rick shrugged as he parked in a field cordoned off to accommodate all the extra vehicles. Already the paved lot was packed with everything from newer upscale imports to old pickup trucks. "Well, funerals aren't necessarily designed to please the dead, they're supposed to help those of us left behind."

"Amen, brother." Red shot him a sour look

as they stepped into the blistering heat and followed the crowds moving toward the church. In spite of the weather, everyone was dressed up for the occasion. The older folks, mostly black, were especially high style—men in dark suits, women wearing somber dresses and amazing hats. The multicultural younger set, obviously friends of Boots's, wore casual or trendy mourning gear.

As they progressed up the walkway, a chilly hand latched on to Red's elbow, and when she spun around in surprise, she was face-to-face with Summer. Her friend was also clinging to the arm of a clean-cut-looking man.

"You remember Paul, don't you?" Summer seemed cool, calm, and radiantly happy in a pale blue sundress that precisely matched her eyes.

As Red tried to place the slim, eager fellow with neatly combed hair even redder than hers, Rick introduced himself to the stranger.

"Summer's told me a lot about you guys." Paul pumped Rick's outstretched hand.

"Well, don't believe everything you hear." Rick cast a suspicious frown at Summer. "I'm not the monster these girls make me out to be."

"Hello, Rick." Summer's icy greeting said it all.

In the meantime, Red had recognized Paul as the clumsy waiter from their high school reunion. She'd also heard that he was Summer's serious new boyfriend. So she smiled and shook his hand, not entirely sure she could trust the only male in their age group who was still wearing his suit coat.

"Where's your daughter?" Red asked Summer.

"We didn't think Gloria's quite old enough to understand a funeral, so we left her at home." Summer beamed. "With her *new babysitter*. Would you believe, we don't need to depend on Creepy Connor anymore?" She gave Paul's arm a loving squeeze. "My honey here introduced me to a sweet Christian girl who lives in my apartment complex. She's one of Paul's students, and she's more than happy to babysit whenever I need her."

"Nice move, Paul," Red said. They'd all heard the horror stories about the druggie neighbor kid who'd been watching Gloria. "Keep that up, and Summer will be indebted to you for life."

He grinned. "That's the whole idea, Red. Make her realize how much she needs me, and soon she can't function without me."

"It's already happening," Summer cooed. "Paul even fixed the leaky pipe under my kitchen sink."

"Jesus." Rick groaned. "What are you doing, man? Trying to make the rest of us look bad?"

"Let's all sit together," Summer suggested.

"Sure, why not?" Red agreed, but she wasn't sure she could take much more of Summer's gushing over her new beau. True, she looked happy and alive, which was more than she could say for Boots, who hadn't fared so well with a murderer she may have met on DATESCAPE.

As they neared the church, Red recalled that their police techs had finally cracked Boots's firewall and discovered a character named *Avatar*, with whom Boots was having a hot cyber affair. Rick hadn't yet interviewed the guy, who was a black video game entrepreneur in Charlotte, but they had learned that the man had been busted for some shady financial practices.

Red hoped Summer's internet catch, Paul, AKA

Bioteach, was the real deal. He seemed too good to be true, but at least he wasn't a complete unknown. He had attended Mooresville High, after all, and now he taught there. Maybe Red simply didn't trust traditional, gentlemanly guys like Paul. Worse still, what if Red was too mean-spirited to abide anyone else's happiness?

On that decidedly unhappy thought, they stepped inside the cavernous metal walls of Family of Christ Church, where they were greeted by a woman who handed them each a memorial program and a cardboard hand fan. Rick's fan bore a colorful picture of President Obama, while Red's was a well-worn relic from a local funeral home, cracked down the middle. When she glanced at the program, she saw a grainy black and white photo of an adolescent Boots. Boots's huge, hopeful smile beamed off the page, and coupled with the rousing gospel music being piped from inside, it tightened a knot in Red's stomach.

"Couldn't her mama find a more recent picture?" Summer's eyes misted with tears.

"Maybe she didn't have one." Red knew Boots and her parents had parted ways years ago. Their daughter's big dreams and progressive ideas did not suit the family agenda.

"I wish I'd known her better," Paul mumbled as they entered the huge sanctuary.

A live band and enthusiastic choir had already brought many members of the congregation to their feet. They were singing *Hallelujah* and waving their arms in the air. Red bet that most of these folks never knew the adult Boots, but it didn't matter now, did it?

"Oh, look, I see Salsa and Lila!" Summer shouted above the music. "We can all sit in that row right behind them."

"Great idea," Paul echoed his girlfriend.

Rick stiffened at the idea.

"Oh, c'mon," Red urged. "Let's sit with them. These girls don't love you, but they won't bite you, either. I promise."

He sighed in exasperation. "It's not that, and you know it. We should sit near the back, where we can keep an eye on things."

"No, *you* should sit near the back and keep an eye on things. I'm not playing cop today."

As Red followed her friends across the aisle to the right side of the church, she caught sight of Boots's white casket smothered in a blanket of flowers, with congregants filing by for one last look at the corpse. Red recoiled in dismay because Boots never would have agreed to an open casket. She would have wanted people to remember her vital and alive, not this way. But as Rick had so aptly put it, this wasn't about Boots anymore, it was about her family.

Red spotted Boots's parents, siblings, uncles, and aunts seated in the front row, receiving guests. She'd never known them well, so maybe she could skip the greeting for now. Apparently, Red's friends felt the same because as Summer quickly took a seat behind Salsa and Lila, they were all looking everywhere but at the coffin. Only Paul strode forward, folded his hands, peeked somberly at Boots, and shook his head. He even spoke quietly to the parents before rejoining the girls.

"They seem like nice people," he said solemnly. When no one answered, he tried again. "And Boots looks real pretty…"

But the women of the TLC were not comforted. Instead, Salsa and Lila reached back to squeeze Summer's and Red's hands. At that moment, Red felt an unshakable solidarity among them, the survivors. At the same time, the fact of Boots being gone hit her with powerful, devastating finality.

"I still can't believe it." Red gasped.

The others nodded in agreement.

"But hey," Lila quipped. "This shindig's not half as bad as I expected. The band and choir really rock, and you gotta admit, Boots always loved a good party."

Red tuned out the words since the sermon wasn't about Boots specifically, but rather it was a generic celebration of life itself. That was good, she approved. She only wished she was sitting with Salsa and Lila instead of Summer and Paul, who were holding hands, behaving more like lovers than mourners.

When James Allen, Boots's assistant from Best Buy, stood to offer a eulogy, his voice cracked, and he broke down in inconsolable tears. Red recalled how Jimmy had claimed he loved Boots, and likely, that was true. He had come today prepared with a video he and Boots had made together for YouTube.

When a giant screen lowered from the rafters, everyone saw Boots singing Aretha Franklin's classic *Respect*, while performing a sexy dance in flannel pajamas. Her voice wasn't great, the dance wasn't graceful, but it was vintage Boots. When it was done, there wasn't a dry eye in the house.

"Wow!" Lila glanced back at Red. "I wouldn't mind having a copy of that CD."

"I'm glad I have my photo of the five of us from the reunion," Summer said. To demonstrate, she took a postcard-sized copy from her purse and passed it quietly around.

Red gasped with surprise because this was the same photo she'd found on Boots's floor the night of the murder, the one she'd almost stolen in a moment of nostalgic need. "Where'd you get this?"

Summer beamed. "Paul gave it to me. I plan to have it framed."

"I want one!" Salsa tugged Paul's sleeve. "Where can I get it?"

Paul actually blushed with all the attention. "I got it online. The high school put up a web page for the reunion, and the alumni posted lots of pictures after."

Red decided to order her copy as soon as she got home, and again she experienced a powerful wave of regret that she'd allowed these dear friends to drift away over the years. At the same time, she sensed a hush descend on the crowd as a new speaker approached the podium.

The regular minister stepped forward with the microphone. "Folks, please welcome Pastor Jonah Ellis from Mooresville's Church of the Holy Redeemer. Pastor Ellis was a close friend of Sister Boots, so we're honored to have him deliver the sermon this morning."

Red's body convulsed with fury to see Ellis's large, equine head nodding benignly at the congregation. As he folded his hands in a brief prayer, then gazed mournfully out at the colorful sea of fluttering fans, she could hardly control her anger at his self-righteous hypocrisy.

"He's got a helluva lot of nerve!" Red hissed under her breath.

"What's wrong?" Summer whispered.

"Long story." Now wasn't the time to tell them they were praying with the man who likely put Boots in that white box. Of all the suspects, Red remained convinced that Ellis was guilty, and as he piously mouthed the scripture in his deep, sanctimonious voice, she longed for revenge.

When she glanced toward the back of the church, she saw Rick get to his feet and fold his arms across his chest. Even at that distance, she felt his anger and knew he was as startled as she was by the surprise appearance of their prime suspect. Red fantasized a scenario in which Rick strode purposefully to the altar, handcuffed the bastard, and then dragged him unceremoniously down the aisle, reading him his Miranda rights.

Instead, much to her dismay, Rick's focus shifted from the suspect to his pocket. Seconds later, he fished out his cellphone, held it to his ear, and then walked right out of the church.

What the hell? Red squirmed in her chair, completely unable to concentrate as Ellis finished and nodded to the group of pallbearers in the front row. Adding insult to injury, Jonah Ellis joined the other five men honored to wheel Boots's casket across the front of the sanctuary, and then they disappeared out a door to the street, to where the hearse was waiting.

Shit! Every instinct told Red that Ellis was escaping, and although she tried to control the impulse, she jumped to her feet. Completely ignoring the protocol, which allowed the family of the deceased to file out first, she half stumbled across Summer and Paul to break into the recession.

"What are you doing?" Summer cried in alarm. Even Salsa and Lila pivoted in their seats, clearly shocked by Red's behavior.

She would explain later. For now, all she could think of was alerting Rick. She needed to tell him Ellis was getting away. Yes, she was crazy, but she was no longer controlled by reason. As she shoved through the startled guests and burst into the foyer, she saw Rick calmly talking on his phone. He was leaning against the wall just outside the building, in a patch of shade, watching the coffin being loaded.

Red rushed to his side and punched his arm. "Look, Ellis is leaving!"

Rick frowned and held her away until he finished the call. Once he'd ended the call and slipped the phone into his pocket, he gave her a look that made it plain he thought she'd gone stark raving mad.

"What do you want me to do, arrest him?"

Red was hyperventilating, and when she saw her panic reflected in Rick's eyes, she realized she'd gone off the deep end. "I just can't stand seeing him here. Boots would be so upset."

"Yeah, I suspect she would be, but I can't do a damn thing about it." Rick took her arm and led her out of the stream of exiting mourners. He walked her across the street and forced her to sit with him on a bench beneath a parched oak tree.

"Why did you leave the church?" She punched his arm again, while Rick continued to stare at her in silence. It was a technique that always worked. So she concentrated on breathing in and out as she watched Boots's family slowly climb into the black limo behind the hearse. Red saw Summer, Paul, Salsa, and Lila step into the sunshine, blink, and look around for her.

Rick didn't speak until he knew she'd regained her equilibrium. "I had to answer the call. It was forensics…"

Red waited as the hearse and limo pulled slowly away. She saw Jonah Ellis fold into a dark gray station wagon and follow them. Rick would tell her when he was good and ready, but by the time the vehicles left the lot and disappeared at the end of the road, she could wait no longer. "So what did the lab say?"

"They got the DNA results back from the good reverend's apple," Rick solemnly replied. "And I hate to tell you this, but Ellis didn't do it. He's not our man."

Chapter Twenty-five

Sometimes Summer couldn't relate to the girls in the True Love Club. She'd tried to convince them to come to Boots's burial, but they all begged off. Red left right after the service with Rick, while Salsa and Lila's excuses were really lame.

"We were not invited, it's a family thing," Salsa insisted.

"Not true," Summer argued. "Paul spoke to Boots's parents, and they said we were all welcome."

Lila shrugged. "Even so, I don't believe in all that graveside mumbo jumbo, and neither did Boots."

"Yeah," Salsa chimed in. "I prefer to remember her alive, not in a hole covered with dirt."

Summer didn't appreciate their attitude, and neither did Paul. She could tell from the cold expression on his face, yet he didn't criticize or correct her friends. Summer and Paul were both believers, so they knew Boots's spirit had already flown to heaven, yet they let Salsa and Lila leave without an argument, and then they headed for the cemetery.

"You can't expect everyone to share our faith," Paul said as they parked and slowly made their way across the brown field to where Boots's family was already seated in folding chairs under a blue canvas canopy.

But Summer was still angry. The others had never been religious, but at least they should make the effort, show some respect. She wondered if the women would feel different if they had children of their own. Since Summer had Gloria, she naturally wanted her daughter to be raised in a church environment, and she thanked God for bringing her Paul, who obviously felt the same way.

She took his arm as they approached the perimeter of the funeral tent, where the other mourners already stood, heads bowed in somber reflection. Was Paul too good to be true? Would he stick by her, as he claimed he would? Summer didn't know, but she believed in his goodness and liked how he smiled down at her, encouraging her through his intense blue eyes.

The merciless sun beat down on their heads as the minister read the Twenty-third Psalm. Like Gloria, Paul had been an only child raised by his mama, who always took him to church. Like Gloria, Paul had been devastated by his parents' divorce and believed in a strong family unit. Once he'd told Summer that she reminded him of his mama, who had passed away, and Summer considered that a high compliment.

"I'm glad we came," she said.

"Me too."

She liked how his red hair lifted ever so slightly in the whisper of a breeze and how he didn't mind being one of only three white faces in the crowd. The only other Caucasian was the young man, James. Now, like at the funeral, the pudgy boy was bawling like a baby, so Summer figured he and Boots had been mighty close.

They watched in silence as one by one Boots's family members placed flowers on the white coffin. One little girl handed a flower to the Reverend Ellis, and then the pastor added it to the collection on the casket lid.

That quickly, it was over.

Everyone moved aside as the family walked away. Summer spotted the cemetery workers standing at the ready in the distance. Soon they would lower the casket and use their shovels, and for a fleeting moment, Summer understood why her friends maybe didn't want to witness that part, but she still blamed them for not coming.

Somehow, it seemed natural that she, Paul, and the white kid hung back until the more connected people left. As those folks drifted toward their cars, and once the parents were safely seated in the limo, only then did Summer notice the heated argument taking place between the kid named James and Pastor Ellis.

She felt the muscles in Paul's arm tense under her fingers as they watched the drama unfold. For some reason, James was screaming at the pastor because he had placed a flower.

"You have no right!" the kid shouted and shoved the tall black man. "You shouldn't even be here!"

"You best stand clear, Summer." Paul gently guided her behind his back. "I don't know what this is all about, but that boy's got blood in his eye."

The two were arguing dangerously close to the casket—and the hole. James balled up his fist and took a swing, but Pastor Ellis ducked away from the blow. When the kid tried again, Ellis caught his wrist in an iron grip.

"Calm down, son," the pastor warned in his deep voice. "This isn't the time or the place."

But James broke loose and butted Ellis with his head. As the big man lost his footing and almost fell into Boots's grave, Summer screamed in alarm. At the same time, she sensed Paul leave her side and approach the fight.

"You stay put," he told her. "Don't move."

By then, they were fighting hard. Absurdly, the kid reminded Summer of an enraged little bull as he kept butting and pummeling with his fat fists. But the strong pastor quickly took the lead, and with one mighty blow, connected with the kid's nose. Blood gushed down the boy's face.

"Stop!" Summer cried as she looked desperately for help, but the crowd had moved on. In the same instant, she saw Paul enter the fray.

Then, almost in slow motion, several things happened at once. The kid dropped to his knees and crawled away on all fours to avoid the next punch, but then he stopped. He wiped blood from his face and reached into the pocket of his baggy pants. When his hand came out, a shiny object glinted in the sun.

"He's got a gun!" Paul hollered as his body seemed to take flight.

Pastor Ellis ducked, while Paul tackled the kid and wrestled something from his hand. Summer cringed at the explosion. When her ears stopped ringing, all three were on the ground. James was sprawled on his back, a look of horror on his face, as Paul held the gun to James's head. Ellis was slowly sitting up, apparently unhurt.

But as Summer gaped in disbelief, a red stain seeped out from under Paul's suit coat and blossomed on his white dress shirt like a rose. The freckles on his face stood out in sharp contrast to his pasty complexion.

"The kid winged me." Paul gasped.

When Summer rushed to his side and knelt in the freshly turned earth, she barely noticed that a few stragglers had left their cars and were running back toward the grave.

Chapter Twenty-six

No way! You gotta be kidding!" Red snapped the aluminum ring on a can of Miller Lite and stared out from her patio.

"Sorry, I'm not kidding." Salsa's voice came from the phone. "Summer is hysterical, and Paul's still in the emergency room. Lucky for him, the bullet passed through the fleshy part of his upper arm and didn't cause too much damage."

The sun had just begun its descent in the western sky, but heat still shimmered above the city beyond Red's apartment complex. She propped her bare feet on the retaining wall dividing her little space from the neighbor's and took a deep chug of cold beer.

"Seems the kid believed the Reverend Ellis was Boots's killer," Salsa continued.

"Well, Jimmy had good reason to think that, but turns out, he was wrong."

"It's all so pathetic. Now the kid's life is ruined, and Summer will never stop talking about how Paul is a hero," Salsa said.

"Is the hero pressing charges?"

"Oh, you bet." Salsa snorted. "In fact, Summer and Paul have both implied that this boy, James Allen, killed Boots himself—in a fit of unrequited love or some such thing."

"Well, maybe he did," Red answered bitterly and took another swig of beer. She'd been dead wrong about Ellis. In fact, the DNA they'd lifted from the pastor's apple had not only cleared the pastor, but also any male of African American descent. Since Boots wasn't killed by a black man, most of the many men she'd dated from the internet, including *Avatar*, had been eliminated.

"But I don't think the kid did it," Salsa said. "I think he's just got a quick temper, like all you redheads. What would Rick think?"

"Since when do you care what Rick thinks?"

"I don't. It's just that Lila said Boots's murder is *his* case."

"Well, Lila is wrong." Red didn't mean to be snippy, but it was a sore subject. On their tense ride home from the funeral, Rick hadn't exactly gloated about her bit of evidence—the apple—being a dead end, but he'd been somewhat patronizing when he told her she could stay on the case.

"But I agree with you, I don't think the kid did it," Red said more gently. "And by the way, I guess Paul *is* a hero."

"I suppose." Salsa's tone was not a ringing endorsement.

"Don't you like him?"

"What's not to like? To hear Summer tell it, the guy's pretty near perfect, and maybe that's the problem." Salsa sighed. "Look how I was attracted to the jerk *Bikerboy*, and where'd that get me? I'm just confused these days."

No doubt Salsa was confused, and Red strongly suspected Salsa's confusion involved Lila, but the two of them would have to work that out on their own. So after a few more pleasantries, including a pledge to get together again real soon, Red said goodbye and hung up.

After a second beer, she heated leftover tuna casserole and ate it on the patio. In the meantime, the luscious aroma of barbecue smoking on somebody's nearby grill made her feel deprived and lonesome. Salsa's love life was in turmoil, so was hers. Dangerous as it was, Red couldn't flush Gina from her bloodstream.

Work was the only distraction. So as soon as she finished eating, she logged onto DATESCAPE and winked at *Paintercat*. They began an online conversation, and she learned he was a retired dentist. He'd had a practice in Asheville but now lived in Charlotte and devoted most of his time to painting those amazing studies of wildcat predators with their bloody prey. Determined to find out more about internet dating, Red had promised to meet *Paintercat* someday soon.

After making that stupid promise, she'd stayed online, hoping to buy that group photo of the True Love Club. Unfortunately, the high school reunion website had been taken down, so now Red would never own that nostalgic picture of the five of them.

Too bad. Lately, her timing was way off. Even her sleuthing instincts were dull and fuzzy. She'd been wrong about everything regarding this case. First, she'd suspected some unnamed serial killer, then the Reverend Ellis, then *Bikerboy* or *Avatar*, and now this misguided kid Jimmy had surfaced as a suspect. What if the cases of Judy the librarian and Boots were unrelated and had nothing to do with the internet or serial crime?

As the molten sun gave its last gasp, leaving behind fiery orange fingers strangling the Charlotte skyline, Red decided it was time to make that call she'd been putting off. She brought a bottle of anisette liquor out to the patio, told herself it would ease her indigestion, lit a citronella candle to ward off the ravenous mosquitoes, but instead of dialing Gina, she lost her nerve and called Dad in Sarasota instead.

As usual, he answered on the first ring. "What's up, monkey?"

Red got the bad news out of the way up front. She told him about Boots's murder and about her funeral that afternoon. As she'd expected, her father was devastated, because of all Red's high school friends, Boots had been Dad's favorite. After making her repeat the entire story twice, the second time including all the false starts in the investigation, she was able to detect the changes in her father's voice as he passed through all the stages of grief.

"God, I'm sorry, honey, how can I help?"

Dad the criminal profiler was back and on high alert. That was a good sign because Red was the same. The only way to climb up and out of sorrow was to buckle down to work.

"You say Boots died on a Friday night?" he asked. "Just like the first woman Judy."

"That's right."

"And although the specifics of the crimes were slightly different, much remained the same," he continued. "The fact that the killer gained entry without a struggle again implies both victims knew their attacker. Judy was drugged, Boots was zapped by a stun gun, but maybe the guy realized he wouldn't have the luxury of time to subdue Boots. Restraints were used in both cases, he ejaculated on each woman's stomach, and twice left a religious calling card behind."

"Yeah but he didn't dress Boots up like a princess before leaving."

"No, but Boots fought back. So either he was angered by her behavior and chose not to play dress up, or maybe he ran out of time."

Red sipped at the sweet liquor and wished she hadn't given up smoking. Obviously, Dad was still clinging to the notion of a serial killer, so she told him about her exhaustive search of the local cold case files, how they revealed nothing remotely similar.

"I hear you, monkey, but serial killers often move around, and sometimes they take a holiday. Maybe your UNSUB once operated in a different state. Maybe he hasn't killed for a number of years because he's been in prison for a while."

Dad was shuffling a whole deck of "maybes" as far as Red was concerned. She squashed a large mosquito feasting on her elbow and decided to move inside just as her cellphone went dead. She barely had time to pee and wash her hands before Dad was back on the landline.

"I've been doing some investigating on my own," he began without preamble. "And your cases sound a lot like the work of a serial rapist who terrorized central Florida a few years back…"

She listened while he described a classic, religiously motivated nutcase who had preyed on middle-aged women more than two decades ago. He had used drugs, restraints, and always left a crucifix behind.

"Yes, but your man never *killed* the women," she objected.

"True, but sometimes they escalate. Consensus was that this sicko was taking his wrath out on older women your age, who reminded him of his mother."

"Thanks a helluva lot, Daddy."

"Well, it's true. You and your girlfriends aren't getting any younger, so you're old enough to be this asshole's mother."

"You're talking twenty years ago. By now, that freak's my age or much older."

"Sure, *he* has aged, but in his mind, his mama never does, so the profile of his victims remains the same."

Red sighed and shoved the liquor bottle out of reach. As was often the case, her father's dogged unwillingness to let go of his favorite bone was giving her a headache. "So do you still have any of your Florida rapist's DNA on file?"

He chuckled and cleared his throat. "Funny you should ask, monkey, because I've been working on that very project. As you know, back in the Stone Ages, we weren't into DNA, but we sure as shootin' saved everything else. In this case, they still have old clothing saturated with the jerk's semen, so you never know…"

"And you've asked your SBI buddies to test those clothes?" It always amazed Red that Dad's former associates seemed endlessly willing to grant him favors.

"Yep, they're testing those clothes next week, so cross your fingers and toes that after all these years, the horny bastard's jizz hasn't dried up like a useless old bread crust."

"That's disgusting. Unless your pals in the State Bureau are totally incompetent, the sample should still be viable."

He offered one of his famous belly laughs. "Don't worry, little girl, we may be Florida crackers compared to your city boys, but we know how to store evidence. Rest assured, the killer's nasty little stain is carefully paper wrapped at room temperature. In the meantime, be careful…it'll soon be Friday night."

"So what?"

"So you and your middle-aged girlfriends, who remind this sicko of his mama, could well be next on this predator's hit list, and Friday's his night to prowl."

"I suppose you want me to observe your old curfew and call the moment I return from my Friday night of wild, indiscriminate sex and pub crawling?"

"You do that, monkey."

And then he hung up.

Chapter Twenty-seven

Red got a call from James Allen's lawyer as soon as she arrived at work Thursday morning. It seemed the kid had named her as a character witness based on the short interview she'd conducted in the parking lot the night Boots died.

"Jimmy told you he suspected the Reverend Jonah Ellis had killed his boss," the lawyer began.

"True, but that doesn't give Jimmy the right to shoot the man."

"What's worse is he shot the wrong man." The lawyer moaned. "But that was an accident."

Red swallowed the last drop of caffeine in her cup and wished everything to do with the Reverend Ellis would go the hell away. "Your client took the law into his own hands. That doesn't speak well for his character."

"Jimmy told you how much he loved Boots, so when Ellis showed up taking control of her funeral, it pushed him over the edge."

Red's headache was proving that no one in her right mind should drink beer, then anisette liquor. Sure, maybe she had a bit of maternal compassion for the straight-A college student who was a victim of his misguided love hormones, but this lawyer's request was nuts. "Why don't you ask Detective Rick Molerno to vouch for Jimmy? He was present at that interview, and he's lead detective on the case."

"I already asked Molerno, but he turned me

down cold."

Now why didn't that surprise her? Rick had been hostile toward the kid from the beginning. In fact, Rick had been the first to tag the unlucky lad as a suspect. Just to be contrary, because she knew it would piss Rick off, Red reluctantly agreed to testify on Jimmy's behalf. "But I can only attest to what I heard, nothing more."

"Oh, thank you, Detective Calendar. You're an angel. I'll forward the court date as soon as I know it."

By the time she hung up, Red realized too late that her testimony would not only annoy Rick, it would also infuriate Summer. Red would be defending the man who shot Paul, Summer's hero boyfriend, so no matter what motivated Jimmy, accident or not, she'd be lucky if Summer ever spoke to her again.

Some days, you just can't win. But the morning did get better. Red managed to completely avoid gossipy Gladys, yet still overheard the delicious news that Miranda, the new officer in homicide and Rick's hot new squeeze, had dumped Rick for a younger cop in vice.

Next Red solved a five-year-old case in which a pair of junkies in ski masks had brutally robbed and beaten an old man in South Charlotte. One punk had left behind a cigarette butt with saliva DNA, which got no hits back then, but today she matched it to a recently released meth dealer who just happened to live two blocks from the police station. When they sent a patrol car to the address, they nailed not only the meth dealer, but also his pal, the other dude who'd helped with the robbery five years ago. Both had confessed.

"Nice work, Red!" Sergeant Darling crossed the aisle to shake her hand. "I just knew you'd be great in the Cold Case Unit. Can I take you to lunch to celebrate?"

Red smiled but politely declined. "Sorry, I already promised the volunteer team. Maybe next time."

"You bet." Darling winked, then briskly walked away.

Fact was, Red felt guilty about ducking out on Manny, Mo, and Jackie on Monday. Although she had since explained the circumstances, the three insisted Red owed them lunch—at least a round of nachos and beer.

So at the stroke of noon, the elderly trio was waiting at Suds N' Sandwich.

"Hey, Red, over here!" Jackie had saved her a place. The guys were already drinking.

As Red crossed the crowded room, she noticed something was missing—that creepy sensation that someone was watching her every move. Call her paranoid, but for two weeks, whenever she ate there, she'd felt eyes boring into the back of her head. Not today, thank heavens. She had chalked that sensation up to stress, and maybe that was accurate because after a successful morning, she was okay.

"Pity you can't drink with us," Manny said.

"Rub it in, why don't you?" Red grinned and sat beside them. Police policy forbade on-duty officers from partaking of alcohol, but since her colleagues were not employees of the CMPD, but rather retired cops volunteering their time, the rule didn't apply.

"Too bad about Rick." Mo smirked. "That little Miranda was a pistol. An old man like Rick needs a young girl to rev his engine."

Red glared at Mo's bald head. Juicy tidbits

spread through the department like chicken pox in elementary school, and these guys were behaving like giggling schoolgirls.

"Serves him right," Jackie piped in. "Miranda was young enough to be Rick's daughter."

"Not quite," Red mumbled defensively. Lately, everyone was pushing her age buttons. First her dad had pointed out that she wasn't getting any younger, and now these three geriatrics were implying that Rick and she were too old to get it on without more youthful stimulation. At least Red's recent indiscretion with Gina proved that she managed quite well, even at the ripe old age of forty-eight.

"Hey, did you hear about my big collar this morning?" She abruptly changed the subject.

Thankfully, it worked. Much as they wanted to dwell on all things sexual, Manny, Mo, and Jackie were easily seduced by a police victory. Soon they were all congratulating Red for bringing the two robber junkies to justice after five long years because the cold case files defined their lives now, and any triumph was well worth celebrating.

Red rewarded herself by ordering a sinful hot roast beef sandwich with mashed potatoes swimming in gravy. Iced tea didn't measure up to a cold beer, but a woman couldn't have everything. In the meantime, her friends' animated conversation floated cloud-like above her head as she ate and drank. While her mind drifted back to the subject of age.

Odd. When it came to Boots, Summer, Lila, and Salsa—women she'd known since her youth— they remained forever young in Red's eyes and mind. She didn't notice their wrinkles, the slower pace, the expanding waistlines because those friends were frozen in time. Just like Red could almost ignore her own aging reflection in the mirror because she felt unchanged inside her skin, her longtime pals seemed ageless.

But strangers her age who wandered into her current life, like Paul, Summer's new boyfriend, did not get such a pass. Maybe to Summer, Paul seemed boyish and vibrant. But Red still saw a forty-something teacher with thinning hair, stooped shoulders, and a judgmental attitude, resulting from what? Too many years standing before wiseass adolescent students? When Salsa chose *Bikerboy*, had she seen a kid full of high-minded liberal ideals? When Red checked out *Bikerboy*'s photo online, she had observed an over-the-hill hippie with an edgy look in his eyes, an edge she now knew was a penchant for rape.

Good thing Red wasn't drinking because her maudlin obsession with aging could easily get out of hand. And as she attempted to pull herself up and out of those reflections, she realized her friends at the table were gearing up to leave. They were joking about how Red was going to pay the bill and giving the waitress a really hard time.

"C'mon, I didn't order chocolate cake," Manny complained as the flustered waitress fluttered around balancing a plate of dessert.

"I should hope not." Jackie smirked. "Your arteries are already clogged."

In the confusion, Red fumbled through her purse looking for a viable credit card and was thoroughly flummoxed when the waitress set the plate down in front of her.

"Wait, I didn't order this either," she objected.

"No, ma'am, it's compliments of that gentleman

sitting at the bar."

Four faces pivoted in unison in the direction the waitress directed, and Red's heart skipped in confusion.

"Who is he?" Jackie's rheumy eyes, while huge with curiosity, were also deeply suspicious.

"Do you know that man, Red?" Mo placed a fatherly hand on her arm.

Taking matters into her own hands, Red passed the credit card to the waitress, picked up the plate of cake, and stomped toward the bar. She did not look back. Instead, she ignored the nervous chatter of her friends as they left and prayed to God for enlightenment.

Who the hell was he? The stranger seated casually on his stool, one expensive loafer hooked on the lower rung, the other planted firmly on the floor as he half rose to greet her, was both utterly unknown, yet vaguely familiar. As Red racked her brain to place him, she couldn't decide whether to be flattered or royally pissed.

The man was undeniably handsome—tall, buff, elegantly dressed in tan slacks and a meticulously pressed designer shirt, open at the collar. His luxuriant black hair was distinguished by salt and pepper at the temples, and his intense blue eyes watched hawk-like as she approached.

"Why did you send this?" Red set the plate on the bar in front of him.

"Chocolate cake, a *heavenly delight,* if the menu is to be believed," he answered in a deep, ironic voice.

"But why did you send it to *me*?"

"It's your favorite, right? If your DATESCAPE profile is to be believed."

Red's brain synapses all short-circuited as she

stared. Was it possible? This audacious stranger looked somewhat like his photo online, yet like all those imaginary aging contemporaries she'd been dissecting during lunch, in the flesh, he seemed both older, and younger, than she had visualized.

"*Paintercat*?" She gasped.

"Right on." He grinned and extended a hand with long, tanned fingers and manicured nails. "Pleased to meet you, *Firebird*."

"But how did you find me?" She had taken great care to remain anonymous and unreachable. Unless, of course, she chose to be reached.

"I wish I could impress you with my superior sleuthing abilities," he smoothly replied. "But the fact is, I simply dropped in for a bite of lunch and recognized you sitting over there with your friends. I must say, your DATESCAPE photo doesn't do you justice."

Red knew he was lying, yet she had taken every precaution in the security handbook to avoid this breach of privacy. Not good. When she shook his hand, she saw a trace of blue paint on his middle knuckle.

"I'm sorry, Red. Don't be mad about the cake. When I spotted you, I couldn't help myself. Besides, you promised we'd meet soon, and I'm afraid I'm not a patient man."

God, he even knew her nickname! Of course, he could have overheard her friends calling her by name. They had been pretty loud.

In person, he looked to be of Cherokee descent. That could explain *Paintercat*'s dark, angular features and perhaps his choice of subject matter. Those Native Americans had been driven from the hills of North Carolina, much like the native mountain cats so prevalent in his paintings.

Red took a deep breath. "I don't appreciate your approach, and I don't want this cake."

"Again, I apologize. It's not fair to keep you at a disadvantage, so allow me to introduce myself. My real name is Sam Redbird."

This was a step in the right direction, his offering up his identity like an unwanted dessert, and he seemed perfectly serious about his name. At the same time, it tickled her funny bone and she couldn't help but imagine what they'd call her if she married him—*Red Redbird*—how ridiculous! Unable to control herself, she laughed in his face.

"Am I that funny?" His eyebrows, much like raven's wings, arched in question. "Does that mean you'll accept a date with me tomorrow night?"

Chapter Twenty-eight

Summer knew Paul wasn't permitted to drive for one full week, so she and Gloria picked him up outside his small ranch house on the outskirts of town and brought him to their apartment for dinner.

"I would have invited you inside my place," he apologized as they filed into Summer's living room. "But the rooms are a mess. With my arm in a sling, I haven't been able to clean."

"We'll take a rain check." Summer pointed him to his favorite spot on the sofa. "What do you want to drink, Paul?"

She knew so little about him, so she'd stocked beer, wine, and even a bottle of whiskey, the brand her ex-husband, Ed, used to like.

"Do you have iced tea or lemonade?"

Summer did a double take. Off hand, all she could think of was Gloria's apple juice in the fridge, but that would never do. Then she remembered the can of frozen lemonade she kept for emergencies. "Sure, I'll be back in a jiffy."

Disappearing into the kitchen, Summer couldn't decide if she was pleased or disappointed. All the men she knew drank alcohol, and she'd been looking forward to a glass of wine or two. Still, she'd rather date a teetotaler than a drunk. She'd prepared the meatloaf in advance. Slipping it into the oven, she suddenly hoped Paul's religion didn't forbid meat on Friday. But he was a Baptist, for pity sake, not a

Catholic.

Willing herself to stay calm and stop worrying, she dumped the frozen lemonade into the blender and churned. At least she could count on Gloria to entertain Paul in her absence. Her smitten daughter had already turned on the TV, and the frenetic, lilting music of a video game danced above their laughter.

Soon Summer was humming to herself, something she hadn't done in years. When she was courting Ed, Friday night dates always involved country western bars, heavy drinking, and bad karaoke. So this quiet evening with Paul was a huge change of pace. She poured two glasses full and carried them to the living room.

"Sit down and join us, Summer." He beamed up at her as he tried to maneuver his controller with his one good hand. "Gloria's beating the heck outta me."

"I'm winning, Mommy!" her child exclaimed.

Gaming wasn't Summer's thing, but she loved that Paul and Gloria were bonding. "No, y'all play without me while I fix dinner." She then recited the menu and was relieved when Paul gave her a big thumbs-up.

"Paul has a surprise for us." Gloria nodded at the bulging backpack he'd brought. "But he won't let us have it unless I eat all my veggies."

"Good deal, kid." Now it was Summer's turn to give Paul a thumbs-up, and when she scuttled back to the kitchen, only slightly jealous that Gloria was more inclined to obey Paul than her own mother, she set the potatoes to boiling. She normally would have used instant rather than bother with peeling and mashing and felt only minimally deprived of that glass of wine she would otherwise have sipped during the task. But this was good.

She gazed out the window above the sink while she washed and snapped the fresh green beans. That big old black storm cloud looked nasty, but they hadn't had a decent rain since last Friday, the night Boots was murdered. The thought sent a shiver down her arms. Was it possible? That so much could happen in one short week? Only two weeks ago, she'd met Paul at their high school reunion, and that night, he was no more to her than a cute waiter who spilled beer.

God did work in mysterious ways.

Chapter Twenty-nine

Salsa barked orders at the cook staff. The guys were moving too slow for a Friday night, but then they never expected this big crowd. The threatening storm must have driven them into the restaurant, but who was she to complain?

She ducked into the restroom to wash her hands and secure the hair back off her moist forehead with a barrette. The kitchen was hot as Hades, and the decibel level, the cacophony of pots clanging, and the staff bitching set her nerves on edge. As she scrutinized her image in the worn old mirror, she looked flushed, frazzled, and irritable. Earlier, she had even yelled at Papa, who was spending way too much time schmoozing with the guests. She'd actually yanked a beer from his hand and commanded him to get back to work.

Maybe her waitress was right. Lucy had asked if Salsa was suffering from hot flashes, and indeed she was. But no way could she blame this bad behavior on the menopause blues. Ignoring the heat, she moved back into the kitchen and volunteered to wait tables.

Thing was, Salsa desperately wanted to be somewhere else. Lila had invited her to an art opening at the Depot, and Salsa really wanted to go. Lila had been working with these artists for weeks, so it was a truly big deal, and although Salsa knew next to nothing about art, she wanted to learn more about what made Lila tick, what inspired her passion. Worst of all, the look of disappointment in Lila's pale blue eyes had cut to the quick. Salsa had wanted to hold her and comfort her, to promise a "next time," but of course, she'd done neither of those things.

"Hey, Salsa, some guy out front wants to talk to you." Lucy was hanging in the swinging door to the dining room, looking hassled and wilted in her uniform.

"What guy?" Salsa snapped. "Is he eating here?"

"Yeah, his order should be up by now. He's having the *camarones a la diabla*, and he's already had a couple of drinks."

"Oh, shit, I'll serve him." Salsa spotted the shrimp simmered in its spicy red hot sauce ready on the hot plate. She added rice, cabbage salad, and four flour tortillas, grabbed a hot mitt, and slid the meal onto a tray. "What's this guy look like?"

"Old, bald, walks with a cane. Table six."

Lucy held the door open as Salsa passed through. Just what she needed, some lonely guy hitting on her. Happened all the time, but tonight she was much too busy for small talk. As she entered the dining room, the sudden blast of air conditioning popped goose bumps on her bare arms, and after the noise and bright lights of the kitchen, she paused for a moment while her ears stopped ringing and her eyes adjusted. Then she carefully wove her way through the closely placed tables to number six.

Sure enough, the seated man was watching her approach, but he wasn't all that old. Bald, yes, and she almost tripped over the cane hung on the empty chair, but this fellow had a ruddy, youthful face. Obviously, he looked different to a college kid like Lucy than he did to her.

She carefully lifted the hot platter off the tray and placed it onto his table.

"Hello, Salsa. Thanks for coming out to see me." His voice was a high tenor and familiar.

"Do I know you?" She slipped off the mitt and squinted at him.

"Aw, jeez, have I changed that much? You refused to be my date for the junior prom. Don't you remember?"

Her eyes twitched as she tried to piece it together. Gradually, his identity dawned on her, but the revelation did nothing to soothe her nerves. "Are you Bill Hoffman from Mooresville High?"

"Yep, but now I'm Bill Hoffman, the parole officer. You better sit down."

Oh, God, was he here about *Bikerboy*, her would-be rapist? Suddenly, she felt weak in the knees. "What do you want?"

"Well, I was hungry for Mexican food, but I'm afraid I also have some bad news."

Just then, thunder clapped outside the building. The loud bang rattled dishes on the tables and stunned the diners into momentary silence. The lights blinked off, then on again, and Salsa sank into the chair across from Hoffman, who had begun to eat in spite of the disturbance.

"What's wrong, Billy?" she asked.

He finished his mouthful, grunted in appreciation, then set down his fork. "The other day on the phone, I told Red that George Burgiss was working at Lowe's those Friday nights when Boots and that other woman were killed, but turns out, I was wrong." He paused for another thunderclap. "It seems George paid another employee cash to punch his time card and work his shift those nights, and the manager just now got wind of the lie."

Salsa felt like he'd punched her in the belly.

Hoffman groaned. "I hate to tell you, but there's more. The landlord says someone went into George's former apartment and took a CD player left behind. Problem was, the intruder used a key, so the cops think your guy is back in town."

Chapter Thirty

Lila almost jumped out of her skin when a thunderbolt hit too close for comfort. At first she believed it hit the weathervane atop the old wooden railroad station, now known as the Mooresville Art Depot, because the paintings on the wall actually shifted with the impact. Moments later, the lights blinked off, then on again, causing all the clients milling around with drinks and snacks to gasp in collective surprise.

At least most folks had arrived before the storm, so Lila should count herself lucky to get a half decent turnout, and although she wasn't properly in the mood, she forced herself to mingle. Problem was, it still hurt that Salsa had refused to come. Lila had even bought a new dress for the occasion, a low-cut blue silk sheath that not only revealed a good bit of cleavage, but also precisely matched her eyes. In her fantasy, Lila had imagined Salsa's dark eyes straying in appreciation to her breasts, while at the same time, Salsa would be enormously impressed by her ability to organize such a gala affair. She would marvel at Lila's graceful ease with the clients, at all the connected people who knew and admired her. But that was not to be.

"Oh, Lila, I love that dress!" Suddenly, Mrs. Pearlstein appeared at her elbow. The woman fingered the fringed white gossamer shawl Lila had thrown around her shoulders in a last-minute attack of modesty. "And the earrings are exquisite with it."

"Thank you, Rachel." Lila's hand flew automatically to her left lobe, where one of the heavy turquoise and silver earrings her ex had sent from New Mexico had begun to droop. "They were a gift from a dear friend in Santa Fe."

"Very nice. Is he anyone we know?"

"No, I'm sure you don't know *her*." In fact, Mrs. Pearlstein and all the other matrons from the various art societies had met her former girlfriend on numerous occasions, before her ex took off with a new lover. Likely, they all suspected Lila was a lesbian, but rather than confront the idea, they preferred to torture her with the male pronoun "he." Hypocrites. She was fed up to the gills with the whole provincial scene.

"Nice exhibit, Lila." Mr. Pearlstein joined his wife, and his gaze did rove to the V between her breasts. "I particularly like all those watercolors by that new fellow Barnes."

"Good, I'm glad you like them, and as you know, they're all for sale." With that not-so-subtle hint, Lila winked and moved on to the next group.

She minded Mr. Pearlstein's ogling less than she minded his taste in art. Yes, she had accepted Jed Barnes's watercolors into the show because she knew his brand of realism would sell, but personally, she hoped to never see another study of a beached sailboat, a crooked birdhouse, or a tobacco barn in winter. Indeed, she longed to include some edgy abstracts or experimental expressionist nudes, but she knew such work would never sell. Unfortunately in this depressed economy, if their little not-for-profit did not generate some cash soon, they'd be forced to close their doors before Christmas.

"Hello, Lila!" A trio of earnest Davidson College

students from just down the road buttonholed her before she reached the next group of viable collectors. "How come *your* work's not in this show?"

Lia loved these kids, had taught them a course in welding as a guest professor, but how should she answer that question? Lila's *Seagull in Flight* was almost completed, but she strongly suspected she'd never exhibit it here in the Depot.

"Maybe next time," she muttered to her young fan club, and then she walked away.

Lila received a second compliment on her earrings from a local jeweler who always bought one painting at every show. "I wish I could carry that kind of stuff in my store, but my buyers are too conservative."

"Thanks, Joe." She wished to God she'd never worn the blasted earrings because so far they'd caused nothing but trouble. They'd come two days ago via FedEx, and Lila's ex had called that evening. For months, she'd avoided her calls, but after receiving such an extravagant gift, she had to answer. Big mistake.

Lila, I want you back, her former partner had sobbed into the phone. *It didn't work out between Linda and me, and now I'm fucked. I really miss you...*

Blah, blah, blah. It wasn't that simple, and by the time they hung up, they were both in tears.

"Are you okay?" Joe the jeweler waved a playful hand in front of her face. "And by the way, how come you keep rejecting my friend Sam's work? In my opinion, he's one hell of an artist."

Now that got Lila's attention, along with a second thunderclap that shook the very floorboards. "You know I respect your opinion, Joe, and I really appreciate your support, but we don't agree about Sam Redbird's paintings."

"I don't get that..." Joe paused to swallow a piece of warm string cheese on toast. "Sam's work is so strong—all those big cats hunting—and kinda spiritual, don't you think?"

"Too violent for my taste." Lila frowned. "Besides, the man's not ready yet. He needs more discipline and practice."

Joe crossed his arms and glared at her. "Yeah, Sam told me you gave him a hard time. He's shown you his art on three separate occasions, and each time, you made him feel like shit."

Lila blinked in surprise. This didn't sound like the mild Joe she'd come to know, and obviously, Sam Redbird had influenced him. She shuddered at the memory of her encounters with Redbird. She and the retired dentist had most definitely not hit it off. It was hate at first sight, that sort of reverse chemistry that sometimes ignites when two big egos clash.

Besides, Redbird's work was simplistic, self-indulgent, and disturbing in its obsession with gratuitous violence. She had suggested training, but her advice had not been received kindly. In fact, during their final meeting, Redbird's anger had escalated to where Lila feared he might hit her. Afraid for her safety, she'd demanded he leave, and once he was gone, she'd been so badly shaken, the incident had lingered in her psyche for days.

"Well, I hope you'll reconsider," Joe said. "In fact, maybe I should save my pennies and invest in one of Sam's paintings rather than make a purchase tonight."

"Yes, Joe, if you feel so strongly, maybe you should."

As she strode away, Lila told herself she should

be ashamed about antagonizing a customer, but she wasn't. God only knew what kind of slander that jerk Redbird had spread about her, but did she care? Maybe she was sick of Mooresville, or maybe she was just mad at the world. Certainly, it annoyed her when her hand shook as she poured herself a full tumbler of champagne.

"Take it easy, Lila. That swill will knock you flatter than a crepe skin if you chug it down."

When Lila spun around to the source of the deep alto voice, she was suddenly face-to-face with *Waterspirit*, the mysterious lesbian she'd discovered on DATESCAPE.

"I mean it, that budget champagne will give you a hangover to die for. That is, you'll wish you were dead."

"Oh, how are you?" For once, the glib Lila was tongue-tied. The woman looked fabulous in a simple, calf-length cream gown that perfectly enhanced her short white hair. *Waterspirit* had the same charming laugh lines at the corners of her eyes and mouth as exhibited in her internet photo.

"I'm fine. Wish you had more modern art in this show." *Waterspirit* smiled teasingly.

"Me too." Tongue-tied *and* stupid, Lila would be mortified if this woman discovered how Lila had tracked her name in the gallery receipts and then stalked her by driving past her home.

"Now, Lila, I know you prefer Jack Daniels on the rocks."

"How did you know?" But *Waterspirit*'s grin said it all. "Oh, God, you saw me on DATESCAPE!"

"Oh, yes, I certainly did, and I was delighted to make that connection."

The woman's eyes focused on Lila's chest, but unlike the disgust Mr. Pearlstein's ogling inspired, *Waterspirit*'s interest lit an entirely different kind of fire in Lila, a blaze centered considerably farther south than her brain. The conflagration spread to her mouth, and she blurted it out. "Well then, will you join me for a proper drink after the show?"

Chapter Thirty-one

Red had trouble choosing an outfit for her Friday night date with *Paintercat*. She'd given up the girly-girl look years ago, so her "dress up" wardrobe was tired, dated, and in some cases, too small. She'd allowed her off-duty duds to dwindle to worn T-shirts and frayed jeans, so as she shoved hangers back and forth in her closet, the only pretend hetero thing she found was an all-purpose black sheath she used for funerals and the occasional obligatory office party. After a quick sniff of the dress's armpits, she judged it to be clean and passable.

At least her feet hadn't outgrown her ancient red high heels, and Red figured since *Paintercat* was an artsy kinda guy, he might appreciate the long Aztec-patterned scarf Gina had bought her on their last ill-fated vacation to Cancun. One drawback to being a tomboy, to feeling more at home working with her dad in the garage than mall hopping with her mom, was the fact that Red had entered womanhood without one clue about fashion.

No problem, she reflected nervously as she flipped the scarf loosely around her neck, with its long tail hanging down her back like a goofy bridal train. She secured the colorful statement with a silver pin and added silver hoop earrings and a touch of red lipstick. She brushed her flaming mane into a loose ponytail, secured with a black scrunchie, and then checked herself out in the full-length mirror.

Not bad. She'd always been able to "pass," and tonight would be no exception. But when she considered walking through a mist of perfume, like the femme fatales in the movies, Red realized her old fragrances had likely gone sour with disuse, so she discarded the idea. Finally, feeling naked without her gun and badge, she locked the apartment and walked to her Challenger.

The dark night air was heavy with ozone, so she could literally smell the rain that was already giving the northern counties fits. As she drove toward the warehouse where she'd agreed to meet *Paintercat*, located in Charlotte's NoDa Arts District, she listened to the police radio band. Its scratchy audio comforted her as fellow officers from Huntersville to Statesville complained about the power outages causing traffic accidents, even a smash and grab at a convenience store in Cornelius, where lightning had taken out the alarm system.

Red hoped the storm would miss the city, but pessimist that she was, she doubted it. She hoped *Paintercat* would monopolize the conversation because she'd never been good at chitchat and judging by the self-confidence he'd exuded at Suds N' Sandwich yesterday, she suspected he'd have no trouble talking. Finally, she hoped this date was not a huge mistake. What the fuck would she do if this man—she should start thinking of him as "Sam," not *Paintercat*—wanted more than a quick drink and conversation?

She'd jump that hurdle when she came to it, not before, and instead, she concentrated on finding a parking space. In the end, she had to park almost a block from the warehouse, which did not bode well for a quick getaway, but she took a deep breath and decided not to sweat it. Telling herself to think positive, she even left her umbrella behind when she locked the car and began walking down the unfamiliar street.

NoDa, or the North Davidson Arts District had never been Red's beat. For several decades, the locals, with help from grant money, had been trying to revitalize the failing commercial area into a thriving arts community. Indeed, a number of trendy galleries, boutiques, and restaurants had sprung up—most failing, some surviving—yet somehow they'd kept up the art crawls, including this one tonight.

Since Red knew next to nothing about this scene, she'd Googled "The Warehouse" where they were meeting and now knew the place had been renovated to include not only artist studio space for rent, but also a nightclub where aspiring poets read their work and new bands tried out their music.

She was greeted at the door by a burly, half-naked fellow whose body was entirely covered by tattoos, so she wondered if the small cover charge was the price of beholding this guy—a work of art in his own right.

"This your first time, lady?" His eyes were deeply suspicious.

Red nodded and squeezed past him into a dim, noisy space crowded with young yuppie types gyrating to heavy metal. Was it that obvious? Did she smell like a cop, or did she just look out of place? She had insisted on meeting Sam in a very public venue, so this definitely fit the bill, and as she shoved through the dancers, where the odor of sweat and beer was overwhelming, she again wondered if she'd made a terrible mistake.

Just when she was poised to turn tail and run,

someone shouted her name above the din. Then she spotted Sam's long arm waving at her, beckoning her to join him at the far end of the room. As Red wriggled into his sphere, he snagged her elbow and guided her through a swinging door into a smaller backroom, where the noise cut off almost immediately.

"Wow." She gasped.

"Yeah, I know. It's a zoo out there."

It took several seconds for her to reconnoiter. This new space was a makeshift café, with varnished packing crates for tables, a long plywood bar nailed to one wall, and the back completely open to the night.

"This used to be a loading dock," Sam explained. He pointed to the concrete deck leading out to the street, where a young man smoking a joint was silhouetted under the misty streetlights. "Now we use it as exhibit space and to enjoy some serious drinking."

As the sweet-smelling smoke drifted into the room, Red reminded herself she was off-duty. Besides, she hadn't busted a kid for pot in years. So she continued to make the emotional and sensory adjustment from the chaos she'd just left and breathed in the scent of rain. Luckily, a row of slowly rotating ceiling fans cut the humidity and kept the area bearable. In the meantime, she was only slightly aware when Sam led her to one of the tables, guided her into one of two director's chairs, and then he smiled.

"Well, what do you think?" His perfect, brilliantly white teeth glistened.

For a moment, that smile impressed her, but then she remembered—*hey, he's a dentist.*

"What?" he demanded.

Red looked directly at him for the first time. Still magnetically handsome, still capable of evoking a sexual response from a department store mannequin, he had every reason to believe he'd excite the same response from her. *Good luck with that, pal.* Tonight *Paintercat* had forsaken his designer persona for jeans and a black T-shirt.

"Guess I overdressed," she muttered.

"No, Red, you look fabulous!"

She tried not to flinch when he reached out and fingered her scarf, his knuckle brushing the underside of her chin.

"So, what would you like to drink?" He shoved a steel mini bucket of whole peanuts across the packing crate.

"What do they serve here?"

"Pretty much anything that comes in a bottle. I'm having scotch."

"I'll have scotch, too, thanks." Looking around, she saw they were alone except for three young women in paint-covered overalls. They were drinking beer while lost in a serious, animated conversation. "Is there a bartender?" Red asked.

"Tonight I'm it," Sam said. "Those of us who rent space here take turns exhibiting, and the featured artist stocks the bar at his own expense. Of course, we only dole out drinks to folks we invite, like those girls over there. They work across the hall from me, so they're always welcome."

"Interesting." Red scanned the walls and suddenly realized the room was completely hung with *Paintercat*'s work. The astonishing, colorful studies of wildcats hunting, lunging at, and devouring their prey were everywhere. Some she'd already seen on the internet, but others were new. In person, the paintings were even more violent than on a monitor screen. The vibrant blood reds, slashes of primary blue and yellow contrasted with the deep greens of background foliage.

"Why didn't I notice before?" She stared at Sam. "This is *your* show. Congratulations."

He shrugged his broad shoulders in feigned modesty, but she could tell he was proud and pleased by her response.

"His work is totally scary, don't you think?" one of the girls said as the three prepared to leave.

"Yeah, Sam's art gives me nightmares," another added.

Red had to admit the texture of the paint, not to mention the large scale of the art, when seen in the flesh were unsettling indeed.

"So how 'bout that drink?" Sam grinned once the girls were gone.

He fetched the scotch and water Red had requested, then sat across from her. "That's a pretty scarf. Great colors."

"Thanks. Now tell me about your art."

Sam began to talk. As she had suspected, he was inclined to carry the conversation, so after the first hour and the second drink, Red knew the bare bones about what motivated Sam Redbird, and it wasn't nostalgia for his dental practice. Since he sold the business and retired, all he cared about was succeeding as a painter.

"When you start this late in life, it's not easy. And when you work with subject matter like mine, no one knows how to deal with it."

"It is pretty raw," she carefully ventured. "I don't know much about it, but clearly, your art is survival of the fittest."

"Yes, life and death." He poured them each another drink. "That's something you know about, isn't it, Red?"

His shoe touched her foot, and she reflexively pulled away. While he talked, his paintings began to seriously disturb her, dragging her back to the two moments in her life when she'd been forced to kill. Her last victim, a vicious street punk who managed to shoot her before she dropped him, had that same panicked look in his eyes—like a doomed rabbit in one of Sam's paintings.

"I'd rather not talk about it."

"C'mon, the waitress at Suds N' Sandwich told me you were a cop, so I went to the police website and learned all about you, Detective Calendar. Exciting career, right?"

"Please, can we change the subject?" Red knew some men were police groupies, and the idea of a woman with a gun turned them on. Was Sam   one of those, waiting for her to titillate him with some violent stories? She also suspected he had somehow learned all about her long before he entered Suds N' Sandwich, so his innocent act was pure bullshit. "Let's talk about your show—what an honor."

"Not really," he answered abruptly and bitterly. "It's no honor. I bought it—like self-publishing a novel. Since I rent space here, they're forced to let me exhibit."

His angry tone frightened her. Like Jekyll and Hyde, Sam *Paintercat* Redbird's personality could turn on a dime. Since Red was no art critic, she didn't know how to respond.

"I've been trying for years to get a show near my home in Mooresville," he continued. "But that bitch at the Depot hates my guts."

Red took a deep breath. That "bitch" he was

describing was her friend Lila. "Well, art is subjective, right? Not everyone agrees."

"True, but this dyke Lila rejects me simply because I'm male. She's allergic to even one whiff of testosterone."

Sam's brutal assault was chauvinistic and homophobic, and it set Red's alarm bells off big-time. She had to make a choice—either tell him to fuck off, that Lila was one of her best friends, or walk away without making a scene. Much as she liked this asshole for exactly the type of online predator they were looking for, she chose the latter.

"Hey, what did I say?" Sam sprang to his feet when Red picked up her purse and headed for the door. "Let's hook up next weekend, okay?"

His furious gaze drilled into her retreating back, a sensation much like being shot by bullets.

"Forget it, Sam. It ain't happening," Red hollered as thunder clapped and she rushed out into the storm.

Chapter Thirty-two

Red had called an emergency meeting of the TLC. She hadn't wanted to schedule it for Thursday because it was inconvenient for everybody to drop everything on a weeknight, yet it was necessary.

"Can Paul come with me?" Summer had begged over the phone. "His arm is healed so he can drive now, and I'd like y'all to get to know him."

"Girls only. Sorry, Summer."

When Red contacted Lila and Salsa, it seemed they'd already made plans together for that evening, so she figured it was no big deal for the two to make a short side trip to Huntersville, which was midway between Red's apartment in Charlotte and everyone else's home in Mooresville, but Red had been wrong.

"Is this meeting really important?" Salsa had whined.

"Yes, and it won't take long. We'll meet for dessert, okay?"

"What kind of dessert?" Lila asked suspiciously when contacted.

"Who cares?" Red had answered impatiently.

"Well, I'll bake something special and bring it along. That way, we won't waste time and money in a restaurant."

In the end, they'd all agreed to meet in the village square in Birkdale, a trendy development on the lakeside of town. The complex included a fashionable outdoor mall with shops, eateries, and a major bookstore. The mall was surrounded by apartments and single-family homes designed to encourage the popular "live, work, and shop in your neighborhood" lifestyle, where everyone walks everywhere, knows his neighbors, and generally replicates Norman Rockwell's Main Street.

Unfortunately, Red arrived late. She'd been held up at the police department, so by the time she parked and located her friends, they were already seated on benches near the bandstand on the green. A German-style beer garden band was loudly performing, part of the village's summer concert series, so Red's voice would have to compete with brass horns and symbols.

"Hi, guys!" She put on a smile.

"You're late." Lila was unpacking a picnic basket as Salsa poured iced tea into festive red plastic cups. Whatever reservations her three friends might have had about this impromptu get-together vanished when Lila distributed her famous glazed fruit dumplings, still warm from the oven.

"Yum. Sit yourself down, Red." Summer licked her fingers.

Red slid onto a heavy, wrought iron bench facing the trio. Since conversation was impossible above the din, she got with the program and bit into a cherry dumpling. "Yum is right. Where'd you learn to bake like this, Lila?"

Lila tossed her long silky brown hair. "Oh, dah-ling, I attended gourmet cooking school for over-the-hill, old maid lesbians. I needed one talent to recommend me."

Everyone laughed but Summer, who couldn't abide Lila's counter-culture humor. Instead, Summer started telling them about the joys of heterosexual dating, which proved to be a recitation of her new boyfriend Paul's many fine qualities. By the time Summer's animated dissertation ended, all the dumplings were gone, and while Red was happy for Summer, all that gushing made her slightly sick to her stomach.

"So how did your big date with *Paintercat* go?" Lila winked.

"Oh, please don't ask!" Red knew Lila hadn't made the connection between *Paintercat* and Sam Redbird, and Red wasn't about to enlighten her. After the rude way Sam had slandered Lila, it was clear there was no love lost between them. Red would take Lila aside and warn her once they were alone together.

"Well, I have some bad news about *my* internet date," Salsa announced when the band took an intermission break. "*Bikerboy,* AKA George Burgiss, is likely back in Mooresville. And what's really scary is that his parole officer now admits that George could be responsible for Boots's and that other woman's deaths."

Red nodded. Hoffman had phoned her as soon as he found out about the timecard discrepancy at Lowe's. "But Bill still doesn't believe George is the killer," she added.

"What the hell is this?" Lila stared at Salsa.

"Sorry, I didn't want to worry you," Salsa murmured as she watched a street pigeon peck at a bit of dropped crust, then twaddle off.

Red sensed the tension between Lila and Salsa, so she quickly filled in the missing details about George Burgiss, including his complete adult criminal resume, which Hoffman had finally provided.

"Is that the same Bill Hoffman from Mooresville

High?" Summer glanced at Salsa. "Didn't he have a crush on you back then?"

"Please forget it, will you?" Salsa growled.

"Is he married?" Summer pressed.

Red held her peace as the two wrangled. Something was definitely going on between Salsa and Lila. They seemed shy and hyper aware of each other. Jealousy? Red refused to speculate. Instead, she waited until a group of grade school kids finished a game of tag and the first stars appeared in the perfect July sky.

"I can't be sure," Red said when the time seemed right, "but in my opinion, George Burgiss is a person of interest, but he's not Boots's killer."

"Why not?" Lila demanded.

Red chose her words carefully. "Because from what we know of George's background, he never lived in Florida."

Three faces gaped at her in utter confusion.

"What does *Florida* have to do with it?" Summer asked at last.

The band was returning from their break, so Red knew she'd have to make her points fast. "It's a long story, but it involves my dad in Sarasota…" She reminded her friends about her father's career as a cop, then later as a profiler. She told them how they'd been unofficially working together on the two local murders, especially regarding the semen DNA the killer left behind. And then she dropped the bombshell:

"So believe it or not, Dad got a hit. The local killer is the same man who raped a number of women in Florida twenty years ago."

As her friends continued to stare, Red recalled how hard it had been to eat crow when Dad gave her the news only last night. Naturally, he had gloated, and

Red had been forced to acknowledge his unexpected success.

"Dad and his friends from the Florida State Bureau of Investigation shared their data with my fellow officers in the CMPD this morning, so now the whole department's trying to piece it together."

Summer's eyes were round as Willow Ware platters. "Was that a feather in *your* cap, Red, or just plain humiliating to have your daddy solve the case?"

"It's not *solved*." Red had actually begun to relax before her dad called because after all, last Friday night had come and gone without incident. The TLC girls had been out and about, and there hadn't been one rape, let alone a homicide, reported in the greater Charlotte area.

"I still think you should watch *Bikerboy*." Lila frowned as she laid a protective hand on Salsa's wrist. "You don't know for a fact he's not from Florida, do you?"

"No, we don't. Unfortunately, Bill Hoffman's records on George Burgiss go back only six years."

"*Twenty years ago*?" Salsa gently moved away from Lila. "How old is this killer?"

"One would assume he's ancient," Red said. "But in fact, he could be our age. If he started at eighteen, he'd be only thirty-eight today."

Summer sighed. "At least that proves my weird babysitter, Connor, isn't doing these awful things. He's just a kid."

"It also proves James Allen, the boy who shot Paul, didn't kill Boots." Red gave Summer a pointed look. "Paul should consider dropping charges."

"The kid still shot Paul." Summer huffed dismissively, then launched into her familiar diatribe about creepy Connor and how Paul had found a nice high school girl to babysit for Gloria—all of it old news.

"So, Red, why did we have to meet in person?" Lila asked. "Couldn't we have done this by phone?"

Red reached into her purse and handed them each a brochure about internet safety, with a special chapter warning about dating sites. "I wanted to see the whites of your eyes when you make me a promise," she told them. "A few weeks ago at the reunion, we made a pact to try DATESCAPE. With the exception of Summer, the experiment has been a disaster. Tonight we must dissolve that pact, and each of you must swear to never go on there again."

The women regarded one another as a new moon peeked out from a cloud blowing in on the night breeze.

"I swear," they said in unison, then sealed it with the old club handshake and bear hugs all around as the band began to play.

Chapter Thirty-three

Thursday evening had not gone well for Lila. After the sobering meeting with Red, Salsa was no longer in the mood for drinks and a movie at Lila's place, so Lila had dropped her off at her bungalow and gone home alone. By Friday evening, Lila screwed up her courage and called Salsa at her restaurant. After seven rings, Papa answered the phone at La Hacienda.

"Buenas *noches*, Papa. *Como está*?" Lila began.

"Lila? *Estoy bien*. Qué *pasa*?"

"Is Salsa there?"

"*Si. Ella está   en la cocina.*"

"I know you're busy, but may I speak to her?"

"*Si*, I will get her."

By the time Salsa answered, Lila already felt guilty about disturbing her at work, on what was one of the busiest nights for any restaurant. "Sorry, I just needed to talk."

"Yeah, I know. I'm glad you did."

Last night when they parted, Lila had kissed Salsa. Again. It was intended to be only a friendly kiss on the cheek, but Salsa had seemed to know that Lila's feelings went dangerously deeper than friendship.

"I'm sorry if I came on too strong last night," Lila whispered into the phone. "But I was hoping we could reschedule. The drinks and a movie are still waiting."

"Will you please stop apologizing?" Salsa sighed.

"I'm sorry," Lila blurted without thinking. Was Salsa angry, upset, or just plain fed up? The film Lila had proposed was *Nina's Heavenly Delights*, a charming lesbian comedy about an Indian family living in Glasgow, Scotland. The straight daughter, Nina, comes home to save her dad's restaurant but ends up falling in love with Lisa, her fellow cook. Lila had hoped Salsa would relate to the situation and laugh.

"Jeez, you just apologized again." Salsa groaned. "I'm really busy, Lila, so please just say what you want to say."

Lila took a deep breath and stroked Georgia's golden head, which was in her lap. It seemed her dog instinctively understood Lila's need for moral support. "Okay, then, let's do it tonight. Come to my place after you finish work."

Silence. Lila could almost hear Salsa thinking, weighing the pros and cons. Lila figured they both understood that accepting the invitation implied a romantic commitment. At least it signaled Salsa's willingness to try something new.

"I don't know what to say," Salsa said at last. "I won't be done until really late."

Lila's spirits soared to the ceiling and fluttered near the chandelier. She rubbed Georgia's head too hard, and the retriever nervously wagged her tail. "No problem. I'll be working late anyway. I'll be out in the shed welding until you get here. You can even bring Taco, if you like."

"For a sleepover?" Salsa laughed. "You realize our dogs are already half in love with each other. Do you think they'll behave themselves?"

Was Salsa flirting? Lila tugged Georgia's ear so enthusiastically that the animal jumped down and hid behind the couch. "Considering how long our dogs have known each other, we must respect them as consenting adults and allow them to make their own decisions."

More silence. "I don't know…" Salsa responded carefully. "Wouldn't you rather ask *Waterspirit*?"

Lila felt like a heavy fist had just punched her in the heart, knocking all the wind from her chest. She never should have told Salsa about her date with *Waterspirit*, how they'd gotten drunk together after the show at the Depot. Lila's brief encounter with the mystery woman from DATESCAPE had been intense, some sexual innuendo and a little touching. To be sure, *Waterspirit* was attractive and intriguing, but the interlude meant little in the grand scheme of things. So why had she told Salsa? To make her jealous? Obviously, the plan had backfired.

"I don't want to see *Waterspirit*, I want to see *you*."

Lila heard pots rattling in the restaurant kitchen and excited voices chattering in the background. Her emotions were walking a tightrope. Would she make it to the other side or fall to oblivion?

Finally, Salsa drew a deep breath. "Let me think about it, okay? Right now, it's too hectic to make a decision. But I promise, I'll come if I can."

And then she hung up.

"So what did she mean by that, Georgia?" Lila walked around the sofa to comfort her traumatized pet. "Is she coming or not?"

Georgia followed her into the kitchen, where the windows to the lake were black. The new moon was too weak to reflect on the water, and the dark silhouettes of the willow oaks were undisturbed by even the whisper of a breeze. It was one of those nights that seemed dead, like the oppressive heat of the day had sucked all the oxygen from the earth, bushes, and trees, leaving nature a wilted corpse.

With that cheery thought, Lila made a sandwich. She had no appetite, but she knew she had to eat, so she slathered two slices of rye bread with Thousand Island dressing, then added corned beef and Swiss cheese. Georgia approved the activity.

"My good girl." Lila cupped her hand and fed Georgia some lean beef. "Forgive me for squeezing your ears?"

Lila was doing it again—apologizing and seeking absolution. It had to stop. She slid the sandwich onto a plate, tucked her cellphone into the pocket of her trousers, and fetched a diet cola from the fridge. Georgia gazed hopefully through big amber eyes as Lila moved toward the back door.

"Sorry, girl, you know the drill. You stay inside while Mama goes out to work."

Sure enough, Georgia did know. She tucked her tail between her legs and went slinking off to her cushion in the corner of the laundry room. Lila heard her softly whining as she stepped into the lawn, locking the door behind her.

Even golden retrievers knew life wasn't always fair, Lila mused as she moved through the dampening grass to the workshop where she made her sculpture. One good thing, though—nature wasn't as dead as she'd assumed inside her air-conditioned bubble. Out here, the cicadas and tree frogs were loudly buzzing, and in spite of the breathless night, she heard the listless washing of waves on sand.

Juggling the sandwich and soda can, she

managed to unlatch the metal door to her studio, elbowed it inward, and then set the food and drink on the little table just inside the door. Reaching backward against the wall, she tripped the row of light switches, and her space lit up like a movie studio.

Lila closed her eyes for one minute, as was her custom, and tried to empty her head of all negative thoughts, indeed any obsession that might interfere with the creative work she was about to do. Her ex-lover, who had been into meditation, taught Lila that trick. This was the same ex who now wanted her back. So the first distraction Lila dispelled was her ex, the second was *Waterspirit*, the third—Salsa—would require more effort.

Opening her eyes, she stared at *Seagull in Flight*, her work in progress, and liked what she saw. The abstract creation featured two four-foot-long curves of thin steel, cut to replicate delicate wings, which had been heated and angled in opposition to each other. Lila had anchored the curves to a silver, conical body, so that the wings were arched in an upbeat reach for the sky. The gull was a mobile, hung from an almost invisible cable bolted to a ceiling beam, and when moved by even a slight breeze, it trailed long wisps of thin aluminum that traced, or echoed, the movement of flight. Lila thought of this echo as the after-tone of a ringing bell.

Tonight's goal was to attach the last three streamers, or tail feathers. When complete, she'd turn on the powerful fans aimed at the sculpture to check its balance and grace.

Lila finished her sandwich and gulped the soda as she planned her activities. She tuned the radio to a New Age channel, where the soothing music reminded her of waterfalls, gentle surf, and yes, birds in flight. The sound system and motor lift for the mobile had been expensive additions but necessary to Lila's health and well-being. She'd learned long ago that using a welding torch while standing on a ladder was dangerous in the extreme, and the music helped clear her mind of extraneous thoughts that might distract her from the hazardous business at hand.

She chose a welding wand with a small tip since the work required a narrow, focused flame. She attached the torch's tube to her acetylene tank, put on her goggles, fireproof gloves, and apron, then turned on the gas. When she twisted down the nozzle to its narrowest aperture, the thin point of fire, blue at the end, cast a hypnotic spell as she began melting the thin rods of copper she used for the welds.

As always, Lila was soon lost in the process, dribbling molten copper onto the seams, forging metal to metal, giving life and meaning to the cold elements as they morphed into a new whole.

She was so engrossed, she never noticed the soft crunch of tires on gravel as a truck with no headlights pulled into her driveway and parked. She thought she heard Georgia barking above the music, but that wasn't unusual. So lost was she that she never saw the tall man in a ski mask until he came up behind her.

"Hello, Lila."

His deep, somehow familiar voice startled her so badly she almost dropped the torch. Through the haze of her heated goggles, she saw several things at once—his eyes gleamed like pure evil from the sockets in his mask, and his dark red mouth leered as he breathed through the third hole. He wore no shirt.

"Who are you? What do you want?" She

instinctively lowered her wand and stepped back several paces until she was trapped against the worktable. The man held a Bible in one hand and a length of her one-inch steel pipe in the other. He wore latex surgical gloves.

"I bring you the word of God," he calmly stated. "And I will punish you for committing a lifetime of unnatural acts."

As adrenaline jolted through her system, Lila was both furious and terrified. All her life, ignorant jerks had sought to make her suffer for being who she was, and she longed to fight back. Yet now, as it seemed clear she might die, she wondered if dropping to her knees and praying to this maniac would save her.

He ceremoniously placed his Bible on the table and shifted the pipe to his right hand. "I don't need the Good Book to preach the Word," he said. At the same time, he began rubbing the front of his trousers and was clearly aroused.

Oh, my god, Lila thought. He intends to rape me. She lifted her gaze to his torso, which was entirely naked. Oddly, the man had shaved off all his body hair, so he looked smooth and innocent as a newborn. He wore five colorful scarves and a heavy gold cross draped around his neck. His appearance was ludicrous, yet it made her sick with fear.

"Fuck off!" she screamed, but the noise coming from her throat was more like a whimper.

"Mind your mouth, bitch. Have you not heard of Sodom and Gomorrah? Don't you know it's an abomination to lie down with another woman?"

As he spewed more filth, little droplets of spittle sprayed from the obscene hole, which was his mouth. When he poked at Lila's crotch with the pipe and described how he intended to teach her the error of her ways, she thought of Boots.

Lila cocked her knee and kicked him as hard as she could in the gonads.

As he roared in pain, he lifted the pipe high above his head. When it connected with Lila's skull, the pain was an unimaginable explosion of sheer agony. But before blood blinded her, she pointed her torch at the smooth white flesh of his chest and turned up the flame. She smelled burning meat and heard the keening of souls in hell just before her world went dark.

Chapter Thirty-four

Salsa invited Taco to join her, and together they climbed into the Honda hybrid and drove west on River Highway, toward Lila's house. It had been a hard decision, one Salsa made while showering after the hard night's work at La Hacienda. She had lingered longer than necessary at the restaurant while mulling it over, then got home around midnight. She realized that she was showering for Lila, and then it hit her:

She had to go.

I'll come if I can, she'd said, but seeing Lila was Salsa's only choice. Her emotions had been in turmoil for weeks, and the attraction she felt was undeniable. Had it been there all along? Since they were adolescents? Salsa had always considered herself straight, and she'd only slept with men, yet her attachments had never felt vital or lasting. When relationships got serious, she ran away, so that now, as she approached fifty, she remained alone and unmarried. Yet she wanted and needed love.

Driving toward the lake, deeper into the country, she powered down her windows and let the humid night air wash over her. She glanced at the melon slice moon and thought about Lila. When Taco lay down on the seat and buried his big head in her lap, she felt the stirring deep inside that Lila always inspired. Fact was, she was scared to death. What did women do together, how did they make love? She'd seen movies and read books, of course, and somehow, she believed that once she was in Lila's arms, nature would take its course. But still she was nervous. This night, this drive, and whatever happened once she got there were irreversible. Her mind, her heart, and every fiber within her knew she could never take it back.

As she slowed and turned left into Lila's neighborhood, Salsa was suddenly startled by a speeding white pickup truck. It was running without its headlights and wobbling all over the road, forcing her off the pavement, almost into a ditch. Damn driver was likely drunk as a skunk, not unusual on a Friday night. Yet as he sped away, the near brush with disaster left her angrily gulping for air. Even Taco was alarmed as he sat upright and barked out the window at the empty road.

Salsa stroked the fur standing straight up on his back. "It's okay, boy, he's gone." She wished she'd seen the asshole's face or gotten his plate number, but no such luck. Mostly, she hoped the incident wasn't a bad omen because when she checked her watch and saw it was after one in the morning, she had a panic attack and almost turned around. "What if Lila's asleep, Taco? She'll think I'm nuts or desperate or…"

But when her golden grinned encouragement, Salsa regained her equilibrium and got back on the road. "You're right. She said she'd wait up for me. And you want to see your girlfriend, Georgia, don't you?"

When they pulled into Lila's driveway, Salsa was relieved to see lights burning in the kitchen and pantry windows, and when she opened her car door, Taco scrambled across her lap to freedom before she could hook his leash.

"Guess we're both over-eager," she muttered

while Taco jumped at Lila's gate.

As Salsa walked across the yard, the rasping symphony of crickets was joined by the mournful hoot of an owl from out near the water. By the time she reached the door to the house, way after Taco, the solo owl was answered by its mate, who was somewhere in the nearby trees.

She rang the doorbell but figured it was unnecessary since Georgia was already jumping at the glass from inside, slobbering and barking. The animals were nose to nose, clawing at each other from either side of the window. If that racket didn't get Lila's attention, nothing would. But as several minutes passed with no sign of activity inside the house, it occurred to Salsa that Lila really was working late in her shed, just as she had promised.

Snapping the leash to Taco's collar, she dragged him off the porch and into the side yard, where sure enough, she saw Lila's workshop lit up like a Christmas tree. Unfortunately, Taco balked, straining at the leash to get back to his girlfriend, but Salsa won that tug-of-war and pulled him through grass already moist with morning dew. Her bare feet in flip-flops were wet by the time she and Taco went slipping and sliding up to the shop. When they got there, Taco stopped dead in his tracks. Hair rose on his hackles as he growled and viciously bared his teeth.

"Will you cut that out?" Salsa smacked his nose. "What the hell's your problem?" She took firm hold of his collar. "Hey, Lila, are you in there?"

No answer. Taco kept growling as Salsa called out again and again. Why didn't Lila hear her? The tiny hairs on the back of Salsa's neck prickled, just like Taco's. Lila had often explained how she got lost in her work, how once in the groove, the roof would have to cave in to gain her attention. But still, Salsa hated to barge in. As she shifted foot to foot, fear and apprehension mounting, Taco took control.

He broke loose and flung himself at the closed metal door. It flew open without resistance and crashed against the inner wall. As the dog charged into the studio, Salsa was momentarily blinded by intensely bright light. She was also stunned by the ripe odor of feces and something else—the stench of raw meat burning on a grill.

Her stomach lurched with the noxious, primal smells. At the same time, the sudden swinging movement of something hung from the ceiling terrified her. When she screamed, Taco ceased barking and howled. More than anything else, the sound of her beloved golden baying—he had never done it before—scared Salsa so badly she sagged to her knees.

When Taco reached her side and jumped at her, his front paws were covered in blood.

"Oh, God, Taco, are you hurt?"

But a quick inspection revealed the blood wasn't Taco's, and the thing moving near the ceiling was only a big silver mobile, Lila's bird, the one she'd been talking about.

Salsa buried her face in the fur of Taco's neck and tried to make sense of it, but no version of reality came out anything but horrible. When the dog moved away, trotting to the far side of the worktable, Salsa crawled after him on all fours and bumped into the body lying there.

As her scream echoed around the room, Salsa saw Lila's beautiful hair swimming in a pool of blood. Lila's eyes were blessedly closed, but her arms and legs had collapsed, twisted at unnatural angles in her own filth. While tears of rage and disbelief poured from Salsa's eyes, bile rose in her esophagus, and she became violently sick.

Once the spasms ended, Salsa gasped for breath and touched the porcelain skin of Lila's face—still warm. And when she laid her cheek against Lila's breast, she heard the faint beating of her heart. *Thank God, she's still alive!* Sobbing uncontrollably, this time with joy and hope, Salsa slid her hand along the bony curve of Lila's hip and reached into her pocket, where the outline of a cellphone was clearly visible. She lifted it out, and with bloody fingers, dialed 911.

Chapter Thirty-five

Salsa lost track of time. Once the ambulance arrived and the medics got busy with Lila, Salsa let go and cried until the tears were all gone. They said Lila had lost too much blood, the pipe had shattered her skull, and she was in a coma. But she still might recover, they said. Miracles did happen.

The Mooresville police and the Iredell County sheriff arrived to deal with the attempted homicide, but as soon as Salsa was able to speak coherently, she used Lila's cellphone to dial Red and begged her to come. Red immediately grasped what had happened and was on her way.

"Looks like you could use a couple of aspirins." The shy EMS nurse with a brown ponytail and buckteeth had been hovering ever since the team arrived. She originally thought Salsa had been injured, had even given Taco a preliminary exam when she saw his bloody paws, but once convinced that neither woman nor dog had been harmed, the nurse attached herself anyway.

"I'll take that whole bottle of aspirin," Salsa answered. She ached from the roots of her hair to the soles of her feet. The nurse assured her the pain was due to stress and shock, but Salsa knew it was the direct result of a broken heart.

"Let's start with two pills." The nurse gave her the tablets with bottled water. "Then we'll see…"

Salsa watched the medics attend to Lila's head

before wrapping it in a gauze bandage, encasing it in a strange helmet. They hooked her up to some tubes and carefully moved her onto a stretcher.

"Will my friend be all right?"

"I hope so." The nurse frowned. "Brain injuries are extremely serious. They'll transport her to Lake Norman Regional. If they can't handle it there, they'll take her either to Charlotte, to Baptist Medical in Winston-Salem, or maybe even Duke."

The ache below Salsa's breastbone intensified. She couldn't stand the thought of poor Lila being shuffled all over the state, but she couldn't bear it if Lila died.

"Are you two close?" The nurse eyed her.

"Yes, friends since high school."

"Well, this is ugly." The nurse nodded at the awful calling card the attacker had left on the floor near Lila's body. "What's that about?"

Salsa glanced at the bloody pipe. A second pipe had been hurriedly placed across it. Together they formed a crucifix. "It's about the killer," Salsa mumbled. "He's a religious nutcase, and he's done this before."

The nurse's nose twitched. "Stinks in here. Smells like burning flesh."

Salsa felt sick to her stomach all over again as she imagined Lila's last moments of terror, but she was proud because Lila had fought back. "She burned him," Salsa told the nurse with certainty. "She's a welder. She fought him off with her torch and saved her own life."

"Do you know that for a fact, lady?" Suddenly, the tall sheriff loomed over her.

"Yes, I know. Lila's a fighter."

"Were you here when it happened?" The sheriff

was joined by a short, uniformed Mooresville cop.

"No, I wasn't here," Salsa snapped. "But I got here soon after, thank heavens."

"How do you know it was soon after?" the sheriff demanded.

"Because I saw the asshole driving away." Until those words left her mouth, Salsa hadn't even considered the relationship between the drunk driver and Lila's attacker. But now it made perfect sense.

The sheriff and the cop glanced at each other, eyebrows raised.

"What makes you think you saw the assailant?" the cop asked.

"Because he was coming from this neighborhood so late at night—no other cars on the road. He was driving without headlights and swerving like a drunk. Almost ran me into a ditch."

"Why would he be driving like a drunk?"

"Because he was hurt, isn't it obvious? Lila torched the guy. If I were you, I'd check the local hospitals and clinics for burn victims ASAP."

Both officers laughed.

"So now you're a detective?" The cop grinned.

"Are *you*?" Salsa glared at him. Their attitudes stank worse than the crime scene, but she was somewhat gratified when the sheriff took the cop aside for a brief conference. Moments later, the cop left the shed, looking red in the face.

"He'll check it out, ma'am," the sheriff reassured her. "Did you get a good look at the vehicle?"

She told him about the battered white pickup but clearly lost points when she confessed she hadn't seen the driver or the license plate.

"Why were you visiting the victim at this

ungodly hour?" he asked with a knowing smirk. "I know Miss Lila from the Depot. Knew her girlfriend, too. What's your relationship?"

"Am I a suspect?"

He laughed. "Not yet."

"Then fuck off!"

Salsa felt slightly ashamed when the sheriff tipped his hat and retreated, saying he'd "catch her later." Even the attentive nurse looked away in embarrassment. But hell, Salsa was at the end of her rope. Even Taco had forsaken her. At the moment, her fickle pooch was accepting multiple dog cookies from a deputy dog lover in the corner.

A hush fell on the room when the medics gently elevated the portable stretcher from the floor and locked it into position to roll. Salsa chanced a peek at her beloved friend, who was now strapped in place under a blanket. The huge, alien helmet on her head made Lila's face appear tiny, like a lifeless porcelain doll, as they wheeled her off into the night.

"At least they got her stabilized," the nurse said, lingering behind.

"But she looks awful, all those tubes…"

"Yeah, really awful." The nurse didn't deny it. "How's *your* pain, ma'am?"

Salsa was numb, but at least her stomach had stopped heaving. "Can you spare some Valium?"

The nurse laughed and patted her arm before leaving. What Salsa really needed was a shot of Novocaine   to the brain to make the nightmare go away. But mostly, she needed Red. And then, like her one and only favor from heaven, Red walked in through the metal door.

"Over here!" Salsa shouted. Red strode across

the room looking shockingly together for two in the morning. She wore a crisply ironed white shirt, with pleats in her dark trousers. She had a gun, a badge on her belt, and a don't-fuck-with-me expression that parted the waters of any resistance. Just when Salsa thought she was all cried out, the floodgates opened, and Salsa's tears poured. So did Red's.

"Oh, God, Red, it was terrible! You should've seen Lila. She's hurt real bad."

"I know, I saw them put her in the ambulance. I'm glad you called me."

"I'm glad you came!" Salsa hugged Red. Only last night, the girls of the TLC had met in Huntersville for Red's warning and Lila's glazed fruit dumplings. "I just don't believe it."

"Neither do I." Red massaged the knot between Salsa's shoulder blades. "But Lila was definitely attacked by the same man. Bastard even left his signature cross."

Of course, it was the same man, and Salsa, who'd always been against the death penalty, decided that in this one case, a lethal injection was warranted. As she watched the cops do their thing, stringing crime scene tape, snapping photos, and dusting for prints, she prayed they would catch him. She'd execute the monster herself.

Red said, "They say it's okay for you to go home now. You've been through hell."

Red was rocking Salsa like a baby. Even Taco noticed the love fest and decided he wanted in on it. Breaking away from the cookie man, he trotted over and snuggled his warm, wet nose into the crook of Salsa's arm.

"I'm not going home. Taco and I will stay here at Lila's, keep Georgia company."

"You sure?" Red pulled away and held Salsa at arm's length, her green eyes filled with concern.

"Yeah, I'm sure. Tomorrow I'll meet you at the hospital, wherever they take Lila. Okay?"

"Yes, okay, I'll be there. But for now, I'll hang with these guys and make sure they don't miss any evidence." Red winked. "It's not my jurisdiction, but I won't be turned away."

"They wouldn't dare mess with you." For the first time in hours, Salsa felt the corners of her mouth curve into a smile. Red's strong presence was both reassuring and downright nurturing.

Salsa collected Lila's house keys. She had spotted them sitting next to a plate holding the crumbs of what looked to be a corned beef sandwich. After another good hug, she said good night to Red, whistled for Taco, and together they escaped into the fresh air, which smelled of honeysuckle, not death.

After the jubilant reunion of Taco and Georgia and after the dogs romped and peed in the yard, they all went to bed. Salsa allowed the dogs to join her in Lila's room. After shucking her bloody clothes onto the master bathroom floor, Salsa showered and slipped naked into the queen-sized bed, where the pillows smelled like Lila.

She couldn't bear to think about how this moment could have been different, nor did it bear scrutiny that she considered prayer. Salsa had given that up when her mother died. It hadn't worked then, it seldom did. But now, as she burrowed into Lila's nest and closed her eyes, she clasped her hands and prayed to the merciful God of Intervention.

Chapter Thirty-six

By the time Red left Lila's place in Mooresville, where the crime scene techs were still at work, and headed home toward Charlotte, she already knew more than she wanted to know about Lila's condition. Listening to the dispatch radio as she drove through the hours before dawn, Red learned that Lila's ambulance had hesitated only briefly at Lake Norman Regional Medical Center. The docs there decided they couldn't handle Lila's severe traumatic brain injury, so everyone agreed that since Interstate 77 was relatively deserted at four a.m. Saturday, they'd transport her directly into the city.

They had taken Lila to Carolinas Medical Center, one of the nation's elite trauma care units. Red's experience with the center involved mostly victims of car wrecks, both cops and criminals involved in disastrous high-speed chases, so she knew the facility was exquisitely equipped. They had emergency surgeons with the latest diagnostic technology, including resuscitation suites and complete rehab care. The good news was Lila had made it there alive, the bad news was that she had to be there in the first place.

Knowing the first few hours were critical to Lila's survival, Red wanted to be near her. So she made a pit stop at her apartment to take a shower, hoping the pulsing water would wash away some of the fatigue, along with the stench of death lodged in her nostrils. She ate two energy bars and drank three cups of strong black coffee, changed clothes, locked her gun away in the drawer—since hospital security would make her life miserable if she took it—then arrived at the center as the first rays of dawn glowed behind the Charlotte skyline.

As Red suspected, she had to show everything but a passport before being admitted to the Progressive Care Unit for TBI patients. As she strode toward the suite where Lila was supposedly in recovery, a young male nurse jogged along with her. He explained that Lila had had a CT scan, which revealed evidence of bleeding in her brain.

"It showed blood clots and contusions," he said breathlessly. "Those increase pressure inside the skull, which can cause additional damage, so the surgeons took her into the operating room to insert a probe through her skull to monitor the pressure."

"A probe through her skull?" Red suddenly felt ill.

"Yeah, for the intracranial pressure monitor."

"God, is she conscious?"

"Oh, no, not at all. After the doc removed the hematomas, he had to repair a small fracture. Luckily, the damage to her brain cells may be limited to the area directly below the point of impact."

"You call that lucky?" Red hesitated until her guide started down the left of two corridors, then she followed him. "She lost so much blood."

"Yes, well, head wounds bleed a lot. Is it true some guy bashed her with a pipe?" The young nurse glanced at the badge on her belt.

Red nodded grimly. "When will she wake up?"

"Hard to say. Doctors sometimes use drugs to put TBI patients into temporary comas because a comatose brain needs less oxygen to function. This is really helpful if the blood vessels, compressed by increased pressure in the brain, are unable to deliver the usual amount of nutrients and oxygen to the brain cells."

"Will they put Lila into a coma?"

The nurse shrugged. "Not my call."

They stopped in a small waiting room with two facing sofas, a coffee table, and the usual complement of out-of-date magazines.

"All I do is watch the machines," the nurse continued. "Right now, Miss Lila's on a respirator, an anti-seizure drip, heart monitor, and of course, the intracranial pressure monitor." He nodded at a metal door with a small window made of safety glass. "She's right in there. Do you want to see her?"

Red most assuredly did not want to see her dear, vital friend reduced to helplessness, but sometimes the imagination conjured an image worse than the reality. "Sure," she said without conviction.

Placing a gentle hand on the small of Red's back, the nurse guided her to the window. He smelled like sweat and disinfectant, and as Red peeked in at the mound on the hospital bed, she felt a little woozy. She couldn't actually see Lila. Instead, she saw a huge, snowball-like bundle where Lila's head should be, but her face was completely obscured by an oxygen mask, and her body was totally swathed in a white sheet. Only Lila's forearms and fingertips were visible, with IV tubes laced to the former and clips attached to the latter.

"Jesus." Red groaned. She pulled at the door handle, but the door was locked.

"Sorry, no admittance, ma'am. One of the

greatest risks now is infection, so *I* can't even enter without a sterile scrub."

"But we'll need to talk to her soon. It's possible she saw her attacker."

"I wouldn't hold my breath, and if you believe in prayer, you might want to try it about now."

Turning away from the window, Red was shocked to see that Rick had slipped silently into the waiting room. He was holding two steaming Styrofoam cups in his hands and appeared to have slept in the rumpled clothes he was wearing.

"Rick, I didn't expect to see you here."

"I've been here since they brought her in. God, I'm so sorry."

When the nurse left the room, leaving them alone together, she searched Rick's tired eyes for signs of sarcasm. He had never liked Lila, but this morning, Red saw nothing but deep regret. When Rick placed the cups on the table and opened his arms, she crossed the room and held him. Or rather, they held each other. "Oh, it was so horrible!" Red sobbed into his shoulder.

"I know."

"How did you find out?" she asked as he guided her to the couch, then sat across from her.

He sadly shook his head. "Well, it's all part of the same case, isn't it? The Mooresville PD keeps me in the loop, so I knew even before you showed up at Lila's place."

"Salsa called me from the scene," Red explained as she tried to piece together the complex, inter-departmental entanglements these tragedies had spawned.

"I know she called you," Rick said. "Salsa's a wreck. She's been phoning the hospital nonstop ever since Lila arrived. I spoke with her twice, brought her up to speed, but the woman's about to implode. I'm sure she hasn't had much sleep."

Red accepted the hot coffee Rick handed her and tried to process. Last night when she'd watched Salsa trudging up to Lila's house with the weight of the world on her shoulders and Taco trotting at her heels, Red had figured Salsa was out for the count. "How did she sound? Was she all right?"

"Not really." Rick stared into his coffee, then took a long sip. "She's running on steam, emotionally shot, but she's coming here as soon as she figures out what to do with the dogs."

Red sighed, then took a gulp of the brew, which proved to be depressingly weak. Lila's incapacity was not only emotionally devastating, but problematic on so many levels. What about her dog, her house, and did she have family who required notification? As Red recalled, Lila's parents had died and she had no siblings. Did she have health insurance or a living will? Red hoped Salsa might have answers to some of those questions.

"I wonder if Lila saw her attacker," Red said.

"Hope so. The crime scene team found no suspicious fingerprints, and though everyone agrees Lila burned the bastard, he hasn't sought medical help." Rick gave her a grim look. "But we know it's the same sicko who killed Judy and Boots, and unfortunately, his pattern would imply that you, Salsa, and Summer are next on his hit list. He seems to be after you girls in the True Love Club."

Red didn't require Rick's insight. She'd figured that out on her own days ago. "Well, what can we do about it?"

"For one thing, I'm stationed here to make sure the sicko doesn't come back to finish the job. If Lila got a look at him, he's feeling mighty nervous about now."

"He'll never get through security."

"You sure about that?"

She wasn't sure about anything.

"And another thing..." Rick growled. "You women were really stupid to sign up on DATESCAPE. I can't believe you went along with it."

"Who the hell told you about that?"

"Summer's boyfriend, Paul, informed the Mooresville cops after that kid Jimmy shot him. He said he reconnected with Summer online. He also told them all about the adventures you, Boots, and Salsa had enjoyed while internet dating." Rick snorted derisively. "Hell, most likely, the killer made up his wish list while shuffling through your profiles."

Red was furious. She'd strangle Paul the next time they met. As for the Mooresville cops, they were like a bunch of silly teenagers gossiping down the grapevine. She saw no point in defending herself and explaining that her excursions to DATESCAPE were for a higher, professional cause—that she was trying to catch the killer. And she was definitely too wrung out to endure one of Rick's self-righteous lectures.

"By the way," she said, "so sorry to hear that Miranda dumped you."

Rick's dark eyes flashed momentarily, but then he just looked tired. "Let's not fight, Red. This isn't about Miranda or even that retired dentist you dated last Friday. This is about making sure all you women stay safe."

Red couldn't even guess how Rick knew about *Paintercat.* For all she knew, he had spies everywhere.

Perhaps the tattooed bouncer at The Warehouse where she'd met Sam Redbird was Rick's fraternity brother. Point was, he was right for once.

"Any luck finding that old white truck Salsa saw leaving the scene?" she asked him.

"Nope. Seems everyone in Iredell County owns one. Listen, the CMPD will keep an eye on Lila here at the hospital. You should talk to Salsa and suggest that she stay at her dad's place above the restaurant until this blows over. Maybe Summer and her kid should visit Summer's folks up in Statesville."

Red knew full well that neither Salsa nor Summer would even consider such suggestions. "Since you're arranging our lives for us, what do you suggest *I* do?"

Rick looked down at his hands. "You shouldn't be living alone right now. Why not ask Gina to move in for a little while?"

Chapter Thirty-seven

Summer had the Monday morning blues. She left the reception area and entered the small surgical wing where her boss, Lake Norman Regional Medical Center's premier gastroenterologist, did his famous outpatient colonoscopies. Soon reception would be filled with anxious patients, all miserable after their all-day Sunday purges. They'd be pale, weak, hungry, and cranky—impatient to be done with the indignities they soon would suffer. And Summer felt out of sorts, too. After a totally shitty weekend, it seemed fitting to spend her morning poking up stranger's asses. *What a life.*

"Good morning, sunshine." Jolene's simpering voice dripped with sarcasm. "Hope your weekend rocked. Mine did."

The disgusting slut was wiping down the bed frames with antibacterial rags, and with each vigorous movement, her big boobs jiggled. Jolene was engaged to Summer's ex-husband, so the fact that she now worked alongside Summer was a pure insult. Jolene was a cleaning woman, Summer was an OR nurse, but Summer's superior status did nothing to lessen her pain when Jolene flashed the big diamond glittering on her ring finger. The bitch should remove her jewelry while cleaning, but Summer knew Jolene did everything just to aggravate her.

"Too bad about your friend Lila," Jolene continued. "You know the EMS brought her here early

Saturday before taking her to CMC."

"She'll get better care there," Summer grumbled. Learning about the attack on Lila had been the final thorn in the crown of a weekend from hell.

Jolene finished with the beds and began folding blankets for the warming oven. "Don't know about you, but I'm scared shitless with this maniac on the loose. Seems like he's going after women your age, and even though I'm much younger, no woman's safe until he's behind bars."

Summer held her temper but imagined how good it would feel to wrestle the stupid little whore down, strap her to a bed, thread a needle into her vein, and pump her full of enough anesthesia to silence her permanently.

"Don't sweat it, Jolene. According to the papers, the rapist only chooses intelligent women."

"Yeah, like lesbians and black girls. That Boots person was also your friend, right?"

The shocking, bigoted remark was a declaration of war, so Summer would oblige her with nuclear holocaust. Only last week, she'd seen Jolene spill a tray of surgical instruments onto the floor. When Jolene thought no one was looking, she'd slipped them back on the tray and left the room. Summer had taken notes, resterilized the instruments, and then filed the incident away for a rainy day. Well, today was that storm. As soon as Jolene left the building, she'd tell the doctor, and Jolene would be unemployed.

"Of course, I feel safe because I have Eddie." Jolene smirked. "It's a comfort having a man around the house. I just know living alone with that little girl of yours is a worry."

"Gloria is a blessing," Summer retorted sweetly. "Just ask Ed. I know how much he misses her, but of course, the courts placed her with me, where she'd be raised in a decent home environment."

Jolene tossed her bottle red hair. "Well, the arrangement suits me just fine, thank you very much." With that final zinger, Ed's fiancée gathered up her stuff and left.

Jolene departed in the nick of time because Summer was primed for murder. Not only was she powerfully inclined to tear out Jolene's hair by the roots, she was also furious beyond belief at herself. She had fucked up big-time with Paul; before Summer went slitting her wrists, leaving Gloria motherless in Jolene's care, she needed to figure out exactly what she'd done wrong. She took a deep breath and composed herself when the doctor walked into the room.

"We have a full house this morning," he told her cheerfully. "Hope you're bright-eyed and bushy-tailed, Summer. Did you have a nice weekend?"

"Not exactly."

"Oh, yes, I heard about your friend. So sorry. Maybe later this week you can take a personal day to visit her."

"Let's hope she wakes up to where she can have visitors."

The doctor never expressed pessimism. It was office policy to whistle a happy tune in the face of any disaster, but today Summer wasn't up for it. They both knew traumatic brain injuries like Lila's usually offered no good outcome, so why pretend?

"I need to visit the restroom," she told him. "I'll be right back."

"No problem. Can't start without you." He set out his instruments, consulted the caseload, and whistled that happy tune as she made her escape.

She locked herself in a stall and sat on the toilet. So what the hell went wrong this weekend? At least Gloria was safely tucked away with Summer's parents in Statesville for the duration. With only a few weeks left before school started, it seemed like a good idea to let Gloria visit with her grandparents, whom she adored. Summer had driven Gloria up Thursday after work, and she'd been all set for a childless, romantic weekend with Paul when Red called that emergency meeting:

"Can I come?" Paul had asked. "I want to get to know your friends."

But Red had said no—girls only—and Paul was pissed. Now that his shoulder was pretty much healed from the gunshot wound, he was restless.

"Sorry, maybe we can hook up after I see the girls," she'd offered. "Gloria's with my folks for a few days, so I'm on my own."

"What do you mean *hook up*?"

"C'mon, *you know*." After almost a month of serious dating, Summer was ready to take their relationship to the next level. But instead of enthusiasm, she'd heard only silence.

"Will you be out late after the meeting?" he said at last.

"Heck no. Your place or mine?"

He cleared his throat. "I don't feel right about this, Summer."

That should have been her first clue. Paul was very religious and somewhat straitlaced about sex before marriage, but hadn't he implied they were headed for the altar? "Why don't I call you when I leave the girls?" she had said.

"Yes, all right." But she'd sensed the hesitation in his voice.

After the meeting, she'd called Paul as she drove home, but he didn't answer. Impulsively, she decided to drive directly to his ranch house to surprise him. It wasn't that late, so she figured she'd catch him watching television. But when she got there, although his car was parked out front, the house was dark except for a weak glow coming from the front hall.

Maybe she was being pushy, but she had parked and approached Paul's front door. She rang the bell, then pounded hard. No response. Curious, Summer pressed her nose against the glass to snoop since Paul still had never invited her into his place. All she saw was an empty hallway and closed doors. Next, she had scribbled a brief, suggestive note, describing in graphic terms what she'd like to do to Paul when they were alone together, then shoved it through the crack under the door. No big deal, right?

Summer had tried calling Paul again Friday night, but when he didn't answer, she began second-guessing the content of her note. Was he offended? When she tried again Saturday without result, she felt her romantic weekend slipping away. Plus, she really missed Gloria. And when she got the terrible news about Lila, she longed to have her cheerful daughter nearby to cuddle.

Late last night, Paul finally answered the phone. She'd never heard him so angry.

"What's wrong with you, Summer? You've been calling nonstop for three days now, and it's driving me crazy! Did it ever occur to you that I'd answer the phone when I'm good and ready?"

"Sorry, I—"

"You should be sorry," Paul shouted. "I haven't been feeling well, so I've been holed up in bed, but who can rest with that constant, infernal ringing?"

"Are you sick?"

"Well, I'm feeling somewhat   better now," he grumbled.

"Can I help? Bring over some chicken soup? Gloria's still at her grandparents, so I'm free."

"Yeah, I know. Free, fast, and loose. Honestly, I must say your note really upset me. I thought you were better than these other women."

Who the hell was he, the morals police? Summer had never considered herself fast or loose. She was simply a woman with the same wants and needs as any human being. "Listen, Paul, I'm sorry I upset you. Let's get together when I finish work tomorrow. For dinner, nothing more."

"Sorry, I'm leaving town for a week."

"Where are you going?"

"If you must know, I'll be attending a seminar for high school science teachers in Raleigh."

"You never told me."

"Who are you, my mother?"

"Summer, did you hear me?" The receptionist's sharp knock on the bathroom door jerked her back to reality. "The patient's prepped and on the table, and the doctor needs you to adjust the camera."

Summer pulled up her pants and washed and sterilized her hands. Moments later, she was in the procedure room, fiddling with the lighted camera at the end of the catheter tube so the doctor could get a clear recording as his probe poked through the colonoscopy patient's anus, traveled up her rectum, and continued its invasive journey up the alimentary canal. All Summer knew at the moment, as the patient groaned in her sleep, was that she, Summer, felt seriously butt-fucked.

Chapter Thirty-eight

Red knew her friends wouldn't take Rick's advice. Instead of moving in with Papa at the restaurant, Salsa had remained at Lila's house to care for both dogs. In spite of her busy schedule at La Hacienda, Salsa had come to the hospital every day, where Lila was still in a coma. Summer had visited yesterday and explained that although Gloria was staying with Summer's parents in Statesville, Summer wasn't about to run home to hide with her mommy and daddy.

"I'm not afraid of this jerk," Summer told Red. "Besides, Paul will be home this weekend, and he'll take care of me."

Red guessed that Summer and Paul had suffered some sort of "misunderstanding." Their spat had left Summer cranky yet certain that she and Paul would work it out.

"I need to clean up my act, Red. I know I can be the kind of lady Paul wants me to be."

So that night after work, as Red propped her bare feet up on her sofa and waited for Gina to finish taking a shower, she thought about Summer's words. The concept of being anyone's "lady" made Red's skin crawl, and she hated to see Summer conform to some prick's self-righteous notion of morality. On the other hand, who was Red to throw stones? While her girlfriends had remained independent during this crisis, only Red had secretly succumbed to Rick's proposition. She had swallowed her pride, thrown caution to the wind, and tearfully begged Gina to keep her company for a few days.

Much to her surprise, Gina had tearfully agreed. And so far, they had not discussed murder, serial killers, or Red's plans for the future. Instead, Gina had loved and comforted Red unconditionally. Gina's tenderness healed her, cradled her in a nest where she could grieve and rejuvenate, and no matter what happened next week, for this, Red would be eternally grateful.

If Gina stayed tonight, it would be the fifth night in a row. Red wasn't clinging to Gina because Red was scared of a crazed predator because she wasn't. Instead, Red hoped that their sweet reunion was a dress rehearsal for a new permanent arrangement. Yet Red feared Gina's passionate mercies were intended only to help Red through this rough patch. Indeed, they both seemed terrified to talk about anything of major significance, so they spent the time making love instead.

"Hey, Red." Gina emerged from the shower, barefoot and smelling of Irish Spring. She wore torn jeans and a soft white T-shirt. Her short black hair was still wet, and she had not gelled and dried it into her trademark Statue of Liberty spikes. She left it natural, just for Red. By the little red nick on one knee, Red realized Gina had also shaved her legs, which Red had never cared about one way or the other. But these gestures were typical of the respectful, almost deferential treatment Red had received ever since Gina arrived. Red also realized how careless she had become over the years with the small, special things she used to do for Gina when they were first together. Another reason Gina left.

"Hey yourself. Have a seat…" Red patted the couch, and when Gina sat and swung her legs up, they played footsie, comparing feet and toes. It was a game they always enjoyed—marveling at how Red's feet were so long and pale, Gina's so stubby and tanned.

"What's for dinner?" Gina asked.

"Chinese."

"Yum."

Red handed Gina a rum and tonic and took a sip of her scotch. While they were together, they'd always chosen those same drinks. Funny how easily they fell back into old habits. Only now it seemed different. They weren't fighting. They also hadn't told anyone, not even Rick, about their fragile new relationship. Perhaps they were both afraid it wouldn't work out.

Red had put down her drink and was prepared to kiss Gina, when her damned cellphone rang. Gina's brother was on the line. "It's Rick. Should I take it?"

A shadow of disappointment scampered across Gina's face, but she quickly recovered. "Sure, go ahead. I'll wait for you in the bedroom."

As she left, Red wished for all the world she could ignore the phone, follow Gina, and leave the whole screwed-up world behind.

"Have you talked to your dad lately?" Rick asked without preamble.

Red waited until Gina closed the bedroom door and was out of earshot. "Yeah, today at work. We spoke for almost an hour, and Dad was really upset to hear about Lila. Also, Daddy's still sticking to the same profile for the killer—middle-aged religious zealot with some serious mother issues."

"Sounds about right. Anything new at his end?"

"Yes and no. He and his buddies at SBI are

combing the obituaries from that year when our rapist was active in central Florida. They're looking at women who died immediately preceding or during that year, women who left behind teenage or young adult sons. Even with computers, it's labor-intensive to search those records from twenty years ago."

"He thinks the guy killed his own mother?"

"Not necessarily, but maybe his mother's death set him off."

She heard Rick pop the tab on a beer. "I have my doubts. I'm afraid your daddy's reaching. All this Freudian mumbo jumbo could be way off base."

"Maybe, but obviously, Florida is the key. DNA evidence doesn't lie, so no matter what, our killer *was living* in Florida twenty years ago."

"Or *visiting* Florida twenty years ago, like every other American."

While Rick talked, Red filled two stove-proof dinner plates with General Tso's chicken and moo shu pork, then slid them into the oven on low. Soon her condo was filled with scrumptious cooking odors.

"So who do you know who hung out in Florida back then?" Rick asked.

Yes, Red's family had lived in Florida before moving to North Carolina, but she was only fourteen when they moved. This was ridiculous. "C'mon, you think I knew the killer?"

"Could be. He definitely knows the other women in your club. The attack on Lila makes that obvious, and it's personal. He could be someone you knew years ago. Maybe you went to grade school together."

"Or maybe he just found us on DATESCAPE. Think about it. This guy killed Judy the librarian, and she was unrelated to any of us girls. The only common thread is DATESCAPE."

"True. So that leads me to believe this psycho homed in on you five after he killed Judy. Either on DATESCAPE, or he saw you all together."

"Yeah, like at our high school reunion." Red completed the terrifying thought.

For weeks, the idea of the high school reunion had been nagging at her, but she'd been slow to admit it. After years apart, the group reunited that night, and all their troubles began soon after. She set the table and started the coffee brewing. Fact was, more than one hundred people attended that event—not only former classmates, but also their spouses and significant others. Most were total strangers.

"Can you get a list of everyone at the reunion?" Rick asked.

"I'm way ahead of you." Red had called the class geek in charge of alumni events and requested the attendance roster, which he had quickly emailed. She'd also asked how she could get a copy of the photo taken of the TLC girls, the one she'd seen at Boots's, the one Paul had given Summer, but the geek couldn't help her.

"I got the list, but I'm afraid it's useless. Once I eliminated all the women attendees, I was left with a bunch of guys I barely remember, plus all the male guests I've never even met. If any of them were in Florida twenty years ago, I'd never know."

"I see your point."

They really needed a break. She and Rick seldom spoke of Lila waking up and identifying her assailant, though they were both praying that would happen. They didn't discuss it, as though talking about it might jinx Lila's recovery.

"Maybe someone on Daddy's list of grieving Florida sons will mesh with someone on my alumni list."

"In your dreams."

Rick was right to be skeptical. The night of the reunion, the auditorium had been dark and noisy, lit only by strobe lights. Of course, Paul had been there. For all Red knew, *Bikerboy* and *Paintercat* were also there because at that point, she'd not yet laid eyes on either man.

Both the CMPD and Mooresville police were working full time to solve the homicides, but so far, they were all spinning their wheels. Since the UNSUB wore latex gloves, they lacked fingerprints, while the ancient DNA was virtually useless without witnesses or motive.

"We need a lead." Rick moaned.

"You got that right. Doesn't this bastard ever make mistakes?"

"Everyone makes mistakes, Red."

Well, that was the truth. When Gina quietly tiptoed into the room, took Red's hand, and looked into her eyes, Red was stunned by the love she saw there. And she wondered—was she making the biggest mistake of all—allowing herself to believe in lasting love again?

Chapter Thirty-nine

The thunder and lightning precisely matched Salsa's stormy mood as she fought for a parking space at Carolinas Medical Center. Seemed like God had hired a heavenly symphony, complete with crashing bass drums and flashing symbols, to counterpoint her anxiety as she struggled to open the Honda's door against the wind that then blew her umbrella inside out. Putting her head down, Salsa butted into the sluicing rain and walked forward, knowing full well her upset was due less to the weather, more to the fact that it had been one full week since they brought Lila here, and she was still unconscious.

No one was allowed to see her. No one could enter the sterile room where Lila still lay like a wired mummy, isolated from all contact with friends. An ever-changing parade of police guards stood outside her door, while her doctors remained either ignorant of her progress, or else they were unwilling to share.

Salsa had been there every day since the incident, but she was unprepared for the gang of visitors who were there today, Saturday. As she navigated the crowded sidewalk and glanced toward the hospital entrance, she saw a long line of folks waiting in the rain to clear security and obtain visitor badges.

At the same time, Salsa worried about how Lucy was faring at Lila's house with the two dogs. She'd bribed their waitress to dogsit for Georgia and Taco because Salsa had discovered that Lila's golden was terrified of thunderstorms. Not just tremble and quake terrified, but "let's tear the house up" terrified. The second night she'd stayed at Lila's, Georgia had gone ballistic at the first big thunderclap and begun shredding the carpet and linoleum. Even Taco was distressed by his girlfriend's misbehavior, partly because Salsa had no clue how to control her.

Salsa had found the number of Lila's vet, put in an emergency call, and learned that somewhere in the house she'd find a prescription for the doggy equivalent of Valium. Unfortunately, once she found the pills and administered the correct dosage, the drug took forty minutes to click in. By that time, Georgia had done some damage. She had wobbled around on all fours looking dazed and unrepentant, while Salsa estimated how much it would cost to replace a half dozen linoleum tiles.

Salsa sighed, wiped the wet black bangs out of her eyes, and then got in line with the other miserable creatures waiting to enter the hospital. As she wondered what the day would bring, she noticed a familiar couple leaving the facility—a couple who absolutely, positively should not be together. Over the years, Red had sent her pictures of Gina, and Salsa felt like she knew the woman. Now, in an unguarded moment, Red and Gina looked like the loving couple they used to be in the photos as they huddled together, linked arms, and prepared to brave the storm. Right before their breakup, almost a year ago, Red had told Salsa that they had been fighting constantly, so that the intimacy they projected now was downright shocking. It made Salsa instantly protective of Red because she knew how devastated Red had been when Gina left her and didn't want to see her hurt again. As Salsa wondered what the hell was up, they spotted her, and like embarrassed teenagers caught necking, they automatically moved apart, put on neutral faces, and moved reluctantly in her direction.

"Hey, Salsa, I didn't expect you'd be here so early in the morning." Red's face was the color of her name.

"Hi, Salsa." Gina refused to look Salsa in the eye. Clearly Gina knew who she was, and Gina also realized that Salsa knew the stormy history of her relationship with Red.

"Why is Gina here?" Salsa bluntly demanded.

"Like you, Gina was concerned about Lila," Red answered coldly and took possession of Gina's arm.

Obviously, Red did not welcome Salsa's attitude in this bizarre situation. "Okay then, so you guys are leaving, and I'm just coming. See you later." She went to the end of the line.

Red sighed and rolled her eyes. "Wait, Salsa, you don't need to stand in line. Allow me to pull a few strings…"

Before Salsa knew what was happening, Red went back into the hospital.

Gina actually giggled as Red flashed her badge, gestured at Salsa, and then whispered into the security guard's ear. Moments later, Red returned with Salsa's visitor's pass, and they all moved into the shelter of the lobby. Ignoring the sullen stares of those left waiting dutifully in the rain, Salsa gratefully accepted the preferential treatment and gave Red a big hug.

"Thanks, I feel like a VIP."

"You *are* a VIP." Red smiled.

Salsa still couldn't figure out why Red and Gina were so happy, but she couldn't stay mad any longer.

"You guys are in a good mood," she ventured.

They glanced at each other, two kids sharing a secret.

"We all have good reason to be happy," Red said. "Lila's awake and talking! They've moved her down the hall to the Intensive Care Unit."

The unexpected news knocked the pins out from under her. Suddenly, Salsa's knees buckled, and she sank onto a bench outside the elevators.

"No way!" She gasped. "Will she be okay then?"

"Looks hopeful," Red said. "They did a gazillion tests on her this morning—put those little electrode thingies on her head, made her blink, wiggle fingers and toes, read eye charts—you name it. So far, she's passed every test, but now she's beat. I think they sedated her because she was asleep when we left."

"You actually talked to her?"

"Red did," Gina said. "She told me that Lila's speech is a bit slurred, but she makes perfect sense. She knows who she is, why she's here, and complains because they're making her perform like a trained monkey."

"Oh, God, that sounds just like her!" Suddenly, Salsa was weeping tears of joy. Passersby likely thought she'd just lost a loved one, when in fact a loved one had just been found. She had so many questions. Would Lila walk again, work again, be able to function like a normal human being? Right now, all that mattered was Lila was back in the land of the living. "Can I see her?"

Red and Gina glanced at each other.

"I guess so," Red answered cautiously. "Some other woman just arrived to see Lila, too. They told that woman she'd have to wait another thirty minutes, until the ICU visiting hours."

"What woman?" Salsa was confused. Lila had no family, and as far as she knew, Summer had been the only other friend to visit thus far.

Red shrugged. "Never saw her before. We determined she posed no danger, then let her through."

"I didn't know her either," Gina added shyly. "But then, I'm out of the loop."

Well, it didn't matter. Lila's health was all Salsa cared about. "What did Lila say to you?"

Another furtive glance at each other, then they helped Salsa to her feet and led her to a quiet corner away from the crowds at the elevator.

"Well, I didn't talk to Lila." Gina blushed. "I wasn't sure she'd want to see me since Red has told her what a shit I've been, so I waited outside."

"Never mind all that, Gina. It's okay," Red said, then dropping her voice to a whisper, she explained that she had questioned Lila about the night of her attack. Although Lila's memory was hazy, she recalled her would-be killer wore a ski mask, so she never saw his face. He had carried a Bible, wore a heavy cross around his neck, and was naked from the waist up.

"The weird thing was the jerk had shaved his entire chest," Red added. "He had no body hair and was naked as a baby."

That creepy tidbit sent chills down Salsa's spine. "But she burned him, right?"

"Oh, yeah." Red puffed with pride. "She zapped him just after he hit her with the pipe. She turned up her torch and burned him bad. She heard him screaming and hopes he died from the wound."

Salsa hoped so, too. "Do you think he's dead?"

Red sadly shook her head. "Well, today is Saturday, and no one was attacked last night. So if the asshole isn't dead, at least Lila slowed him down. But no one's found his body, and since Lila didn't see his face, we're back at square one."

So there was good news and bad news. As much as Salsa wanted revenge, Lila's miraculous survival was all that really mattered.

Red touched her shoulder. "Lila asked about you, Salsa. Your name was the first word she said when she woke up."

"You told her I've been here, right?" Red's revelation brought fresh tears to Salsa's eyes.

Red winked. "Sure, I told her, so if I were you, I wouldn't keep her waiting." Red gave her a gentle nudge toward the elevator.

And Salsa was happy to oblige.

Chapter Forty

As Lila swam in and out of consciousness, she decided the experience was much like being trapped inside her dream, where she was locked in the old Manhattan warehouse where she'd learned to weld. In this new, expanded version, it was still night, the cavernous space still included tunnels without end and the cold, inexplicable sense of loss. But now the devils and demons stalking her were not faceless haunts but one man. He wore a mask with an obscene hole for a mouth. He had a smooth, hairless body. His hands were pipes, and a fiendish cross hung around his neck.

In this dream, the pain was real, sometimes intense, sometimes muted to a dull, flat-lined confusion where she felt nothing at all. When she tried to form words or names in her mind, the result was a floating alphabet soup, where the letters, sometimes mixed with numbers, never worked together. Mostly, she was swimming underwater in a pool where she never broke the surface. Sometimes she felt panic, sometimes submission, but the dream never ended.

Until today.

That morning, before the tests—the poking and prodding—put her under again, Lila thought she saw Red and told her the dream. She was sure it was Red, but then she saw Gina, floating like a ghost in the hallway, and since the two of them together was impossible, she realized she was hallucinating. But now, in spite of the sedative they'd given her, she heard chatter in the hallway, smelled food cooking, and felt the touch of warm fingers on her cold left arm. When she opened her eyes, she saw a tall, willowy vision with short, angel white hair.

"Hello, Lila, it's Grace," the vision said.

Light streaming in from the window hurt Lila's eyes, and she couldn't lift her head for a better look.

"How are you feeling? You remember me. We drank Jack Daniels together after the Depot art show."

But Lila couldn't remember. All that came to mind was the word *Waterspirit*, but that made no sense.

"You look pretty good—considering," the spirit said.

At the same time, Lila became aware of a second shadow, shorter and broader, and different warm fingers on her right arm.

"Don't listen to her, Lila," the short one said. "Believe me, you look like hell, but it's good to have you back."

The new voice was filled with love and laughter. Lila knew her but couldn't place her name. All she knew for sure was that she had two beautiful women there fighting over her. Not a bad thing. They were arguing about powers of attorney and something called a living will, and while Lila almost grasped those concepts, they wouldn't come clear.

"Lila told me her ex-partner lives in Santa Fe," the spirit said. "We should call and tell her what has happened. I'm sure she'd want to know, and very likely, the two of them made arrangements about these things."

What things? Lila didn't like the sound of it, and the word "Santa Fe" made her feel sick, but she couldn't tell them *no*.

"Call her ex?" the short one said. "No, not a good idea."

Both sets of fingers tightened on Lila's arms. If a catfight broke out across her bed, Lila would be hurt even worse. Where were the nurses? Throughout the long ordeal, they had barged uninvited into her room day and night. They stabbed her with needles, even washed her private places too hard when she silently screamed for them to stop, so where were they now?

"Are you Salsa?" the spirit asked. "Lila told me about you, and I warned her—never get involved with a straight girl."

Hearing the name *Salsa* brought Lila to life inside her useless body, and when she stared at the short figure, her mind focused. At the same time, she suddenly felt   safe and warm and wanted the other woman to go away. Lila remembered how the therapist had asked her to open and close her hand, so with her right fingers, she wrapped around Salsa's fingers and squeezed hard. The gesture did not go unnoticed.

"Oh, did you see that, Grace? Lila can use her hand!"

"Very good, Lila!" the spirit said, but she didn't sound pleased. "Should we tell a nurse?"

"No need to tell me." A third figure hobbled into the room carrying what Lila recognized as the dreaded bedpan. "We already know Miss Lila has her motor skills. Last night, she almost knocked this outta my hands."

Lila wasn't as pleased as she'd expected to be by the aide's arrival, so she moved her tongue around, moistened her lips, and worked to find words. After a few false starts, sound broke through her heavy sedation.

"Please leave," she said with a clarity that surprised everyone.

"Now, Miss Lila, are you asking *me* to leave?" the aide said.

"No." Lila pointed at *Waterspirit*. "Her. Please leave." The warm fingers on her left arm tightened momentarily, then released as the spirit stepped back.

"I am so sorry, Lila," the spirit said before finding her way out the door. "I should have realized we had one too many women in this room." She gave Salsa a dirty look, and then she was gone.

The aide placed the hated bedpan on a side table and folded her arms in disapproval.

Lila crooked her finger and beckoned. "Both come close." Much to her surprise, Salsa and the aide understood. When pretty Salsa leaned over her, Lila felt the tickle of her hair on her cheek and smelled her spicy skin.

"What is it?" Salsa asked.

"Can you hear me?" Lila said.

Both said yes as Lila tightened her grip on Salsa's fingers. "Then listen. I want her—Salsa—my power of attorney. Do you understand?"

"I hear you," the aide said.

"Oh, are you sure?" Salsa's big brown eyes watered.

"Yes, *you*," Lila said before slipping off into the dream. But this time, Lila wasn't in the scary warehouse, but rather in a land with blue sky, fresh water, and green fields—a place she'd never been before.

Chapter Forty-one

Red was determined to escape work early Friday evening, before the night cops arrived and before the usual weekend shit started happening. So she sprinted down the hall and knocked on Rick's door, and when he opened with a huge conspiratorial grin on his face, she saw he was even more eager to split than she was.

"Let's go," he whispered. "Let the next shift deal with the druggies, drunks, gangbangers, and other assorted crazies. I'm outta here."

"Amen."

They took the back stairs rather than risking small talk in the elevator, and as they jogged down the steps, Red still couldn't believe that Rick had agreed to come to Lila's party. Gina, Salsa, and she had cooked up the idea to celebrate Lila's second week anniversary in the hospital with a bedside picnic and a streamed movie. The notion had even attracted Summer's Good Samaritan Seal of Approval, so she'd offered to bake a chocolate cake and supply two candles. Since Mexican cuisine from Salsa's restaurant seemed too spicy, Salsa had given up the idea of making this a surprise party and had simply asked Lila what she wanted to eat.

"Big Mac, large fries!" Lila had exclaimed, much to everyone's shock and dismay.

"Oh, man, her brain is really scrambled," Red had teased.

Lila scoffed. "I'm sick and tired of eating

anything puréed and healthful. Gimme red meat *now!*"

Red had hoped to watch a thriller with a wild car chase, while Salsa, who was hooked on the television *Survivor* series, figured the "survival theme" was appropriate to Lila's situation. Summer and Gina voted for a good romance, but they were all doomed to be disappointed.

"*Gone with the Wind,*" Lila had insisted.

Rick had been present at the time. "No way." He groaned.

"Way. It's my party, right? Would you rather see *The Sound of Music*?"

"Maybe I'll eat and run, skip the movie," Rick had said.

So today, when Rick and Red burst from the bowels of the CMPD building into the bright light and oppressive heat of the August afternoon, Red was surprised that Rick was still coming.

"I'll pick up Gina, then stop by McDonald's," she said as she moved toward her Challenger.

"I'll bring the beer and wine." Rick waved as he ducked into his Crown Victoria, then sped away.

As Red went about her errands, she sang along with the radio and even giggled at the deejay's lame jokes. It was a relief to now have Rick in the loop regarding her and Gina. They'd told him several days ago that they were back together, and he'd been thrilled. He'd even been hopeful that this time was the charm. Red sure as hell hoped so.

Point was, Red was happy—happier than she'd been in months. Gina and she were coexisting in perfect harmony. They were still a little guarded and unnaturally attentive to the nuances of each other's feelings. They had still not discussed the future, so Red dared not hope it would last. But for now, in spite of all the ugliness of the outside world, she felt safe inside.

Gina and she arrived at the parking lot of Carolinas Medical Center at the exact same moment as Rick, and they parked in adjoining spaces. Rick's backpack, filled with alcoholic beverages, was slung over his shoulder. Gina and Red collected their white paper bags adorned with golden arches and stuffed with junk food, then they all linked arms and headed inside.

Somehow, they wheedled their way through security with their alcoholic contraband. Rick even made it past Lila's protective nurse by flashing his hundred-kilowatt smile. When they entered Lila's private room, Salsa was already there, feeding Lila nachos, one by one.

Salsa and Summer were wary of Gina being back in Red's life, but for now, they had forged an unspoken agreement to give Gina a chance. Like Red, they were holding their breath and wouldn't exhale until they were sure the relationship would work. Lila, however, was Red and Gina's biggest cheerleader. Although they'd never met in person, from the moment Lila woke up and found Gina in her hospital room, she'd given Gina a fragile hug and whispered, "Welcome to the club."

So Red watched Lila nibble the nachos and loved her all the more for her unconditional support. Red held up the bag of burgers and told her, "Hey, don't spoil your appetite!"

"Not a chance," Lila mumbled through a mouthful.

Lila seemed to be improving every day. Her speech was still somewhat slurred but understandable, and while she couldn't stand or walk, she was able to swing her legs off the bed and wriggle her toes.

"Nice turban, Lila," Rick said as he set a six-pack of Bud and a bottle of chilled chardonnay on the hospital tray.

"I like it." Lila patted the colorful cloth tied around   her head. "Salsa chose it for me."

"Well, I offered to buy her a fancy wig, but Lila refused," Salsa said. "So I bought her some hand-painted scarves at the artists' co-op. They cover the bandages just fine."

Everyone laughed as Red distributed napkins and Rick popped the top on a beer. Somehow, Lila managed to look fashionable in the makeshift head wrap, and someone, likely Salsa, had applied Lila's makeup.

"You're lookin' good," Rick said as he passed Lila a paper hospital cup filled with wine.

"No alcohol for you, Miss Lila!" The nurse, who had become Lila's determined guard dog, poked her stern face in the door. She waggled her finger and folded her arms across her considerable bosom.

"Aw, you're no fun." Lila stuck her tongue out at the nurse but dutifully refused the drink. When Red handed Lila the strawberry shake she had requested, Lila transferred it to a plastic safety glass with a bendy straw and made a face. "Next time, bring vodka and I'll spike my juice. *She'll* never know."

"Oh, yeah, I will. And go easy with them fries, Miss Lila. That salt will send your blood pressure through the roof, are you hearin' me?"

"Yes, ma'am." Lila saluted as the nurse retreated.

"Mind if *we* indulge?" Red lifted the bottle of chardonnay, then passed cups to Gina and Salsa.

Lila said, "I shall take vicarious pleasure in your excess. By the way, where's Summer? I promised that bodyguard posing as my nurse that I'd go easy on the fries, but I said nothing about chocolate cake. Summer's still bringing the cake, right?"

"Absolutely. When I phoned her last night, it was already in the oven," Salsa confirmed.

"She probably got delayed at work," Gina said.

"Yeah, performing colonoscopies is a shitty job." Rick sniggered.

"Up yours, Detective Molerno!" Lila toasted him with her milkshake.

Everyone laughed, and Red was happy that even Lila, who'd been critical of Rick, thanks to Red's complaining emails over the years, now seemed to enjoy him. "Should we start eating without Summer?"

"You bet." Rick tore into one of the food bags, took a huge bite from a burger, and then dangled a fry from the corner of his mouth. "Pass the ketchup. Nothing worse than cold, greasy fries."

Following his lead, they all dug in. Red was hungry enough to gobble all six of the chicken sandwiches she'd purchased along with the Big Macs but set her limit at two. In the meantime, she noticed Salsa was barely eating a thing. Instead, she was carefully cutting bits of chicken into bite-sized portions for Lila, then feeding them to her with a plastic fork. The tender gesture caused an ache somewhere deep in Red's chest behind her heart. Not indigestion.

Red had told Gina about the growing attraction between Lila and Salsa, and they were both worried about the two women. Gina was more hopeful about the relationship than Red because in her misguided youth Gina had believed she was straight. Unlike

Red, Gina had slept with men until she realized that men provided neither the emotional nor physical satisfaction she craved. But Red remained skeptical. What would happen to Salsa and Lila's relationship once Lila left the hospital? How would Lila survive financially if she could never work again, never create the sculpture that so defined her? And would Salsa be willing to love and support a disabled person?

Pushing those worries aside, Red glanced nervously at the big round clock mounted on the wall above Lila's bed. "I wonder what's keeping Summer."

"What time is it?" Lila said.

"Six thirty." Red stared at the clock, which was like those found in public school classrooms coast to coast. When Red had been hospitalized after the gunshot wound that almost shattered her knee, the same type of clock had been prominently displayed where she could see it. It made the hours, days, and weeks in rehab drag unbearably. At least Lila's clock was out of sight, hopefully out of mind.

Rick finished his third burger, second beer, then wiped his mouth with a napkin. "Look, girls, I gotta bounce…"

"Rick can't deal with Scarlett O'Hara and Rhett Butler doin' their thing." Gina scoffed.

"True," Rick admitted. "But before I go, I need to talk to you, Salsa."

"So talk already." Salsa looked up, surprised.

"Not here, out in the hall."

Red sighed as Rick tucked the remaining beers under his arm and trudged toward the door. Subtlety had never been his strong suit, but he commanded attention, so Salsa obediently trailed after him, a pained look on her face.

"What's that all about?" Lila asked Red.

"I think he wants to discuss George Burgiss, the jerk who tried to rape Salsa."

"And Rick figures I'm not *man enough* to hear about it?" Lila snorted.

Red shrugged. "Something like that. He doesn't want to upset you." But clearly being left out of the loop agitated Lila even more.

"Have they caught the creep?" Gina asked.

"No, not yet, but they've had a sighting."

"What the hell does that mean?" Lila demanded.

Red took a deep breath, unsure how much to reveal, since the truth was disturbing indeed. Burgiss had recently started a fight with two yokels at a nearby redneck bar. He'd cut the locals with a broken bottle but escaped before the police arrived.

"Someone spotted Burgiss at a bar," she answered neutrally.

"But he got away?" Gina asked.

"Right."

"Fuck." Lila folded her long white fingers into a fist and pounded her tray. "And I suppose the cops don't have a clue where he's hiding."

"That's about the size of it." Red hated to admit that even after two sightings—first at his abandoned apartment, then the bar—the authorities were nowhere. Everyone figured Burgiss had a secret hideaway, which remained as elusive as the man himself.

"Red, do you think Burgiss is the one who tried to kill me?" Lila's slightly slurred speech tripped on the question.

"Honestly, I really don't know."

They waited in miserable silence until Salsa stomped back into the hospital room, her face flushed with anger.

"Well, Rick wasn't much help," she snapped. "The stupid Iredell cops couldn't shoot a sitting duck if it flew up and pooped on their heads."

Everyone blinked in surprise, then laughed in spite of themselves.

"As opposed to us dumb Charlotte Mecklenburg cops, who can't catch that duck if it hops off its nest and lays eggs on our breakfast plates?" Red fired back.

Salsa groaned. "I didn't mean to dis you personally, Red, but jeez, why can't *someone* catch *someone* before it happens again?"

The question had no reasonable answer, so Red glanced at the clock again and wondered about Summer. "I don't get it. It's after seven, and Summer's still not here."

"She said Paul would be back in town tonight. He's been at a teachers' conference all week, so maybe she ditched us for him," Salsa said.

"If she did, I'll kill her." Red gathered up the soiled sandwich wrappers and dunked them into the waste can. She placed the cold burgers she'd set aside for Summer on the nightstand. "It doesn't make sense. If Summer went to the trouble of baking a cake, why not bring it?"

"Maybe she gave the cake to Paul," Gina grumbled. "You say Summer's crazy for this guy, but she wouldn't dare dump us—at least without calling first."

Suddenly, Red had a bad feeling as she rummaged through her purse and found her cellphone. "I'm calling Lake Norman Regional Medical Center to find out if Summer's still at work."

Red dialed Summer's office and listened to the

recorded message, which she switched to speaker. The office was closed for the day, but the message offered an emergency number. Gina wrote it down.

"Is this an emergency?" Salsa asked.

Red was beginning to think so. It wasn't surprising that Summer's office was closed for the weekend, but this being Friday night, the killer's night to prowl, she didn't like it one bit that Summer had stood them up. Wordlessly, she entered the number Gina handed her and connected with an actual human voice:

"Front desk. How may I direct your call?"

After convincing the receptionist that this was not a medical emergency, but rather a police emergency, the flustered woman patched her through to Summer's boss. The good doctor did not take kindly to having his happy hour interrupted.

"I hate to tell you, Detective, but Summer never showed up for work today. She left us high and dry. It was a nightmare."

"Did she call in sick?"

"No, damn it, and that's not like Summer. Our cleaning woman, Jolene, told me Summer has a new boyfriend who was due back in town today. She figured Summer bailed on us to be with him."

The doctor sounded not only angry, but also slightly inebriated, and whoever this bitch Jolene was, she'd done Summer no favors. Red figured she'd reached a dead end. "Thanks anyway, sir."

"Is Summer in trouble?" he asked.

"I sure as hell hope not." She hung up without ceremony.

"Maybe Summer's really sick," Salsa said hopefully. "Call her house."

Red was already dialing Summer's home landline. A tiny voice picked up on the first ring.

"Mommy, is that you?"

Gloria sounded scared, and she was probably hungry. After hearing her story, Red was just plain scared.

"Grandma and Grandpa dropped me off at church, then went home," Gloria explained. "Mommy was supposed to pick me up, but she never came, so I walked home by myself."

"Who's with you now?"

"Nobody. I'm home alone."

Chapter Forty-two

A long time ago, when she was about Gloria's age, Red found herself home alone. Back then, it was safe to walk back and forth from school, so Red had left her second grade classroom and shuffled through the autumn leaves to the surprise party Mom had planned for Linda, the orphan child who had been placed in foster care with the Reynolds family down the street. Red had heard the grownups talking about how poor Linda wasn't adjusting well, so they thought some birthday presents, a cake, and balloons would be just the ticket to cheer her up.

But when Red got home, her front door was locked, and the house was dark. She figured everyone was inside hiding already, waiting to jump out at Linda when she arrived, so Red crawled in through a loose basement window to a silence as big as the sound inside the seashell she'd found at the beach.

She went up to the kitchen, but no one was there. While she waited for the others, their plastic chicken clock above the refrigerator slowly moved its big hand, and the sun was an orange marble above the back fence until it rolled out of sight. No use waiting for Daddy to come home because he patrolled at night and always missed dinner. She waited while goose bumps grew on her arms, while strange, creepy noises climbed on the stairs and tears streamed from her eyes.

Now she gripped the steering wheel tighter as her Challenger sped north on I-77 toward Mooresville and remembered how she felt back then, like *she* was the orphan child. Hopefully, Gloria was not feeling so alone.

Of course, Red had called Rick as soon as they'd discovered Gloria's predicament. He had just arrived home from the hospital, and they debated calling the Mooresville police to look in on Gloria, but in the end, they decided a gang of cops at the door would unduly alarm the child. Considering Red could get there in thirty minutes, it seemed the best plan. But Gina had disagreed. Gina wanted to let Rick handle it, so they had argued. And it had escalated. Standing outside Lila's hospital room, shouting in whispers, Gina called Red a *cowboy,* and she called Gina *controlling.* So they had parted angry, and Salsa had driven Gina home.

The night of Linda's surprise party, Mom got home around eight and found a shivering, bawling nervous wreck—or so family legend had it. Mom had been sick with worry and ready to smack Red upside the head for getting her "signals crossed." It turned out the party was never planned to be at *Red's* house. Instead, it took place at the *Reynolds's* house. All the neighbors were in an uproar, ready to form a search party for poor lost Red until Mom found the "silly, forgetful girl" had been home all along.

As Red slowed and turned into the Oakmont Apartment complex, she hoped Gloria had gotten *her* "signals crossed" and that Red would discover a perfectly rational explanation for Summer's absence, for her leaving an eight-year-old on her own. When she spotted Summer's old tan Toyota parked in its usual spot, Red exhaled in relief. Apparently, Summer had come home.

She rang their bell, heard what sounded like a

chair being dragged across the floor, and then sensed an eye at the peephole. After an eternity, the child opened the door but left the security chain engaged.

"Are you Gloria?" Red gently asked.

"I'm not supposed to open for strangers."

"But I'm not a stranger, am I? We just talked on the phone, remember?"

"Are you Mommy's friend?"

So Summer wasn't home, after all. "Yes, Gloria, I'm your mommy's friend Red. Please let me in so we can sit down and talk, all right?"

Red must have been convincing because soon the child released the chain and retreated down the hall as Red entered. Red closed the door behind them and turned on more lights. Eventually, Gloria took her hand and led her into the kitchen, where the child had eaten one slice of the chocolate cake Summer had baked for Lila.

"I was hungry," Gloria explained. "I hope Mommy won't be mad."

"I'm sure she won't be."

Not good. As Red settled at the table with Gloria, it seemed clear that Summer not only never made it to work, she also never left the apartment complex, at least not in her car. So where the hell was she? Surely, Summer wasn't frittering the day away with one of the neighbors, so had someone picked her up? Voluntarily or otherwise?

"Where's my mommy?" Gloria demanded.

"We should call your father."

"No!" Gloria shrieked. "Daddy would be mad at Mommy for leaving me alone. He'll take me away from her, and I'll have to live with that slut Jolene."

Red blinked in surprise. This was the second

time in less than an hour she'd heard the name *Jolene*, and whoever Jolene was, she was not a family friend. Obviously, domestic issues beyond Red's understanding were in play, but calling Summer's ex did not seem like a good idea.

"Okay, should we call your grandparents to come stay with you?"

"No!" Gloria stomped her foot, ran from the table, and into the living room. "I just spent a whole week with Grammy and Grandpa. I love them, but they're no fun." The child picked up a remote, plopped onto the couch, and turned on a video game.

At the same time, Red's phone vibrated.

"Why didn't you call me?" Rick snapped.

"I was about to." Red partially closed the door to keep their conversation private. "I'm here at Summer's, and Gloria's okay for the moment." She brought him up to date.

"So who took Summer?" Rick asked.

"That's the ten-thousand-dollar question, isn't it?" She knew they both feared the worst.

"The local cops will be there soon," Rick said. "They'll cordon off the area and conduct a door-to-door search. One of the neighbors must've seen her leave."

Red doubted it. The sense of loss was overwhelming. She was convinced the killer had abducted his next victim. Her gut told her Summer was in mortal danger, yet the entire combined police forces seemed helpless to do anything about it. As she watched Gloria playing through the crack in the door, she felt like a terrified orphan all over again.

"What'll you do with the kid?" Rick said.

"Are you coming?" Red swallowed the lump in

her throat.

"I'm already on the road. Sit tight and wait for me."

Red joined Gloria on the couch. The frenetic action of the video avatars jerking around on the muted screen, responding to the girl's concentrated commands, cast eerie, unnatural colors on the child's face.

"Don't worry, we'll find your mom."

"Yeah, I know. Why don't you call Paul?" Gloria brightened.

Gloria was a mind reader because Paul was next on Red's list. "Great idea. What's his number?"

"How should I know? It's in Mommy's phone."

Red groaned. Undoubtedly, Mommy's phone was with Mommy. But it was an interesting idea. She must remember to ask Rick about the possibility of tracking Summer through her GPS, assuming she had downloaded an application.

"What's Paul's last name?"

"Don't know, but he's really nice. I'm sure he'd watch me until Mommy gets home."

Another dead end but no problem. Red knew Paul was a biology teacher at Mooresville High, so she'd call the school and get his info.

"Miss Red, can I show you something?" Suddenly, Gloria was all smiles. Apparently, the thought of Paul as her babysitter totally appealed to the girl. If anything, Gloria was an even bigger fan than her mother. Red watched as Gloria reached under the couch and pulled out a glossy travel brochure.

"Check it out." She shoved the colorful brochure into Red's hands. "Disney World! Isn't it awesome? Paul promised to take me and Mommy this Christmas, soon as school is out. We'll stay at a big hotel with palm trees and free breakfast, right near the park. Paul's been there lots of times, and he's best friends with Mickey Mouse."

"No kidding?" Maybe the relationship between Summer and Paul was more serious than Red realized.

"Honest. And guess what else?" Gloria grinned, exposing an endearing gap between her two front teeth. "When Paul was a little boy, not much older than me, he got a job at Disney World feeding the alligators. He kept working there until him and his mommy moved away."

"Paul lived in *Florida*?" Red tried not to panic.

"Sure, most of his life. He went back to Florida after high school and only came back to stupid Mooresville because of his job." Gloria made an ugly face.

Like most kids, Gloria figured the grass was greener everywhere than it was at home. But at the moment, Red was preoccupied with the math, and the numbers were indisputable. Unless he'd been teaching at Mooresville High for more than two decades, Paul had been living in Florida twenty years ago, just like their killer.

"Excuse me, Gloria, I need to make a phone call." Red moved outside to the front stoop and closed the door before the child could protest, then located the number of the high school alumni geek she'd recently called about the reunion attendance list. He answered on the first ring.

"Hey, Red, I didn't expect to hear from you again so soon."

"Hey, Randy, can you give me the phone number for a teacher at Mooresville High? His name is

Paul, and he teaches biology."

"Oh, sure, Paul Miller. Nice fellow. My daughter's in his class."

Within seconds, Red had Paul's vital statistics, including a home address. Although Randy wanted to take a conversational walk down memory lane and relive their high school glory days, she cut him off and dialed Paul. Unlike Randy, Paul's phone rang ten times before he answered, and the man sounded exceedingly annoyed by the interruption.

"Yeah, what do you want?"

Red realized he didn't know who was calling. She hadn't yet established a relationship with Paul, she wasn't in his digital directory, so she'd popped up as an unknown caller. "It's Red, Summer's friend," she quickly explained. "I need to talk to you."

He paused. She listened to the void while Paul struggled to adjust his attitude. When he spoke again, his tone was smooth as maple syrup.

"It's great to hear from you, Red. What's up?"

Rather than reveal her hand, she decided to downplay. "We expected Summer to come to a party for Lila at the hospital today, but she never showed. Is she with you?"

More silence. "I've been out of town."

Was that an answer? Red didn't think so. "Well, have you heard from her lately?"

"Not really."

Red's pulse rate escalated, and heartbeats thudded in her ears. Paul definitely didn't sound like a loving, concerned boyfriend. If anything, he seemed completely uninterested. "Where are you now, Paul?"

"At the grocery."

"Well, never mind. Please tell Summer to call if

you hear from her."

After saying their brief goodbyes, Red disconnected and gazed out at the twilight parking lot, where a teenage boy was slumping against a lamppost, smoking a cigarette. She suspected he was the kid Summer always talked about, the weirdo who babysat for Gloria.

"Hey there!" Red shouted, trying not to sound like a cop. The kid ground the butt out with the toe of his sneaker and sauntered over. "What's your name?"

"Connor," he mumbled.

Red told Connor that Summer was delayed, and she needed him to watch Gloria for a couple of hours. To emphasize, she fished a twenty from her purse and pressed it into his moist hand.

"Cool." Connor slid past her into the house like he owned the place and high-fived his video pal. Soon Connor and Gloria had booted up the sound and were engaged in heavy competition.

It seemed all right. The kid was sullen but hardly Jack the Ripper. Red told him to make Gloria a peanut butter sandwich, then firmly closed the door behind her and ran to her Challenger.

No point waiting for Rick, he'd only try to stop her. Gina would be furious if she found out that Red was striking out on her own, but Red would deal with them both later. As her heart continued to race, she plugged Paul Miller's home address into her GPS, then headed down the dark highway toward the country north of town.

Chapter Forty-three

It was fully dark when Red located Paul's neat brick rancher in the suburbs above Mooresville. The neighborhood was older, heavily wooded with large lots, but many of the homes had fallen into disrepair. Several had signs out front indicating they were for sale by the bank—foreclosures—and while the place didn't seem dead, it was definitely sleeping. The street lacked proper lighting, with only an occasional Duke Energy security bulb mounted atop an electrical pole, casting deep shadows on the lawns. For a Friday night, it seemed odd that not one kid was outside playing, so Red guessed most of the residents were older, possibly retired.

As she parked a block down the road from the rancher, it also struck her as strange that an eligible single man like Paul Miller would choose such a quiet neighborhood. Even on a teacher's salary, he could afford a condo or townhouse closer to the action. Had he inherited this house? Had it once belonged to the infamous "mother" in Red's dad's profile, the mother who drove her son to rape and kill?

The chilling thought propelled Red to retrieve her Smith & Wesson from the console. She unstrapped it and clipped the holster to her belt. She untucked her shirt, so its tail would hide the weapon from any curious neighbors with their noses pressed to windowpanes. Finally, before exiting the vehicle, she speed-dialed Rick. If she should encounter trouble in this unlikely, seemingly benign setting, it was only fair to give him a heads-up as to her whereabouts and the circumstances that brought her here. Unfortunately, her call went directly to his voicemail, and as she left a hasty message, she pictured him at Summer's house trying to cope with Gloria and Connor. Kids were not Rick's forte.

In spite of Red's jitters, the image brought a smile to her lips. She could almost hear Rick scolding her for approaching Paul without backup. At the same time, he'd be whining about being left to deal with the kids on his own. But much as Red looked forward to hearing Rick mouth off, she knew she had to mute her phone, at least for the moment. One couldn't hope to sneak up on a suspect with a phone chirping in one's pocket.

So she turned down the ringer and slipped out to the sidewalk, where the day's heat still rolled up in waves from the hot concrete. Attempting to blend in, which wasn't easy for a middle-aged, six-foot-tall, redheaded cop, she strolled toward Paul's house, certain that curious eyes were watching her every move. As she drew close, trying not to be disheartened because his place was completely dark, she reminded herself that Paul might still be at the grocery store, as he had claimed. Seemed reasonable. If the man had really been away at a conference for a week, he needed supplies. On the other hand, maybe he hadn't been away at all. Maybe Paul was holed up the whole time inside the house, licking his wounds and recovering from the burns Lila had inflicted with her welding torch.

What if he was hiding inside right now? What if those eyes Red felt watching her didn't belong to the retired neighbors but to Paul himself? Staring at the dark picture window to the right of his front door, was it her imagination or had the drapes parted for only a second?

She stubbed her toe on an uneven crack in the sidewalk and almost tripped. *Get a grip!* Furious with her clumsiness, she took a deep breath and willed her heart to slow down. She was out of practice, hadn't been on the beat for years, but that was no excuse for behaving like a clueless rookie. Did she want Paul to be gone? Hell, yes. Or did she want to catch him hiding inside with Summer? Well, yes again, that was the point, wasn't it? Saving Summer before it was too late?

Red took another deep breath before starting down the path leading to his door. Her fingers trembled as she touched her gun and folded the shirttail back just enough for easy access. She was in charge, right? She was an officer of the law with a viable reason to investigate. Yet she couldn't help but recall the shocking, searing pain when that bullet tore into her leg in that dark alley years ago, and she imagined how much worse it would be to take a slug point blank in the chest if a killer was waiting right behind that door.

Enough already. She stood straight and moved purposefully down the walkway bordered by lovingly tended annuals—impatiens being the only flowers she recognized—and told herself: *How bad could Paul be if he cares for his garden?* She rang the doorbell, then knocked hard for good measure.

While she waited, Red heard a lonesome radio playing from inside a distant garage and the muffled roar of traffic from the interstate, which lay beyond the suburb's buffer forest. Next she peeked inside but saw only a dimly lit hallway and closed doors. A large stack of mail was piled on a little table with a lace tablecloth. Well, the mail made sense if the man truly had been out of town, but the lace seemed out of place. *More shades of the dead mother?*

She left the porch and walked over to Paul's two-car garage, also dark. When she peered inside, the blackness prevented her from seeing much of anything except the fact that no car was parked within. "Nada," as Salsa would say.

Paul wasn't home.

When Red left the garage to check out the backyard, she breathed more easily and felt free to snoop. She knew if a body needed burying, it was likely stashed in a shallow grave behind the shed, right? Now convinced that she was alone and out of harm's way, she was also rapidly convincing herself that Paul was innocent, so of course there was no body—let alone Summer's.

She relaxed her grip on her weapon and carefully stepped through a narrow passageway between the garage and a tall privacy fence. Brushing away the long fronds of a willow tree, which was leeching water from the ground around Paul's pump house, she emerged into a moonlit clearing containing his working garden—rows of corn, tangles of beans, and a tomato patch. Nothing sinister there—no freshly turned earth or abandoned shovels.

After walking Paul's back half acre, joined by a feral cat that followed a few paces behind her, Red felt a little foolish as she pictured Rick arriving with guns blazing—figuratively speaking—to rescue her from nothing at all. But when she parted the willow fronds to squeeze back through the passageway to the front, she was instantly aware of a subtle shift in the atmosphere. Something was different.

Squinting through the bushes between the garage and privacy fence, she saw that a white pickup truck with a portable roof covering the truck's bed was now parked directly across the street. As she tried to understand why this truck was sounding alarm bells in her head, the cat yowled near her feet, and something struck her from behind.

Before Red could fight back, a strong arm angled around her throat, cutting off her windpipe, lifting her off her feet and holding her against his muscled body. Terrified, she struggled to reach her gun, but with his other hand, the attacker beat her to it. His fingers fumbled at her belt, and then her weapon fell to the ground.

As Red elbowed the monster, the rough wool of a ski mask scratched the side of her face. She smelled his hot breath while he choked her. Just as she was about to pass out, another pain—like an electric knife to the small of her back—screamed through her entire body.

And then there was nothing.

Chapter Forty-four

Rick found the kids playing video games. Although he'd never met Summer's daughter, Gloria, let alone the sulky teenager Connor, the pair had let him in without question—never even asked to see his identification.

"What's wrong with you?" he scolded Connor. "Didn't anyone teach you not to open up for strangers?"

"You kiddin' me, man? You even stink like a cop, why would I doubt you?"

Resisting the urge to smack the smirk off the punk's face, Rick let it drop. If this juvie lived in Charlotte, he'd be a perfect candidate for their Gang of One program for at-risk teens. As it was, the only thing Rick cared about was catching up with Red.

"How long ago did the police lady leave?" he asked Gloria.

"You mean Miss Red? Only a few minutes ago. She was going to see Mommy's boyfriend...I think." The child smiled, exposing a cute little gap between her two front teeth. "Paul's really nice. He's taking us to Disney World."

"No, Paul's an asshole," Connor said.

Rick frowned at the boy. Either he had a problem with adult males or a long-standing crush on Summer, but Rick preferred to leave the psychobabble bullshit to the guidance counselors.

Glancing through the window, he saw his backup arrive. The two patrol cars parked out front—

no sirens, no spinning lights—low key, like they promised.

"Want some chocolate cake?" Gloria grinned.

"No thanks, doll, but maybe the guys who came to help find your mom would like some." He nodded at the response team. They were already knocking at the front door. At the same time, Connor sprinted toward the back exit.

"Catch you later, Gloria," he called before leaving via the patio.

Rick suspected Connor had history with the Mooresville police, but again, it wasn't Rick's problem. So after a brief meet and greet with the officers who would search the complex, interview neighbors, and generally look for evidence of foul play, Rick said goodbye to Gloria and left the building.

Hopefully, everyone was overreacting, and he'd find both Red and Summer at Paul's, chatting away over coffee. But as he drove toward the suspect's house, the more certain Rick became that Paul was their man. When Red told him about the Florida connection, it all made sense. Although Rick had met the uptight redheaded teacher only briefly at Boots's funeral, he could picture Paul as the judgmental mama's boy from the profile. Red's dad had described this nutcase down to the letter. Paul had never been married. Rick didn't know whether Paul was a religious fanatic, but he wouldn't doubt it. And as far as Rick was concerned, anyone who sneaked around on the internet looking for dates—or victims—was already weird.

Feeling a little lost, he followed his GPS into a down-at-the-heels development he'd never seen before. Having grown up in Mooresville, Red knew this town much better than he did, and besides, quiet suburban neighborhoods gave him the creeps. As a city boy, Rick liked his danger loud, crowded, and spilling out into the streets, not lurking behind drawn window shades like here.

When he turned into Paul's road, his sense of unease increased. Why the hell hadn't Red waited for him instead of charging off half-cocked on her own? Her garbled message in his voicemail had pulsed with an urgency bordering on panic, and he prayed she wouldn't do anything stupid.

As he slowed to a crawl, Rick heard a radio playing softly from a brightly lit garage. It was an oldies tune, the Righteous Brothers' *Unchained Melody*, one of his favorites. The garage door was open, with an elderly man crouched inside cleaning his lawn mower. His white-haired wife was standing above him, watching with a tender look on her face. Surely nothing bad could happen in this Norman Rockwell neighborhood.

But then he spotted Red's car parked along the curb up ahead, and his fear went into overdrive. The shiny bronze Challenger, Red's pride and joy, was apparently unoccupied, and when he parked behind it, he confirmed that Red had indeed moved on. She'd left the vehicle a full block from the suspect's house, so passive surveillance had never been her plan.

He strapped on his shoulder holster and gun, then exited his Ford. He tried the Challenger's passenger door and found it unlocked. Either Red had left in a tearing hurry or been extremely preoccupied. He opened Red's console and saw she'd taken her weapon. Well, that was good…and bad…because ever since her last shooting incident that left a street punk dead and Red wounded, she had been gun-shy. Though she'd never admit it, Red was afraid to use her weapon. She didn't want to shoot a human being again. But she was courageous and would do her duty. What Rick feared most was that inevitable moment of hesitation between drawing down on a suspect and firing—a moment of soul-searching that could get Red killed.

Feeling something like panic, he quickly abandoned Red's car and rushed toward the small ranch house where Paul Miller lived. Gun in hand, he strode down the path to the door, accidentally trampling some silly flowers bordering the sidewalk. If Red's fatal flaw was her conscience, then his was his temper. He had a reputation as a hothead in the department, and Red was always telling him to slow down and think before acting.

To hell with that.

Rick rang the bell and pounded hard with his fist. "Open up, Miller! I know you're in there."

Although the house was dark and silent, Rick's gut told him the killer was hiding inside, and while all he could see was a dimly lit hallway with closed doors, his imagination ran wild. He pictured Red and Summer gagged and chained to beds, or much worse.

Should he break down this door or seek entry elsewhere? As he jogged over to the locked garage, he shivered in spite of the sweat pouring down his back. He saw no car inside, only deep shadows and the usual shit folks stored in garages. At the same time, he heard a loud crash coming from behind the house, from the backyard. Damn!

With adrenaline flooding his system, Rick located a narrow passageway alongside the building and carefully made his way through the bushes, his right arm extended, his left hand locked on his right wrist to steady his aim as he pushed through a curtain of willow fronds.

Crouching, he spun around the corner into a grassy clearing lit by moonlight. Off to one side was a garden, where every cornstalk took on threatening, human characteristics. Several thick tree trunks afforded cover for the enemy, while close to the rear wall of the building, a sudden movement accompanied by an unearthly yowl caused Rick to drop to his belly in a defensive roll. When he braced his elbows for a clear shot, he was staring into the wild green eyes of an alley cat who, if anything, was twice as terrified as Rick.

"Jesus Christ Almighty!" he cursed under his breath as the cat arched and circled the upturned trash can that had obviously caused the racket he'd heard out front. The cat sniffed at some dried coffee grounds and ripe banana peels, gave a disgusted meow, and then galloped out of sight into a hedge row.

Feeling ridiculous, Rick struggled upright and wandered toward a small, shiny object catching the moonlight. As he walked, the urgency drained from his muscles, and he sensed he was alone in the night—no imminent danger in the yard and likely none inside. The images of a maniac's trophy room filled with photos of all his victims or the torture chamber with chains faded from his imagination as he approached the object and picked it up.

At first it appeared to be a broken picture frame, its metal border mangled, glass shattered. But as Rick turned it over in his hand, the backside was smooth as human flesh, with tiny round holes embedded in the skin for a camera and speaker—it had once been a cellphone. As he looked more closely above the burnished silver Google band, he saw a colorful decal of a miniature Betty Boop and froze in shock. It wasn't just any cellphone, it was Red's, with the one cartoon character she adored, the decal she used to identify all her personal possessions, so Rick had no more doubt. Red was gone.

And the killer had taken her.

Chapter Forty-five

Once upon a time, Red fell out of a tree in the woods behind the playground, and the big kids put her in a wagon and rolled her back to the school. The hard steel bed of the wagon jolted her broken arm, and the pain ricocheted through her body while the sun bounced in the blue sky until stars exploded and her head went black. Next she was sick to her stomach, and then she was dead.

But now, as bile rose in the back of her throat and she coughed, her hot breath blew backward, and she realized she was gagged. The stinking, stretchy tape flattened her lips so she couldn't get air, and instead of sun and blue sky, she saw only a dark lid right above her head. The pain was in her back, not her arm, and when she shifted her weight on the vibrating steel floor, she discovered her wrists and ankles were bound, and she couldn't move.

She cried when she remembered what had happened, and the salt stung her eyes. She recalled the strong arm around her windpipe, the rough mask against her cheek, and the excruciating electric charge from a stun gun. So the killer had abducted her, and now she was in his truck.

Stupid. Stupid. Stupid. The road beat under the tires, sending Red's spine into spasms of agony, and she had no idea how long they had been traveling. Two minutes, two hours, two days? The occasional flash from other headlights moved across the narrow rectangle of window in the rear of the truck cover, but they offered few clues other than the fact that not many cars were on the highway. They were traveling at a high speed, so likely they were on an interstate in the middle of the night.

With what little strength she had, Red struggled to free her hands and feet, but the restraints wouldn't budge, and the effort brought on a fresh flood of tears. But this time, the tears weren't self-pity or fear, but rather anger. As she thought about Boots, Salsa, Summer, Lila, and especially Gina, she was furious with herself for allowing this to happen. Red was supposedly a seasoned officer of the law, yet she had impulsively blundered into the killer's trap. She'd let her emotions cloud her judgment, lost her weapon, and become his latest victim. Rick would be incensed. First, he'd want to strangle her for her stupidity, but then he'd be hell-bent on revenge, an attitude that sometimes made him stupid, too. Gina would go through all the stages of grief, starting with denial, ending with an acceptance that their relationship was doomed. Red had not changed. She was still the bull-headed, unthinking, risk-taking cop Gina despised. Even if Red survived, she wouldn't get another chance.

She hated herself for putting Rick in danger, and the thought of losing Gina again was unbearable. But in the end, as the pain in her back burned through her shoulders and seared down through her hips and legs, to where she feared she would pass out, Red hated the killer most of all. She owed it to herself, to all of them, to stay strong. Somehow, she would turn the tables and defeat this bastard—rip his throat out or stab him in the heart, if he had one.

Yet she knew she was hallucinating, and as the

nose of the truck angled upward, as though they were climbing to the top of a mountain, the incline slid her body against the tailgate, and the shock made her vomit into her gag. Suddenly, as she struggled to catch her breath, she was falling from a great height, from that tree long ago, and as the blinding sun electrified the insides of her eyelids, then went black, she knew she was dead all over again.

Chapter Forty-six

The abandoned Challenger and smashed cellphone proved to be ample cause for a search warrant. Rick had called the Mooresville police, explained the situation over an hour ago, but as he paced in Paul Miller's front yard, it felt like an eternity. Logan, the Charlotte detective in charge, had reminded Rick that the wheels of justice turn slowly, and in this case, obtaining the search warrant involved bothering a particularly cranky old judge after hours, but to hell with that. All Rick knew as he deliberately stomped on the flowers along Miller's sidewalk was that every minute of delay hurt Red's chances of survival.

For all he knew, Red and Summer were imprisoned inside the creepy ranch house, so it took every ounce of his willpower not to break in forcibly. Truth be told, he had already tried to pick the locks with the handy set of tools he'd stolen from a breaking and entering pro some years back, but no go. Miller had installed multiple deadbolts both front and back, so the place was like a fortress. Rick fantasized about shooting off the locks, then kicking in the doors, but he heard Red's voice in his head telling him to cool it. Such action would not only jeopardize the case they might build against Miller, but also land Rick a suspension, or worse.

Once satisfied that he'd sufficiently messed up the suspect's flowers, Rick wandered down the block to the garage with the radio. The old guy had finished cleaning his lawn mower, and now he and his wife were seated on the front stoop sipping iced tea. After counting to ten, another trick Red had taught him to calm himself, Rick approached the couple and introduced himself. After explaining how his partner had disappeared while visiting Paul Miller, the two stared at him in utter disbelief.

"So did you see anything?" Rick prompted.

The husband reached down beside the steps and brought out a bottle of Jack Daniels. "Care for a nightcap, Detective? My wife can fetch another glass. You look like you could use a drink."

Rick's jaw dropped in surprise. Not iced tea, after all. "No thanks, I'm on duty." He gaped at the man. "Have you seen Mr. Miller?"

The wife chuckled and touched her husband's hand. "Not for several weeks, mister. Paul's a teacher, don't you know? He's been gone to a conference up in Raleigh, best I recollect."

"But he was due home today," Rick pressed.

"Not so's you'd notice, Detective." The husband smoothed his white mustache. "I've been workin' outside all day, and I've not seen hide nor hair of Paul."

"Did you see his car?"

"No, sir. We don't get much traffic on our street, and I'd take notice if I'd seen Paul drive in or anyone else, for that matter."

"Yes, you would, honey, but even you come inside from time to time to answer a call of nature." The wife giggled again and looked meaningfully at Rick. "He don't miss much, mister, but he's human."

Next the pair launched into a litany praising Paul Miller. He was a perfect neighbor, perfect gentleman, lived "clean and quiet," and to hear them tell it, Miller ranked up there somewhere between sliced white bread and Jesus Christ. In the meantime, Rick shifted impatiently foot to foot, and his throat burned for a taste of the whiskey.

"We've known Paul since he was a teenager. He's almost like a son to us," the man said.

"Yes, him and his mama lived in that rancher when Paul was in high school. She bought the place after her divorce, when this development was new. They moved back to Florida for a spell, but we were happy when Paul came back to teach," the wife added.

"What about his mama?" Rick grumbled.

"Well, she passed on." The wife shrugged. "He don't like to talk about it, and who can blame him? Those two were real close."

As Rick watched the happy couple, he figured the others in this neighborhood would hold the same high opinion of Miller. They'd never question why the guy kept his house locked up like Fort Knox, why he never married. Miller fit the profile Red's daddy constructed to a tee, and now, as Rick thought about Red's father, it occurred to him that he needed to make an unpleasant phone call to Captain Calendar and tell him his daughter had been abducted.

"Let's just say Paul *did* come home today, and I missed him..." the elderly husband conceded. "If your partner met up with him, maybe they went out to dinner."

"That's right!" The wife winked. "Lately, Paul's been steppin' out with a lady friend, but he don't tell us much about that."

Rick was getting nowhere, so he quickly excused himself when a Mooresville patrol car turned onto the street and stopped at Miller's rancher. In fact, Rick broke into a trot and met Detective Logan and his partner at

Miller's front door.

"Let's rock n' roll." Logan held up a search warrant and nodded. He knocked and rang the bell.

"If he's home, he's not answering," Rick snapped.

"Then we move to Plan B." Logan pulled a house key from his pocket.

"Is that a master key?" Rick watched as Logan effortlessly opened the door.

"Nope, it's a copy of Miller's own key. The man's very security-conscious. He left it with us and informs us each time he leaves town, so the cruiser can keep an eye on the place and enter in case of an emergency."

"No shit." Rick scoffed. He broke into a sweat as they entered the silent foyer, with Logan in the lead. So Miller was a conscientious, law-abiding citizen—a cop's best friend. Well, he may have these guys fooled but not Rick. Logan passed out gloves before they began turning on lights, and as Rick worked his hands into the latex fingers, he lingered behind at the hall table to check out the piled-up mail as the others moved down the hall. He inspected the dates of cancellation. Sure enough, some dated back two weeks, but if Miller hadn't yet been home, how the hell did the mail get neatly stacked on the table? By rights, it should be lying in a heap under the slot in the door.

So the bastard had returned. As Rick peeked at the bills, bank statements, and junk, he noticed a framed photo on a little easel. Taking a closer look, he realized the picture depicted Summer, Salsa, Boots, Lila, and Red at some party—the high school reunion. Son of a bitch! How did Miller get hold of this, and why was it so prominently displayed? As more sweat pooled under his collar, Rick slid open the narrow drawer in the hall table and found three more copies of the same photo. A memory tugged at the back of his mind, and then it came clear. The night Boots was murdered, he'd seen this same photo of the True Love Club on Boots's hall table.

Damn. Trying to stay focused, Rick attempted to piece it together. He knew Miller was a teacher with a legitimate connection to the girls' high school, so maybe the man had a perfectly reasonable explanation for possessing these photos. Rick would be sure to ask Salsa or Lila about this as soon as possible. On the other hand, and more likely, Miller had used this photo as his calling card the night he killed Boots. The theory had always been that Boots welcomed her attacker into her condo since there had been no signs of a forced entry. So had Miller offered to sell or give the photo to Boots, thereby gaining her trust?

In Rick's tortured mind, the answer was an emphatic yes. Unfortunately, the killer had worn gloves at all the crime scenes, so even when the Mooresville cops checked the photo for prints, they'd found nothing. He got his breathing under control and followed Logan and his partner deeper into the hall, keeping the information to himself for the moment.

Miller's small formal parlor was neat and prim as a spinster's underwear—no one ever went inside. Across the way, the dining room was the same. The big cherry table smelled of lemon oil, and the china cabinet was crammed with sentimental porcelain figurines of children.

Behind it, Miller's kitchen was spotlessly clean, reeking of cleanser and bleach. Even his refrigerator was appropriately empty of all perishables—no milk carton rings on its plastic shelves, the freezer filled with individually wrapped portions of meat, meticulously folded into cellophane. Both bathrooms were equally pristine.

"A bachelor lives here?" Logan seemed incredulous.

"Hey, the guy's Mr. Clean." His partner snorted derisively.

The dead mother's bedroom was the only space showing traces of dust, as though it had been sealed off as a shrine many years ago. The second bedroom had been converted to Miller's den, with science textbooks filed alphabetically on the shelves, his computer keyboard covered with its original plastic sheath.

Rick tapped the hard drive. "You need to impound this. Let your techs explore Miller's internet browsing history." As he thought about DATESCAPE, the violent website that ensnared the women of the TLC, he felt sick to his stomach.

Finally, when they entered Miller's bedroom, Rick's hope plummeted altogether, for the immaculate space offered no clues other than a monastic single bed made up with hospital corners, a reading lamp, and a shelf holding a collection of souvenir cups.

"All clear," Logan stated the obvious. "It would seem whatever happened to Detective Calendar happened outside."

"So it would seem." Barely able to conceal his disappointment and his guilt, Rick exited the back door and stepped into the yard, where the feral cat had ventured out of the bushes and was giving the spilled garbage a second sniff.

He took out his phone, glanced at the pale moon, and thought about Red's dad. Would he still love Rick like a son when he broke the news?

He made the call.

Chapter Forty-seven

The deep, droning voice nibbled at the edge of Red's consciousness, and as she slowly focused and realized her predicament, it was all she could do to keep from screaming. Not wanting to call attention to herself, afraid to move, she kept the tension in her eyelids neutral so the monster wouldn't know she was awake. The monotonous, sing-song voice didn't sound like Paul or anyone else she knew. He was reading from the Bible, but he wasn't reading to her.

Working through the pain, which had blessedly been replaced by a numb sensation throughout her body, Red listened more carefully as the monster continued to scroll through scripture detailing the virtues of cleanliness, of washing away one's sins, of bathing in God's words, and other garbage. Not that she believed religion was garbage, but from this lunatic's lips, it sounded filthy, vile, self-serving, and threatening as hell.

His voice came from the far side of the room. Apparently, he was stationary and seated, his energy flowing to another person, not to her. Daring to open her eyes only a slit, Red saw she was lying on an old-fashioned comforter on a hardwood floor. The comforter stank of must, but the floor was meticulously clean. Her wrists and ankles were bound with wire to the legs of an antique iron bed, and beyond the far legs of the bed, she saw the monster's large bare feet planted on the floor and the wooden legs of his chair.

She couldn't see his face or his upper body, so likely he couldn't see her. Emboldened, she opened her eyes wide and realized the room where she was imprisoned had no windows, so she had no concept of time. Was it day or night? The springs of the bed sagged with the weight of another human being, and even before Red heard her fellow prisoner's voice, she knew.

"Are you clean?" the monster asked.

"No, Father, I am not clean," Summer replied.

Red's heart shattered. Her dear friend sounded like a drugged zombie. Had the man broken her so completely?

"Ye call me Master and Lord, and I shall wash your feet..."

What was all this *father* and *master* crap? Red's wounded heart surged with helpless loathing as she listened to the monster untying Summer from the bed. As his feet moved, Red saw long strands of silk flutter. Had Summer been bound with those? Fortunately for Summer, they seemed insubstantial restraints. Unfortunately for Red, her wire ligatures were far more challenging.

Soon Summer's pale feet and bare legs appeared as he helped her to stand. The monster was leading Summer slowly from the room, in a direction designed to keep Summer from spotting Red, but Red decided to play dead. At any moment, he might look back to check on her, and unless she too wished to be subjected to a bath, she had better be a good actress.

Hoping for an Oscar-winning performance, Red closed her eyes and willed every muscle in her body to go slack. They progressed slowly. The monster hummed a familiar hymn, while Summer staggered beside him. Red waited until she heard the door close, heard him twist the deadbolt, and then she cried.

Chapter Forty-eight

Salsa took hold of Lila's fingers and held on tight as Rick Molerno delivered the bad news Saturday morning. The minute hand on the hospital clock jerked with each word, keeping syncopated time with the sounds coming from Rick's mouth. His lips were surrounded by at least one day's growth of black bristle, and his dark eyes were rimmed with red. As the vile, unthinkable information about the abductions of Summer and Red spilled out, Salsa found it almost impossible to concentrate.

"Bottom line—I fucked up," Rick finished.

Lila's fingernails dug into Salsa's hand, and by the stunned expression in Lila's pale blue eyes, Salsa feared the news had been one shock too many. Rick was clearly in misery, mopping his face with his hand and unable to meet her gaze, but Salsa couldn't find it in her heart to forgive him. Boots was dead, Lila was flat on her back, her future almost certainly altered for all time, and now Summer and Red were gone.

"Seems like everyone in law enforcement fucked up. What's wrong with you people?" Salsa demanded.

Rick stared at the floor. He'd told them that after his visit, he was going to the airport to pick up Red's dad, Max, who was flying in from Sarasota. Rick claimed Max would probably "kill him," and as far as Salsa was concerned, that was okay.

"We put out an APB on Paul Miller, so the moment he surfaces, we'll arrest him," Rick said.

Salsa glanced at Lila, who rolled her expressive eyes. During their long hours together at the hospital, they'd discussed the case nonstop. Somehow, speculating about the killer's identity was easier than talking about more personal matters, and while they both disliked Paul's uptight personality, they considered him a wimp, not a killer.

"Are you sure it's Paul you want?" Salsa asked.

Rick scowled. "Gimme a break. I told you what happened." He crushed the empty cardboard coffee cup he was holding, then stomped across the room and jammed it into the waste can. "How do you explain the photograph? The freak had it displayed like a fucking trophy of his conquests."

"Okay, we saw that photo at Boots's funeral. Summer showed us the copy Paul had given her, and he told us we could buy it online," Salsa said.

"But why did he need so many copies?" Rick snapped.

Salsa shrugged. In spite of all the evidence, she still had doubts. When she thought about Paul, his perfectly combed red hair, self-righteous attitude, and geeky persona, she could understand how he'd fool Summer, who was desperate for a husband and father for her child. But she couldn't imagine him murdering Boots, overpowering Lila, and certainly not capturing Red.

"What about Paul's DNA?" Lila spoke up for the first time. "That result should solve the mystery once and for all."

Salsa smiled at Lila, relieved that she was still able to process after hearing Rick's news. Lila had been making steady progress. In spite of the traumatic brain injury, her cognitive functions were fully up to speed. Except for details about the night of the attack, her recollections of all past events were completely restored. But Lila still suffered from nightmares, and when she awakened after one of those, she tended to backslide, sometimes for hours.

Salsa tenderly smoothed the little worry lines creasing Lila's forehead but resisted an impulse to kiss them away. That impulse had become almost irresistible during the long recovery when it seemed their small moments of physical contact were the quickest path to normalcy. At first, Salsa had been frightened by her need to touch Lila, but gradually, it began to seem all right. Now she only kept her hands, and her lips, off Lila when others were in the room.

"About Paul's DNA…" Rick returned to the bedside, his hands folded, his head bowed in disgrace. "They'll have to get another search warrant."

"Fuck!" Lila shouted. "What the hell?"

"Yeah, I know," Rick muttered. "I want you to know that I tried last night, but like you said, Lila, the whole scene was fucked."

The two women listened in astonishment as Rick described his total meltdown at Paul Miller's ranch house the previous evening. After searching the backyard, Rick went back into the house, where he found Paul's comb. It included enough trace hair and follicle to provide a good sample, so Rick had tried to impound it—forcibly. The move ultimately resulted in a fistfight between Rick and Logan, the Mooresville cop. It also netted Rick a twenty-four-hour suspension from the case.

"They call it a cooling-off period." Rick snarled. "Seems I was trying to violate Paul's civil rights because the warrant wasn't specific to DNA collection."

The clock slowed to a standstill, and the sounds of the hospital staff in the hall—the chattering and preparation of the patients' breakfast trays—faded to muted background noise as they all considered the consequences of the delay.

"So how long will this DNA business take?" Lila asked.

Rick rocked on his heels and gazed at the ceiling. 'They'll have the damned comb in the lab by this afternoon. Another couple hours for the result, if they expedite."

"Well, shit, let's hope they *expedite* then," Lila stated the obvious.

Again Salsa touched Lila. The turban had slipped back too far on Lila's forehead, exposing a new growth of fine brown hair, soft as duck down. She adjusted Lila's turban and smiled to hear Lila cursing—*fuck, hell,* and *shit*—all in the space of a few minutes. It was a good sign. Lila had never been shy about using profanities; she kept it under control unless truly riled. So Lila's fighting spirit was alive and well, and Salsa hoped hers was, too.

These past two weeks, Salsa had swung like a pendulum between hope and despair. She hadn't suffered nightmares like Lila's, but her near-rape by *Bikerboy* had shaken her badly. She was neglecting Papa, the restaurant, and even the dogs. But her complaints were minor compared to what had happened to the others. Salsa knew Red's abduction would have devastated Gina, but so far, Salsa had been afraid to contact her. Salsa had despised Gina because of the emails Red sent describing the pain Gina caused. When she finally met Gina several weeks ago, Salsa had been cold. Now, since she'd come to know Gina and like her, she didn't know how to comfort her. She wished she'd never allowed those preconceived notions about Gina and her brother, Rick, to poison her mind.

"Any news about George Burgiss?" Salsa asked Rick.

"Yeah, have you caught him yet?" Lila's frown deepened. *Bikerboy* had always been Lila's prime suspect.

Again Rick hung his head. "Sorry, no. Burgiss has disappeared from the face of the earth, so we screwed up again."

Salsa agreed the cops had screwed up, but she decided not to pile on. Rick was already sufficiently beaten down from flogging himself. Since Lila had landed in the hospital, Salsa had adjusted her opinion of Rick. At the moment, he seemed to be a lousy policeman, but obviously, he still cared deeply for Red. Salsa was certain that Gina had given Rick hell on steroids for losing Red. The only person Gina was likely to blame more than Rick was Red herself. That had always been the issue between Red and Gina, hadn't it? Now that Red had again placed herself in harm's way with disastrous consequences, Gina must be crazy with grief and fury.

"Don't you have a plane to meet?" Lila asked Rick.

"Right, Red's dad."

Moments later, Rick slunk from the room like he was going to a funeral, and once he was gone, Salsa sat on the edge of Lila's bed.

"I don't know what to think," Salsa said, choking back tears.

"Best not to think at all," Lila gently took hold of Salsa's arm, coaxing her to lie down beside her.

"Close your eyes and rest with me for now. It will still hurt as bad tomorrow, but as my favorite heroine once said: *Tomorrow is another day.*"

Chapter Forty-nine

The next voice that swam into Red's nightmare was female. Summer's hoarse whisper brought her fully awake with hope, but when she flexed her wrists and ankles, they were still bound. Nothing had changed.

"God, Red, I'm so sorry!" Summer moaned. "It's all my fault. I told him you'd go to my apartment to find me, and he caught you there."

As Red struggled to concentrate, she felt a lethargy in her muscles and a fogginess in her head that went way beyond fatigue. She'd been drugged, and by the drunken way Summer's tongue tripped on words, so had she. On a positive note, the pain in the small of Red's back had receded, so the monster's stun gun had done no permanent damage.

"Summer, did he hurt you?"

Her friend began to weep. "I can't think straight, but I know he injected me with something that morning he took me, and it made me feel numb all over."

"Did he rape you?"

Summer cried harder. "Not unless he did it when I was asleep. I know he wants to, but he's scared." Summer's tone was scornful. "The lunatic says I'm like a dirty house, and he can't come in until I'm clean."

"Jesus, he's insane! When did you realize I was here?"

Summer coughed, then swallowed. "I heard him drag you in sometime last night...I think. Or it could've been last week. I'm living in the Twilight Zone here."

Red understood. She too had lost all sense of time, and with no windows, she had no idea if it was day or night. "Where the hell are we?"

"Not sure. By the way Master describes it, I'd guess we're in the mountains."

"What's with this *Master* crap?"

As Summer spoke, Red noticed her breathing was shallow and restricted. Next Summer suffered a sudden spasm that shook the mattress, which was suspended near Red's face.

"Oh, please, Red. If he tells you to call him Master or Lord or even Jesus Christ, you better say it like you mean it, or he'll hurt you real bad."

Red waited until the bed stopped shaking. "What's he done to you?"

"Can't talk about it."

Even though she'd been only half conscious, Red believed she would have heard screams or a struggle if the monster had abused Summer on the bed. "Did he take you out of this room?"

"He took me to the bathroom!" She sobbed.

Summer's misery convinced Red all over again that somehow she had to escape and kill this bastard.

"And no matter what..." Summer choked. "Don't swallow the big pill. It'll knock you out cold. Spit it out or hide it under your tongue. Once it made me throw up, so then he had to give me the bath."

Red mumbled something she hoped sounded encouraging, but she had no control over this situation. Whether or not Red avoided the pill, she stank to high heaven, so sooner or later, the monster would bathe her. "Where is he now?"

"He says he meditates and reads the Bible, but I think he's off eating or playing with himself," Summer spat out the words. "He'll come back all excited, so no matter what, pretend you're asleep."

Summer was only trying to help, but her submissive attitude toward their abductor was infuriating. If he came for Red, she'd kick him in the balls rather than be led to the damn bath, which sounded more like a torture chamber. She'd scratch his eyes out before succumbing to the Stockholm syndrome, as Summer seemed to have done.

"By the way, Summer, he didn't grab me at your apartment. Paul abducted me at his own house."

"Paul's house?" Summer responded dreamily.

Summer didn't know, or else she was in denial. She had obviously blocked out the true identity of their captor. By all accounts, Summer had been in love with Paul. "Have you ever seen this bastard's face?"

Red waited while Summer endured another coughing spell so intense it seemed she'd cough her lungs out. As Summer tried to catch her breath, Red wondered if she had contracted pneumonia lying naked on her back after the dreaded bath. Some drugs also suppressed the immune system, so what the hell was the jerk dosing her with?

"Sorry, no, he always wears that mask."

Summer then launched into a breathless, nonsensical description of the monster as a hairless monkey with huge, colorful hands and a cross burned into his skin. As she continued to rant, her voice got weaker, and her words lost all context. By the time Summer faded completely and stopped speaking, Red felt desperately alone, and it was more obvious than ever that they had to escape. If not for Red's sake, then for Summer's because she was seriously ill.

Red fought despair by jerking at the wires binding her to the bed. For a while, the pain kept her anger alive, but then she realized the wires had broken her skin. She was bleeding and cold.

When the door finally opened and the monster's bare feet silently entered the room, Red shivered uncontrollably, as though the chill had blown in along with him. He was singing a hymn, high and off-key, in a voice barely human, as though his vocal cords had been altered by design, or by drugs, and Red recalled that strange, robotic sound from when he was reading the Bible. No wonder Summer didn't recognize the man, if indeed he was a man.

Terrified by the unearthly presence, Red closed her eyes and willed her body to stop trembling, so as not to attract his attention. But when he knelt on the floor beside her and she smelled his odd scent, oily and sweet, she knew she had failed.

Chapter Fifty

Captain Maxwell Calendar had not changed since Rick last saw him three years ago, before Gina and Red split up. Back then, Max had been more like a father to Rick than his own dad had ever been, but Max had been cold and disapproving toward Gina. He'd even taken Rick to Florida, where they'd kayaked on the brackish inlets and gone for long walks along the Gulf of Mexico, but today all that was history.

"How could you let this happen?" Max demanded as Rick navigated his Crown Vic through the loops of traffic at Charlotte Douglas Airport and headed back toward the city.

A shameful heat crept up Rick's neck. "I screwed up, Max. The answer was there all along, but I just didn't see it."

The retired police profiler shook his head of bushy white hair and frowned straight ahead through the windshield. His intense blue eyes were remarkably like Red's, but unlike Red, who had always guarded her fair complexion from the sun, Max's face had acquired the patina of creased mahogany leather after years of tropical exposure.

"So you believe this Paul Miller is our man?"

"Yes, sir, I do. All the evidence points in his direction."

"But where the hell is he?" Max gave voice to Rick's thought but neglected to complete the sentence—*and where the hell has he taken Red and Summer?*

Rick was living the agony of losing his partner, but Max had lost his daughter, which was unimaginable. In spite of Max's ridiculous rejection of Gina, Red and Max had remained soulmates, a relationship Rick envied. Their closeness had made Gina extremely jealous at times, while Rick had a deep-seeded fear that he'd never be smart enough or tough enough to rise to the professional heights of Max at the top of his game.

"What about the women's hard drives?" Max asked.

"We're on it. The techs have analyzed the internet activity on all five women's computers. All had positive hits on DATESCAPE, but we knew that already. Unfortunately, it would require an act of Congress with permission from the Supreme Court to compel DATESCAPE to give up more personal information about their clients than what's already in the public domain, that is, the profiles already online."

"Doesn't matter," Max interrupted. "We know DATESCAPE's the link, and I Goddamn guarantee Miller's hard drive will show hits not only on *our* women, but many others."

"Yes, sir." Rick had brought Max up to speed on every detail of the case from Boots's murder, Salsa's encounter with *Bikerboy*, and the attack on Lila, to the abductions of Summer and Red. "I still think that photograph is important."

"Yes and no." Max growled. He leaned forward in his seat belt, snagged his briefcase out from under his feet, and lifted out a typed report. "My pals in Tampa got busy and generated this history on Mr. Miller. It includes every fucking detail of the sorry asshole's life—every school he attended, every bill and credit card—more than his poor dead mama would ever want to know..." Max gave the paper a vicious flick with his fingernail. "And everything I read here tells me Miller fits the profile—from his lack of commitment to a woman to his devotion to the Baptist Church, where the little fuck wanted to be a minister. Even the timelines *could* work..."

"But?" Rick sensed that Max was unconvinced.

"It all proves nothing." Max shoved the report back in the briefcase and stowed it away. "Didn't your department tell you? Miller's alibi checks out. He did attend the teachers' conference in Raleigh, but naturally, none of the organizers can vouch that he attended the classes. He could've signed in, then split, for all they know."

"You got this information from the CMPD?" Rick gripped the steering wheel harder.

"Sure did. For the most part, your team is on the ball, Detective Molerno."

"Sorry, Max. I made a mistake. They took me off the case for twenty-four hours."

"I know, they told me. Suspended, right?" Max chuckled.

Was there anything Max did not know? "What about the photograph?" Rick asked defensively.

"Same deal." Max sighed. "Inconclusive. Paul Miller attended Mooresville High and the recent reunion. Likely, he took photographs that night, so possibly the reprints were gifts for the girls, nothing sinister in that."

"Bullshit." Rick ground his teeth. "I was at that bastard's house last night. I saw Red's smashed phone, saw the way the sicko lives. He did it, Max, all of it."

"You feel it in your gut, hotshot?"

"Yes, I do."

Two grown men in a pissing contest. As Rick steered into the parking lot at Carolinas Medical Center since Max had specifically requested to see Lila, the absurdity of the situation hit home. After all, Rick and Max were on the same team. Both were insanely worried about Red, both helpless to do anything about it, but was that any reason to fight? Rick glanced at Max, saw the tension coiled inside him, the blood in his eyes, and suddenly, he looked much older than his seventy-five years.

"Truce?" Rick extended his hand.

Max swatted his hand away but then winked. "Watch your driving, Molerno, or you'll be up on manslaughter charges for running down a nurse."

Rick swerved, narrowly missing a Pink Lady volunteer, then managed to park without incident. As both men exhaled, Rick felt the animosity melt away, but then Max checked his watch.

"It's one thirty," Max said. "She's been missing what, fourteen hours?"

"Maybe more." Rick struggled to put it together. Last evening, he'd left Lila's party around six thirty. Red must have arrived at Summer's around seven thirty, then left by eight. So likely she'd been abducted by nine last night, meaning she'd been gone, as Max said, about fourteen hours. "But Summer was taken Friday morning before work, so she's been gone almost thirty hours."

They sat together in miserable silence and watched the Saturday afternoon visitors stream into the hospital. Neither cop wanted to state the obvious, but they knew the statistics. In cases involving sex-related abductions, most victims did not survive the first three hours. After twenty-four hours, the odds dropped to less than one percent that the victim would be found alive.

More than likely, both women were already dead.

Chapter Fifty-one

Gina Molerno slumped in Red's patio chair. She was oblivious to the sun beating down on her head, the flies buzzing around the toast she hadn't eaten, and the upbeat chatter of residents from Red's complex driving off to their carefree Saturday pursuits. Ever since Rick called with the news of Red's abduction, she'd felt like she'd been chained underwater, unable to breathe or even drown—the preferable outcome.

Her brother's call woke her from a deep sleep. Her dreams should have been heavy with dire premonitions, but instead, Gina had dreamed of making love to Red in the bed still perfumed with her lover's unique scent—part Irish Spring, part sex. In Gina's fantasy, it did not matter that they'd argued yesterday, that her last words to Red were shouted in anger because she knew Red would be back and they'd make up with a fervor more erotic than the dream.

But their sweet reunion never happened.

Gina couldn't think straight. She dragged herself into the air-conditioned living room, flung herself down on the couch and clutched her cellphone to her breast. She couldn't eat, sleep, or drink herself to death. She could only wait for the phone to ring.

Finally, it did—Lila and Salsa calling from the hospital. Gina heard the grief and uncertainty in Salsa's voice as she begged Gina to join them. Salsa claimed she wanted them to wait together for the resolution—

solidarity in sisterhood and all that shit. They meant well, but seeing Lila, broken and emotionally fragile in her bed, would only serve to remind Gina how sick and brutal this monster was. And now he had Gina's beloved Red—and Summer.

So Gina politely refused their invitation, then sank into a memory of Red's recovery in a hospital bed after a bullet had shattered her leg. Gina had stuck with Red during the long months of healing and rehab. Gina had said her prayers and shed all her tears. But then when Red got better and announced that she was returning to police work, to risk injury and death all over again, Gina had imploded and bowed out of Red's life—until now.

What the hell was she doing here? Living in Red's house, eating her food, and sleeping in her bed? This time, Gina feared neither prayers nor tears would save her lover, so when the phone rang again, she almost didn't answer. But the caller ID said it was Rick.

"Any news?" Gina was terrified to hear his answer.

"Nothing new on Red and Summer, but I picked Max Calendar up at the airport, and we just arrived at the hospital."

"Good for you." Gina hated Captain Calendar as much as she loved his daughter. The man was brilliant, Red adored him, but he was a fucking homophobe. During their eleven years together, he'd made Gina's life miserable—like a nagging toothache.

"I'm sorry, sis, but I had to call him. He had a right to know."

Grudgingly, Gina knew Rick was right, but she wanted no contact with the man. She bit her tongue and remained silent.

"Max is going to help find Red," Rick soldiered on. "And there's something else…"

Gina held her breath.

"While Captain Calendar's in town, he was hoping to crash at Red's condo. Is that okay?"

Wiping away tears, Gina put on her big girl pants and came to a decision. "No problem. Tell Calendar he can stay as long as he wants because I'm leaving."

Chapter Fifty-two

Red flinched at the killer's touch. His fingers felt hot against her chilled skin as he methodically untwisted the wires binding her hands and feet. She avoided looking into the eyes behind the wooly mask because such directness could seem confrontational to someone with a deranged mind. Instead, she took Summer's advice and remained passive.

He abruptly stopped singing a hymn. "You stink. Can you walk?"

His voice was high, almost robotic. He was deliberately altering it, so as not to be recognized.

"Did you hear me, bitch?"

Suddenly, he struck her across the face with the back of his hand. The sharp pain vibrated to the back of her skull, and she tasted blood in her mouth. Every instinct, all her training, screamed for her to fight back, but she restrained herself. Due to her weakened condition, she'd be no match for the fucker. She glanced at his hairless chest, branded with a scar shaped like a cross from Lila's torch. Summer was right, he did look like a monkey. With body hair, he'd definitely resemble an ape.

"Yeah, I can walk," she answered. He yanked her to her feet, where she swayed on wobbly legs.

Another reason for Red's hesitation was the gun tucked in the back of his waistband, out of reach. Her gun! Seeing her faithful Smith & Wesson in the killer's possession was the final affront. She suspected he knew how to use the weapon but not as well as she did. If the slightest opportunity presented itself, she'd reclaim it and blast him through the gates of hell.

"Move your ass." He roughly maneuvered her out in front of him, stiff-arming her to walk several paces ahead toward the open door. The position made it impossible to grab the gun.

Red stole a peek at Summer, but the sight of her naked, bruised body and the terrified plea in her blue eyes caused her to quickly look away.

"Where are we going?"

He grunted and pushed her forward.

Red tried to take it all in—a small antique bureau against the wall opposite the bed. A pitcher, plastic cup, steel wash bowl, bottle of pills, and what appeared to be a hypodermic needle were neatly laid out on its surface. Tools of the killer's trade, she thought grimly as he shoved her through the door. Summer said he'd injected her the morning of her abduction. With a needle like that one? What the hell was in it? And what about that ridiculous old wedding gown hanging on the closet door? Had he stolen it from a Tennessee Williams stage set?

As Red stumbled into the hallway, blinding light stunned her vision. Although the shades were drawn in the adjoining rooms, she realized it was daytime—early afternoon by the slant of the sun. Had she been captured only the night before?

Inevitably, they moved into a large bathroom at the end of the hall, and the monster locked the door behind them. It wasn't the torture room Red had visualized, with cracked tiles and a grubby shower, but rather a state-of-the-art space. A modern garden tub was already filled with swirling, scented water, while a silent exhaust fan kept the spotless mirrored wall free of steam.

The killer touched a button near the door, and organ music piped into the room. Did the maniac intend to bathe her or baptize her? She noticed an open Bible and candles set up like a shrine on the granite countertop between the twin sinks, and had she not been terrified, she would have laughed out loud at the absurdity of the scene.

"Get in!"

He pushed Red toward the tub, causing her to crack her bad knee against its porcelain rim. The old wound hurt like hell, but the pain only sharpened her desire to strike back. When he swatted Red's bare bottom to urge her on, her hands knotted into fists, and she longed to pound him within an inch of his life.

As she climbed in, she caught her nude reflection in the mirror and had never felt more exposed. While the monster rocked on his heels, enjoying the view of her backside, she imagined the leer on his face beneath the cowardly mask. She wanted to rip it off and claw his prying eyes out.

She ground her teeth to keep from spitting out obscenities as the pervert threw a washcloth and soap at her and said, "Begin thy cleansing." When Red attempted to lower herself into the bath, he commanded her to keep standing, forcing her to bend and dip, an indignity he seemed to relish.

Scalding water burned her lower legs, while goose bumps prickled her upper body. And as Red raised her arms, she gauged the distance between her and the gun but realized a lunge was impossible. Somehow, she'd have to lure the monster closer.

"Allow me to assist," he said. But before he approached, he pointedly lifted the Smith & Wesson from his waistband and set it on a shelf, far out of reach. He snatched the washcloth from Red's hand.

She heard heavy breathing under his mask and realized the animal was sexually aroused. His voice dropped a full octave to a hoarse growl, and she figured it was now or never. When he dipped and lathered the cloth, then reached between her legs, she stiffened her hand and chopped him in the throat.

He reeled backward coughing but quickly recovered his balance and came at her in a rage. He locked her in a bear hug that momentarily knocked the air from her lungs. She leaned over and bit his shoulder, drawing blood, and he roared in fury, cursing words that were far from biblical. Clenched like wrestlers, Red could do little against his superior strength but bite him again and claw his back with her fingernails.

The monster howled in pain, drew back his fist, and slammed it into her stomach. When she doubled over, he got his hands around her neck and began to squeeze. Already weakened by the long ordeal, Red's knees buckled as she gasped for air, and when she sank into the burning water, his fingers became a hangman's noose.

Red was losing consciousness. Would she be strangled or drowned? At the last minute, he released her. The back of her head cracked against the hard porcelain as water closed in above her face. Reflexively, she closed her mouth and held her breath. At first, she saw stars, like in the comic books, but then she saw his huge hands playing in the swirling water. Like Summer had said, there were colorful dots of primary red, blue, and yellow on his palms and knuckles.

Where had Red seen this before?

As her hair fanned out in the whirlpool, like a blood red stain, suddenly she knew. The monster was an artist, and the sickly-sweet smell on him was linseed oil. Jesus Christ Almighty!

The knowledge fueled Red's will to survive, and her face exploded up and out of the water. Taking him by surprise, she grabbed onto his mask with both hands and jerked his head downward, smashing his forehead on the rim.

Coughing, screaming, gasping for air, she repeated the attack. The second pounding sent the monster to his knees. They locked arms. She used him like a brace to leverage herself up and over the edge, and suddenly, they were rolling together on the floor. When he went for Red's throat, she went for his face and managed to work the mask up and off his head.

For a split second, they froze. The pressure eased on her neck as they gaped at each other. Sam Redbird's forehead gushed blood from its impact with the tub. The blood flowed into his eyes but did not diminish the hatred she saw there. It was the primal lust of the predator, the *Paintercat*, and Red fully understood that if she didn't kill him, then he'd kill her.

Chapter Fifty-three

All hell broke loose when Rick and Max stepped off the elevator on Lila's floor. The rookie cop who'd been guarding Lila barked into his radio, requesting backup. The rookie was screaming for the security guards on the first level to use the stairwell and join him on the eighth floor ASAP.

"What the fuck?" Max's white eyebrows shot up. He'd been trailing Rick through the labyrinth of the medical center, but now he shoved Rick aside for a better view. "It looks like your officer's in trouble."

Jockeying past Max to retake the lead, Rick saw young Joey Janowski waving his pistol at the emergency stairs. The staircase was walled with safety glass, and far below, the hospital rent-a-cops were climbing upward like ants in a maze.

"I saw him, Detective Molerno!" Janowski shouted. "It was him, the man in the APB, the dude with the red hair!"

"You sure?" Rick's adrenaline kicked into overdrive. Paul Miller was on the premises.

"Yeah, he was headed for Miss Lila's room bold as brass when I spotted him. When I drew my weapon and told him to stop, he turned tail and ran down the stairs."

"Shit!" Max cursed. "The dumb bastard's come back to finish the job."

Rick agreed. Did the stupid fuck actually think he could take another whack at Lila unnoticed? The newspapers had been following the story since Lila was attacked, and lately, the reporters had taken a warm and fuzzy slant about how well Lila was recovering, how she was talking and remembering everything. No doubt Miller feared she'd identify him unless he took matters into his own hands.

Following Janowski as he entered the stairwell, it occurred to Rick that with the security guys charging up from below and the CMPD closing in from above, Miller would be caught like the monkey in the middle. Unless, of course, Miller realized his predicament and ducked out one of the many doors leading to the interim levels.

Janowski was panting hard as he clattered down the metal steps and waved his gun like a madman.

"For Christ's   sake, don't shoot him!" Rick yelled. If Miller had stashed Red and Summer away in some remote hideaway, they'd never find them if Miller was dead.

"Holster your weapon, son!" Max shouted at the rookie, but Janowski was on a tear. The kid likely figured catching a serial killer would be a giant step up the ladder of his career, and he wasn't about to let a superior officer like Rick steal his glory.

Rick and Max were close on his heels, but still Rick saw no sign of Miller below. Taking a chance, he tapped Janowski on the shoulder at level five and pointed at the glass door. "He went that way. I saw his head moving down the hall!"

"Are you positive?" Sweat poured down Janowski's pink cheeks.

"Positive. Go get him, Officer…"

Taking the bait, Joey Janowski shoved through onto level five, while Rick and Max kept climbing lower.

"You're a tricky son of a bitch, Molerno," Max said.

"Thanks, I'll take that as a compliment."

"You do realize you just sent our only firepower on a wild goose chase?"

"I realize that, Max, so start praying Paul Miller is unarmed."

Rick and Max were working like a team now, just like in the good old days when they'd taken a two-man kayak down the Peace River, paddling and dipping in perfect rhythm.

"Did you see that?" Rick nodded at the slowly closing door two flights down.

"Yeah, buddy. We're on the right track."

Advancing more slowly now, Rick felt Max's hot breath on the back of his neck as they arrived on the landing at level three. Rick paused to peer through the chicken-wire glass window and was startled to see Miller only two yards away, fast-walking toward a red exit sign.

"That's him," he whispered to Max, and then he shoved through the swinging metal door and shouted, "Hold it right there, Miller! Police!"

Instead of fleeing like before, Miller stopped moving and slowly faced them. His fair complexion was blotchy pink, but every hair was in place, his white dress shirt perfectly pressed, as always.

"What do you people want?" he whined in an unnaturally high voice.

"Show me your hands!" Rick bellowed.

Miller trembled violently as he held out his arms. He had a cheap gift shop bouquet clutched in his right fist.

"Why'd you run?" Rick demanded as he strode up to Miller, who was obviously unarmed and seemingly harmless.

Miller squawked, "Some crazy man with a gun was chasing me."

Rick realized that since the rookie was in plain clothes, it was possible Miller didn't know he was a cop, but the Mr. Innocent routine made Rick want to strangle him on the spot. His heart thudded double-time, and his fists coiled with rage.

"Where is Detective Red Calendar?" Rick grabbed Miller's wrist, and the bouquet fell to the shiny linoleum floor. At the same time, Rick sensed the hospital security guards had arrived. Two guards had followed them in from the stairwell, and two more exited the elevator at the end of the hall.

"Go easy, Molerno." One of the guards moved in close. "We've got him."

"What the hell are you talking about?" Miller struggled in Rick's grip. "I don't know anything about Red."

"You came here to pay Lila a visit." Max crowded in. "You figured it would be easy to finish her off when she was flat on her back, without a welding torch to defend herself."

"Are you nuts?" Miller's gaze flipped wildly back and forth from Rick to Max. "My neighbors told me some Charlotte cop came around. What's your problem?" He broke loose and gave Rick a shove.

Rick shoved back hard. Miller staggered, lost his balance, landed on his backside, and began crabbing across the floor on all fours. Rick grabbed him by the seat of the pants, landing a few solid punches as they rolled against the wall.

"Get off him, Detective!" Suddenly, Officer Joey Janowski entered the fray, joined by the two guards. He grabbed Rick's right arm, while one of the rent-a-cops secured his left. With considerable effort, they got Rick under control and pulled him away from Miller.

"Jeez, man, I thought you were suspended," Janowski panted. "What are you doing? They'll kick you off the force."

At the moment, Rick couldn't care less if they fired his ass. All he cared about was Red—and pounding a confession out of the punk hiding behind the security guards' legs.

"Use your head, boss. The DNA results will come back soon, and we'll nail this bastard," Janowski said.

"I want my lawyer," Miller blubbered.

Throughout, Max had remained uncharacteristically subdued. What was wrong with him? Rick wondered. Didn't he care about his daughter? With two guys still pinning his arms, Rick watched in disbelief as Max crossed the hall and extended a hand of friendship to the quavering Miller.

"Let me help you up, son."

Clearly, Miller trusted this benign father figure, but when he lifted his hand to accept Max's aid, Max latched on to Miller's shirt instead. With one mighty upward thrust, Max yanked the wimp upright, tearing his buttons off. Next Max ripped the shirt open as Miller squealed in protest. Finally, Max strong-armed the prisoner around so everyone got a good look at his chest.

"I decided not to wait for the DNA results," Max said.

Rick, Janowski, and the hospital security guys

were all momentarily stunned by Max's burst of violence. They all gaped at the wriggling prisoner's bare chest. Rick saw unblemished white skin stretched across Miller's scrawny rib cage   under a thick cover of silky red hair. No burns, no scars.

"Shit," Rick muttered softly.

"Double shit," Max concurred. "I don't know what this joker's guilty of, but he sure as hell never attacked Lila." He shoved Miller toward Janowski. "He's all yours, son. Good collar. We still have the fact that Red was abducted at Miller's house, but…"

Rick mentally finished Max's thought: *but Miller's not our man.* As the depressing truth sank in and the adrenaline retreated, Rick felt like not only a fool, but a failure. They were back at square one. As he thought about Red, the shame and exhaustion overwhelmed him.

"I'm pressing charges!" Miller pointed his finger at Rick and Max. "You're both crazy."

Even Janowski seemed subdued as he read the Miranda rights to Miller, like a kid who'd found the Cracker Jack prize not to his liking. He took Miller into custody, then nodded toward Max. "Who is this guy, Molerno? Should I arrest him, too? He *did* assault the suspect."

Rick sighed. "Cut him a break, Joey. This man is Red's father, so under the circumstances, you can't blame him for acting out."

Janowski's beady little eyes narrowed as he considered his options. In the end, he shook his head and spread his hands. "I see your point. Red's good people, and I'm sorry for your loss, sir," he said to Max.

"She's missing," Rick snapped. "You make it sound like she's dead. And in case you've forgotten,

Joey, Red is my partner, so cut me some slack, too. You never saw me touch the suspect, right?"

Looking extremely uncomfortable, Janowski blushed to the roots of his blond hair. "No, sir. I didn't see nothing."

"That's what I thought. So call it in, Janowski. Do you need help getting Mr. Miller back to the station?"

"No, sir, I got it covered."

"Then what are you waiting for?" Rick turned, took hold of Max's elbow, and led him down the hall toward the elevator.

Sensing another explosion, Max reversed roles, took Rick's elbow, and firmly steered him aboard the elevator, which arrived just in time. Once they were safely aboard, heading back to Lila's floor, Max sadly shook his head. "Look, I'm sorry Miller wasn't the one. They'll have to cut him loose. I thought we were one step closer, but instead, we're two steps back." He looked Rick in the eye. "We need to look at any men my daughter met online."

Chapter Fifty-four

Leveraging up on his elbows, Redbird looked around the familiar room and realized he was still among the living, neither heaven nor hell. And his ultimate prize, the red-haired harlot, lay on her face only three feet away. Her head was bloodied by the broken urn he had thrown. His head was bloodied by the beating she gave him at the tub, yet he had prevailed.

Was she dead? Slithering across the floor, he held two fingers to the pulse at the base of her bruised neck and found life, but he couldn't afford to let Red live now. She'd seen him without the mask.

Like a child deprived of the toy he most coveted, he was deeply disappointed—and angry. By the spirited way she fought, breaking Red would've been the most rousing challenge ever. Judy the librarian was easy; she'd admitted her sins without a fuss. Boots had fought back, and he'd been forced to kill her prematurely. Summer was guilty by association. She hung out with the other harlots; he'd been following Red and had seen them all together at Birkdale Village. He'd checked out Summer's shameless profile on DATESCAPE, so Summer must also repent.

But for now, he'd eventually have to kill Red and dispose of the body, a near impossible task here in Mother's land of the living dead, where the proximity of neighbors made him feel like an animal at the zoo. Where the nosy old folks watched his every move.

But Redbird had options. He still had time to experience the thrill of Red's conversion, her tearful submission to God's will as she confessed her sins under Redbird's strict tutelage. Emboldened by the thought, he clamped his jaw shut and endured the agony as he struggled to his feet. He waited for the wave of nausea to pass, then stepped across Red's body to survey the damage in the mirror. *Dear Lord, give me strength.* A large wound stretched horizontally across his forehead, and his nose was broken. His face was caked in dried blood, and one of his canine teeth had cracked inside his mouth, penetrating his inner lip. The tooth repair would be costly, even if one of his former colleagues gave him a professional discount.

Redbird frowned at his once-handsome face, then he gave Red a swift kick in the side. His ribs screamed in protest, so undoubtedly, the hellion had broken one or two. He wasn't a vain man—*remove far from me vanity and lies*—but he did depend on his good looks to attract sinners unto him.

So he was damaged, but the warrior's cross still glowed on his chest, under the bite marks on his shoulder, and the cross was his to bear. And bear it he would, until his mission was complete. Like his namesake, Samuel, who ministered to the Lord even as a child, Sam Redbird cleansed his face and hands. He wrapped his ribs with an elastic support bandage and injected his throbbing mouth with an appropriate dose of Novocain. Unfortunately, the dose he'd given Summer to subdue her had been too strong. It had suppressed her respiration and over-stressed her heart, yet Summer would survive long enough to repent. She would still be in the bridal bed when he returned after dealing with Red. But in the meantime, Summer must be sustained and restrained.

He gently spread antibiotic cream on his face, applied sterile gauze, then opened the drawer under the sink where he kept his supply and donned a freshly washed mask. Stepping over Red, he left the room and locked the door behind him.

Once Summer was secured, Redbird prepared the truck for one last transport, this time to his hunting cabin deep in the mountains above Boone. It was the home of his heart, a small log structure, reachable only by an abandoned timber trail. It was off the grid, the lair of the *Paintercat*, where he killed deer and made art.

Two Demerol later, the dream became a hallucination in living color. He clothed Red in one of his old running suits, rolled socks onto her feet, and was able to lift her dead weight with ease. As he drove northeast, from highway to secondary roads, from day into night, *Paintercat* was invincible. He dodged the oncoming headlights and soared above the yellow ribbon of the centerline. Red taillights burned in a cobalt blue sky—the primary colors of his paintings. God's golden finger pointed the way into the lost woods.

The final retreat.

Chapter Fifty-five

Most critically ill patients die in the early hours of morning, two to three a.m. At least that was the theory of Lila's spinster aunt, the queen of all things morbid. So as Lila lay awake, recalling how her aunt loved to take pictures at funerals, never weddings, she was suddenly fully awake and turned on the light beside her hospital bed.

She glanced at the watch Salsa had brought her. It was after three a.m., so Lila wouldn't die tonight. It seemed as good a time as any to finish reading the report Rick had left with her. He'd given a copy to Salsa, too, so they could both peruse the printouts taken from the TLC women's computers. These included internet logs detailing every communication going out and coming into the women's email, complete with original texts and responses. While this seemed like a gross invasion of privacy that offended every liberal bone in Lila's sorry body, it also titillated her curiosity.

Naturally, she began by reviewing her own history, and much to her relief, she hadn't written anything too incriminating. Aside from a little casual flirting with *Waterspirit* on DATESCAPE and the renewal of her subscription to *Lesbian Connection* magazine, her personal report only made her blush once.

Next, of course, Lila pried into Salsa's email, hoping nothing would make her excessively jealous. She also hoped Salsa had written something extra nice about Lila to someone—whomever that might be. Instead of anything juicy, however, she was disappointed to find a number of recipe exchanges between La Hacienda and other Mexican restaurants, mostly establishments on the Left Coast specializing in organic menus. BOR-ING. Salsa supported the GRRCC, a golden retriever rescue club in Charlotte, and this was more interesting since their mutual pets, Georgia and Taco, were both rescues. Finally, Lila read the notes to and from *Bikerboy* on DATESCAPE and got the green-eyed jealousy jolt she'd feared. So she stopped. Who needed it? And what right did she have, really, to be so possessive?

After Boots's history, Lila gave up reading altogether. Not only had it been unbearably sad reliving Boots's full-of-life personality in her enthusiastic communications, but it was depressing to be the voyeur in Boots's very active love life. Lila recognized some of the dates' names, like *Avatar*, the last man Boots met online, but the other long string of men Boots had dated and bedded were total strangers. To each her own.

Picking up where she left off, Lila took a sip of water and turned to Summer's and Red's files. That afternoon during their visit from Rick and Max, who were both considerably shaken by their encounter with Paul Miller, Max had been particularly eager for Salsa and Lila to check out the files:

"That's why I wanted to see you today," Max had explained, shoving the reports into their hands. "I was hoping you two could take a look and shed some light. After all, you girls know each other better than anyone."

"Good to see you again, too, Max," Lila

responded wryly. She'd had nothing against Red's dad when they were in high school, but Red had mentioned in emails how abysmally Max had treated Gina when she was with Red. Lila was unsure if Max had a problem with gays in general or just Gina.

"So this is an official visit?" Salsa grinned. "Silly me, I thought you came to catch up with my scintillating personality."

Max actually blushed to the roots of his white hair. "Yeah, sure, that too…" he stammered.

Lila couldn't help herself. "Say, Max, isn't it great that Red and Gina are back together? I haven't known Red to be so happy in years."

Captain Calendar's blush faded to a sickly shade of gray as he gave Rick a questioning look. When Rick nodded, the fearless profiler seemed to shrink into himself. Max cleared his throat. "I don't know what to say, except I'm sorry. I was an asshole regarding Gina and Red. I was wrong. In fact, I always liked Gina…" He again glanced at Rick. "I know they were good together, and I apologize for my ignorant behavior."

Rick seemed stunned. After catching his breath, Rick said, "Don't apologize to us, Max. You need to apologize to Gina and Red."

"God willing, I'll get a chance to do just that."

Lila shook her head as she opened the binder to the last two reports. Red's dad had been a favorite in high school. All the girls loved Max's gruff manner and profane language and had teased him even then. So they all felt betrayed when they heard he had rejected Red and Gina. Had Max changed? Had he "evolved" on the issue of gay rights, like most of America? Lila sincerely hoped so. Because they were all older, not necessarily wiser, and their present crisis was no laughing matter.

They'd all need to pull together to get Red and Summer back.

"I can't believe Miller is innocent," Rick had said that afternoon as he paced the small room, blaming himself for every wrong turn the investigation had taken. "Obviously, he didn't attack *you*, Lila. The lack of burns on his chest proves it. But Miller might be guilty of all the rest."

Max laid his big hand on Rick's shoulder. "Cross Miller off your list, son, he's not the one."

Lila and Salsa agreed, and while Lila hated to admit it, she'd come to believe that *Bikerboy* was also a dead end. Lila concurred with Max, that if they were going to find a new lead, it was likely hidden somewhere in the data from the computers.

"We can't go charging off half-cocked anymore," Max told Rick. "Especially now that you're suspended from the force for six more hours."

"Like I give a damn?" Rick had shouted.

Max winked at the women. "Rick's temper has put *him* out of commission, but *I*, on the other hand, am a free agent, and no one tells *me* what to do."

As the men prepared to leave, Lila was amazed that Max, who used to be as volatile as a lit fuse, had such a calming influence on Rick. Still Max, always the outlaw, was likely to take matters into his own hands, so in spite of his advanced age, Lila was oddly comforted to have the renegade on their team.

Lila adjusted her pillows and skimmed past Summer's report. Now that Paul had been eliminated, Lila believed the answer lay somewhere in Red's online activity. All day, she'd been getting bad vibes concerning Red's abduction. When Lila touched Red's dossier, the vibes got stronger, and her pulse rate accelerated. She turned pages directly to DATESCAPE and began to read. Although Red was totally opposed to internet dating, Lila knew she'd gone online to look for clues to Boots's killer and connected with some dude called *Paintercat*.

Suddenly, the text beneath Lila's fingers burned up through her arm and exploded in her chest. Was she having a heart attack? When she turned the page to *Paintercat*'s art and then to his headshot, she immediately recognized Sam Redbird. Next she visualized him with a naked, hairless torso, five colorful scarves, and a heavy gold cross. She saw little droplets of spit spray through the mouth of his mask as he lifted the steel pipe high above his head.

The report slid from her lap and landed on the floor, but somehow, Lila pressed the emergency code button near her fingertips. As the pain got worse, she felt hands all over her body, and someone gave her an injection. Lapsing into semi-consciousness, the pain blessedly subsiding, Lila's clarity was astounding. Her mind was like static electricity, fireworks that finally coalesced into a single beam of light.

Red had never told Lila she was dating Sam Redbird, and Lila had never told Red how many times she had rejected Sam's violent art. If Lila had known, she would have warned her friend about the hatred in his soul.

While the medics worked their magic, determining that Lila had suffered neither a heart attack nor a stroke, all that mattered was the phone just out of reach on her night stand. She began swatting the hands away, and as soon as she could speak, Lila screamed to the orderly that she needed to make a call. When they tried to shush and placate her, Lila reared up on her elbows.

"Listen, you fuckers, bring me the damn phone right now, or I'll hold my breath and die on the spot!"

It worked. The orderly quickly found Rick's mobile number on the business card stapled inside the report, and then he dialed. Rick answered immediately, and the orderly placed the phone in Lila's hand, helping her hold it to her mouth and ear.

"What's up?" Rick was half-asleep.

"I hope you're off suspension," Lila gasped, "because I know who took Red!"

Chapter Fifty-six

If Red didn't kill Redbird, then he would kill her. She recalled escaping *Paintercat's* chokehold as they fought on the bathroom floor. She had made it to her feet and was running toward the shelf holding the gun when he threw something at the back of her head. She slipped on a wet spot, but after that, her memory died.

Now, as she listened to the rumble of his truck tires pounding uneven ground, she realized the monster was still alive, and they were on the road again. She had the mother of all headaches, and her body felt like he'd backed the truck over it a couple of times before they got underway. Jesus, Mary, and Joseph! Was he unstoppable? Like the bloody Energizer bunny?

Red knew she had inflicted major damage during their tussle on the bathroom floor, but now he was hauling her off somewhere new and driving like a madman. The truck swerved wildly back and forth, its headlights jumping up and down as they climbed what seemed to be a mountain to nowhere. Had Sam Redbird lost his mind? Or maybe he was badly hurt, which was entirely possible, and no longer in control of his motor functions. If this were the case, she prayed the mountain had guardrails.

Hurt or high on drugs, Redbird was definitely slipping because this time he had neglected to bind Red's hands or feet. That was okay by her. Either he'd left in a tearing hurry, or he figured she was out for the count. *No such luck, asshole.*

In her previous life, Red couldn't cry, but now she couldn't stop. In spite of the tears blinding her, she was determined to kill the monster as soon as he came for her. When she thought about Boots, Lila, and especially Summer, tied naked and helpless to that bed, she vowed to avenge them all—even if she had to rush through bullets from her own gun to kill him.

As the terrain got rougher, *Paintercat* slowed down but not much. Branches from low-hanging trees pummeled the lid of Red's box, and she rolled around like a bruised marble when he took the curves. But at least with her hands free, she could guard against the worst punishment. When the vehicle finally came to a full stop, she heard him drunkenly singing a disjointed version of *Abide with Me* and guessed his words were slurred not by alcohol, but more likely by painkillers. Could dentists prescribe controlled substances? She figured they could.

As *Paintercat* slammed the door of the driver's seat and made his way back to the tailgate, Red did a quick inventory of her condition and the odds. Aside from the headache, when she ran her hands up and down her limbs, she encountered no unusual pain other than the general fatigue wrapped around her like a heavy shroud. Close as she could figure, she hadn't eaten in two days, and instead of solid sleep, she'd been unnaturally comatose much of that time. He had dressed her in a flannel running suit and a long-sleeved jacket with a hoodie—hot as hell in August. And instead of shoes, she wore knit athletic socks—not ideal foot gear for   rugged mountain terrain. Her clothing alone stacked the odds against her, but the clincher was the gun. If *Paintercat* still had her Smith

& Wesson, biting and clawing wouldn't cut it.

She heard him fall against the truck's hatchback, and he cursed as he fumbled with the lock, confirming her assessment that he was impaired in some way. Still, without a weapon, Red stood no chance of escaping alive. Making a snap decision, she opted to play possum and see what happened. If he was drugged, he might not realize she was faking. At the very least, attempting to haul her from the vehicle would make his life a misery. There would be plenty of physical contact, maybe an opportunity to reach inside his waistband for the gun and gain an advantage.

Suddenly, the hatch sighed open. *Paintercat* lowered the tailgate, and his big hands closed around Red's ankles. She willed herself to go limp and tried not to respond in any way as he dragged her out. The motion caused the jacket to ride up toward her shoulders, and her bare back scraped against the steel ribbing of the floor. A strand of her hair snagged on a bolt and was torn out without ceremony, but still she did not scream. Luckily, the night outside was dark as pitch, so he couldn't see her grimace, but if the bastard dropped her on the road on her poor abused head, she'd holler loud enough to wake the Cherokee dead, whose spirits undoubtedly roamed these woods.

Thankfully, *Paintercat* pulled her off the truck with only minor insults to the heels of her feet, which fell deadweight and bounced on the dirt. Huffing and puffing, he was running out of gas and stank like a locker room as he hooked his hands under her armpits and pulled her across roots that tugged at her clothing. Next he dragged her through a blanket of pine needles. Twice he stopped to rest, panting and coughing, but he didn't loosen his grip on her.

Finally, they arrived at what felt like a crude set of steps, which presented a logistical problem for her captor because Red's butt and ankles kept catching on the risers as he tried to haul her up. When he grunted and dropped her like a bag of dirty laundry and her throbbing head hit splintered wood, she could endure no more. She risked opening her eyes only a crack, and in the weak moonlight, she saw the monster doubled over on the stoop of what appeared to be a rustic log cabin. He was dry heaving, clutching his ribs, and sure enough, her gun was tucked in his waistband.

Red had to make her move. Rolling onto her stomach, she pushed up with her hands and knees. *Paintercat* was in such agony, he had not yet noticed her. Although her muscles felt like jelly, she lifted her arms, lunged forward, and tackled him just below the waist. He yelped in surprise as they went down together, toppled off the landing, then had the wind knocked out of them as they hit the hard ground.

But Red was on top. Balling her fist, she punched *Paintercat* in the face, and he yowled in pain. She pummeled his ribs, and he squealed like a pig at slaughter, but she still couldn't reach the damn gun.

In self-defense, *Paintercat* reached up, got his arms around Red, and crushed her against his chest in a bear hug, so she could throw no more punches. Suddenly, they were rolling through weeds and brambles, locked together like lovers, until they hit a fallen log.

Red reached around the fucker and found her gun. When he realized what she was doing, *Paintercat* roared and wrapped his leg across her, pinning her to the ground, but the move came too late. Her fingers closed on the rubber grip of her weapon, and she freed it, only to have the monster grasp her shooting wrist before she could fire.

But she twisted her wrist and pulled the trigger. The explosion shattered the silent void of night, and somewhere deep in the forest, an owl screeched in fright. *Paintercat* began keening. He curled into the fetal position and tucked his left hand between his knees. Near as she could tell, she'd shot his hand, maybe blown off a couple of fingers.

As Red crawled a few paces away, took a two-handed aim at his heart, her arms shook uncontrollably as she prepared to take his life. She saw his face in the moonlight. It resembled pounded red flank steak, and his eyes were stretched wide in terror.

While she hesitated, saying a silent prayer for forgiveness, suddenly, *Paintercat* cocked his knee and kicked her under the chin. She flew backward as her jaw collided with her brain. She bit her tongue, nearly severing it. Dazed and dizzy, she somehow stood upright, but when she backed up to aim again, her traitorous legs gave out, and she stumbled backward, right over the edge of a cliff.

The extreme incline sent Red barreling downward at escalating speed. Not knowing where she would land, she reached out in desperation, grabbing at small branches along the way, hoping to break her fall. Naturally, she lost her gun, but there was no going back. Finally, she crashed into a rock ledge part way down the slope and stopped.

Once she caught her breath, she looked up and saw *Paintercat* silhouetted against the dark sky at the top of the hill, howling like an injured wolf. Cradling his injured hand in the crook of his right elbow, he loped a few paces down the incline after her but quickly stumbled and gave up. Then, folded forward at the waist and swinging his good arm like a demented ape, he disappeared back over the rise in the direction of the cabin.

Red wasn't sure how long she lay against the rock recuperating. Time no longer had meaning, and while she figured she was less hurt than her pursuer, she was in no shape to wage war. She was dehydrated, her battered head was spinning to where it was impossible to think straight, her heavy clothing burned like a fever, and her feet were torn to shreds inside the ruined socks.

Sweet Jesus, she prayed, hoping the pain would go away so she could make a plan. As she stretched flat and lay still, aligning her spine and listening to the forest sounds, she heard the mournful call of a nightingale, the buzz of wood frogs, and the nearby rush of water on stones. When she was able, she crawled on all fours through the dark until she saw the sparkle of moonlight on a creek, until her fingers touched the cold, blessed water.

In some small way, Red's prayer had been answered. She dipped in and held her aching wrists in the current. It stung her scratches and cooled her pulse. When she believed her body would tolerate it, she cupped her hands and filled her mouth. First she rolled the liquid around, rinsed away the blood, and spat it out. Only then did she swallow—only a little. At first the frigid water shocked her system, and she gagged, but once it traveled down to her stomach, it seemed to spread through her capillaries, veins, and arteries like a healing life force. The more she drank, the force grew stronger, so she drank until she could hold no more.

Red washed her face and arms, dribbled the cold down her neck, through the valley between her breasts, and eventually peeled off her socks and soaked her feet. The welcome numb sensation tracked up her legs like anesthetic, so when she was ready, she carefully put the socks back on. The little protection they offered was better than nothing, and the small relief from the creek was better than a bottle of aspirin—almost—because even her headache had receded.

Yet she was still not ready. The bone-deep fatigue made it difficult to move, let alone run. Searching for her weapon in the dark was a fool's mission—hopefully, *Paintercat* would not find it first. But for now, she needed sleep.

Red got to her feet, grateful to find her limbs still worked, and holding her arms out in front defensively, she groped her way along the creek. When she walked into an area soft with pine needles and a row of wild raspberry bushes, she got down and discovered a cave-like opening in the bushes and crawled inside to shelter. Ducking under the brambles that caught at her hair, she moved in as deep as possible and lay down in her nest. It would have to do. She drove the night dangers to the back of her mind, including marauding bears and the illusive painter cat, the monster's namesake. She thought a few minutes about Gina, then closed her eyes and fell into a deep, dreamless sleep.

Chapter Fifty-seven

Rick and Max hadn't slept at all that night, so now, as they sped north toward the mountains, they sucked strong coffee and hoped the caffeine buzz would not addle their brains.

"How the hell does Sam Redbird afford three properties?" Max grumbled as Rick drove.

"He's a retired dentist, and you know how damn much they charge."

"Have you ever met this guy?" Max demanded.

"No, for Christ's sake. But an ex-cop pal of mine works as a bouncer at The Warehouse, a nightclub down in the arts district. He clued me in when Red dated the bastard."

"She dated this psycho, and you never figured him for a suspect?"

"She was doing research for work," Rick answered defensively. "So will you please lay off?"

As soon as Lila had implicated Sam Redbird with her phone call in the wee hours of last night, the entire CMPD went into high gear, concentrating on the suspect's real estate. They discovered he owned a condo in Mooresville, rented studio space in Charlotte, and had inherited a townhouse in a retirement community in Weaverville in the mountains near Asheville. He also owned a hunting cabin with no address, located in the highlands near Boone. The cops had come up empty in Mooresville and Charlotte. The Weaverville police were currently checking out the retirement community where Redbird's mother had lived until her death a little over a month ago. And now, as the sun began to rise off to the right of Interstate 77, Max and Rick were headed to the highlands and a cabin that did not appear on any map.

"I don't like the looks of that sky," Max said. "It's pink as a bloody shrimp cocktail. Where I come from, that's bad news—means a storm's coming."

"Yeah, I know. Remember the old rhyme: *Red sky at morning, sailors take warning; Red sky at night, sailors' delight.*"

"Sure, I used to quote that to Red." Max chuckled, but then both men fell silent. Neither wanted to talk about Red, yet they worried nonstop.

"So you really think Sam Redbird's the one?" Max replaced Rick's empty Styrofoam cup with a fresh, steaming coffee from the gray cardboard carrier between his feet.

"Yeah, I do," Rick answered grimly. During the raid on the dentist's home in Mooresville, Detective Logan found no incriminating evidence at first glance, but he did find plenty of potential DNA. This time, Logan did not insist on a search warrant. Instead, Logan had tagged and bagged everything from Redbird's toothbrush to his hairbrush and sent them straight to the lab.

"So they cut Paul Miller loose?" Max sipped at his coffee.

"Soon as his DNA results came in, he was home free. Turned out the little prick spent less than twenty minutes in lockup." Rick frowned at Max. "He was royally pissed. You'll be lucky if he doesn't sue your ass for that assault in the hospital."

"Hell, I'll buy him a new shirt." Max shrugged.

Rick's police band radio crackled, and an unfamiliar voice came through the static:

"Detective Molerno? Sergeant Campbell here, Weaverville PD. We have entered the suspect's home in Lone Oak Village, and we found her!"

Campbell's words so excited Rick that he swerved into the left lane directly in the path of a barreling semi-trailer. Just in time, Max snatched the wheel and yanked them back on course.

"You better pull off the road, son, or you'll kill us both," Max said.

"Hold on, will you, Sergeant?" Rick shouted at the speaker. Fortunately, he spotted a truck stop ahead and pulled off the highway, cutting   the engine. "You found Detective Calendar? Is Red okay?" He took hold of Max's hand and held on for dear life.

"Does she have long blond hair?" Campbell asked.

Rick's heart dropped to the soles of his feet. "No, sir, I believe you've found her friend Summer."

Max and Rick stared at each other. Max slowly shook his head. "The blond woman—is she alive?"

Sergeant Campbell cleared his throat. "Tell you the truth, at first I thought she was dead. Never seen anything like it. Poor gal was naked as a jaybird, all trussed up to the bed and pale as the sheet she was layin' on. Pulse so weak, it was hardly there. They took her directly to the hospital."

While Rick was happy for Summer, he couldn't find it in his heart to express it properly. "Sergeant Campbell, did you find another woman there, too?"

"No, sir."

"How about a man?" Max bellowed. "Any sign of that murderous mother fucker on the premises?"

Taken aback by Max's outburst, Campbell gulped. "The only person on location was the blond woman. Now if you'll excuse me, I got me a crime scene to deal with."

"Did the blond woman tell you anything at all?" Rick quickly interjected before the sergeant signed off.

Campbell paused. Rick could almost see the country cop scratching his head, trying to decide how much he should confide to a pair of crazy cops from the city. Finally, he spoke. "Well, now, she did say her redheaded girlfriend was dead in the bathroom. We checked. The lady was mistaken."

"Any signs of a struggle in the bathroom?" Rick couldn't seem to draw enough air into his lungs as he waited for Campbell's response.

"Other than a broken urn, a small amount of blood, and some water on the floor, we saw nothing outside of the ordinary."

"Did Summer say anything else? Where the man took her friend?" Max demanded.

Sergeant Campbell sighed. "Look, the woman passed out. She's unconscious on her way to the hospital. Nothing. Nada. Anything else?"

"Yes, Sergeant, please have the doctors call me when Summer wakes up, *capiche*?" Rick signed off and gazed at Max. "Now what?"

Max's eyes were rimmed with red. "Now we step on it and get to Boone. Turn on your goddamn siren and stick a cherry on the roof."

"But where do we go once we get there?"

Chapter Fifty-eight

The first thing Red heard was a mockingbird dancing in the bushes above her head. Its many songs were disorienting, like a flock of mixed species. It sounded like jays, cardinals, chickadees, titmice, nuthatches, mourning doves, and even a white-throated sparrow had landed to compete for the bumpy little berries dangling above Red's face. At first, she thought it was a dream and giggled. Daddy had forced Red to learn bird calls, which had been really weird and amazing to a girl who preferred more active pursuits. As she slowly opened her eyes, feeling safe as a child awaking on a down comforter, she saw a thick canopy of small leaves and black twigs. Above that—a violent pink sky. She blinked and tried to understand.

Then, unfortunately, she remembered. The awful knowledge hit like a baseball bat to the chest, taking her breath away. The *who, what,* and *where* she was were so entirely surreal and terrifying that she froze, and more stupid tears flowed down her face. Refusing to believe, she snatched the berries and stuffed them into her mouth, as though the sweet/tart taste and sticky purple juice would restore her reality to childhood, where she was safe and Daddy would protect her. She ate greedily, out of control, until the mockingbird fled the bush, and the panic slowly subsided to something resembling calm, or perhaps defeat.

Time still had no meaning. As Red stared

unblinking at the evil sky, which foretold of a coming storm, she wondered if she could simply stay in her bush forever, living off berries and drinking from the creek. She'd seen a foreign movie like that once. Swedish, she thought, about star-crossed lovers who ran away to live in the wild.

They died.

Red pictured herself naked from the waist up, free of the monster's stinking jacket, her red hair tangled and filled with brambles, her face and mouth stained blue from the berries as she danced through the mountains like a madwoman. The image was so absurd, she suddenly laughed out loud, then clamped her mouth shut.

Because *Paintercat* was still out there somewhere. He was up in his cabin licking his wounds, bandaging his hand, preparing his next attack. He was making his way down the hill, searching the brush for her gun. He was standing above her, the barrel of the Smith & Wesson pointed at her head.

Or else, he was dead.

But Red knew he wasn't dead, and she had bungled her one chance to kill him. She was a stupid, cowardly woman. Maybe she deserved to die, but Boots, Lila, and Summer never deserved what they got. And Gina would never forgive her, even at her funeral. As her anger rekindled, she realized it was too late for Boots, but maybe not for Summer. But unless Red took action and made her way out of this mess, Summer would never be found. Summer would become *Paintercat*'s next victim, and it would be Red's fault.

The anger turned to rage. It propelled Red to her hands and knees and she crawled out of the cave of brambles. It brought her to her feet in a pre-dawn world stained pink and silenced by the hush before the storm. As she stood there, scenting the air like an animal, she smelled pine, damp earth, but not the enemy. He was still holed up in his lair.

When she looked around, every instinct alert to danger, Red saw the dense, sleeping forest and the steep hill where she had fallen. As she tried to get her bearings, she felt oddly strong, rested, and absolutely determined to finish it this time. She saw a thin line of smoke moving straight upward on the eastern ridge, in front of the rising sun, so she knew the way to his cabin and began to climb.

As Red moved through the dense underbrush, she grabbed onto bushes to ascend the grade. Briars clawed at her socks, pulling them loose and threatening her foothold, so finally she removed the stupid things and left them behind. Ignoring the pain, she tried to think of herself as a barefoot savage and kept going. About midway up, where she'd lost the gun, she realized it was impossible to find it, which meant *Paintercat* couldn't find it, either. Or so she hoped.

Red's moment of truth came when she prepared to emerge from the valley and into his yard. The second she poked her head up, she would become vulnerable. Having no illusions about *Paintercat*, she was certain he was a hunter, so his cabin in the wilderness was undoubtedly stocked with the rifles he used to kill innocent prey. And although Red's uncles had asked her to hunt with them during deer season, she had never wanted to murder Bambi and couldn't understand why anyone else would.

But that was a different story. Red listened, heard nothing resembling human activity, and then quietly eased up and over the edge. The old white pickup truck offered a measure of cover, so she sprinted across the short distance and ducked low behind it. Easing forward, she peeked over the hood and saw the log shack was less than twenty yards away, with a kerosene lamp lit on a table near the single window.

While her sense of self-preservation told her to run away in the opposite direction, her training insisted that her only option, if she planned to attack, was the element of surprise. Red needed to get behind him, sneak up on him. With any luck, the monster was sleeping. But then luck had not been on her side lately.

When she looked around the cabin, planning her approach, Red was shocked to see that *Paintercat*'s house had fallen into disrepair, and the open space surrounding it looked like a junkyard. Weeds grew in the sagging window boxes, and a broken sofa lay upside down near the door, its springs and stuffing exposed. Twisted, rusty auto parts littered the driveway, so that the scene bore no resemblance to the ultra-neat house where Red had originally been held captive. It seemed the monster had a split personality. He maintained a highly civilized existence in one life but shed his camouflage altogether here in the mountains, where his evil flourished unrestrained.

The only positive aspects of that depressing thought were the junk bunkers. Using the sofa and auto parts as cover, Red scampered from behind one to another, eventually working her way around to the back of the cabin without attracting *Paintercat*'s attention. The rear offered a different way to hide— behind a man-made mountain of discarded artist's canvases piled in the narrow space between the back wall and the dense forest.

These abandoned paintings had clearly not pleased the artist, for they had all been viciously slashed to ribbons, so that Sam Redbird's familiar subject matter—prowling wildcats and gutted prey—was now a gruesome graveyard of torn images. Somehow, these eviscerated canvases were even more terrifying than the imagined arsenal inside because they chronicled *Paintercat*'s madness and the violence it provoked.

Red squatted behind the carnage and waited for whatever might happen next. There was no back door, so she couldn't mount a rear assault. In the meantime, the tortured sun had sneaked up behind her, illuminating the cabin, front yard, and the dropping mountain panorama beyond with its strange rosy glow. Thunder rumbled in the distance.

And then the front door slammed. Fear vibrated through Red's body like electric shock, and suddenly, *Paintercat* was fully visible just around the corner. Fortunately, the man was looking the other way, out across the cliff where she had fallen the night before. He was most certainly not dead, but she had known this all along. His wounded hand was swathed in a clean, professional bandage, but his other hand—the right one—grasped an automatic hunting rifle. Red was no expert on this kind of weapon, but she believed it was a Winchester with a scope, the type of gun that took the sport out of hunting, leaving   no chance for Bambi. Now why was that no surprise?

Paintercat stretched, coughed, belched, then spat off the mountain in the general direction Red had fallen. On their one and only date, Sam Redbird had been urbane and sophisticated. Up here, he was a pig. And clearly, his one goal was to track her down and finish her off.

Red watched him wobble unsteadily as he began climbing down. He often tripped, cursed, and then righted himself, and that was the good news. He was drunk, drugged on pain meds, or seriously injured, and all those ailments helped level the playing field.

The bad news was, Red had nothing to play with. The moment *Paintercat*'s head dropped below her sight line, she counted to ten—a trick she had taught Rick— and then ducked around the corner and into his cabin. Having nothing to fear, the cocky son of a bitch had left the door unlocked, and having no one to impress, the pig's interior was indeed a sty. Figuring he would kill Red quickly, *Paintercat* had left the kerosene lamp burning. The flickering shadows revealed a squalor of empty food containers, dirty dishes, unmade bed, unfinished paintings, but no Bible anywhere in sight. The place stank of linseed oil and cigarette smoke.

A thorough search convinced Red that *Paintercat* had taken his cellphone and car keys along with him. It was too much to hope for a landline phone, with no electricity out here in the boonies. But she did find one item of interest—an old bow and arrow set—which *Paintercat* had abandoned in favor of the rifle, the more reliable killing machine. The bow and quiver of aluminum-tipped arrows were now part of the dusty mantel décor, but she removed them and eagerly assessed their condition. When she cranked up the tension, the bow arched perfectly. Its string was intact, and for the first time in days, she felt like Lady Luck had finally smiled down on her.

Red located a pair of antique binoculars and some leather moccasins. Pulling on two pairs of the monster's socks, she then tightened the moccasins and felt minimally prepared. Because even though her male relatives had never convinced her to hunt live game, she had been on the high school archery team. At that time, she could sink an arrow into the hay bale bull's-eye with the best of them.

A long time ago.

Red cracked the door and lifted her binoculars to be sure that *Paintercat* hadn't doubled back. She saw no sign of him. But the early morning had turned gray, and mist fogged her lenses. A steady rain fell on the far horizon. Collapsing the bow, she strapped on its harness and secured the set to her back. The thunderclaps were louder as she left the cabin, and lightning crackled on a far distant ridge as she headed downward, tracking into the eye of the storm.

Chapter Fifty-nine

The Boone police were on it. They had set up roadblocks where they might prove helpful, commandeered a firefighter's helicopter to fly low over the rugged terrain where Redbird's cabin might be located, sent available units to explore roads in the general vicinity of where the county survey indicated Redbird maybe owned land—but when all was said and done, Rick and Max realized the cops didn't have a clue how to find Red.

Rick pulled to the curb on Main Street when he noticed a trio of old-timers sheltering from the rain. They were tucked in under the eaves of the original five and dime store, warming a bench and watching the world go by. Rick and Max agreed the information they needed would more likely come from these local geezers than from the tourists or sleepy-eyed Appalachian college students who were just beginning to drift out onto the rainy streets to face the morning.

"Those guys are fixtures," Rick explained. "They see everything and know everyone in town." He slid one quarter into the meter. "I hope they're willing to talk fast."

"I suspect it goes against their nature, but it's worth a shot," Max agreed.

Three sets of suspicious eyes watched their approach from beneath the brims of identical straw visor caps. Rick knew folks from the hills needed to be finessed with preliminary conversation and small talk, but today they'd have to skip the niceties. He got straight to the point, gave them a detailed description of Sam Redbird, and asked for directions to his cabin.

"I knowed you boys was cops soon as you stepped outta that vehicle," the fat one said.

"Yessir, what's this fella done?" The skinny one asked as he watched a scantily clad coed dismounting her boyfriend's motorcycle across the street. "Is he one of them rapists or a pervert?"

When neither Rick nor Max were forthcoming with details, the third man carefully spat a stream of tobacco juice into his empty paper coffee cup and frowned. "You know they got a lunch counter inside. Today's special's the meatloaf. Don't 'spose you gents would care to join us for a meal?"

"Please, sir, do you know Mr. Redbird or not?" Max pleaded.

"Redbird's a name you're not likely to forget. Is he Cherokee?" the fat one asked.

Rick interrupted, "Listen, guys, are you going to help us? I'll leave money and y'all can buy lunch."

"We don't want your money, mister," they chorused.

Rick had crossed the courtesy line. Money bribes usually worked in the city, but not up here. Now the men were insulted, so they'd never cooperate.

But then Max, who was closer to their age, stepped up and looked each man in the eye. "Redbird has kidnapped my daughter, do you understand? He'll hurt her, maybe kill her, if you don't give us directions. I'm begging for your help."

Suddenly, the three were nodding and talking low amongst themselves. Someone brought out a napkin and drew a crude map with a blue laundry marker. He handed it to Max.

"Yessir, we know him. Claims to be a man of God, but I say he's the devil's spawn."

"Never did fit in up here." The skinny one tore his gaze from the coed. "Thinks he's some sort of *artiste* and brags how he's a hunter."

"I've stumbled across his land a time or two, and this map'll get you there, but with the storm comin', you'll need four-wheel drive. Allow a couple hours."

Never underestimate the power of groveling, or as Red would say, leading with the truth. Rick gave Max a smile of thanks and shook the locals' hands. Moments later, they were back on the road, but as Rick glanced miserably at his watch and wondered how in God's name they would locate landmarks like "a lightning-struck tree at the fork in the road," he decided he'd try a different approach in God's name…

He said a silent prayer.

Chapter Sixty

Redbird expected to find Red unconscious in the rubble where she'd fallen the night before, but when he half collided with the rock ledge himself, the bitch was gone. *Dear God, give me strength.* He wanted to pray for guidance as he made his way to the creek, but he was too angry to summon the Lord in his present condition. He wanted to quote some scripture suitable to his situation—a passage about war, victory, and vengeance—but his fevered brain couldn't make the words come together. Mostly, he wanted to leave little Sammy Redbird behind for *Paintercat* because *Paintercat* would not whine about his lost fingers and the virulent streaks of red infection now spreading all the way up to his elbow.

No, *Paintercat* would deal with it. He was God's warrior, His avenging angel with a divine right to take an eye for an eye and never hesitate. Thunder boomed and lightning struck nearby, so little Sammy lifted his ruined face to the first curtain of rain and begged for the transformation to happen soon. He prayed to sweet Daddy Redbird, who had appeared to him in a dream last night. In the dream, the Reverend Redbird was not the groveling, pussy-whipped wretch Mother had made him, but rather the preacher in his prime, shaking the Good Book in his right hand and pounding the pulpit with his left. His long black hair was glossy as the raven's wing, fire and brimstone smoked from his mouth.

Strengthened by the image, *Paintercat* was back again and ready to hunt. Emboldened by the knowledge that the harlot could not have traveled far, he followed the creek to a stand of bushes where she had clearly spent the night. Ignoring his pain, he knelt to touch the bed of pine needles, which conjured her image plain as day. He saw her tears, felt the throbbing in her head and torn feet, and knew he was on the right track.

Having often followed prey through this terrain, *Paintercat* knew the lay of the land more intimately than he knew the sinful streets where he had languished during his professional years. He knew there was only one passable trail. It descended ever downward, sometimes treacherously steep, to the inevitable sheer edge of a cliff, a drop-off, the dead end where all his deer had met their maker.

He paused to make sure he was locked and loaded, then sighted through his scope. The storm had arrived, so the sheeting rain made it difficult to spot through the fogged-up lens, but in the end, he wouldn't need it. Because, when he did find Red, they'd be as close as they had been in the Charlotte pub, where disguised as a homeless man, he had watched her from behind his newspaper. Close as they had been on their date, when she so rudely brushed him off.

And just like the game *Paintercat* had tracked and killed over the years, Red would be forced to choose between the cliff, where she would fall to her death some hundred feet below or stand and fight. All his four-legged victims had chosen the latter. Big mistake. *Paintercat* wondered if Red would be that brave. Considering how she'd hesitated when she'd had the chance to shoot him, he assumed she lacked the courage.

Relishing the look of sheer panic in Red's eyes as she faced her final seconds of life, he stopped to rest. Leaning against his killing tree, he glanced down at the bones of last season's deer. Because of the long, arduous trek up to the cabin, he had learned how to slaughter and dress his prey on site. Then, utilizing a heavy tarp connected to a chain tied to his truck's tow ball, he had carefully dragged the meat uphill and taken it to the local storage locker.

The turkey buzzards and vultures had picked the deer's skull and legs clean, dust to dust, the Lord's way. And as the pain in *Paintercat's* arm radiated through his chest, making it hard to breathe, thunder crashed and rolled across the mountain range, now shrouded in fog. Nature's timpani echoed from ridge to ridge, and once he fancied he heard the faraway beating of a helicopter's wings. Water soaked his hair. It steamed off his fevered skin, making it difficult to focus: *And the rain descended, and the floods came, and the winds blew, and beat upon his house; and it fell not: for it was founded upon a rock.*

And God told him Red was near. *Paintercat* scented her fear, her sinful flesh close at hand, and readied his rifle. He balanced the stock of his .300 Winchester Magnum in the crook of his infected elbow and gripped the trigger plate with his strong right hand as he moved toward the edge. He knew she was there, cowering in the brush or backed against the wall with nowhere to go.

When he neared the drop-off, *Paintercat* heard angels singing in the wind. He also heard a twig snap behind him halfway up the ridge. Startled and panicked, he spun around and spotted her red head floating above a knee-high boulder where she had taken cover, and before he could wonder how she had managed to gain the advantaged position, he dropped to one knee and took aim.

Red's burning bush was a beacon in the fog. It illuminated her face like a halo, so he drew his bead, held his breath, and gently squeezed the trigger. The explosion filled the valley, and the rifle's recoil kicked his wound with the searing fury of hellfire, knocking him backward onto his butt, and yet he rejoiced. He had heard the bullet shatter rock, but he also heard Red's unearthly scream as it connected with her body, and when he scrambled back to his feet, the red halo was gone.

The hellion was dead.

Paintercat's victory howl joined with the angel chorus and vibrated through the storm. He turned his face upward to heaven, and the healing water streamed down his neck and shoulders. She had fallen behind the rock.

But when he looked to the boulder, he saw Red's ghost rise like a heathen spirit from the grave. He stared in disbelief as she slowly stood to her full height in the shimmering mist and opened her white arms. He squeezed his eyes, then blinked twice as she lifted a heavenly harp and fit it to her shoulder. She laced a silver arrow and aimed it at his chest. Still *Paintercat* did not believe it as the ghost stretched the instrument and let the arrow fly. It came to him in slow motion, twisting its feathers like a speeding bird.

Its beak entered his heart. It tore through flesh, muscle, and bone, then buried its fiery head in his beating organ, just before he stumbled backward and into free fall.

Chapter Sixty-one

Red slumped forward on the rock and watched Sam Redbird fall. In a strange, suspended moment, the monster seemed to float, arms outspread in the currents above the valley, a look of stunned disbelief in his eyes as he spiraled downward, ultimately swallowed by the fog.

As the bow tumbled forward from her hands, his death a given, she thought she should cry, but no tears came. A piece of shattered rock had grazed her side, but when she fingered the surface wound, still no tears. Through the veil of exhaustion and pain, she thought of Boots, Lila, and Summer and felt only relief. She thought of her beloved Gina and her partner, Rick. It was over. All that remained was the long way home.

She prayed she could find her way.

Epilogue

Daddy and Gina pushed Red's wheelchair into Lila's hospital room. Red was still groggy from the pain meds. Rick, Salsa, Summer, and Paul were all there, eager to hear the final chapter. Red told her story, then looked up at the two significant men in her life.

She wondered why it took them so damn long to find her.

She remembered next to nothing about that fateful day.

"Better late than never," Daddy said.

"Red looked like a monster from a horror movie," Rick told the audience. "We almost left her there."

Red stared at Summer and Paul Miller, seated side by side on the couch, holding hands. Red was pleased to know that Paul had dropped the charges against James Allen, the kid who wounded him at Boots's funeral. Maybe Paul wasn't so bad, after all. And now, after a week in the hospital, Summer was ready to go home and carry on with the rest of her life, whatever that might bring.

Red searched Summer's eyes. They would always share a bond of terror.

"We have good news," Salsa said. "Lila's coming home next week!"

"Salsa will be living with me for a while." Lila smiled.

They made no secret of their love, yet Red still doubted they could actually make a future together. She hoped she was wrong.

Gina took Red's breath away.

Gina and Daddy were learning to know each other, getting on surprisingly well.

A Florida vacation with Gina? Red looked adoringly at her lover, who looked back with that special gleam in her eye. Red desperately hoped they'd get back together permanently, but for now, it seemed a bridge too far.

Red would cross that bridge soon, but not until the nightmares stopped.

"Are you listening, Red?" Summer said. "I know this has been the worst month of our lives, and it all started with the reunion. But when ten more years have passed, do you think we can do another reunion?"

"Why not?" Paul chimed in. "I'd be willing to play bartender again." He winked at Summer. "And maybe even sign on to DATESCAPE, for old time's sake. You never know who you'll meet online." He gave Summer's hand a fond squeeze.

Red looked from face to face in utter disbelief and enunciated her next words with absolute clarity:

"Thanks anyway, but I'll take a pass."

THE END

About the Author

Kate, a longtime art gallery owner and passionate writer, lives with her family on a lake in North Carolina. When she is not writing or creating driftwood sculpture, she enjoys swimming, boating, and playing with her cats.

Other Books by Kate Merrill

Romance
Northern Lights (as Christie Cole)
Flames of Summer
Beloved Enemy (as Elizabeth Whitaker)
Framed

Diana Rittenhouse Mystery Series
A Lethal Listing
Blood Brothers
Crimes of Commission
Dooley Is Dead
Buyer Beware
Amanda Rittenhouse Mystery Series
Murder at Metrolina
Homicide in Hatteras
Murder at Midterm
Assault in Asheville
The Mayberry Murders
Blue Silk Stalkings

Red Calendar Mystery Series
The True Love Club

Miss Addie's Gift: Portrait of an American Folk Artist

Too Many Damn Yankees in Queen Charlotte's

Court
A collection of Short Stories

www.ingramcontent.com/pod-product-compliance
Lightning Source LLC
Chambersburg PA
CBHW020342010826
48973CB00005B/1234